Solar Wind

Carole Ann Lee

Dedication

To my family: Rod, Dave and Shauna for their love and support.

Acknowledgements

As always thank you to William C. Dietz, one of the finest writers in the Scifi genre, for the inspiration to write Nick Banner's and Zeke Slater's stories.

Thank you to my friend, Holly Smith for such a beautiful cover and for your insight and suggestions that helped to make Zeke worthy of his role in this book

You are simply the best, Holly, and always will be.

CHAPTER ONE

Port Chance, Quade's World:
20 A.C. (After Colonization) Earth Date: 2106

Slater rolled to his side, bringing Celeste with him. "Thank you," he breathed, pressing a kiss to her damp forehead.

A slow smile tugged the corners of her mouth. "My pleasure, Captain." Stroking the tightly corded muscles banding his ribs, she felt his heart kicking her palm. "Rest assured there's more where that came from."

"There is, huh?" His voice was husky from the passion they'd just shared. He squeezed her gently. "Ahh, Celeste...if only I could stick around long enough to take advantage of your sweet offer."

Even now as she watched all six-foot-three of him rise languidly from the bunk, Celeste easily read the male power he emanated, the heady virile control he unconsciously held over women. Zeke Slater was a magnificent lover--merciless in his demands, yet at the same time always carefully attentive to his companion's responses. And it was this potent combination of opposites that women found irresistible.

Rising upon her elbows, she watched him cross the room, tawny, sun-streaked hair spilling across his brow as he gathered his clothes off the floor. "Take me with you," she said, her voice a soft pleading purr as he began dressing. Celeste's hopes rose a notch when his hand stilled on the fly of his pants and he smiled as if weighing her words.

"Take you with me where?" He studied her with an intensity that totally addled her brain.

"Come on, Slater," she pleaded. Celeste was stunningly gorgeous, and she knew it as she armed herself with the perfected pout that always got her what she wanted.

Zeke returned to her side, the mattress dipping beneath his weight as he sat down to pull on his boots. "Celeste, we've been all through this before."

Tossing the cover aside, she scrambled to her knees and moved up behind him. "I guarantee you wouldn't be sorry," she whispered, wrapping her scented arms about him, her deep russet hair draping about his shoulders.

Slater's laugh filled the small cabin. "Sorry? Hell, I'd never survive."

"Sure you would." Dipping her head, she gently kissed the jagged scar marring the burnished flesh just below his right shoulder blade. If asked, Zeke would simply laugh and say it was a souvenir. Rumor said it was a grim reminder of a place called Steel and a rescue mission he'd been involved in.

Celeste tasted her way back to his ear. "I'd go easy on you," she cooed. "I promise."

Slater grinned. "You would, huh?"

"Will you at least think about letting me keep a dwelling for you here in port?"

Celeste felt Zeke's body stiffen, and with practiced ease she pressed her firm breasts against the hard-muscled contours of his back. "I know we've been through this before," she purred, pressing her lips to the outer shell of his ear, "but lots of other captains do it."

"I'm not other captains." Gently peeling her arms from about his neck, he rose to his feet. "Come on, Celeste, get dressed. *Solar Wind's* scheduled to lift in two and a half hours, and I still have a slew of things yet to do."

A rush of heat surged through her as she climbed off the bunk, her lower lip pouting in a display of pique. "This arrangement of ours is getting embarrassing."

"Oh, yeah?" He turned to face her. "How's that?"

"All of my friends are aware that I'm the only one you seek when you come to port, and--"

"You'd rather I see someone else?" he interrupted with endearing puzzlement.

"Of course not. It's just that it's becoming noticeable that this is a nowhere arrangement for me."

A muscle clenched along his jaw as he retrieved her fluidly soft dress off the floor and handed it to her. "Don't spoil the evening, Celeste. I've never led you to believe there could be anything more. Besides, we set the rules ourselves. Remember?"

Oh, yes, she knew the damnable rules. And it was true; to remain uninvolved was as much her idea as his. However, between her desire to move up in social rank along with his prowess as a lover, Celeste found herself willing to bend a rule or two.

She dressed quickly, soft fabric hugging every curve as it settled into place. "But what if I want more?" As soon as the words were out, Celeste knew she had just made an irrevocable mistake.

He glanced up, studying her a moment. "Then I'd say it's time to move on."

She came forward. "Look..." she whispered, drawing herself up against him, "We're good together, Slater."

With a soft chuckle he tweaked her nose. "Yeah, I have to agree with you there."

Rising up on her tiptoes, she cupped his face. "So what do you say?"

Second after second ticked by before he finally answered, "You'll have no trouble finding some eager pilot willing to accommodate you."

It wasn't the first time she'd badgered him about keeping a portside dwelling. But this time she'd crossed the line, and it was obvious her arsenal of beauty and feminine charm held no weapon powerful enough to repair the damage.

"Captain?"

With an air of dismissal, he moved to the wall and pressed a small intercom pad. "Slater here."

"They're preparing to load up, Boss."

"On my way."

Damn him. As easy as that, it was over. Celeste's gaze dropped to the sexy black lace teddy lying rumpled at her feet, and with a rush of indignation she swiftly kicked the fragrant item beneath the foot of his bunk. She'd not be so easily forgotten. Finally, with a sigh of resignation, she stepped into one sandal then the other and came forward.

"Hey..." Placing an arm about her, he drew her near. "I understand they're opening a new 'Made On Earth' shop in the spaceport mall," he said good-naturedly. "Eight weeks ago half my hold was filled with their inventory." Reaching for her hand, he pressed a sizeable cluster of credits into her palm. "Check the place out."

"I don't want your credits, Zeke. There's never been credits between us, and I don't want it now."

"I know," he said, gently cupping his hand over hers. "But I want you to buy yourself something pretty."

"But--"

"Besides, you're going to have a new condo to decorate before you know it."

Pulling out of his embrace, she faced him toe to toe. "But I don't want a condo with anyone else."

Celeste knew instinctively as he quietly escorted her off ship, she would not be invited back.

~ * ~

Running an experienced eye over the belly of his ship, Slater always insisted on performing his own pre-flight check. The way he saw it, there were four things you just never turned over to someone else's care: Your ship. Your gun. Your credits. Or your woman--in roughly that order. It was a rule that had been firmly ingrained over the years.

Finally making his way up the ramp, he entered the main hatch of the *Solar Wind*. No high security consignments this trip. No customs, and no time-consuming red tape to go through at the drop. With a little luck this would be a slide-in-slide-out run.

4

Easing into the command seat, he watched the U-shaped screen snap to life as he entered destination coordinates into the NAVCOMP. With a final pause he swept the perimeter vid-cams across the surrounding landing zone. To starboard, a private yacht was just lifting. To port, several nearby freighters were taking on freight, and the biker he'd noticed earlier was still circling the LZ. No one seemed particularly interested in the *Solar Wind*, and that was just fine with him.

"I said I'm not moving until I see Captain Slater."

Slater's pre-flight preparations were suddenly shattered by a familiar voice coming from the open hatch.

"And I already told y' the captain's busy," came an equally disgruntled reply from *Solar Wind's* First Officer, Frank Reno.

"Look, just because I'm homeless doesn't mean--"

"Thaaat's right. It don't mean a thang. It ain't got nothin' to do with how y' live. It has to do with the fact ee's busy."

"Then I'll just wait right here until he's not."

"Frank--" Slater called without taking his eyes off the console.

But Frank wasn't listening. He was too preoccupied addressing the shoddy young man standing just outside the main entry. "The captain can't be bothered right--"

"Frank," Slater tried again, this time with a little more volume. "It's okay. Let him come in."

"But, Boss--"

"It's all right. I've got a few moments."

"I need to talk to you, Captain," the young man broke in. "Gibby asked me to give you something important."

"I tried tellin' him yer busy," Frank interrupted, "but he don't seem t'--"

"Its okay, Frank." Stifling a sigh, Slater finished entering the final sequence into the onboard computer before swiveling about. "Come on in, Leon. I have a few minutes."

"I won't take long, Captain." Spearing Frank with a scowl, the rangy youth took off his hat and stepped inside the ship's main hatch to wait. "And just to let you know, sir, my name's Wolf today," he said proudly.

"Then, Wolf, it is." Grabbing what he figured to be his last breath of fresh air, Slater rose to his feet and bounded down a short flight of metal stairs to the entry. "Come on back, while I get us both some coffee."

Ignoring his First Officer's set features and fixed stare, Slater led the way down the corridor and into the galley. "Have a seat, Wolf," he said, motioning toward a built-in booth and hoping that whatever the kid had to say, he'd make it quick. Zeke suspected it had been a long while since Leon had considered any personal hygiene. Without a doubt his unique essence would take a serious toll on the ship's atmosphere.

Leon eased into the booth, clearly making a point of ignoring the canister of biscuits sitting in the middle of the table--a point that didn't escape Slater's notice.

"You hungry?"

"Nah, I just ate. But thanks."

Slater nodded. Truth was he probably hadn't seen a decent meal in weeks. But unless it was handled just so, a simple offer could backfire into an insulting handout. Slater knew the ritual. "Well, in case you change your mind," he said, shoving the container toward Leon. "I'll get us some coffee then you can tell me what's going on."

Had the biscuits not been offered, Leon would never have touched them. But since they were, Slater figured several would be stuffed into a pocket by the time he returned with the coffee.

"Here you go, man," he said, handing the young man a steaming mug.

"Thanks."

"On the house." Zeke settled into the booth across from Leon. "So what's up?"

Wrapping both hands about the warmth of his mug, Leon leveled his gaze. "Gibby wants you to know that there's trouble about to go down."

Slater halted his mug half way to his mouth. "What sort of trouble?"

"Some guy on a jet bike is out there on a serious manhunt. And he's got a T-30 stashed beneath his jacket." Leon shrugged. "Anyway,

Gibby figured you might want to put in for an early departure before all hell breaks loose around here."

Slater's eyes narrowed. "Yeah, I noticed the biker," he said, setting his coffee back down. "But I didn't notice the weapon."

"It's concealed. The only reason we noticed it is because we've been watching him for a while. I doubt he's going to give up until he finds who he's looking for.

"Oh, and there's one more thing..." Leon paused to dig into a pocket. "Gibby found this lying out on the landing zone not far from here." Sitting in the center of his outstretched palm was a woman's delicate hair comb adorned with five sparkling jewels.

There was little doubt of the comb's value as Slater reverently lifted it from Leon's grubby hand. "Where did you get--"

"Gibby found it laying out on the LZ."

Slowly turning the comb over in his hand, Slater leaned back in the chair and thoughtfully lifted his gaze. "Somebody's got to be missing this. I suspect the authorities should be notified."

The kid huffed a laugh. "I'm sure they should, but you're the only one Gibby trusts with it."

"Me?"

"Said he wants you to hang on to it until the owner's found."

"But I have no idea when I'll be back this way."

"Just the same, he wants you to hang onto it." Leon took another sip of his coffee then rose from the chair. "Well, I'd better be on my way."

"Wolf, wait a minute." Rising to his feet, Slater reached into his hip pocket and fingered out a credit clip.

Leon held up his hand. "Look, Gibby and I--we don't want money for doing the right thing."

"If you or Gibby should find the owner or need to get a hold of me," Slater said, withdrawing a small card from the clip, "contact this sector. They'll know how to reach me."

Wolf accepted the card. "Okay," he said studying the contact information.

"And...as for both you and Gibby," Slater added, withdrawing a folded credit, "I appreciate the forewarning about the trouble." Laying the credit on the table, he slid it toward the young man. "Consider this a reward."

Leon started to protest when Zeke withdrew another credit from the clip. "Plus," Zeke continued, "eventually somebody's going to be happy to see this comb again and will also want you to have a reward. I can collect from them later."

Several pondering moments passed before Leon finally glanced up. "I suppose there's nothing wrong with accepting a reward."

"I'm telling you, man, people do it all the time."

"Okay," he muttered, snatching up the tender and stuffing it into a pocket. "But Gibby isn't going to be happy about this."

"Well then, Wolf, you just tell Gibby it's the only way I'll hang on to this comb for him."

A wide, toothless grin spread across Leon's young face as he rose from the booth. "I'll tell him, Captain--and thanks."

It was with mixed emotions that Leon made his way back down the boarding ramp. Technically, everything he had said was true. But it was what he hadn't said that was eating at him--the minor little detail he had deliberately left out of the telling.

He liked and respected Captain Slater. In truth, Slater was one of very few who treated him and Gibby with genuine kindness. He just hoped he wouldn't be too angry when he discovered the girl.

And he would discover her. There was little doubt of that.

~ * ~

"Good heavens! Why in lasers did y' have t' invite 'im in?" Frank asked, furiously fanning the air. "Whew-eee!" Striding to the nearby controls, he switched the air filter on high.

Zeke laughed.

"And then," Frank went on, "when y' invited 'im to sit down fer coffee and a friendly little chat...hell, I was beginnin' to think y' were gonna ask 'im t' stay fer breakfast too." Snatching the canister of biscuits off the table, Frank stomped directly to the trash.

"Frank, I need you to put in a request for an immediate lift," Zeke said, ignoring his First Officer's on-going tirade.

"Already in the works, Boss. Clearance should be comin' through any moment."

"Good." Slater's attention was riveted on the comb as he turned it over in his hand once again. "You know what this is, don't you?"

"Yeah, a woman's hair bauble."

"It's a little more than that." On a hunch, Slater carefully pressed what looked to be a touch point along the top ridge of the comb. Immediately a miniature compartment snapped open revealing a tiny hidden micro disc no larger than one of the jewels decorating its surface.

"I'll...be...damned," Frank murmured.

CHAPTER TWO

Within minutes, clearance had been confirmed and *Solar Wind* was lifting for space in a thunderous roar. Having entered a code into the onboard computer, Slater watched as crucial data began flooding the screen. Speed. Altitude. Fuel Consumption. E.T.A. It was all there--an electronic version of "Relax, I've got everything under control."

Quade's World belonged to the Sector Five Star System--a backyard neighbor to Earth's own solar system and originally discovered during Earth's so-called "Race For Space" era. Thanks to the dimension-twisting realm of travel called hyperspace, a five hundred and fifty-year void between the two star systems was now reduced to a little over eight weeks.

"Boss, what do y' make of this?" Frank asked from across the helm, his eyes fixed on an overhead monitor.

Rising from his seat, Slater moved to stand behind his First Officer. "Make of what?"

"Portal Screen B." He hitched his chin toward a pulsing red indicator.

Slater paused, his eyes following Frank's. "Looks like something's shifted back there."

"Yep, that's what I figured, too, but check this." Frank's craggy gray brows drew together in concentration as he tapped in another directive. "Unless I'm mistak'n', I'd say we picked ourselves up some live freight back at Port Chance."

In silent speculation the captain's eyes narrowed as he watched the security vid-cam quickly replay the last sixty seconds of activity.

"You want me to run a backup on the sensors, Boss?"

"No, I've got a better idea." Descending the short flight of stairs to the corridor, Slater snagged his leather jacket and holstered weapon off a hook, wrenching them on as they made their way toward the ship's hold.

Lights snapped to life, and a host of familiar scents greeted them as they entered the cargo bay. It was a pungent mixture of imported rarities, exotic spices, and the distinctive odor of raw textiles.

"Help!" came a muffled, yet decidedly feminine voice. "I want out!"

"Y' hear that?" Frank asked, his breath forming in the chilled air.

"Over there." Slater's eyes were focused on a stack of shipping modules lined along the starboard wall. "That damned Celeste," he muttered.

"Celeste? Y' don't think she'd be so foolish as t'--"

"I wouldn't put anything past her." The sleek blue-black barrel of Slater's weapon quietly slid from its holster as they wormed their way through the tightly stacked freight. If nothing else, he'd give her the scare of her life.

The muffled sounds came again. Stronger. More urgent. The insistent kicking and thumping coming from the far corner.

Thunk! "Somebody, get me out of here!" Thunk! "Dammit! I'm freezing." Thunk! Thunk!

"Since when did we start haulin' talkin' veggies?" Frank asked, grinning as they drew to a halt before a fresh produce pod.

A muttered curse was Slater's low-voiced reply as he disengaged the lock on the vented pod. "All right, Celeste! Come on out." And with a swift upward motion that belied the weight of the cumbersome lid, he threw it back on its hinges.

"It's about time somebo--dee..." Kira Delaney's voice trailed into quivering silence as bright overhead light spilled into the pod--even as Slater's lips formed an unspoken curse.

Frank's long, breathy whistle finally broke the silence. "Y' want me to check the next crate over for Celeste?" he asked, his gravelly voice dripping with unmasked laughter.

No response.

~ * ~

Squinting against the glare, it took a moment for Kira to realize she was eye-level with the business end of a Sheldon mini-blaster. In numb fascination she slowly rose to her knees, ignoring the pain in her cramped limbs. Her gaze slid beyond the bore of the weapon to taut-muscled thighs and narrow hips clad in dark leathers. With a hard swallow, her silent perusal inched upward, lingering briefly upon a magnificent torso with shoulders so broad they seemed to block out all else. At last her eyes came to rest on the grim face of the man towering before her.

And their gazes locked.

"Kira." Slater's flat statement clearly linked disbelief with reluctant recognition. In truth, he looked as though he'd just opened the lid on Pandora 's Box.

Slowly rising to her feet, Kira extended a frigid hand. "Well, Slater, are you going to shoot me or help me out of here?"

Lowering his weapon, he reached for her hand.

"I'll say this much," she added as he helped her up and out of the produce pod, "you certainly know how to make a girl feel welcome." The façade of nonchalance was taking every ounce of self-discipline Kira possessed.

With a muttered curse he released her, leaving her to slump against the edge of the container while he re-holstered his weapon. Next, he began shrugging out of his taubear-hide jacket. "Here," he said, draping the garment about her shoulders.

The butter-soft leather was heavy; his lingering body heat heaven to Kira's chilled flesh.

"You'd better have one hell of an explanation. That's all I can say."

"Zeke, I can--"

"How the devil did you manage to slip past security?"

"Look, I can explain everything if you'll just give me a--"

He huffed a soft laugh. "Yeah, I'll just bet you can."

Frank stood there eyeing the exchange with amused curiosity while Slater, with a heavy sigh, glanced briefly away. "Next port..." he said, his eyes cutting back to meet hers, "I'm putting you on the first liner bound for home."

"But, Zeke--"

"You know what, Kira? I'm afraid I'm really not up for one of your wild stories at the moment." He turned to make his way toward the exit.

"But, you won't believe--"

"A single word."

A strained hush filled the air as she stared at Zeke Slater's retreating back. Offering the older man a lame smile, Kira summoned as much dignity as her depleted strength would allow and started after Zeke--her frozen, cramped limbs protesting every step. "But, it--it's different this time."

That stopped him. He turned to face her. "Okay. I give. What is it this time? Customs? Port Security? An irate vendor? Tell me if I'm getting warm." Without giving her a chance to answer, he added, "I do know one thing. If those security vids caught you climbing into that produce crate, you can bet your sweet ass they know exactly where you are. Next, they'll be notifying us of your presence and arranging for me to hand you over to the authorities at the next drop." He smiled blandly. "Four years...and nothing's changed, has it?"

"It isn't like that at all." Kira followed him out of the hold on shaky legs. Time certainly hadn't altered his low opinion of her. That much was obvious. To him she was still Renn Delaney's little hellion. "Why is it you've always chosen to believe the worst of me?" she asked, half-running to keep up with him.

"Experience, sweetheart." He turned to face her while waiting for a safety lock to cycle open. "Unlike some people I know, I make it a point to learn from mine."

Kira peered up at him, striving to see beyond the mockery and blatant distrust etched upon his handsome face. She knew what he was referring to--the untimely death of a mutual friend, Lance Girard. She was with Lance at the time of his death and it was no secret Zeke believed her responsible--by association if nothing else.

Tension arced between them, taut with unspoken words. Only sheer determination kept Kira from backing down. "You're wrong about me."

"I doubt that."

"I'll...uh...go help Talbot at the controls," Frank muttered, quickly brushing past the couple.

They both ignored him.

One corner of Zeke's mouth rose lazily. "Your daddy know where you are right now?"

Stunned by the question, Kira simply stared at him.

Zeke's lip curled. "I didn't think so." He turned and resumed his trek toward the bow of the ship. They were just entering the ship's living quarters when Kira caught her reflection in the shiny metal fascia of an instrument panel. A faint bruise colored her right cheek; a darker one marred her left temple. The rest of her, from head to toe, was smudged with residue from the pod's previous consignment. That, combined with her hair in such wild disarray, she looked more like a medusoid than a woman. Even her once stylish outfit was now filthy and torn at the knees.

Following Zeke down the narrow passage, she noted three private cabins lining the port side. "You uhh...wouldn't happen to know where I might freshen-up...by any chance?"

That brought him to a halt. Releasing a compressed sigh, he swung about to face her. Several heartbeats passed before he finally said, "Follow me."

The cabin they entered seconds later, though not extravagant, was beyond what Kira had expected--obviously Captain's Quarters judging from the size. "Thank you," she said, truly meaning it.

He hitched his chin to the left. "You'll find the lav through that door. Help yourself to the shower if you wish, but go easy on the water."

"I promise."

She thought he would turn to leave, but instead he remained, frowning as he slowly assessed her disheveled appearance. "That bruise at your temple looks nasty. You sure you're okay?" Strange as it was under the circumstances, the question seemed sincere.

Kira forced a smile. "I'm fine. Really. I just need a couple of minutes."

He regarded her a moment longer then saying something she didn't quite catch, he turned for the exit.

The instant the panel cycled closed, Kira's brave smile faded as everything suddenly came slamming back--everything she had so carefully tucked beneath a pretense of careless nonchalance.

Vivid memories of the past few hours resurfaced. She had worked late tonight. Charlie had offered to walk her out to her vehicle. Old Charlie--he'd been a security officer at the complex for as long as Kira could remember...

By the time they'd reached her ground runner, they were laughing over an incident that had happened when Kira was a child--a time when she had accidentally set off perimeter alarms while picking flowers on the company grounds.

Charlie laughed. "I'll never forget the shocked look on your face. You were--" his words died mid-sentence.

"What is it?" she followed his gaze. "Charlie, what's wrong?"

The answer came with blinding speed as he shoved her to the ground. "Honey, stay down until--" his next utterance was a soft gasp as a blue lance of energy stuttered out of the darkness. Charlie landed hard on the pavement beside her, his lifeless stare a memory Kira would never forget--her scream, a sound that still echoed in her ears.

Another sharp crack of energy lashed out, this time spewing sparks as it raked down the side of her shiny red ground runner.

A blue haze drifted in the air. The stench of hot metal, ozone and burned flesh filled her nostrils. There was no time for tears as she quickly belly-crawled to the opposite side of the runner. With shaky hands she aimed the remote and pressed until the side panel slid open.

The ride to the spaceport was wild--the decision to head there, spontaneous. The image in the rear vid-screen, however, confirmed her worst fears. Her sporty little ground runner was no match for the jet bike bearing down on her. Within moments of entering the terminal, Kira stashed the runner in a shadowy niche and was darting behind the massive landing jack of a nearby freighter. There she remained, heart pounding and too scared to move while the biker, with his thermal-visor in place, slowly navigated the spaceport--one painstaking aisle at a time.

Overhead, the freighter's hull radiated the heat of a recent reentry, the pinging of cooling metal ticking out the minutes. For the moment, she was safe. Her thermal aura would not be easily detected beneath the heat of the freighter's hull. She couldn't stay here indefinitely. It wouldn't be long before the cooling vessel would no longer cloak her thermal image.

She had been eyeing a cluster of abandoned cargo pods when a sudden discharge of steam surged from an overhead vent, scaring a muffled scream into her throat and her feet into action.

With a physical jerk, Kira's thoughts suddenly slammed back to the present. How could she have known the lid was on "auto-lock?" How could she have known that what had seemed the perfect hiding place would in fact become a prison?

And the only clue as to how she had ended up on board Zeke's freighter was a low, gravelly whisper... *"Just stay quiet and we'll get you to safety. Once the ship lifts, honey, you need to scream like hell. You hear me? Make as much noise as you can. You'll be rescued."*

So, what was she to do now? How much should she tell Zeke? He would want answers soon, and she seriously doubted he'd settle for half-truths. Just from his thunderous expression, she suspected she'd come awfully close to being jettisoned out of the nearest air lock.

Zeke Slater. His name tumbled through her mind. It was obvious he'd changed in the four years since she'd last seen him. Hardened was more the word.

And very capable of dumping you off at the nearest spaceport without a backward glance, a silent voice added.

Obviously he hadn't heard of her father's recent death, Kira thought, or he wouldn't have asked about him. Maybe he wouldn't be quite so angry if he knew. But deep inside Kira knew she could never use the tragedy of Renn Delaney's death to gain anyone's favor.

So, what are you going to tell him when he demands an explanation? Are you going to tell him that you're in trouble--again?

Nearly groaning aloud, Kira rose and headed for the lav.

No, she didn't dare tell him that either, although he probably already suspected as much.

Quickly stripping off her soiled clothing, she adjusted the shower and stepped in. A couple of Zeke's personal toiletries sat on a narrow shelf. Refusing, however, to use anything of his, Kira opted instead for a simple rinse-off. It was humiliating enough just having to use his shower.

Renn's death had not only thrown her into a tailspin of grief, it had also left her trying to manage his half of Major Metals. With all there was to learn, it was no wonder she hadn't noticed the subtle increase in supplies being channeled through the company. Only recently had it become clear that somebody was breaching corporate security--using her I.D. to authorize special purchases.

Now, like a bad dream, here she was on board Zeke Slater's ship, bound for who knows where. Zeke. Again, she pondered the change in him. She supposed time had a way of doing that. After all, she too had changed. No longer was she the reckless teenager he obviously remembered. Although she'd play hell convincing him of that, particularly in light of the fact that he'd just found her hiding on board his ship. He'd never in a million years believe how she had wound up there. She wasn't sure she believed it.

The stark reality was Zeke Slater saw her as a stowaway, and that put her legitimately at his mercy. She'd already conjured up several scenarios of merciless consequences.

Maybe she should tell him the truth after all.

And just how merciful do you think he's going to be when you tell him about Charlie?

Well, she just wouldn't tell him about Charlie. But then, that would only leave more unanswered questions. So, on second thought, maybe she'd better make up a story after all.

CHAPTER THREE

Kira tenderly touched the sensitive bruise at her temple, unable to recall exactly how she'd received the blow. In truth, it was hard to think right now, let alone try to figure out how she was going to deal with Zeke.

Being particularly mindful of the water, she hurried with her shower. By the time she emerged, a pair of dark pants, a belt and a white tee shirt were lying on a small shelf just inside the lav. Deciding not to dwell on the fact that at some point her privacy had clearly been invaded, she gratefully reached for the clean garments.

Opting not to wear the pants which were far too long, Kira tried on the shirt instead. It hung to mid-thigh and looked more like a short dress than anything. Cinching the belt about her waist, she tucked the excess length into itself. Not exactly stylish, but it was clean and would do until her own things were ready.

She sensed his presence the instant the privacy panel slid open. Zeke was stationed before the view port, staring into the star-studded blackness surrounding the ship. At last he turned to face her, taking in her appearance with candid distraction.

"I assume these were set out for me?"

His response was a curt nod. Crossing the cabin to the lav, he retrieved the pants she had chosen not to wear. "Here," he said, firing them at her. "Put these on. I won't have you parading around in front of my crew in that getup."

"Actually, if it's all right, I'd prefer to wait right here until my own things are dry."

18

"Suit yourself." Again, his eyes swept over her, and despite his apparent lack of interest, he looked...intrigued. At the moment, Kira wasn't sure if that was good or bad.

She moved to the bunk, casually took a seat on the foot of it and began putting on her shoes. "This place is actually quite comfortable," she said, feigning an air of casualness.

"Yeah, well don't get too comfortable."

"Someone special?" she asked, spying a wispy edge of black lace peeking out from beneath the bunk. Retrieving a seductively delicate teddy from the floor, she dangled it loosely off the tip of her finger. "Surely this isn't yours," she went on, watching his scowl deepen with recognition.

Three strides and he was standing before her, wordlessly snatching the fragrant scrap off her fingertip and tossing it haphazardly to the side. "Why are you here, Kira?"

"I already told you, I did not stow aboard."

With a smile of pained tolerance, Zeke dropped down beside her. "I know what you've told me," he said with extreme patience. "It's what you haven't that concerns me."

"What if I were to tell you..." she paused. Sliding closer she placed her hand on his arm, intensely aware of the powerful biceps bulging beneath his shirt. "I mean, what if I simply wanted to see you again?"

Of all the things she could have said, why that? Instant heat crept into Kira's cheeks. Had she lost her mind? What happened to the story about trying to rescue a litter of chae kittens? How she'd accidentally fallen into the cargo pod trying to get to them and--oh well there was no point in going over it now. The path had just been set--such as it was. She had no choice now but to follow it through.

The silence was tangible. Kira stole a quick glance in Zeke's direction. "I-I mean," she said with a nervous laugh, "what has it been...four years?"

His sights were set dead ahead, his expression unreadable. Easing her hand from his arm, Kira silently regarded the clear cut lines of his profile, saw a muscle jerk along his jaw and his eyes narrow ever so slightly.

At last he turned to face her, his steely regard piercing the short distance between them. "Now, you want to try the truth?"

"What do you mean?"

"There's not a chance in hell I'm buying that one." Rising to his feet, he moved to stand once again before the small view port--his back rigid. "We don't even like each other, much less--"

"I'd hoped to change that."

You're playing with fire, a small voice warned.

Slater's head came around, their gazes locking. "Change it?" he repeated flatly. "Into what?"

"Friends...?"

His eyes narrowed. "What the hell are you up to?"

"Nothing."

He paced back to stand before her. "Who else knows you're here?"

"No one." She swallowed, his gaze so intense it was difficult to meet, but she did so unflinchingly. "Look, Zeke, I know things have been a little strained in the past, but if you'd just--"

"Strained?" He laughed. "Sweetheart, strained doesn't even come close."

"Okay. So we didn't like each other very much, but--"

"Now you're catching on. The last time you pulled a stunt like this, Renn had a swarm of bounty hunters tracking me with orders to shoot me on sight. Thanks, but no thanks."

Kira rolled her eyes. "Oh please. They were hardly bounty hunters."

"Close enough. Point being: arrangements have already been made for your return trip home."

"What do you mean?"

"Next port and you're out of here."

"Who did you talk to?" she asked, suspicious.

"Renn. Who else?"

Kira's mouth fell open. "You spoke to my father?"

"I did, and he sounded none too happy."

"But..." A surge of panic shot through her at the realization that someone was posing as her father. No way was she going back on those arrangements. Problem was it was a little late now to start spilling the truth. Zeke would never believe her. Not now. Not after the lies. "Zeke, please, let me make my own arrangements. I promise I'll--"

"Sorry. It's a done deal."

"But, if you will just let me stay on until I can--"

"Not a chance."

Determined to change his mind, she lounged back on splayed palms, allowing age-old instinct to take over. Even as the borrowed shirt rode her thighs, Kira's gaze remained steady. "I promise you won't be sorry."

"What?"

With a careless shrug, her eyes slid to the sexy black teddy crushed beneath his boots. "I'm not suggesting that I could replace her, but perhaps I can--"

"Repla--?" With a frown, Zeke's eyes followed hers to the floor. A pause. "Good god, I hope not!"

"Perhaps I can make you forget her," she bravely forged on, ignoring the obvious consequences of such an outrageous suggestion.

He absently nudged the provocative scrap of lace with the toe of his boot. "She's already forgotten." In the next instant total awareness suddenly dawned. Zeke's narrowed eyes slowly lifted to meet hers, their gazes locking for several unnerving heartbeats. "What are you doing?" he asked, his voice a mere whisper of disbelief.

His eyes swept over her, lingering briefly upon her legs, her breasts then back to her eyes. "What the hell?" he said beneath his breath. "What are you doing, Kira?"

"Nothing," she whispered, humiliatingly conscious of his frowning scrutiny.

Again his eyes moved over her, taking the deluxe tour this time. It was a look meant to intimidate, and it did exactly that--effectively stripping her in every possible sense of the word. "Well, you'd better define nothing, because from where I stand it's a hell of a lot more than nothing."

Unnerved, Kira swallowed, her stomach clenching under his burning regard. Those eyes. Stars, how could she have forgotten those gray eyes? Four years ago she hadn't yet experienced the brunt of his sultry gaze. But now...

"Are you coming-on to me?" he asked, his tone incredulous. "Because if you are, you need to understand something. I'm not the same man you used to know. I might be good at fitting in when and where I have to, but underneath I'm port-hardened. You understand what I'm saying?"

Kira forced her chin up to meet his gaze squarely. "Yes."

"Good." He smiled slowly. "Then you won't be too shocked when I explain what I look for in a playmate." Her jaw dropped as he began listing a few preferences. "So what do you say? Think you can handle it?"

Silence.

"That's what I thought. Now sit up!" It was an order Kira dared not challenge at the moment. Pulling herself into a sitting position, she swung her legs over the foot of the bunk and faced him, her cheeks flaming as his gaze went from her face to her breasts to her legs then slowly back up again.

"What?" she asked, unsettled by the sheer intensity of him. "What are you thinking?" His nearness was so galvanizing she was scarcely aware of holding her breath.

Slater didn't respond. For a moment he simply stood there pinning her with an unreadable gaze. "I'm, uh..." Reaching for her hand, he pulled her to her feet, the scent of leather and cold steel filling her senses.

"I'm--uh..." Again he hesitated, his voice a husky rasp. When his heated focus shifted to her mouth, Kira's stomach coiled. God help her, she was about to get what she'd asked for.

"I'm just wondering..." He closed his eyes for a moment. When he opened them again, some of the heat was banked. "...where the devil you're going to sleep," he finished in a rush of words. With Kira firmly in hand, he turned for the door.

"Where are you taking me?" They were heading toward the cargo bay.

"To your new quarters."

Kira twisted against his grip, but for all her trying she might as well have been manacled by a band of iron. Surely he wouldn't make her stay in the hold.

Or would he? Knees bending with her own conclusions, she frantically dug in her heels. "You had better not be taking me back to the cargo bay!"

That brought him to a halt, and he turned to face her, amusement lurking in his eyes. "Is that where you think you're going?"

Up went her chin. "Just in case, I am not budging!"

"Is that right? Well then, I guess I owe you an apology."

"For what?"

"For this." With a muscular twist that wrung a gasp from her lips, he scooped Kira up, hoisting her across his shoulder. "Right now I'm in no mood to fight with you, Kira."

"Damn you, Zeke!" Kicking and squirming, she pummeled his back with her fists. "Put me down this instant." Grabbing hold of his belt for leverage, she managed to sock him hard in the small of the back and felt a measure of supreme satisfaction at his resulting curse. Yet, Slater's purpose never wavered as his booted feet echoed down the corridor.

With her hair falling upside down around his hips, Kira watched the deck bobbing along beneath her. "You're going to regret this."

"I sure as hell am." With a muttered curse, he yanked the shirt she was wearing--his shirt--over her backside, securing it beneath a steely arm.

"You sorry son of a--oomph!" A seemingly innocent adjustment of her weight stopped Kira's discourse, mid-sentence. The disruption however was only a brief reprieve. "If you don't put me...down this very minute, I swear you're--oomph!" Another slight adjustment and her belly bit deeper into his shoulder.

"Need any help, Boss?"

Muscles flexed even tighter about her thighs. "Nope. Got it all under control."

Kira lifted her head, bracing splayed hands upon the small of Zeke's back to peer through her tousled hair. She should have guessed.

The older man Zeke referred to as Frank was lounging against the bulkhead, taking it all in with amused interest.

Silently she cursed him too, as Zeke's long strides continued carrying her farther down the narrow corridor.

At last he came to a stop. With a doubled fist he hit the touch pad and waited while the door cycled open. "Legs," he said upon entering the tiny cabin, "it's small, but it's all yours." He set her down on her feet.

Glaring at him, Kira flipped a russet lock of hair from her face. "If you think for one instant you're keeping me penned-up in here..."

"You're not confined. Though I assure you, that's next if you cause me any trouble. And just so you know, we've got a little over two weeks before we set down on Lilo."

"Zeke, please don't put me off on Lilo," her tone softening. "Let me make my own arrangements. Please. I promise I will do it, and I won't be any trouble in the meantime. You won't even know I'm around."

He laughed. "Yeah, and zipcats don't have fangs. Sorry. Lilo's it. Next stop after that is Echo and I'm sure as hell not keeping--"

"Oh, that would be perfect. I could--"

"Not a chance."

"But--"

"No."

"I really need to see Grant. I was on my way out to a chartered flight," she lied, "when I..."

Zeke was smiling, clearly not buying a word of it. "When you what, Kira?"

Silence.

"What is it you have to see Preston about that Renn can't handle?"

"For your information, it's professional."

"Ahh...professional," he drawled. "Yes, of course. I recognized the professionalism the instant I found you hiding in a produce pod."

She stared past his shoulder. "For the hundredth time, I was not hiding. I had nothing to do with coming on board your ship, but obviously there's no sense trying to explain it."

"Explain it?" He blinked in feigned confusion. "But, I thought-- Kira, didn't you already explain it? Something about coming on board to reconcile our differences. How was it you put it--helping me to forget about black lace? You mean that wasn't true after all?"

"Zeke, I..." Her face flaming, Kira's words trailed off at his look of mock disappointment.

Suddenly, in a flash, all pretense was gone. "Next port and you're off," he said. "Until then, you're not confined, but again one sure way to lose that privilege is to cross a designated Security Line. They're clearly marked on this vessel, so no excuses." With that, Zeke turned for the exit.

Kira watched the door close behind him as he disappeared into the passageway. With a heavy sigh, she sank down onto the edge of the tiny bunk, needing a good cry, but refusing to give in. Crying had not seen her through life. Determination had, and what she needed now was a plan.

Brushing another lock of hair from her face, Kira considered the turmoil of the last three months. In truth it was almost too much to deal with--the grief over her father's death, the hectic rush to learn the corporate side of Major Metals, the rumors that Major Metals was using slave labor. But the eventual discovery of embezzlement is what sent her into a course of action that not only landed her in her present predicament, but cost Charlie his life. He had died saving her. There was little doubt she had been the target--the very reason the biker chased her to the spaceport. But who? Why?

Truth was, Grant Preston's offer to buy her half of the company was beginning to look better by the minute. And yet, letting go of the only connection she had left with her father was beyond thought.

~ * ~

The *Solar Wind* was little more than a vapor trail by the time a shiny black ground runner slid to a halt before the main entrance to the Port Chance Spaceport. Leaving the vehicle on standby, two men--one hideously burn-scarred, the other with unusually bright blonde hair--climbed out, made their way across the circular drive and entered the terminal.

Shouldering their way through a crowd of newly arrived passengers, they approached the communications center. "Did you get it?"

The young clerk paused and looked up. "You forgot to tell me there's a classified status on this particular freighter. I need a code, Kendyl. You hear what I'm saying? Geez, I could lose more than my job for even trying to access this information."

"No one's going to find out. So, what did you come up with?"

"What'd I come up with? Absolutely nothing. I'm telling you without a code, I get zilch. She's listed as *Solar Wind* and that's it."

"Well, I don't have a damned code, so figure something else out."

"You just don't get it, do you? There is nothing else. Without a code, my hands are tied."

Standing off to the side, the man with bright hair whispered, "You sure it's him?"

"Of course it's him, you idiot. Who else would put a classified code on a damned freighter?"

"If he's got a woman on board, you can have Slater and I get the woman."

"Shut up, you moron." With a muttered curse, Kendyl slapped fifty credits down on the counter "All I want is the next stop. That's all."

"Without a pass code," the clerk enunciated slowly, "I can't even verify that the *Solar Wind* has a toilet, let alone give you their next port-o-call."

All of them had failed to notice the attractive redhead who'd moved closer to the conversation. "You're wrong about a woman being on aboard the *Solar Wind*," she said. "I just came from there and believe me, the captain's alone."

Was that a note of jealousy he heard in her tone? For an instant Kendyl wanted to laugh out loud. She was just the wild card he needed. He reached into a pocket and pulled out a copy of a security photo and handed it to her. "Unless this is you climbing into that produce pod, sweetheart, he's got a guest with him. See the serial number on the front?"

She nodded slowly.

"That particular container was listed on *Solar Wind's* manifest," he lied. Kendyl had no way of knowing that. A classified ship's manifest was as private as their itinerary. Nevertheless, he waited for her response.

Silence. Just watching her study the picture made his burned-scarred face hurt with restrained laughter.

Slowly, she lifted her chin to meet his icy glare straight on, never batting an eye at his gruesome visage nor giving away the hurt and anger he knew she was hiding. "I can tell you *Solar Wind's* first port of call, but that's it."

"That's all I need, darlin'."

"They're headed for Lilo," she said as her fingers curled about the credits.

"Not so fast." Kendyl's scar-roughened palm clamped down, nailing her hand and the credits to the counter. "And just how do I know you're telling the truth?"

"You don't. But then, do you hear me asking what exactly you're going to do with that information?" She smiled. "The captain's a friend of mine. I'd hate for anything to happen to him. So it looks like we just have to trust our instincts." With that, she jerked her hand, credits and all, out from beneath his. "Gentlemen..." she drawled as she turned away.

CHAPTER FOUR

Over the next two weeks Slater tended to his duties, avoiding Kira like the plague. All he wanted was to get to Lilo, unload his cargo--stowaway in particular--and get back to normal routine. Having Kira on board was putting things in a serious cramp. Conversations now had to be guarded. Plans and strategies were confined to private quarters. And to make matters worse, his extended 10-man crew members were now relegated to living in the secret smugglers hold with orders to remain there until he said otherwise. Despite the fact that the space was set up to accommodate short term living, tempers were flaring over the inconvenience. Zeke, nonetheless, had no choice but to stand by his decision. He wasn't about to explain the extra crewmen, or anything else to Kira.

Precious few knew Slater's true occupation. Though he appeared as a hotshot pilot, the ruse was simply a front for a dangerous job that required a larger crew working at his side. In reality, Zeke was a privateer for a secret alliance of merchants whose goal was to search out and cripple pirate ships menacing the trade routes. Any plunder recovered in the process, all the better.

To the unknowing eye, *Solar Wind* seemed nothing more than a tired thirty-five-year-old freighter that had seen more than her share of hyperspace. Yet, despite appearances, nothing could have been farther from the truth. The ship was thirty-five all right, but she was also in excellent running condition. The puddle of number two lubricant that dripped from her starboard landing jack came from a specially installed tank located within the landing jack's housing. A flip of a switch set the leak into action. The flip of yet a second switch had *the Wind* sagging to starboard with a low groan. The use of both deceptions simultaneously had anyone believing her starboard hydraulics were shot, and more than once the sham had come in handy.

Solar Wind was the result of months of planning and revamping. Her electronics and covert weaponry were not quite two years old. Her beefed-up drives were routinely upgraded, and as a result, she was more than capable of pushing through space as fast, if not faster, than anything out there.

Having once belonged to a smuggler, the ship already had secret storage compartments in a dozen various places. But the hidden smuggling hold at the stern was a bonus no one had expected. With a bit of redesigning, it concealed a large storage area with living accommodations that included provisions for meals and hygiene.

And it was here Slater's hand-picked crew would remain until Kira could be safely ushered off ship.

Her legs alone will be permanently etched upon your mind, won't they, pal.

Ignoring the silent voice, he pondered the fact that she had to be up to something.

But what really leaves you a little shaky--is that for one fleeting instant, you actually considered her offer. The inner voice laughed. *Didn't you, old man? And it was there in your eyes for her to see.*

What the devil was she doing out on the docks at that time of night, he wondered?

She's developed into more of a woman than you ever imagined possible, hasn't she?

Shut-up! he shouted silently. I don't even like her, let alone--

The voice laughed. *Since when did liking her have anything to do with it? It's called lust, old boy. The body can do it without even involving the mind.*

"I don't know what the all-fire hurry is." Entering the helm, Frank's gravelly voice jolted Slater from his present torment. "We sure as lasers are makin' good time."

Frank Reno was an energetic man nearly twice Slater's age. Besides being First Officer, Frank was also ship's cook, medic, captain's mentor and, last but far from least, a trusted friend.

"Yeah, even better time than I'd hoped." Taking another sip from his mug, Zeke mulled over the interesting changes that had slowly come over Frank during the past two weeks. Little Miss Stowaway had him falling all over himself. Just this morning Frank had made temberberry biscuits--a rare delicacy coming from the modest galley of the *Solar Wind*. In truth, Slater couldn't remember a time when the cuisine had been so...creative. Let him pamper her if it makes him happy. She'll be off-ship soon, and then they could all get back to normal routine.

"At this rate we should put down at Lilo in about..." Frank paused while processing an estimated E.T.A on the MAINCOMP, "about twenty-six hours."

Setting his mug down, Zeke raised his arms over his head and stretched. "Twenty-six hours and looking good."

Frank suddenly cleared his throat and rose from his seat. "Uh, I'm not so sure about the looking good part, Boss." The laughter in his voice was Zeke's first warning. "Yep, from the looks of it, I'd say you've got a small rogue asteroid approachin' astern. And judgin' from the look on 'er face, you're gonna have to do some fancy maneuverin' to avoid a collision with this one." Looking suspiciously like the proverbial rat abandoning ship, Frank high-tailed it for his place on the other side of the helm.

Zeke braced himself. Smothering a groan, he donned his most pleasant smile and turned to find Kira bearing down on him with crewman, Steve Talbot, sheepishly in tow.

"Morning, Kira."

Ignoring his amiable greeting, she drew to a halt at the base of the short flight of stairs and glowered up at him. "You care to explain the subsurface monitors in your hold--the ones for Major Metals?"

His smile died. "I beg your pardon?"

"Monitors," she repeated, still glaring. "You've got two crates of them, destined for Major Metals on Echo."

Undaunted by his stare, she went on. "For your information, Zeke Slater, that shipment is unauthorized and I demand to know what it's doing in your hold."

"Someone give you permission to go snooping about in the cargo bay, Kira?" he asked softly. Zeke's gaze slid briefly to Talbot, who shrugged in helpless apology. The young crewman's only assignment over the past two weeks had been simply to entertain Kira and keep her out of trouble. A task he had heroically carried out until this moment.

"I wasn't snooping. I had asked if I could go back there because I couldn't find something, and--"

"Something..." Zeke repeated.

"Yes. Something that I was sure I had lost inside that stupid crate. And now I demand an explanation about those monitors."

Several heartbeats of silence passed in which Slater's riveting gaze never faltered. Then, as if coming to a decision..."Frank," he said softly, "you've got the con."

"Yes, sir."

Holding eye contact with Kira, Slater descended the stairs in two bounds and closed the distance between them. She inhaled sharply as he caught her arm, spun her about and propelled her right back the way she had come.

"Legs," he murmured in a clipped undertone for her ears only, "you're hardly in a position to be demanding anything, sweetheart, much less challenging me before my crew."

She tried squirming free but failed. "You owe me an explanation--"

"I owe you nothing." They were approaching her tiny cabin. "You remember me saying that if you caused me any trouble you'd be confined to quarters?"

"What?"

He pressed the access pad and the panel slid open. "I meant what I said. If you need anything," he added, steering her inside, "the com-switch is right there on the wall to your left."

Kira spun about to face him. "You can't do this!"

"I'm sure either Frank or Steve will be more than happy to get anything you need." With that he palmed the pad, closing the panel between them. Touching it one more time, he heard the audible snick of the lock.

"Don't you dare lock me in here, Zeke." Thunk! Thunk! "Zeke! Open this door!" Thunk! "You hear me?"

Setting his jaw against the twinge of regret and self-disgust, he crossed the narrow corridor where he lingered against the bulkhead, listening to her protests. She was muttering something he couldn't quite make out. Something about unauthorized monitors.

Geez, Slater... You could at least hear her out.

With a curse, he shoved his hands into his pockets and reminded himself that Kira Delaney was trouble in the worst way.

Minutes ticked by. Still rationalizing his behavior, he paced back to the panel. Kira was continuing to babble on. Something about Echo. Still, it was hard to catch all that she was saying.

At last, bracing an outstretched palm against the doorframe, Zeke blew out a long slow breath and closed his eyes against the mounting sense of responsibility stealing over him--a feeling he neither wanted, nor could shake. Hell, he wasn't her guardian. Besides, there were a thousand and one reasons why he couldn't let her stay on board, even if he wanted to, which he didn't.

The inner voice wasn't convinced. *You were curious about her years ago. Remember? It was her eyes that first caught your attention. And now... Admit it, Slater, the instant you saw her in the cargo bay you wanted her. In fact, you thought damned hard about accepting her outrageous offer before hauling her out of your cabin like a madman.* The voice laughed. *You thought about it later that night too. Didn't you, ol' boy?*

With a muttered oath, he stubbornly denied the memory of Kira's blatant invitation; denied the fact that he could still envision the rounded upsweep of her breasts, the hem of his shirt riding her shapely thighs...those legs alone...

The weeping coming from the other side of the panel had grown softer, reduced to an occasional hiccup. If only he could make out what she was saying. Zeke remained braced against the wall, oddly wanting to go to Kira, yet just as determined not to.

At last with a heavy sigh, he straightened and woodenly made his way back up the corridor where he rejoined Frank at the helm.

He didn't need to see the look on his First Officer's face to know the man was about to make a comment.

"Down right feisty, ain't she?" Frank's gaze remained on the controls.

Ignoring both the remark as well as that lazy knowing smile that Frank was so good at, Slater ascended the stairs to the helm. "Where's Talbot?"

"Last I saw 'im, he was high-tailin' it towards the back."

Without comment, Slater moved to the command console and dropped into the pilot's seat. Hundreds of tiny colored indicators winked at him as he focused his attention on the console. From there he checked the exterior sensors. It was all busy work since alarms would be screaming throughout the entire ship if there was anything out there to worry about.

Problem was, he needed something to do--anything to rid his mind of a willful little hellion with dark auburn hair, green eyes, and sexy legs that wouldn't quit.

Damn, he hated redheads. Why was it he always seemed to gravitate to women with red hair?

In spite of his efforts to avoid her over the past two weeks, Kira's image had remained emblazoned upon his mind. Every stunning detail, including a few specifics he refused to acknowledge.

"Wonder what she meant when she said that shipment of monitors weren't authorized?" Frank muttered without looking up from the console.

No response.

Reaching for his mug, Frank rose from his seat and made his way to the base of the steps where he refilled his mug from a beverage dispenser.

A muscle in Slater's jaw clenched. "I don't care what lies she's concocted, she's off at the next port."

Frank ambled back to the helm. Placing the mug to his lips, he took a tentative sip. "Leapin' lasers! This stuff's strong enough to grow hair on the roof of yer mouth!"

Slater frowned. "I said--"

"I heard what the devil y' said. I ain't deaf. Hell, go ahead. Put her off at the next port if that's what it takes to get that perpetual scowl off yer face. Who's gonna miss 'er anyway? Certainly not you."

Strained silence filled the air. Frank set his coffee down and eased into his seat. "Galdern bursitis been actin' up again," he muttered, grimacing as he worked the muscles of a stiff shoulder. "Gonna have to get in for another one of them pulse treatments when we get back."

Focusing his attention on the monitor, Slater tapped in a code and ran an experienced eye over the data flooding the screen. Since Kira had come aboard, he'd performed maintenance checks on just about every system accessible. Never had the ship been so thoroughly gone through and so completely organized as it was now.

"Y' ever bother to at least find out 'er story?"

"Nope." Slater continued scanning the monitors. He'd long ago learned to ignore Frank's knack for turning a question into a taunt. "It's not like she'd tell the truth, Frank."

"Yer so busy condemin' 'er at every turn. What if she's an innocent? Y' ever think of that?"

"Innocent?" Slater laughed then turned to his First Officer. "This isn't the first time she's pulled this stunt. Besides, everything's just a little too coincidental for my peace of mind. The sooner we get her off ship, the better. And in the meantime, I want answers."

"Wouldn't y' at least think we'd 'ave heard from her daddy by now?"

Slater was wondering the same thing. He'd lied to Kira when he'd told her they had already talked to Renn. He'd said it mainly to get a rise out of her. He could almost see the thoughts scrambling through her mind. Shock. Fear. Desperation. In just that order. But it was the fear that was eating away at him. Something wasn't right.

Truth was, all Frank had done was leave a message indicating that Kira was with them and would be returned once they set down on Lilo.

The next day a message arrived in standard form stating that there would be an arranged charter waiting for her.

That bothered him too--bothered him far more than it should. For one, why hadn't Renn responded personally? From finding Kira in the hold to no word from Renn, the whole thing was strange.

Running the cursor down the manifest, he busily highlighted a few specifics on the list. At last, with a heavy sigh, he turned to face his First Officer. "She can't stay, Frank. It's too damned dangerous. For everyone involved."

No comment. Nevertheless, Slater braced himself for the inevitable. The old man seemed to possess an uncanny ability for seeing straight through to certain people's inner feelings--namely his. Furthermore, Frank didn't seem to have any qualms about offering opinions, or advice for that matter, especially when he knew certain people weren't particularly interested in hearing it.

Withdrawing a pipe from his pocket, Frank slid the teeth-nicked stem into the corner of his mouth. "If y' ask me--"

"No one's asking, Frank." Slater's gaze remained on the screen, looking but not seeing. "Don't you find it a bit odd that she just happens to materialize at the very time we're taking on that shipment of monitors?"

"All I'm sayin' is, stowin' aboard is a serious offense and--"

"You're right on the money there." Slater leaned back, suppressing a heavy sigh. He had no sooner convinced himself there was nothing to feel guilty about when the memory of Kira's soft weeping filtered through his thoughts. He could still hear her muffled voice pleading with him through the closed panel.

Several minutes of silence passed before Frank spoke up again. "I thought y' might be interested in knowin' that after y' escorted her outta here, I ran a check on that shipment she was complainin' about."

No response.

"I found somethun' interestin'." Frank drew slowly on his pipe and waited.

Slater huffed a soft laugh and continued running a systems check. Never taking his eyes from the screen, he entered a directive into the computer and brought forth a glowing red schematic of the ship.

Frank watched a thin ribbon of smoke curl off the stem of his pipe and continued waiting. Several long and silent moments passed before Slater finally turned to pin his First Officer with a hard stare. "Is there a point you're trying to make?"

Frank shrugged. "It's probably nothin'--but, like I say, I did a little checkin' of my own. I checked their scan authorization against the one we have in our system."

Slater's brow lifted.

"Its close," Frank went on, studying his pipe with idle interest. "So close in fact, it passed our primary scanners without a hitch. But just for the hell of it I ran a detailed computer analysis, comparin' it directly to the voice pattern we have on file."

He had Slater's full attention now. "And...?"

"And it ain't her. She's right. That shipment ain't properly authorized."

Slater's narrowed eyes held fast. "What are you saying?"

"I'm not sure." Conversation momentarily lapsed as Frank raked back his unruly gray hair. "I even ran a backup. Same results." Frank leaned back in his chair and drew meditatively on his pipe. "Alls I know is--if the girl don't know more than we do, then we got ourselves a little problem."

"Well, in case you hadn't noticed," Slater cut in, "we've had ourselves a little problem from the minute we found Kira onboard. She isn't here by accident, Frank. She slipped through security for a reason, and I intend to find out why."

As far as Zeke was concerned, the timing sucked. They'd carefully orchestrated each detail of this mission and had worked hard securing the contract for hauling shipments. It was a dicey plan at best, but they were too damn close to their goal now to start believing in coincidences.

"What if she don't know what's going on?" Frank mused. "Maybe she's being used and she don't even know it." He absently stuck his pipe between his teeth.

Exhaling a slow breath that puffed out his cheeks, Slater once again turned control over to Frank and rose from his seat.

Descending the flight of stairs, he entered the corridor, passed the wall of storage lockers, the lav, the galley, and finally drew to a halt before Kira's tiny makeshift cabin. The lock disengaged with a click. "Kira?" he said, activating the intercom, "It's me. I'm coming in."

He waited a moment. No response.

Without hesitation, Slater touched the access pad and the door hissed open. Clutching the top of the doorframe, he peered inside. The cabin was dark; the only illumination was streaming in from the corridor behind him. "You awake?"

Still no response. He let go of the frame and stepped inside. Touching a switch to his right, he activated indirect lighting. There, in the shadows, lay Kira, curled up on the bunk, silently watching him.

"We need to talk."

"I didn't invite you in." Her sullen voice was barely audible.

"Pardon me?"

"I said...I didn't invite you in." She turned over and faced the wall. "So go away."

"Not until I get a few answers."

"Well, you're going to have a long wait," she said to the wall.

"Then I might as well take a seat and get comfortable."

That brought her head around. "Not unless you want to discuss that shipment of subsurface monitors."

He came a step closer. "All I do is haul freight, Kira. That doesn't make me a part of some conspiracy or whatever it is you're suspecting. I pick up a consignment. I take it to its drop. It's that simple."

"I thought you're supposed to run a compliance check on everything that comes on board."

"We do. Look--we can talk about the monitors later. What I want are some straight answers."

"I already told you." Sitting up, Kira rose from the bunk, meeting him toe to toe. "Number one," she said, stabbing him in the chest with her finger, "I did not stow aboard. You got that, Slater? And two, I have no idea how I got here."

"And you expect me to believe that."

"I don't care whether you believe it or not. It's the truth."

"Okay. Let me see here. I've got two stories to choose from. The first is that you came aboard to mend our differences and to form--or should I say ignite--a friendship. A bit ridiculous, yet--tempting just the same." Kira blushed. He ignored it and went on. "Now, the second story is far less intriguing, but just as ridiculous. Supposedly, out of the blue, for no apparent reason, you found yourself locked in a produce pod--in my cargo hold."

Her jaw set, Kira remained stubbornly silent.

Slater folded his arms. "Tell me, Kira, does this happen often-- miraculously winding up in cargo holds? I mean, it could be a real pain if you were discovered by the wrong sort of captain."

"And just where do you figure you fit in?"

He stared at her for several heartbeats, his gaze intense. "Don't push me."

"I'd like you to leave--now."

"I'm not going anywhere, until I get answers."

"Well you've got a long wait, because I don't have the answers you're looking for."

~ * ~

Port Lilo:

"*Solar Wind*, this is Lilo Control. You have confirmation for Docking Bay Twenty Nine."

Slater's eyes were fixed on the instrument panel. "That's an affirmative. Initiating descent now."

Kira had stubbornly stuck to her story, giving no clue of her reason for stowing aboard. He might have been tempted to believe her, had he not known her. The problem plaguing him now was whether their cover was blown or not.

He wanted her off ship, and yet, no matter how hard he tried to tamp it down, there was a sense of uneasiness that just wouldn't go away.

He should be celebrating the fact that he would soon be ridding himself of her. Instead, a nagging feeling had been troubling him for the last several hours. Call it premonition. Instinct. Whatever the hell it was, he didn't like it.

At regular intervals a soft chime broke the silence, signaling designated drops in elevation.

"Frank, I want the cargo loaded, and this ship ready to lift in one hour. Less, if you can do it."

"You got it, Boss."

It wasn't long before the proximity alarm was sounding as the ground seemed to rise up beneath them. Rooster tails of dust coiled about as the *Solar Wind* danced mere inches off the blackened surface toward its assigned berth. Slater's gaze slid briefly to the external VIDSCREEN. Lilo's spaceport consisted of docking bays--dozens of them, each defined by large glowing neon numbers. Leaning forward, he made an adjustment on the console then reached overhead, completing the task with a flip of a toggle switch.

Frank cleared his throat. "Knowin' what it takes to change a voice pattern, I'd be willin' to wager she either knows more than she's letting on, or that little gal's in way over her head."

Silently denying similar concerns, Slater calmly made another adjustment on the control panel. "Decreasing forward motion by ninety percent."

"Zero-one-zero 'til we're in," Frank responded, and with a shrug added, "Of course, that's just my opinion--about Kira, I mean."

"Right."

"Know what else I think?"

Slater's jaw tightened. Frank was going to tell him regardless.

"There's only one way to bamboozle a voice scanner." He shot Slater a brief glance. "And hell, Boss, nobody drags out the heavy artillery unless they're serious."

No response. His hands calmly moving from one control to the next, Slater gave no indication of his mirrored thoughts or mounting concern. Oh, he'd tried asking Kira about the voice patterns, even started to tell her about Frank's findings, but she'd have none of it, refusing to even talk to him. Fine. He'd play her little game.

"I just wish we could connect with Renn before puttin' 'er on some chartered flight."

Slater slid him another hard look, well aware of what the older man was doing. Both he and Talbot were so thoroughly besotted with Kira, all she had to do was bat her lashes over those big green innocents and they were reduced to blithering idiots.

"Alls I'm sayin' is, her life could be in danger," Frank went on.

With a lopsided grin, Slater slowly shook his head and proceeded to guide the *Solar Wind* into her assigned bay. "She's got you and Talbot so snowed you don't know what the hell you're talking about." He entered a command into the MAINCOMP, killing power to the thrusters as he gently lowered the ship onto her landing jacks.

Turning to face Frank, he added, "Why don't you ask little Miss Stowaway about her adventure to Kelly's Haven, Frank. She was a stowaway then too. Oh, and while you're at it, ask her how Lance Girard died."

"I ain't defendin' 'er. I'm just wantin' to avoid another casualty, that's all."

Trying to ignore him, Slater made a final entry, shutting down most of the system and placing the rest on standby. He waited patiently while bank after bank of indicators winked out in response. At last he released his safety harness and stood up. "You ready?"

Muttering beneath his breath, Frank rose to his feet.

"I'll go get Kira," Slater said, descending the stairs to the corridor.

"You want me to do anything, Captain?" Talbot asked.

"Yes. While we're gone, I want a detailed backup on literally everything in our hold--in particular anything tagged for Major Metals. I want to know what it is, where it's from and exactly where it's going."

"I'll get on that right away," Talbot snapped, still blatant in his eagerness to make up for escorting Kira to the cargo bay.

An exhaust-tainted breeze greeted them as the main hatch irised open. "Let's go," Zeke barked over the descending whine of *Solar Wind's* turbines.

40

"I don't believe this," Kira shouted back. "Whatever happened to good old-fashioned hospitality?"

He reached for her elbow and began ushering her down the ramp. "It went out with prop planes and parachutes."

"You just won't give me a chance, will you?" she complained.

"Nope."

"Why have you always expected the worst of me?"

"Don't take it personally, Legs. I also expect Greegs to bite if given the chance."

Upon reaching the base of the ramp, Kira jerked free of his grip and marched on ahead. Her heavy hair, haphazardly piled atop her head, bounced with every step she took. "I'd think you'd at least--"

"Spare me the wounded heart. Besides, after the last time you stowed aboard, I would think you'd understand my position."

"Oh, please...I can't believe you're still dredging that up. What was I...eighteen at the time?"

Zeke's long strides brought him effortlessly abreast of her. "Let's put it this way, you were old enough to know better. Geez, Kira, if you hadn't tripped that motion detector when you did--"

"A mistake I sorely regret."

Grabbing her by the wrist, he spun her about to face him. "You're missing the whole point. You have no idea how close I came to shutting down life support to the cargo bay."

"Sure, I do. You've reminded me enough." With that she snatched her hand from his grasp and resumed her trek across the landing zone.

"Four years--and still the same."

She ignored him as he fell into step beside her. "Easy," he cautioned, cupping her elbow and guiding her over a cluster of fuel lines stretched across their path.

"You know of course, just because you put me on a charter doesn't mean I'm staying." Again she tugged her arm free.

"That's true, but once I see you safely aboard, my responsibility's over."

"How gallant."

Without comment, he directed her toward the entrance of a small and crudely constructed terminal. As with most mining outposts, luxuries were an uncommon commodity, and Lilo was no exception. The place was rough, dirty, litter-strewn, and smelled incredibly bad. In short, Kira found it a hellhole--heavy with a variety of nasty odors that ranged from undefined bodily odors, to the stench of exhaust and raw fuel that had made its way in from the landing zone.

CHAPTER FIVE

Kira regarded the tattered, mural-sized map hanging at the head of the stairs. Various mines were depicted in faded red. Many were clustered together, while others were spaced farther apart. It was the word UNCHARTED, however, that seemed to take up most of the topography as it slashed across the map in bold letters.

Once they'd reached the top of the steps, Zeke again caught her elbow. "This way," he said, steering her off to a rundown seating area. "Wait here, while I arrange for your passage."

"I'll tell you what, Zeke. While you're doing that I'm going to visit the facilities."

"Kira, this is not the sort of--" His eyes narrowed suspiciously. "You realize you're on your own if you take off. I won't come looking for you."

"Well, that's certainly a relief," she drawled, sending him a sugary smile. "I'd hate for you to come storming the doors of the ladies' lav just because I happen to take a little longer at this sort of thing than you do."

He gave a quick sweep of the area. "Five minutes. I mean it."

The condition of the terminal's entrance should have been her first clue as to the squalid condition of the restroom. But even worse was discovering that the facility was one big community lav where privacy was virtually nonexistent. Although there were three commodes with privacy panels still intact, modesty, Kira discovered, came with a price tag.

And the problem was, her credits--what little she had with her-- were tucked in a tiny travel pac, presently slung over Zeke's shoulder.

With a heavy sigh, she weighed two options, neither of which held much appeal. One was to swallow her pride and forgo privacy. The other entailed making a trip back to find Zeke.

She opted for the latter.

"You want me to go in with you?" He was dead serious as he handed over more than enough credits from his own pocket. Truth of it was, she had anticipated amusement lurking in his eyes, but instead found solemn resolve.

"No, I'll be fine."

"Make it quick."

A short time later, Kira emerged, expecting to find Zeke lounging against the wall just outside the lav. Instead, he was a short distance away talking with someone who looked suspiciously like another pilot. Probably arranging the chartered flight. There was no way she was taking that flight only to end up dead at the other end. Besides, even if she were to leave now, how would she track the monitors, or learn where or to whom they were going? If she could just get a message off to Grant, alert him of the *Solar Wind's* arrival and incoming consignment. Then she'd gladly leave everything in Grant's capable hands. Kira quickly glanced about, noting a sign near a back exit indicating that a Communications Center was located in a building on the far side of the landing zone. With a quick glance back at Zeke and a sharp intake of breath, she turned for the exit.

Once again the stench of a spaceport greeted her as she stepped out of the building onto the tarmac. Darkness had settled in quickly, and overhead the vast spiral of the galaxy stretched across a moonless sky. Resolved in her decision, Kira quickly began making her way across the LZ, sidestepping service equipment and fuel lines snaking across her path.

"Well, well, looks like we found ourselves a piece of lost baggage."

Kira's arm was grabbed from behind. "And in such a hurry too." came another voice.

Sheer fright swept through her as she struggled vainly to break free. "Let go of me!"

The grip tightened. "Now is that any way to treat someone who's just trying to be friendly?"

Screaming was a distant thought. It would have taken more concentration than Kira possessed at the moment. Besides, who would hear her? Trying for a figment of rationality, she quickly gauged the distance to the Communications building. If she could free herself long enough--

"Just try it," he said, following her glance, "and you aren't going to like the consequences."

"But we will," the other man chimed in.

Before either of them knew what she was about, Kira brought up a swift, accurate knee. But she wasn't quick enough to escape before she was grabbed again. "You want to play rough, do you?"

"Make her pay," the injured man roared, his scowl murderous as he wilted to one knee. "Teach her a lesson!"

Suddenly, she was being roughly backed into the shadows. "You won't be so high and mighty when I get through with you," he said shoving her up against a stack of cargo pallets. With that, he grabbed the front of her shirt and yanked hard. A final twist popped open the top three fasteners. "I'll show you what--"

"Let her go."

It was a deep voice--taut with rage, and one that Kira immediately recognized. Peeking around the brute pinning her against the pallets, Kira caught sight of Zeke.

One might have thought he was engaged in nothing more than casual conversation. Yet, Kira easily sensed the fury hidden beneath that air of cool nonchalance. "You're going to be sorry now," she whispered, squirming unsuccessfully to break free.

With lazy regard, Zeke's gaze dropped to the hand manacling her wrist. "You want to release her, or shall I do it for you?" His languid tone was deceptive, yet the calm warning was perfectly clear when the bore of his weapon leveled on the man's upper arm.

Still, it took the audible snick of the weapon's trigger mechanism to spur the assailant into action. Spitting on the ground, he released Kira and stepped back. "You won't get away with this."

Zeke stared at him hard, his tawny hair rising and falling in a sudden breeze. "Step away, Kira." His eyes remained locked in silent combat with her captor.

"Now, with two fingers," he calmly instructed, "I want both of you to very slowly remove your weapons from their holsters and place them on the ground."

"You have no idea who you're messing with, mister."

Zeke's eyes grew openly amused. "Your weapons."

Reluctantly, both men slowly withdrew their handguns and placed them on the ground.

"Now, kick them over here." Without lowering his weapon or even sparing Kira a glance, he shrugged out of his jacket and thrust it at her.

Thankful for the covering, Kira slipped into the jacket.

As instructed, the guns were kicked over. "You're a dead man, mister."

Zeke ignored the threat. "You okay, Kira?" he asked, still without looking at her.

"Yes."

"You think you can collect their guns for me?"

"Yes." Feeling a sudden surge of strength, Kira pushed up the sleeves of the jacket and moved to gather the weapons. "I'd be real careful about issuing idle threats," she hissed to the one who'd just threatened Zeke. "You have no idea who you're messing with either."

"Kira! Just get their damn guns, will you?"

Snatching up the last of the weapons, she returned to Zeke's side, purposefully avoiding his heated glare.

"Drop them in there," he said with a nod to a large lubricant vat sitting off to the side, "then get behind that crane and, for godsake, stay there." Once she had done as he'd asked, he addressed her attackers. "You boys just out for a little fun tonight? Or are you following orders?"

No response.

Zeke started to advance on the men. "Maybe Port Security can get more out of you."

As quick as a striking viper, a small handgun materialized in the hand of one of the men. And in a moment frozen in time, Kira watched white fire belch from its bore.

Zeke dropped to one knee, his own gun roaring twice in response. And then there was silence.

"Kira?"

"I'm all right."

"Sonofabitch! Ahh, dammit!" Zeke was still muttering curses as she stepped out from behind the crane. Clamping a hand over a wound in his left arm, he used the toe of his boot to nudge one of the men onto his back. For a long moment he simply stood there studying him. Finally lowering himself to one knee he single-handedly dug through the man's pockets. From there he moved on to the next body.

Kira moved closer. "Oh, Zeke, you're hurt!" A bright red stain was spreading rapidly.

Without comment, he examined the second man in much the same manner as he had the first.

"Zeke, you need to--"

"You ever seen either of these men before, Kira?"

In a numb, detached sort of way she glanced down at the bodies sprawled before her. "Never. Why? Who are they?"

"I was hoping you could tell me." Rising to his feet, he stared at a security printout. "They each had a copy of this on them."

Trembling inside, Kira stared at the image. "What is it?"

"It's a printout from a security cam. Nice job, Legs. You've managed to drag me into your mess this time."

Silently, she studied the picture. Zeke was in the foreground, inspecting the wing tip of the *Solar Wind*. "How do you suppose they got--?"

"Who the hell's on your tail?" he interrupted, his tone accusatory.

"No one. Did you ever stop to think that maybe they're on yours?"

A sidelong glance was his only response as he snatched the printout from her hand, stuffing both copies into a back pocket. "It's one thing being caught on a routine security scan. It's quite another, finding my picture crammed in some goon's jacket."

"Don't go blaming me. I'm as much a victim as you are." Her gaze drifted to Zeke's injured arm. The flow of blood was not being staunched, even by his grip. "Zeke, you're losing so much blood!"

He shot her a hard look. "Let's get the hell outta here." His resentment was unmasked as he took off across the landing zone with Kira half running to keep up.

"Zeke, I am sorry about this. I really am. I never dreamed anything would happen. I'd planned on coming back. Honestly. I only wanted to--"

"Shut up, Kira!"

~ * ~

"Don't ask me how that slug missed hittin' a main artery," Frank muttered, his voice drifting into the corridor. "The way you were bleedin' I thought it had."

Silence as Frank set to work.

"Yer just damn lucky. That's all I gotta say".

"Just patch me up."

Still wearing Zeke's jacket, Kira moved to the entrance of the galley and peered inside. He was slouched in a chair, his jaw clenched, most of the color drained from his face. His bloodied shirt had been stripped away, and his arm was positioned on the surface of the table for Frank's solemn inspection.

"What can I do to help?"

Zeke never glanced up. The telltale twitch of a jaw muscle was the only acknowledgment of her presence.

"Hot water," Frank replied. "And lots of it."

"Done." Stepping into the galley, she hurried past Zeke, skillfully avoiding his thunderous expression as she made her way for the sink. Once there, she found and filled a large container with steaming hot water.

"Right over here," Frank directed without looking up.

It was then she saw the full extent of the damage to Zeke's left bicep, how the heavy slug had torn a vicious furrow through the main tendon. "Is there anything else I can do or get?"

"Not right now, but stay close."

Lapsing into silence, Kira's eyes slowly lifted to meet Zeke's penetrating gaze. His eyes, now smoky with pain, were an irreproachable indicator of his mood--and for several heartbeats she felt herself held immobile by their intensity.

Then his eyes slid closed and he stiffened, an indrawn breath hissing through his teeth as he wordlessly endured Frank's probing examination. An elusive dimple flashed in his right cheek then disappeared. "Damn it, Frank," he gasped, grabbing the edge of the bench with his free hand.

Kira flinched. "Isn't there something you can give him that would ease the pain?"

"Nothin' that wouldn't knock him out," Frank replied, "and right now, I need him alert."

Unable to watch any longer, she glanced away.

"Kira, there's a second med kit in that far storage cabinet," Frank called out, "Would y' get it?"

She hurried to do his bidding, her heart wrenching at the sound of yet another low growl. Though Frank kept to his task, Kira sensed something was wrong. There seemed to be a sudden urgency in his tone, a deeper frown as he continued probing the injury, removing bits and pieces of Zeke's shirt along with some sort of strange purplish residue.

"Hurry." His tone had turned rough.

Quickly setting the kit down, she opened it and stepped aside. "What's wrong," she whispered, noting Frank's expression had indeed moved from concern to visible alarm.

He didn't answer. The silence stretched on, taut with tension as his look continued to darken. Helpless to do anything but wring her hands, Kira remained close by, watching as the older man tenaciously worked.

With the exception of a stifled gasp every now and then, Zeke had begun to fall silent.

"How y' doin' son?" The fear in Frank's voice was obvious.

"I'm--okay," came a sluggish response. "...Tired."

Zeke's reflexes seemed to be getting progressively lethargic. Kira felt a host of inner alarms at his hesitation, the dispassion in his tone, and his eyes not quite tracking before drifting closed.

Frank had obviously noticed it too. His head jerked up with a frown. "Stay with me Capt'n!" he ordered sharply. Turning, he quickly rifled through the med kit. At last, finding what he was looking for, he grabbed a small container, opened it and feverishly began smoothing a silky-looking salve directly into the open wound.

Frequently, he would lift his head, nervously gauging Zeke's responses as he worked. And each time, Kira watched his scowl deepen. "Dammit, Slater," he bellowed, "I said stay with me!"

Zeke's body jolted. "...I--am."

"The hell you are," Frank growled. "Kira." He caught her roughly by the elbow and propelled her a few steps away. "I don't care how," he whispered harshly, shoving a small vial into her hand, "just get a dose of this stuff into him."

She nodded, glancing down at the tiny bottle of clear liquid in her hand. "Injection?" she asked.

"No. By mouth. Water, juice, whatever it takes. Press right here for a measured dose."

"I'll get it down him, Frank," she promised. Rushing to a storage cupboard across the galley, she retrieved a drinking glass. Working quickly, she retrieved a carafe of juice from the cooler and poured a small amount into the glass. Next, she added one dose of the medication as Frank had instructed. At last she hurried back to Zeke's side. "Here, drink this."

No response.

She touched his shoulder and spoke a little louder. "Zeke?"

Slater opened his eyes, regarding both her and the glass with unmasked annoyance.

"Its just juice. Drink it."

Wordlessly his eyes drifted closed again.

"Zeke, you've lost a lot of blood, and you need--"

"No."

"Hold still will y'!" Frank barked, trying his best to pinch the wound together and apply an epidermal adhesive at the same time.

"Drink it, Zeke," Kira persisted. "It will help with the pain."

At that he half-laughed. "I don't need--" But his words were cut off with another groan as Frank applied sudden pressure to his arm.

"You're as thick-skinned as an Azar, aren't you?" Kira goaded. "Of course you don't need any help."

Zeke's scowl increased. "All this concern isn't--going to work, Kira. You're still--in big--trouble."

"Frank, do you keep any Scotch around here? At least that will help take the edge off of things."

"Now you're talkin'," Zeke drawled.

Yeah, Kira figured he'd go for that. She shot Frank a private look that plainly asked if it was okay to mix this stuff with alcohol.

"In the lounge." Frank's verbal answer included a discreet nod of consent.

The ship's lounge/galley formed a large circular area in the middle of the ship. The lounge was on the port side, and the galley on the starboard with the main corridor dividing them right down the center. Hurrying into the lounge, Kira found a half-filled bottle of Terran Scotch. She measured out one shot, then released another dose of the drug before rushing to Zeke's side. "I promise I'll confess everything just as soon as you're feeling better."

"Damn right...you will." This time he readily accepted the offered drink. "And I'd better have--straight answers."

"I promise."

Without hesitation, he tossed back the harsh blend in one burning swallow.

"The truth," he added hoarsely.

"That too," she answered gently, closely watching him.

Even now, he was undeniably sexy. Despite having not ever been on the receiving end of his masculine appeal, Kira was far from immune to the heady male allure. Zeke Slater was a killer combination of seductive magnetism and just enough boyish charm to create a potent mix that most women found endearing and hard to resist.

"Just as soon as Frank is finished here," she said, snatching up his empty glass, "you're going to lie down. Then afterward, I promise that we will--"

"The hell I am!" That stubborn set of his jaw plainly emphasized his determination.

Kira didn't argue. In silence, she waited as Frank tore open a package of mediwraps and finished binding Zeke's injured arm to his side. "There," he muttered, critically eyeing his work. "I've done all I can for now." With a sigh, he gathered up both med kits and turned for the storage wall.

Kira's glance moved back to Zeke, taking in his heavy-lidded eyes, dull and glazed with pain. Just when she was beginning to feel thankful that she'd managed to get the medication down him, suddenly his good arm lashed out and his hand clamped about her wrist.

"Whadya put--in the Scotch?"

"Nothing."

"Don't give me that. You put something--"

"Zeke, it was just something to--" She gasped as his hand tightened with surprising strength.

"Damn you!" Releasing her abruptly, he rose from the bench, swaying on his feet as he towered above her.

"Zeke, please. Sit down."

He frowned--his eyes glassy. "You drugged me." Anticipating what was about to happen next, Kira lunged forward as he staggered, his legs buckling. The next instant, his inert weight was taking her down with him, pinning her to the deck beneath his body.

"Lord help me, darlin', are y' hurt?" came Frank's grizzled voice, taut with concern. She could hear his footfalls getting closer.

"I'm all right. He's just heavy."

"Don't you worry, I'll have that big fella off y' quicker than a hyper jump."

Within moments, Kira felt Zeke's weight being lifted.

Exhaling with the effort, Frank hoisted his captain's limp body over his shoulder and laboriously began making his way down the passageway. Kira rushed on ahead to Zeke's cabin and quickly turned down the cover on his bunk.

"What's wrong?" she whispered, watching as Frank eased Zeke's relaxed body down onto the mattress.

"I wager he's gonna be here for a spell, so help me get 'im undressed. You get his boots while I loosen his pants."

"That sedative couldn't possibly be working so fast, and why did we give it orally instead of by injection?" she went on, her attention on getting Zeke's boots off as Frank began unbuckling Zeke's belt. "Is there something you're not telling me?" she asked as the first boot fell to the floor with a thud.

"Yes." Without further explanation, Frank began loosening the waistband of Zeke's pants.

"But, I thought--"

"You got those boots off?"

"Almost." A final tug had the second one dropping to the floor.

When Frank glanced back up, Kira realized that *Solar Wind's* First Officer was looking as though he'd just lost his best friend. "What aren't you telling me?" she asked, her heart in her throat.

Dragging his bleak gaze away from his captain, Frank began, "That was no sedative, Kira. It was Stenzoid. An antitoxin. And this particular medicine works best when given orally."

"Antitoxin? But, that's...for--"

"Poison."

Kira's gaze flicked back to Zeke. "But...I don't understand."

"Kira," he said, raking a hand through his wiry gray hair, "there's a whole lot you don't understand."

"But, he'll be all right, won't he? I mean, it was a flesh wound. Wasn't it?"

Using his sleeve, Frank mopped his forehead. "Truth is, darlin', I don't know if e's goin' to be all right or not." He studied Kira for a long moment. "What sort of trouble are y' runnin' from, girl?" He shook his head and with a meaningful nod toward Zeke added, "If...he makes it through this, he'll be askin' that same question. And, I can tell y', he won't be settlin' for anything but the truth."

Tense silence filled the room until at last he asked, "Y' ever heard of coated slugs?"

"No."

He nodded. "I knew we were in trouble the instant I seen that residue." He paused, his gaze flicking back to Zeke.

"My guess is that slug that ripped though his arm was coated with Tenacide."

Kira stared at him, remembering the purplish residue she'd watched Frank frantically remove from the wound.

"It works like an insurance policy," he went on, his tone turning cold. "If the slug don't get the job done, the poison will."

Silence followed as Kira's gaze gravitated back to Zeke.

"Once it enters the bloodstream, it works fast," Frank added. "But if I've done my job, and if luck's on his side, he'll pull through. If not..." his voice trailed off and Kira watched a muscle work along his stubbled jaw. After a moment, he added, "At least he's got three things goin' for 'im. One: the slug laid the flesh open rather than puncturin' deep into the muscle. Two: with all that bleedin' he done, along with the cleanin', it should 'ave flushed out good. And three:" he said, his gaze lifting to meet Kira's, "that boy's just too damn stubborn to let it get the best of 'im."

CHAPTER SIX

"So, what happens next?" she asked quietly.

Frank slowly shook his head. "We wait." Several moments of silence followed as they both looked upon the man lying so still and helpless. At last Frank pulled a chair closer to the bed and with a heavy sigh, lifted his old man's eyes to meet Kira's. "Here, have a seat. I'm gonna spell Talbot at the helm. If anything changes, you call me, okay? The intercom's on the wall, right by the door."

Over the next four hours, Kira never left Zeke's side. One of the first things she did was clean the blood that had dried on his hands and under his nails.

She was mopping his brow with cool water when Frank returned. "How's he doin'?"

Kira straightened. "He feels a little feverish."

"Here, let me take over for y'."

"I'm all right, Frank. Really."

"Just for a little while, honey," he insisted. "It's been nearly six hours since it all began, and for now he's stable. And that's good. So you go get yourself somethin' to eat and a bit of rest."

Kira's focus remained on Zeke's still form. At last she rose from the chair. "Okay. I'll take a break, but I don't think I can sleep."

"If you do nothin' more than lie down for a spell then you can take over for me while I'll do the same."

With a nod of compliance, Kira turned for the door.

"Try to rest, Kira," he called after her, his tone serious. "This ain't over yet, and I can't have y' faintin' from exhaustion on me."

The galley was dimly lit when she entered. Filling a glass with cold water, she took a long drink. Food was the last thing she wanted, but for Frank she forced down a commercially prepared meal. Afterward, she indulged in a quick shower.

She traded Zeke's leather jacket for a baggy button-up shirt and a pair of slip-on pants, rolling the length into cuffs. Removing his jacket, however, had brought with it a pang of regret. If he hadn't given her his jacket, he would have still been wearing it at the time he was shot. Knowing how durable taubear hide was, Kira couldn't help but wonder if most of the poison wouldn't have been deposited on the leather instead of in his wound. Maybe Zeke wouldn't be lying here now, unconscious and fighting for his life.

And, a small voice intruded, *if you hadn't taken off in the first place, the entire scene could have been avoided.*

Carrying her guilt with her, Kira lowered her weary bones onto a small wall-bed in the lounge that Frank had let down for her use. Three hours later, she awoke only marginally rested but unwilling to stay away any longer.

Frank was just finishing up redressing Zeke's wound when she returned. The bond was tangible between this older man and his captain; a bond she suspected went beyond mere station.

He finished adjusting the sheet at Zeke's waist and turned to face her. "Feelin' better?"

"Yes, thank you." She moved to the edge of the bunk. "How is he?"

He shrugged. "The same."

Kira stared down at the man lying in such stillness, watching the throb of pulse at his throat. "But...he's going to live, isn't he?"

A moment's hesitation then Frank said, "For now." He lifted a container of clear gel. "I just finished puttin' this on 'im. Between this and the injections I've been givin' 'im, it should help with the fever."

According to Frank, the first twenty-four hours were the most critical of all, but until the fever broke and Zeke regained consciousness, the instructions were that he was to be watched around the clock.

Frank and Kira took turns--one attempting to sleep while the other stood vigil. Every hour Zeke's body was sponged down with the gel, and every four hours the wound was redressed with a special salve Frank called Acuel.

By the end of the second day, Zeke was in such a feverish state, Kira seriously doubted that anything was helping. "Don't you dare give up!" she whispered. "Fight, dammit!"

It was odd that he didn't thrash about or mumble deliriously. Instead, he just lay there burning up, his skin dry and hot to the touch. By the third day, something unseen startled Zeke awake. Bolting effortlessly into a sitting position, he looked at her in unfocused confusion before falling back against the pillow.

Sometime during the fourth night, Zeke grabbed a fistful of her hair and held on. "Don't leave me!" he grated out. "Dear God, don't leave me!" And all of heaven's anguish showed in the depth of his stormy eyes. It took every ounce of Kira's strength just to pry his fist open enough to extricate her hair. And then it was over. As quickly as it began, Zeke once again lapsed into unconsciousness, his breathing hard and labored.

"I won't leave you," she vowed. "I promise I'll stay right here." She wondered how many levels there were to unconsciousness and whether he could even hear her, let alone understand.

The waiting was the worst part, although Frank kept insisting that each new day was another milestone. To Kira's way of thinking, Zeke was only growing weaker, the poison claiming new territory with each day. Soon it would all be for nothing, this war they were waging.

She fell asleep that night exhausted, leaning forward in the chair with her head and shoulders resting on the edge of the bunk next to Zeke.

~ * ~

Slater came awake by degrees, gingerly testing each new level before moving on to the next. Gradually focusing his blurred vision on the ceiling, he willed the cabin to stop spinning.

He'd been dreaming of an angel, a gentle guardian whose eyes were as green and shimmering as the skies of Nimora. He could still feel her cool hands caressing him all over; hear her comforting voice. And when the pain and heat had been at its worst, he remembered clinging to her desperately. Her touch, her voice--the only anchor keeping him from being sucked down into the bowels of darkness.

But it had all been a dream, and for now he needed to focus on reality. Ever so slowly, his eyes took in his surroundings, straining for some sort of connection between the dreams, the throbbing pain throughout his body and the utter weakness he was feeling. It wasn't until he began to move that reality broke through the fog with excruciating clarity. He'd been shot. He remembered that much. He'd been winged in the arm by two goons trying to--Kira! Was she all right? Jerking his head up was a mistake that sent spears of pain shooting through his body.

And then his gaze settled upon her. Swallowing hard, he closed his eyes and dropped his head back onto the pillow. For what seemed an eternity, he simply lay there feeling the pressure of her arm lying across his chest and remembering the touch of cool gentle hands on his fevered body. A ripple of sizzling awareness surged through him as once again he opened his eyes and glanced down at her.

One hand rested beneath her cheek. Her lips, slightly parted, looked soft and dewy. Her dark auburn hair, impossibly long and thick, trailed wildly over one shoulder and onto his bunk. Unruly tendrils had even managed to snake their way across his belly.

It was then a groggy memory cut across his thoughts--one of ensnaring his fist in a handful of hair. And it was so damned silky. He remembered not wanting to let go--remembered that part vividly, afraid she'd leave him if he did. He recalled an angel's voice, coming from somewhere beyond the wastelands of semi-oblivion, talking to him, begging, pleading, commanding him to fight for his life, forbidding him to die.

Slater's eyes slowly drifted down to the small, warm hand cradling his own in the center of his chest. Had his angel been more than just a fevered dream? Had Kira been the one at his side during those long hours? Was it, in fact, her voice he'd heard coaxing him not to give up? From their joined hands, his gaze was drawn unbidden to the gaping neckline of the--

Everything inside him went dramatically still. The little hellion was wildly and gloriously naked beneath her shirt--correction, his shirt. Oversized and dipping low, the front opening gave him an unhampered view that left nothing to the imagination. There was only one conceivable response for a situation like this, and Slater's body responded with inevitable idiocy.

He was stunned...breathless...appalled... And the weird thing--the really disturbing thing--was that he didn't even like Kira. She not only wasn't his type, she got on his nerves. How the devil could someone who didn't even attract him induce the lust and turmoil going on right now in his gut? Not that in his present weakened condition he could do anything about it even if wanted to. Which he didn't, despite the fact he was rock hard.

Knowing what he must do, several agonizing heartbeats passed before he reluctantly tore his eyes from Kira's succulent bounty. It was time she woke up, and with a deep breath, he lifted her clasped hand to his lips before gently replacing it on his chest.

Kira stirred, blinking slumberous eyes open, and for a frozen moment neither she nor Slater moved. Heat simmered between them as they stared at one another. He watched her eyes widen as awareness gradually settled upon her features. He had always thought Kira's eyes were incredibly sexy. Yeah, he'd noticed, long ago, but never had they seemed more stunning than at this very moment.

"You're back," she whispered.

"Barely..." With blatant curiosity he witnessed the exact moment Kira became aware of the intimacy of their joined hands upon his chest. Next came the instant she realized the private view she was providing. Cheeks flaming, she bolted upright, adjusting the neckline of the shirt in one fluid motion.

"How long have I been out?" he whispered, trying not to break through the threshold of pain any more than he already had.

"A few days," she said, quickly rising from the chair. "I'll go get Frank. He wanted me to let him--"

"Kira. How long?" he repeated. Weak as he was, it was next to impossible to sound commanding.

She released a sigh and turned to face him. "Five days."

It took a moment for Slater's befuddled brain to assimilate that smidgen of news. "Five days..." He lowered his voice to a whisper, staving off the intensifying headache. "That's a bit excessive for a winged arm, wouldn't you say?"

"I wouldn't know, but I'll go find Frank."

"Don't bother. Soon as my head quits spinning, I'll find him myself."

"But you shouldn't be getting up. Here, let me fix your pillow." With a stifled groan, he allowed her to adjust his pillow. "There now," she said, her voice sounding almost breathy, "isn't that more comfy?"

Hell no, he wasn't comfy. His head was killing him and his arm was bound so tight he was sure the circulation had been cut off. Even worse were the thoughts he'd been entertaining ever since he awoke to find her sleeping at his side...and that didn't even count the looking he'd done. Yeah, he looked. Shamelessly took his time, in fact. What normal guy wouldn't?

But that's not the point, is it Slater? What really appalls you is the fact that right now your gut is burning--for Kira Delaney, of all people.

Choosing to ignore the inner taunt, Zeke continued questioning Kira. "People don't pass out for five days from a winged arm. And they sure as hell don't wake up feeling the way I do right now." The worst hangover he could ever remember wasn't this bad. The roaring in his ears alone was as if he'd been standing too close to a Mark 6.

"Zeke, I know you're hurting. And I'm truly sorry that I was the cause."

If she only knew.

He groaned softly as he changed positions. "What the devil were you doing out there anyway?"

"I uh...was on my way to the communications building to send a message...home."

Zeke frowned as she went on. "Look, I know that you don't trust me, but--"

"You got that right." His smile was completely joyless. "I have one bitch of a headache, and every muscle in my body swears that I've been hit by a runaway freight sled." Once again he swung his feet over the edge of the bunk, this time managing to sit up.

"Frank said you shouldn't be getting up."

Holding the sheet in place with his bandaged arm, he sat there a moment. "What was in the Scotch?"

She stared at him blankly.

"What was in the damn whiskey, Kira?"

"Stenzoid," came her whispered reply.

"Stenzoid."

"Yes. It's an--"

"I know what the hell it is."

She swallowed, "Frank said I was to give it to you."

He favored her with another tight smile. "He said to give me Stenzoid."

She nodded slowly.

"In the Scotch," he added in the same unemotional tone.

"Well, no, that part was my idea."

"Although I'm dying to ask why, I'll save that one for Frank."

"I'll, uh, go get him." She turned for the exit before he could get in another word.

~ * ~

"They're not just illegal, Frank. I know of only a couple of places you can even get them."

"Yep. A guaranteed funeral in every slug," came Frank's easy drawl.

Kira lingered in the corridor outside Zeke's cabin, listening as Frank filled Zeke in on the past five days.

"What the hell are we up against?"

"Beats me. I tried askin' 'er, but it's sorta like askin' the bulkhead, if y' know what I mean."

"I guess it was too much to ask for a quiet stop to unload cargo and certain unwanted passengers."

"So it seems," Frank agreed.

"I'll lay you odds those men were on hire. And I'll also wager she knows why. Hell, they both had a security printout with them. In fact, there should be one over there in my pants." A moment of silence passed, some rustling noises, then...

"Damn," Frank whispered.

"Nice, huh? I'd be willing to bet they knew the instant we touched down."

Still hidden from sight, Kira swallowed and leaned back against the wall. Dear God. All she wanted right now was to get to Echo and out of Zeke Slater's life.

"I'm telling you, the sooner we get her off ship, Frank, the better. We can't afford to have our position jeopardized any further than it's already been. What have you heard from Delaney, by the way?"

"That's the curious part. Nothin'. Not even a failed attempt."

"I want to know what the hell she's up to. Our entire operation could be blown if we're not careful."

"We'll get it figured out, Boss. But right now there's no need for you to be worryin' about anything but gettin' well."

Kira turned and hurried toward the galley. The conversation was winding down and the last thing she needed was to be found eavesdropping in the corridor. Besides, she'd heard enough to confirm her worst fears. Zeke and his crew were up to something--Illegal, no doubt. And judging from their unauthorized cargo, she'd be willing to bet that Major Metals was in the firing line. For now she'd play it cool as though she suspected nothing.

Kira was sitting at the booth quietly nursing a mug of coffee when Frank appeared. "Stubborn as they come," he muttered. "But at least he's better."

~ * ~

Two days later there was even more improvement in Zeke's condition. Kira stood in the open doorway to his cabin with a cup of Frank's specially brewed tea. "You wanted to see me?"

"Yes." He was standing next to a set of storage lockers, looking stronger, yet still ashen.

Kira stepped inside his quarters. "You should be sitting down."

"I'm fine."

"Hardly. You're swaying."

"I said I'm fine."

She shrugged. "Frank says you're to drink this while it's still hot."

"Put it over there for now," he said, hitching his chin toward a nearby desk.

Kira set the tea down then turned to face him. His attempt to get dressed was a disaster. With the exception of two misaligned buttons, his shirt hung loose and open, as did the top studs of his pants, and judging from his still damp hair, he must have attempted a shower of sorts. Most of the color had been leached from his face, and beads of sweat dotted his temple--both manifestations of pain and exhaustion.

"I suppose I could use some help with the shirt, huh?"

"I'd say so." She wondered how long he had struggled with it before admitting he couldn't do it by himself. And although she tried not to notice--didn't want to notice--his chest filled her vision. The same taut and powerfully muscled expanse that she had faithfully sponged down more times than she cared to remember. "Let me fix it for you." Being careful of his injured arm, Kira undid the two mismatched buttons and realigned the shirt, much as one might do for a child. The only difference being, the man patiently waiting for her to finish was no child by any stretch of the imagination. And nobody was more disturbingly aware of that fact than Kira at the moment. How she could loathe someone and be attracted to him at the same time was beyond reason.

Silence hung heavy between them as she briefly checked his bandaged arm. "How you ever managed to keep this dry, I'll never know."

"Magic," he said on a wearied exhale.

Working quickly, Kira didn't linger over the chore.

At last leaving the yawning waistband of his pants for Zeke to figure out, she stepped back. "Now, for that tea. Frank says you're to drink it all on an empty stomach."

"Dump it. What he doesn't know won't hurt him."

"Fine with me...but he'll ask, of course, and naturally I'll have to tell him the truth."

"Naturally," he sneered. Accepting the mug, he took a few tentative sips, made a face then downed the remainder in two gulps. Setting the mug down, he leveled his gaze on her. "You ready to answer a few questions?"

"About what?"

He smiled blandly. "I've got lots of time, and not a damn thing to do but stay here and recoup."

The soft warning was not lost on Kira. "Meaning what?"

Zeke waited about three beats. "For starters, until you're ready to talk, we'll be sharing this cabin. You and I."

"...You can't be serious."

"Remember that first day, and your little proposition for passage?"

"I beg your--I never--that was not a proposition!"

"Oh yeah? Then why you were so damn scared?" One corner of his mouth quirked in amusement. "I figure it won't take much before you're telling me everything I want to know."

Two heated spots seared Kira's cheeks. "I'm not scared of you."

He stared at her for several intense moments before saying in a low whisper, "Don't challenge me, Kira."

CHAPTER SEVEN

"You're actually going to keep me here?" she asked in disbelief.

"Yes."

"For how long?"

"That's up to you." He gingerly crossed the cabin to a desk where he proceeded to make an entry into the mainframe. "In the meantime," he added, "you might as well make yourself at home."

"I will do no such thing."

He shrugged. "Fine. Then don't."

With a frenzied glance over her shoulder, Kira turned and made a dash for the door. The audible click of a lock brought her whirling about to face him--her mouth stubbornly compressed. "I'm not staying in here with you!"

Zeke remained where he was, his gaze little more than stoic resolution. "You know what to do to remedy the situation."

~ * ~

Several hours had passed by the time he was quietly slipping out of his cabin, locking Kira inside. She'd called his bluff, leaving him no choice but to make good his threat to confine her to his quarters. In truth, it amazed him that it had actually come to this, particularly in light of the fact that he'd confined her once before. Dammit, he wanted answers. And he wanted them now. Did she think he wouldn't follow through?

Amid tears of anger and frustration, Kira had finally fallen asleep in a chair near the portal, but not before she'd called him every name she knew, along with a few he was sure she'd made up.

Wondering what the devil he was supposed to do with her now, he made his way to the helm. Unfortunately, confining her to the same tiny cabin she'd used before was no longer an option. In reality it was a mini cargo hold that doubled as extra living quarters only when it wasn't being used for storing special freight that demanded unusual conditions. The consignment Frank had loaded on board at Lilo included several large medical pods of rare and highly unstable medicine that required a constant temperature and a pressurized seal.

Literally, there was nowhere to put Kira, aside from moving Frank or Talbot out of their quarters--an option Slater refused to even consider. Like it or not, Kira would share his cabin, and he'd better not hear one complaint--not one damn word.

He'd already personally sent off two memotorps to her father before they'd even arrived at Lilo. Frank had sent another message later explaining the circumstances that had caused them to miss her charter. Just this morning he'd instructed Talbot to renew the message. The whole thing was odd. Considering the urgency of the messages and the fact that it was Kira's safety in question, it wasn't like Renn not to respond immediately, let alone personally.

It was in this agitated mood that Slater ascended the stairs to the helm. "Any word yet from Delaney?"

"No, sir." Talbot's tone was cool.

Slater didn't notice. "What did you find out on that audit?"

The young crewman turned to face his captain. "That shipment of subsurface monitors is the only consignment in our hold destined for Major Metals Mines. And I double checked the computer listing."

"Good. Who's it going to?"

"Somebody named Grant Preston."

Zeke shifted. Preston again. Something was going on. Kira was either playing dumb or she truly had no knowledge of it. With a scowl, Slater turned and bounded back down the steps, passing his own cabin, the galley and finally coming to a halt before Frank's open door.

"Come on in, Boss." With his pipe clamped tightly between his teeth, Frank was sitting at his desk, staring intently at the terminal.

"There's still no word from Delaney."

Frank grunted a soft response without so much as looking up.

"And you got off another message?"

"Yep. I had Talbot do it. That is, after I convinced him y' weren't beatin' yer roommate to a bloody pulp."

Zeke scowled. "What are you talking about?"

"From the sound of things, the kid wasn't so sure. Just a friendly suggestion. From now on, any discussions the two of you have, try keepin' it down."

"And just what would you have me do? Gag her?"

"Alls I'm sayin' is, for a while there, the boy was ready to storm your quarters."

"A mistake he would have regretted."

"Yeah, that's what I told him. Oh, and by the way, word came through from base this mornin'. There's a freighter headin' toward us with seven tons of integral spectrometers that don't belong to em."

"Good. I need the diversion."

Frank grinned. "I figured y' might."

"How long before we link up?"

"Eight days. Only thing is, accordin' to my calculations, by the time we overtake 'er, we'll be well over the line."

Crossing boundaries as a harmless merchant freighter was one thing. Crossing boundaries as an avenging privateer was quite another, and damn risky. Not that they hadn't taken the risk many times. The problem now was Kira. Slater knew only too well that as long as they were within the neutral boundary, they were under the protection of the CUP, Coalition of United Planets. If captured on the other side as a privateer, their marques from the Coalition would be worthless. The *Solar Wind* would be confiscated, and there would be no mercy for her crew-- including innocent passengers.

Frank grinned. "Hell, when do we let little things like boundaries stop us? I went ahead and entered the coordinates into the NAVCOMP. On your approval, I'll lock 'em in."

"If only we didn't have Kira on board," Slater muttered.

Frank's eyebrow rose. "But think of it, Boss. Seven tons of specs. We'd be fools to pass this one up. And who knows what else we'll find on board? Why, we'd have 'em crippled, raided and be back across the boundary 'fore they even know what hit 'em."

Slater nodded in agreement, and after another long thought-filled moment said curtly, "Stowaways be damned. Lock in the coordinates."

"Good as done, Boss." Frank rose from his chair, tucked his pipe into his pocket and made for the exit. Slater followed the older man out into the corridor, their steps keeping pace until he turned into the ship's lounge while Frank continued making his way to the helm.

Reaching for a shot glass, Slater grabbed a bottle of Terran whiskey out of a cabinet and poured himself a measure. It wasn't something he did often, but occasionally there were times, like now, when he needed a drink. Who the hell was trailing them? How much longer before he'd hear back from Delaney. And in the meantime--what the devil was he supposed to do with Kira?

Ten minutes later Frank was joining him. "Everything's all taken care of, Boss. We should be interceptin' 'er right on schedule. Oh, and that shadow that's been tailin' us, it's just about off our long-range scanners."

"Good."

Eyeing Slater's arm critically, Frank said, "I see yer not wearing the sling I fixed for y'."

"That's right."

"Y' know it's gonna take a helluva lot longer to heal without support, don't y'?"

"I'll take my chances."

~ * ~

On board the Moon Runner:

"You wanted to see me?"

68

"Yes." Konto lifted his gaze from the monitor. For several long moments he simply stared at Ben Hagen. Finally, he said, "Who's responsible for those two bungling idiots on Lilo?"

"What do you mean?"

"Just what I asked."

"My connections on Lilo knew exactly what we expected--"

"And what did we expect? What exactly were my orders?"

"To capture Slater and hold him until we arrived."

"And did they follow through?"

Hagen paused. "Their attempt failed, sir."

"You know, it's a sad thing when we allow others to make mistakes that we end up having to pay for. Don't you agree?"

"Look, this isn't my fault. I did my part."

Konto was through listening. "You failed, Hagen. I have no further need of your services." He motioned for the thug standing just outside the door, "Mr. Landry, would you show Mr. Hagen off the ship?"

"What!" Hagen shrieked.

Withdrawing his gun, Landry stepped forward.

"Now wait just a damn minute! You can't do this!"

"I'll be at the helm," Konto added as he brushed past.

"But...but we're in space!"

Oblivious to Hagen's screams, Konto made his way down the companionway.

"You got a fix on their ship yet?" he asked upon entering the helm.

"She's going like a Marotti out of hell. We have a fix, sir, but at this rate, not for long." The young techman turned to face Konto. "And they've increased their velocity. Again."

"And what exactly are we doing to rectify the situation?" Konto's eyes swept across the control board.

"We're wide open. Yet, even at this speed, they continue to pull away from us." The young technician released a compressed breath. "And to be truthful, I don't know how much longer we can keep this up."

Konto swore crudely. Again he glanced over the controls as red-lit indicators pulsed out their warnings. He watched as the helmsman entered another directive.

"According to this, sir, they're exactly two days and thirty-four minutes ahead of us and gaining steadily."

"What the hell are we following?" Konto half whispered.

"I can't even venture a guess, sir."

Leaving his post, another crewmember joined in the query.

"She's fast like a Mach Three-Forty."

"Or a Stardart," the helmsman added. "If I didn't know better..." Lost for words, he shook his head. "The one thing I do know, she's too damn fast to be what she appears."

"The *Solar Wind's* a damn freighter," Konto snapped. "We should have three times her speed without even trying. Kendyl mentioned nothing about chasing some tricked-up star-runner."

"When we left Port Chance, they were a mere one hour ahead of us. By the time they left Lilo they were six hours ahead of us. Now, having slipped into hyper speed, they've increased that distance and are still gaining. Whatever she is, she's not standard. Plain and simple, sir, we can't match her speed."

Konto cursed again. "I want that time factor shortened, and I don't give a damn what it takes to do it."

~ * ~

Slater stood in the open doorway of his cabin like a stone statue, one hand braced upon the entry plate.

If he'd thought to find Kira still curled up in the chair where he'd left her, he couldn't have been more wrong. In frozen disbelief, he slowly took in the total effect of his newly renovated cabin.

"I changed my mind about making myself at home," she offered cheerfully. "I hope you don't mind. Things were just a bit drab for my taste. And since I'm going to be here a while, I decided to dress things up a bit. What do you think?" She stepped back to admire her handiwork.

"What in hell's blazes have you done in here?"

Kira's expression plunged dramatically. "You don't like it?"

Without a doubt she had gone through every locker, cabinet and drawer she could access to find what now garishly embellished his cabin.

His gaze slid to the viewport, which was bedecked with a black lacy valance that looked suspiciously like the teddy she had found beneath his bunk that first day. Heart-shaped "doilies" had been cut from a couple of his shirts and were placed beneath virtually everything possible. The bed sported a coverlet, made from what looked to be an extra blanket. But it was the dozen or more diamond-shaped holes festooning the top of it that held his rapt attention.

"You know, this is really interesting, Zeke." She held up the memory gem for emphasis. "I've heard of these but have never actually seen one before."

His eyes narrowed and he exhaled slowly, only then realizing that he'd been holding his breath. His muffled curse was barely audible as he stepped fully inside the cabin, the panel cycling closed behind him.

"That's you on a jet bike, isn't it?" she added cheerfully.

His jaw clenched.

"You couldn't have been more than what, a teenager when this was taken? Oh...I also saw you riding a beautiful horse. I didn't realize you rode horses, Zeke."

If she'd been looking for the right button to press, she'd just found it. In two strides he was standing before her, his hand outstretched.

With a heavy sigh Kira placed the crystal sphere into his palm. "I was only looking at it."

"Kira, I want everything put back the way it was."

"I'll be more than happy to, but only if you'll let me stay on until Echo."

"Don't issue ultimatums. I guarantee you will right this cabin regardless."

"Look, if its money you want, you'll be well paid for your troubles."

"Paid?" The brackets around his mouth deepened ever so slightly. "You couldn't begin to afford me."

"Probably not, but I bet Major Metals could."

"And how much do you think I should charge for the trouble you've already caused? Course I'd have to add hazard pay to the bill," he went on. "But you know what? I'd gladly forgo any payment just to have one long vapor trail between you and me."

Kira looked at him sharply.

"But since that isn't possible right now," he went on, "I'll settle for some straight answers. Starting with, who's after you?"

"No one."

"Don't play dumb."

"I'm not! I know nothing about someone following us."

"The hell you don't. My guess is you were running from someone on a jet bike the day you stowed aboard this ship. And ever since, someone's been on our tail."

"Zeke, please believe me. I had no idea--"

"The only reason you're still around is because I happen to think too damned much of your father to just dump you off somewhere. Which I might add is a helluva sight more than you must think of him, or you wouldn't have stowed aboard in the first place." It was a well-aimed crack and judging from the look on her face, he'd struck home.

"I've got a call in for him now. Once we hear back and calibrate a new rendezvous point, you're outta here. I don't give a damn how sorry you are, and believe me I care even less about collecting any recompense. The only thing I'm looking forward to is the vast relief I'll experience in just knowing you're off my ship.

"And..." he added, spanning the cabin with a wave of his hand, "Get rid of the frippery."

"Frippery? I happen to like it," she snapped, clearly lying.

"Get rid of it." His glance shifted to take in the cabin. "When I return, this place had better be back in its original condition."

Up went her chin.

Ignoring her rebellious glare, he stepped forward, capturing her stubborn little jaw. "You're a stowaway, Kira, simple as that. Try using your creative imagination on exactly what that could mean."

A moment of thick silence and eye contact passed. "I am not a stowaway," she mumbled against the pressure on her chin.

Unbidden, his eyes once again drifted to her mouth. Swearing inwardly, he resisted the impulse. "You know...somehow I don't believe you realize your true position here. Maybe I should spell it out."

She blinked, her bravado visibly withering as his hand shifted to caress her cheek. "Bottom line," he said softly, "I'm fresh out of patience. I want answers, and I'm quite capable of doing whatever it takes to get them. You understand what I'm saying?"

She nodded.

"Excellent. So while you're cleaning things up, you think about what I've said."

CHAPTER EIGHT

He turned to leave when she added, "And just so you understand, Zeke Slater, bullying won't work with me."

He turned to face her. "Legs, you have no idea how bullying I can get. Continue to buck me at every turn, and I won't hesitate to rid myself of the problem."

She tensed. "You wouldn't."

"Who's to stop me?"

At that she half-laughed. "You're joking."

"Don't bet on it."

"You're just trying to scare me."

"Am I?"

"But you just finished saying that the only reason I'm still on board is because of--"

"Your father. That's absolutely true. But if you keep pushing your luck, there's no telling what I might do."

She fell silent as he palmed the door. "You've got two hours."

"Don't hold your breath," she whispered as the door cycled closed and the lock clicked behind him. He wouldn't jettison her off the ship. He may have changed, but not that much. It was just a scare tactic.

"Don't bet on it." Zeke's words tumbled through her mind. And with that memory came the assurance that one way or another Zeke Slater would indeed impose some form of unpleasant discipline should she fail to obey.

~ * ~

74

"Now that y' have 'er just where y' want 'er, what are y' gonna to do with 'er?" Joining Slater in the helm, Frank made no pretense of hiding his amusement.

"What do you mean, where I want her? I want her off my ship. That's where I want her."

"Coulda' fooled me. I remember tellin' y' she could have my cabin. But, apparently, y' want her holed up in yers."

Slater tensed, his gaze focused on the controls. The only outward indication that he'd even heard the subtle rebuke was the twitch of a jaw muscle.

Frank could be insufferable when he wanted. Yet the relationship between the two men went far beyond mere station. There was an understanding, a mutual respect, and in his heart, Zeke knew the old man was right. He should have grabbed at the offered cabin. Especially since he didn't have a clue as to what he was going to do with her. And, more importantly, what he intended to do if she challenged him by not putting his cabin back in order.

As if reading his mind, Frank's easy drawl broke into his thoughts. "Would y' at least listen to a suggestion?"

~ * ~

Nearly an hour had passed before Kira made the decision to restore Zeke's quarters to its former state. She was just folding the last article of unscathed clothing and placing it back in the storage chest when the lock on the entry clicked off.

"It's me," came the grizzled voice from the other side. "May I come in?"

Frank... "Yes, of course." Kira closed the door on the locker and started for the portal just as it cycled open."

"Boss thought y' might be gettin' hungry," he said, entering the cabin with a tray of food.

Kira's eyes widened upon closer inspection. There was an assortment of meats, breads, and fresh fruit. Off to the side sat a small dish with some sort of dipping sauce and a glass of juice. "This hardly looks like prison rations," she teased, truly glad to see Frank.

Frank beamed, his eyes gleaming beneath droopy lids. "Looks tasty, huh? We took on fresh supplies at Lilo, and Boss said t' be sure and give y' the good stuff." He grinned and added, "But I was gonna anyway. I even brought y' some of the finest wine y'll ever put t' yer lips."

His urging was hard to resist. Crossing the cabin to a small table, Kira took a seat as Frank set the tray down before her.

"Go on," he said, "give it a try." Sweeping back a nearby chair, he flipped it around and straddled it.

"Honey fruit?" Kira asked, reaching first for a juicy piece of the golden-fleshed fruit.

"Yep," he said, beaming with satisfaction as she took a tentative bite and sighed.

"And this?" she asked curiously, picking up a moist orange-colored wedge of fruit.

Frank grinned. "Darlin', that's called a tangerine. Boss brought back six cases of 'em for ship's larder on his last trip to Earth. Good, huh?" He grinned, watching her lick juice from her fingers and waited expectantly as she next selected a slice of meat and dipped it in the dish of sauce.

"Ummmm..." With sauce clinging to the corner of her mouth, Kira reached for a napkin.

"I thought y'd like it." Frank's weathered face reflected his delight.

"You want some?" Kira asked, dabbing her mouth with the napkin.

"Nah, I've already eaten." Leaning forward, he draped his forearms nonchalantly across the back of the chair. Finally, after a long moment of silence, he spoke up. "Would y' mind if an old man asks a favor?"

Kira looked up from her meal. "Not at all."

Frank took a deep breath and squared his shoulders. "I ain't never seen the Capt'n in such a foul mood as he's been in lately."

She stopped eating. "You mean, since I came aboard."

He nodded.

"Pardon me, but unless my memory fails me, Zeke Slater appeared to already be sufficiently ill-tempered at the time he found me locked in that crate." She reached for the glass of wine and took a tiny sip. "I'm not totally responsible for his grumpiness, Frank."

"Fair enough. But the point is, you are responsible for yer own actions." He glanced away for the space of a heartbeat. "Maybe..." he began, his eyes flicking back to her, "if y'd just try being a bit more...cooperative."

Kira's expression stilled. Setting the glass down, she smoothed the napkin in her lap. "Just what is it you're suggesting?"

"Well, for starters, why don't y' try humorin' him instead of provokin' him at every turn like y've been doin'."

"Humoring?" she repeated, eyeing him skeptically. "Well, there's not a whole lot of options with that. You must either mean humoring him as in one: making up answers to questions I have no answers for, or two: reporting immediately to the nearest airlock. Or perhaps you mean throwing myself upon his bunk like some dockside harlot."

Frank frowned. "That's not what I mean, and y' know it." He paused then added beneath his breath, "Though I have t'admit, it'd probably smooth the edge off that hellish mood he's been in lately."

Dipping another slice of meat into the sauce, Kira asked with mock innocence, "What would? Throwing myself off the ship or into his bed?"

Somewhere in the wake of Frank's engaging grin, she found it difficult to be irritated with him. A reluctant smile tugged at the corners of her mouth, despite her efforts to maintain her curt control.

"I'm sure we could come up with somethin' a little less..." he paused for the right word.

"Drastic?" Kira's expression grew serious. "He has no right to treat me--"

"That's where yer wrong, Frank interrupted. "He has every right."

"If he wants me out of his hair so bad, then put me off at the nearest port."

"What he wants most of all is answers to a few questions. Besides, he tried puttin' y' off, in case y've forgotten. And look where it got him." Frank shook his head. "If that poisoned slug had been embedded just a little deeper, we'd 'ave lost him for sure."

In her mind's eye, Kira could still see Zeke facing down the two hoodlums who had attacked her. That was the easy part--envisioning him standing there like a warrior in her defense. The hard part was remembering his hooded eyes as he fought to remain conscious, struggling against the poison that had already begun entering his system. She could still hear his muttered curse as his legs buckled, and the feel of his weight as it took her to the deck with him.

"Y've stowed aboard a damned freighter," Frank said, his gravelly voice breaking into her thoughts. "Believe me, yer wrong about Slater's rights. As Capt'n, 'e's got every right. While yer rights, darlin', are still sittin' dirtside back at Port Chance."

"Yes, I'm well aware of my puny status on board this ship. Zeke took perverse pleasure in making sure there were no misunderstandings."

"'Then let me just say this in his behalf. Any other Capt'n might 'ave left y' to yer fate on the nearest dock, like so much baggage. And that's only if y' were lucky." He paused, allowing his words to sink in before continuing. "Chances are any other Capt'n would 'ave taken a fancy to y'--in which case, y' would 'ave already been a ride-under for him and half his crew by now."

Ignoring the dockside slang, Kira forced a stiff smile. "Rather a moot point, wouldn't you say, in light of the fact that he has me presently locked within his private quarters?"

Frank wasn't the least daunted by her insinuation. "Yes, but unscathed, nonetheless." His tone softened. "Like I said, any other ship, any other Capt'n and yer fate would've been very different."

Kira sniffed. "Maybe. But, since your idea of jumping into his bunk is about as appealing as being jettisoned out of an airlock, I can assure you Slater won't be getting from me whatever it is you think he needs."

Frank released a breathy whistle. "Now there y' go again, readin' more into it than what I said. I wasn't suggestin'--"

"Besides," Kira interrupted, "I assure you, finding me in his bunk would only fuel his temper. Not cool it."

At that last comment, Frank simply looked at her, his eyes brightening with private laughter. "All kiddin' aside," he said, "watch yer step with him. He's not a man to trifle with and y've been pushin' him hard lately."

"Me?" Kira stared at him. "That's not true, I've been--"

Frank put his hands up in mock defense. "It's been a while since he worked for Major Metals. He's not the same man y' used to know, and I guarantee his tolerance level is a far sight lower."

"Yes, I already figured that out."

"Anyway," he added, softening his words with a sideways grin, "me and Talbot are gettin' tired of catchin' all hell because he's pissed at you about somethun'."

With a sigh and a half smile of her own, Kira laid her napkin aside. "Okay," she said. "For you, Frank, I'll try. But don't get your hopes up, cause I think he might be a tad upset with me right now."

Frank grinned. "That's an understatement."

"Well, I almost didn't change it back, you know."

One bushy gray eyebrow rose. "Exactly why I volunteered to bring in yer dinner?" Shaking his head, Frank fell silent, his gaze shifting to the viewport across the cabin. Soft light slanted shadows across his face, and in the quiet that followed, Kira studied the grizzled, gray-haired old man, sensing his life had been one long vapor trail of regret. And yet he seemed content enough on board the *Solar Wind*. She wondered at the bond between him and Zeke.

At last, sensing there was more on his mind, she asked, "What is it?"

Frank's gaze returned to her. Seconds ticked by in which he simply studied her.

"What?" she asked again.

His eyes narrowed. "Darlin', the man put his life on the line for y'. Damn near lost it in the process. He deserves some answers."

Kira turned away from his knowing stare. "Despite what he thinks, I did not stow aboard. If he can't...or won't take me to Echo, then let me off at the next port. I'll be off his ship and out of his life. And we'll both be happy."

Time passed in which Frank continued to study her. Finally, he said, "It may not be that easy. We've had a shadow on our scanners ever since Port Chance."

"Yes, he told me. But I assure you, I don't know who's following us or why."

"He figures you do."

"I'll tell you what, Frank. I'll make Zeke a deal. You tell him that if he agrees to take me to Echo, I'll answer his questions as best and as honestly as I possibly can."

"And if he refuses to accept those terms?"

"Then he can forget the answers. It's that simple."

Frank's expression stilled. "I don't think you're gonna want t' broach that idea to Slater. He won't take it well."

"Well, those are my terms." Kira looked away.

With an ironic smile, Frank shoved his hand through his hair. "Considerin' he almost died on yer account, y' really should think about what yer doin', especially if there's somthun' he should know."

"Look, I am truly sorry that Zeke was injured on Lilo. If I'd only known, I would never have left the terminal."

"What the devil were y' doin' out there all by yerself, anyway?"

"I was on my way to the Communications building to get a message off to...to my father."

"I see." Shaking his head, he looked briefly away. "Must take some pretty hi-tech equipment t' do that."

Kira frowned. "To do what?"

"Get a message off t' yer daddy."

She grew still.

"If you don't say somethun soon," he added with quiet emphasis, "I'll be forced into tellin' 'im myself. And I assure y', he ain't gonna like hearin' it from me. In fact, he's up there right now wonderin' why he ain't heard back yet. For all I know, he's already sendin' off another message--this time demandin' a response."

Kira swallowed and glanced down into her half-filled glass. In the silence, the ship's drives hummed around them. The ventilation hissed softly. At last, she looked up. "How long have you known?"

"About your daddy?"

She nodded.

"A memo came through just this mornin' from Major Metals, and before I go any further, I want you to know I'm awfully sorry for your loss, honey. Nevertheless, be thankful it was me who intercepted it." Frank removed his pipe and a small pouch from his pocket. Using tiny pinches, he methodically began compressing tobacco into the bowl. Finally, he shoved the unlit pipe into the corner of his mouth, resealed the pouch and stuffed it back into his pocket. "If Slater finds out about this from anyone other than you..."

With a sigh Kira, looked away. If she told Zeke everything, she would lose her bargaining power. Besides, what guarantee did she have that she could even trust him--or Frank for that matter. At last she turned her eyes back upon Frank. "You tell Zeke if he wants answers, I'm willing to bargain."

"Bargain," Frank repeated blandly.

"Yes. He takes me to Echo, I'll answer all of his questions." She shrugged. That seems fair enough, wouldn't you say?"

"Echo." Frank shook his head slowly. "You really don't want to give him an ultimatum, honey. Listen, I'll talk to him and see what we can work out."

"Just tell him what I said, Frank."

Again he raked his hand through his hair. "Think about what yer doin', girl."

"I already have."

He took the pipe from his mouth. "Y' realize Slater won't consider this bargainin'. He'll see it as defiance."

CHAPTER NINE

"She said what?"

Frank calmly withdrew his pipe from his pocket. "Y' heard right."

Slater's jaw tensed as he finished making his entry in the day's log. "I don't make deals. You know that."

"Yep." Cupping his hand around the bowl of his pipe, Frank touched a flame to the tobacco and began puffing it to life. "That's what I tried tellin' 'er." Smoke escaped with his words as he went on. "But she says she refuses t' answer any questions unless you agree to take her to Echo."

"Not a chance. In fact, I'm to the point of putting her off at the first attainable station. By the way, a bulletext came through from Newton Enterprises while you were serving the Princess her evening meal. They've got a rush shipment of positrons tagged for Echo and are willing to pay double credits."

Frank released a breathy whistle. "We should be able to adjust our schedule for double credits."

Slater reached for the tangerine he'd retrieved earlier from the ship's larder. "I figured it'll set us back some, but not so that we can't make up the difference." The zesty scent of citrus drifted into the air of the small lounge as he began peeling the fruit.

Fresh Terran-grown produce was a rare delicacy on board the ship. But with a recent trip to Earth, Frank had taken the opportunity to stock up on several varieties of fresh fruits along with a selection of prime Terran beef.

"I take it yer gonna put the girl off first?"

"Next port." Easing his thumb between two wedges, Slater separated the tangerine in half, sending a pungent spray of juice into the air. "The sooner the better," he added beneath his breath.

The memory of her half sprawled upon his bunk would be forever burned into his soul. Even now, summoning the image induced forbidden thoughts of touch and taste...and scent. Her mouth alone--

Don't even think about her mouth, a silent voice warned.

Glancing up, found Frank studying him with knowing eyes.

"So, how's the arm."

"Sore." He had the distinct impression that Frank had changed subjects to hide his amusement.

"Can't say it surprises me. First y' refuse to keep it bound to yer side. And now y' ain't even wearin' yer sling."

"Am I going to have to hear this all over again?"

Frank shook his head. "Nah. I'm done tellin' y'. Done feelin' sorry fer y' too. Y' can take yer sweet time healin' cuz that's apparently the way y' like it."

"Good. I trust that means we're officially finished with this discussion then?"

Frank shrugged. "It's yer arm."

"At least we both agree on that. Now, can we return to more urgent matters?"

"Y' want my advice about the girl first?"

"Hell, no! If I left her up to you, you'd have her at the helm piloting the damn ship. What I need you to do first is to verify Newton's shipping code against the one we have on-system." Slater pulled off another segment of fruit, frowning in thought as he ate. "And as for Kira, I've already requested a listing of any commercial liners headed for Quade's World as well as all available private charters."

Silence.

Reading more into Frank's silence, Slater stared at him. "We can't keep her, Frank. It's too damn risky, as you well know."

"I know that," he snapped around a puff of smoke. "It's just...after what happened last time and all. I still say she's in a heap of trouble."

"All the more reason." Slater glared at him. "She'll be fine. I'll personally escort her safely on board." He knew what was going through Frank's mind. His own flood of emotions were running the gamut; everything from severe annoyance to mild attraction to a growing sense of concern that he didn't dare acknowledge, let alone give in to.

Frank was staring at him again--his pipe anchored in the corner of his mouth, his look pensive.

"You got something else on your mind?"

"Yep."

Slater separated another wedge from the tangerine. "Well..."

"Y' ain't gonna like it."

Zeke merely looked at him.

"It's about Delaney."

"And...?"

"I got a response back this morning."

Slater sat forward. "You're just now telling me?"

"I wanted to give the little gal a chance to tell y' herself."

Slater's mouth curled. "Tell me what?"

"That her daddy's dead. Killed 'bout three months back in some minin' accident."

"Renn's dead?"

Frank nodded.

"Dead..." Zeke whispered. "Why didn't we hear about this?"

"Dunno. Except three months back, if you'll recall, we weren't anywhere near Quade's World to hear the news. Maybe it was old news by the time we got back around. Hell, I don't know."

"All this time I've been trying to get in touch with him, and she never--"

"Maybe she tried tellin' y'. Did y' ever think of that? In the beginning, y' know, you didn't give 'er much of a chance."

Slater slid him a scathing look.

"Anyway, yer supposed to contact that Preston guy if y' have any questions."

"Preston." A muttered curse deepened Slater's scowl. "Never could understand why Delaney went into partnership with him in the first place." He paused, thinking out loud. "All this time...and she never said a word."

"She may still come through, Boss."

That earned him another look. "A little late, I'd say."

"Y' never know, there may be more we don't know."

"That's a distinct possibility I'm not about to overlook." With that, Slater quickly concluded his entry into the compulog.

"What are you going to do?" Frank asked, around the stem of his pipe.

"Actually..." Slater began with a silken thread of warning, "I believe Miss Delaney has grossly underestimated me. In fact, I'd say it's time for a little lesson, starting with the merits of intimidation."

Frank's brow lifted, his expression stoic. "Some lessons are best not learned at all," he muttered beneath his breath.

"I want to know who's on our tail, Frank."

"Maybe she don't know."

"She knows."

Frank didn't respond, just drew on his pipe.

"So far, she's suffered nothing worse than being locked inside my cabin. I guarantee, if faced with an unpleasant consequence or two, she'll come free with the information." With a determined sigh, he rose from his chair. "If you should need me, I'll be in my cabin--shocking our stowaway into a few answers."

Withdrawing his pipe from the corner of his mouth, Frank studied a thin ribbon of smoke trailing off the tip and murmured, "That could prove to be a lesson neither of y' will soon forget."

Slater paused at the portal. There were times when the old man's gut instincts strangely echoed his own.

~ * ~

Kira gave the cabin one last sweeping glance after Frank had left. If her hunch was correct, it wouldn't be long before Zeke would be bursting through the door. She braced herself, wondering if she was truly prepared for the fury that Frank had alluded to.

The better part of an hour ticked by, and no Zeke. Once again, her gaze strayed to a framed picture, and for a long moment she stood there studying it. Zeke was standing beside a dark-haired companion, whose muscular build and rakish good looks were an equal. What a pair they were, with their arms draped over the other's shoulders, lifting tankards in a brazen toast to some attained conquest. Both wore insolent grins, and Kira could only wonder at the reason.

Next to the picture sat the very object that had put fire in Zeke's eyes as he snatched it from her hand. The memory gem, as it was called, was a sphere-shaped object. The base had been planed so that it could rest on a shelf or desk.

By itself, the memory gem looked like a glob of solid crystal. But upon holding it, body heat became the catalyst in bringing it to animated life. Trapped within the memory gem was a personal selection of videos.

Intrigued, Kira once again picked up the forbidden object and carefully clasped it in both hands. Holding her breath in anticipation, she waited as a picture gradually materialized within its transparent depths. There, before her eyes, stood a much younger Zeke, appearing to be in his mid-teens. His long sun-streaked hair hung well below his bare shoulders. A soft breeze lifted the tawny mane off the back of his neck and tossed a heavy lock down across his forehead. He was talking to someone, yet the globe presented no audio. In fascination, Kira watched as sunlight glinted off the dark teak of tanned skin and youthful muscle. So detailed were the images, she could even glimpse a fine sheen of perspiration dappling his shoulders. But it was his face that commanded the most of her attention. Even at his young age, Zeke Slater's rugged handsomeness held heartbreaking promise. He smiled, and that familiar muscle clenched along his jaw line. Her breath caught at the sight.

A small girl soon entered the scene and Kira watched with interest as Zeke drew his arm about her and said something that made her laugh. A younger sister, perhaps? She was pondering that question when the scene changed again. This time he was sitting in a flagrant pose, astride a shiny black jet bike. Long dark-clad legs were extended out on each side of the bike, grounded by booted feet. Muscular arms stretched out before him to grasp tall widespread handlebars. Zeke's hair remained unfashionably long, and with a toss of his head, he flipped an errant wisp off his face. Though still youthfully rangy, the dark short-sleeve T-shirt he wore clung flawlessly to muscular biceps that belied his young age.

Finally, with a sigh, Kira placed the globe back on the shelf. Zeke was not only older now, but she suspected very much different from the person in the memory gem. The passage of time could bring about many reasons for shaping decisions in life. After all, in just three short months hadn't her own life been turned upside down? Glancing away, she considered Frank's suggestion to level with Zeke. Should she tell him about the unauthorized supplies being filtered through the company? Dare she confide in him about the rumors of Delaney mines being run by slave labor? Tell him about Charlie and the real story of how she had gotten the bruise on her temple? How she truly had no idea of how or why she had ended up on board his ship? She laughed softly. Not that he'd believe her. More than anything she needed to tell him of her father's death. If she didn't, Frank would for sure.

Without warning, the lock disengaged and the panel cycled open. "So, you want to negotiate."

A tiny flicker of alarm coiled in the pit of her stomach at hearing the audible snick of the lock sliding back into place.

Kira watched him cross the cabin to his desk. His easy masculine grace belied the exasperation she sensed lying just beneath the surface.

"The least you could do is knock before just barging in. I could have been in a state of undress, for all you knew."

Slater's faintly amused gaze lifted from the computer. "These are my quarters. I'll come and go as I please. And...since you've brought up the subject of undress, I've been doing a little re-thinking. I figure as long as you and I will be sharing this cabin, what the hell, I might as well take you up on your offer."

"What offer might that be?" she asked warily.

Slater came around from behind the desk, slowly unbuttoning his shirt. "Come now, Legs, surely you haven't forgotten."

Kira took a step backward. "You mean the bargain that I talked to Frank about?"

He shook his head slowly. "I mean the sweet little offer you made right over there on my bunk."

"But, I never--"

"Now that I've had time to think it over, I have to admit it does have certain advantages."

"Zeke, I didn't..." Her voice trailed off as he advanced upon her, tugging his shirt from his pants. Kira retreated, one step at a time until the backs of her legs came up against something hard. "You're not serious," she whispered, just as she tumbled into the seat behind her.

Leaning forward, he clamped his hands over the tops of hers, pinning them to the arms of the chair. "I'm very serious." His shirt hung wide, exposing an impressively defined torso with sleek muscles that angled into the waistband of his pants. "You knew all along I was trying to reach Renn, and yet you said nothing. Why?"

"Zeke, I--"

"Who's tailing us?"

"I already told you, I don't know!"

He leaned forward, crowding her space. "I'm trying very hard to remain a gentleman here, Kira," he said, almost too quietly.

"Let go of me!" Despite his injury, Zeke's grip was like iron. He was completely and implacably determined.

"What's it going to be, Legs?"

Up went her chin. "What do you want me to do? Lie?"

He smiled. The air thickened. Zeke's hooded eyes swept over her, lingering on her mouth, and then her breasts. When his gaze returned to her face, Kira knew exactly what he was thinking. Her insides coiled. Nervously she moistened her lips, his avid gaze following every movement. "I'm not afraid of you," she whispered lamely, all too aware of his size, his heat, his scent...his nearness.

"Yes, you are." His tone was gentle and seductive and somewhat amused as he leaned forward, his head slowly descending.

"Slater, I am warning--"

He touched her mouth gently with his own. "Still time to change your mind," he whispered against her lips.

"Don't! I already said--"

This time his mouth claimed hers in a searing kiss that turned Kira's bones to liquid. She moaned, but he only deepened the kiss, angling his head for better purchase. Her heart slammed into her ribs, sending a coiled jolt straight to her belly.

The tip of his tongue slid along the crease of her lips, seeking entrance. "Open for me, baby. I gotta taste you."

With another moan, she turned her head away. Zeke growled in response and gently nipped her earlobe, running his tongue around the outer shell of her ear before returning to her mouth.

"Zeke, please--" No sooner had her lips parted than he plunged in, sending his tongue deeply and sensuously inside. The warm glide of his tongue against hers made her gasp, sending another surge of wild sensation southward. Withdrawing slowly, he thrust inside again...and again.

Dazed, pliant and utterly bemused, it was then Kira numbly realized that at some point he had drawn her up into his arms.

War had definitely been waged and underestimating him was a grave error. This assault was more effective than any other means of bending her to his will.

His hands slipped to the small of her back as he pulled her tighter into the cradle of his hips. Trembling, Kira stifled a moan at the undeniable imprint of his male body upon her belly. "Zeke..." she implored.

At last he succumbed, his lowered head nestled in the hollow of her shoulder, his mouth pressed to her throat. "You want me to stop?" came his deep, gentle voice.

Torn between fury and undeniable desire, Kira could only nod in answer.

"A few answers, baby. That's all--and I'll back off."

Again, she nodded and whispered, "All--right."

~ * ~

Major Metals Mining site, Echo:

Evening fog had begun rolling in, settling low over the jungle. Only the tallest of trees mushroomed above its billowy stratum. Deep in thought, Grant Preston stood before the window of his office, watching the encroaching mist swallow up the lights of the various outbuildings.

He smiled inwardly. It paid to have connections. And thanks to just such a connection, a particular segment of Lilo's security vid-footage had been transmitted directly to his private receiver for evaluation.

The footage clearly depicted Kira being ushered off the freighter, *Solar Wind*. Once again he depressed a key, zooming-in and freezing the picture for a closer look at her "escort."

Zeke Slater... He had it figured she'd stowed aboard a ship, and with *Solar Wind* being the one that had left port first, it was a logical guess that she'd chosen that ship. What he hadn't figured on was learning that Slater was piloting that particular ship: the very ship transporting the consignment of subsurface monitors.

The botched effort on Lilo was unimportant now. They'd get both Slater and Kira once they arrived on Echo to deliver the monitors.

The thing that bothered him was that every freighter chartered to carry their consignments was to be cleared first. Neither *Solar Wind* nor its captain had been processed through the proper channels. Yet they'd somehow been cleared just the same. With a foul curse, Preston turned his pale eyes on the screen where a frozen close-up of Zeke Slater's face stared back at him. "So you want to play hero, do you? I'll be happy to oblige. We'll be ready for you."

~ * ~

Zeke sat back, staring at Kira. "So, what makes you think Renn wasn't killed in an accident?"

"I don't have proof." She looked up from studying her hands. "It's just that..." she shrugged, "a bunch of things have been happening ever since...his death."

"Like the monitors," Zeke offered.

She nodded. "And...other things." Her voice broke on the last two words and looking away again, she fell silent.

CHAPTER TEN

At last she turned back to him. "Surely now you can understand how important it might be for me to go to the mine that collapsed on my father--if nothing more than to touch the soil that buried him."

"You could have done that three months ago. Why are you so hell-bent on getting there now?"

"I've told you."

"Kira, did Renn always make his own inspections?" he asked, changing the subject.

"On occasion. Why?"

Slater shoved his hands into his pockets in silent contemplation. After a moment, he asked, "Did Renn leave any notations or logs of any kind? Anything to document his discussions with Grant?"

"Yes. In fact, just recently I found a memo-disc from Grant saying he suspected sabotage to the very mine that collapsed. He wanted Dad to come there. That's one of the things I want to talk to him about. Plus," she added, "I wanted to go over the company ledgers with him."

"Ledgers," Zeke repeated. "You lost me there, sweetheart. You stowed aboard my ship so you could go over the company records with Preston?" At her stubborn look he added, "Am I grasping this correctly?"

"No."

"Well, sure as Saturn has rings, I can't seem to figure out where I went wrong."

"First of all," Kira ground out, "for the hundredth time, I... did...not...stow aboard your ship. And, second, I have proof that everything I'm telling you is true."

"You have it with you?"

"Yes."

"Get it."

"I can't."

He smiled and looked away. "Why doesn't that surprise me?"

"Zeke, I had it with me. At least I did before I ended up on board your ship. That's why I had Talbot take me back into the cargo bay. I was looking for my hair comb. I thought it might have fallen inside the crate."

That brought his head around. "What's it look like--this comb?"

"It's fancy," Kira answered. "Has a few jewels set into it. Why?"

"Wait here." Within seconds Slater was handing over the comb Leon had left with him. "This it?"

"Yes. Where did you get--?"

"You lost it out on the tarmac."

Kira glanced up from checking the comb over. "Thank you."

"So what's on that microchip?"

It shouldn't have surprised her that he had recognized the comb for what it really was. Removing the tiny microchip, she handed it over to him. "I copied everything from the company records onto this. I think Grant's message to my father is included as well."

Accepting it, Zeke crossed the cabin to his desk where he entered the tiny chip into the terminal. "You have a password or something?" he asked, his eyes glued to the screen. Kira gave him the security code, and within seconds they were quickly scanning the manifest. The first thing Slater pulled up was Grant's memo to Renn.

Renn,

The deeper I get into this, the more obvious it's becoming. I'm beginning to believe one of the mines is being sabotaged. These last few days in particular have been revealing. I need you to come as soon as possible--G. Preston

Zeke settled hipshot on the edge of his desk. "So...you didn't actually see your father's body. Is that right?" he asked, his eyes still studying the message.

"No. I was told that the cave-in was so massive, they closed that tunnel rather than try to recover the...bodies."

That brought his head around, and he stared at her in that intense way of his. "Who told you that?"

"Grant was the one who first notified me of my father's death."

He cursed beneath his breath. "So, what you're saying is, you only have Grant's word on your father's death--on everything for that matter?

"Yes... Why?"

"Nothing." Once again, he returned his attention to the manifest.

"Why?" she repeated. "What are you thinking?"

"It's just...I'm not sure I buy it, that's all."

"You don't think he's dead?" She couldn't help the hope that leapt into her heart.

"Let's just say, I'm reserving judgment." Warming to the subject, he went on. "Kira, did Renn have any enemies that you know of?"

"None."

He paused. "What about Preston?"

"What about him?"

"Did he and Renn always get along?"

"You're not suggesting..." Kira drew in a breath. "Grant Preston, for your information, is a trusted family friend and my father's business partner. You have no idea how kind he's been to me, Zeke. Even going so far as to offering to buy me out immediately so that I wouldn't have this burden to worry about."

Zeke's eyes narrowed. "What was your answer?"

"I thanked him and told him no, of course."

"And his response?"

Irritation shot through her. "It was simply a courtesy offer, Zeke. Just what is it you're suggesting?"

"I'm not suggesting anything. But I'm sure as hell not taking Preston's word on anything, either."

"What have you got against him?"

He ignored her and returned his attention to the screen.

"You don't even know, do you?"

"I have reason," he said without looking up. He took a deep breath. "Let's put it this way: I didn't like Preston's ethics when I worked for the company. I doubt they've improved."

"My father trusted him, Zeke, or he would never have been in business with him."

"Yeah, the guy's the next thing to a saint," he muttered. "So, how come he didn't level with you about the sabotage? All this time has passed and he's said nothing? Wouldn't you think he'd enlighten you about--"

"Maybe he didn't want to say anything until he knew for sure what they were dealing with."

With a dubious sigh, Zeke turned back to the computer and entered a directive. Immediately, the screen changed, bringing forth the company log for Major Metals.

6/25/21 15:13--Another shipment of iridium alloy lost to pirates. This marks the tenth heist in less than six months. Preston and I have no other recourse but to suspect treason from within.--R. Delaney

Several silent moments passed as Zeke read and reread the log. Finally, he asked, "Is this your father's last entry?"

Kira nodded. "He left for Echo that next morning."

Zeke scrolled forward, stopping to skim through ensuing memos that had been entered since Kira had taken over. At last he came to a stop and studied one particular entry.

9/26/21 12:20--Once again, the records were in disarray this morning. I'm becoming convinced that this is not merely my own lack of business skill. In requesting up-to-date statements from all of our accounts, I discovered some bills are being paid twice, while others not at all.--K. Delaney

Dragging a hand through his hair, Zeke made no comment, just studied Kira's notation a moment longer before entering a directive that brought forth the company ledger.

"Explain."

"Okay," she said, stepping forward. "See this green section? These are the records from two years ago." After giving Zeke a moment to examine the list, she asked him to scroll forward. "And this gold section is the following year. The blue," she said, as he continued to scroll the manifest forward, "is six months ago."

Zeke frowned. "So, what is it I'm looking for?"

"For example," Kira said, having him bring the first list into parallel alignment with the last, "notice the number of invoices for intrinsic augers back then, compared to the records just since I've taken over."

Kira waited while Zeke studied the two charts. At last he said, "There's nothing to compare. There are no augers listed at all in the first list."

"Precisely. Now..." She had him bring up another portion of the ledger. "Notice how, just since I've taken over, things start to pick up."

Kira watched as Zeke began highlighting specific objects on the manifest. "Do you know if the mines were producing more during this period?" he asked, without looking up.

"No. If anything, productivity was down."

His brows drew together as he returned his attention to the screen. Unable to help herself, Kira gave in to the urge to study him as he examined the manifest. Without thinking, she touched her tongue to her lips, and a tiny shudder tripped southward. She tasted him all over again. Her knees weakened at the mental imprint his body had made upon her.

She took in his wide shoulders, flexing with casual strength beneath his shirt as he moved. Her gaze traveled up to the nape of his neck where shiny sun-streaked hair cascaded loosely about his shoulders. And it was just as silky as it looked too. She knew that because--

"So," Zeke began, jolting her from her reverie, "the mine's showing a decrease in yield, yet the records show an increase in new equipment?"

"Yes. And, if you'll notice, it really seems to go crazy right about here," she said, pointing mid-way down the list. Opening up more and more to him, Kira went on to explain how she'd become aware of purchase orders that she had not authorized--yet they bore her personal ID code. "Eventually I worked out a system where I secretly kept track of everything I individually approved."

"And...?"

She had him scrolling to yet another list of figures. "Now, this is a list of purchase orders I personally okayed. And this list over here are orders I know nothing of...yet it shows that I approved them."

Silence engulfed the cabin as Zeke leaned back and continued to study the monitor. "And this all began after his death?" he asked, scrolling the manifest backward.

"Apparently so."

"It makes sense," he murmured. "It would be a damned sight easier to pass something under your nose than your father's."

Kira turned to look at him. "What's that supposed to mean?"

"Just what I said," he answered without looking up. Entering a directive into the computer, he watched as it produced the anticipated results. "Your lack of experience, Kira, would make it a hell of a lot easier to pad an order without being noticed. What's important here, though, is not how but who?"

"So, now will you take me to Echo?"

"You still haven't explained why you stowed aboard. And don't give me that bullshit about not knowing how you got here. We've had someone on our tail ever since Port Chance, and I need answers. Now."

With a sigh, she glanced away. After a moment she said softly, "You're not going to believe me."

"Try me."

When she continued to hesitate, he added, "Start at the beginning--and I want the whole story."

She held his gaze, wanting so badly to confide in him, longing to lay everything upon his broad shoulders. Even so, she wasn't sure whether he'd even believe her, or whether she could bear it if he didn't. "It's a wild story, Zeke."

"Wild's right up my alley."

Kira bit her lip. "Okay." With a sigh of resignation, she began unfolding the story of how she had been working late that night and of the sniper waiting in Major Metals' parking lot. Tears were welling by the time she told of Charlie's death and how she had to leave him lying there.

To his credit, Zeke didn't interrupt as she related the wild chase to the spaceport and how she'd hidden from the gunman in the produce bin.

"So, you were the one that biker was after."

"You saw the biker?"

"Yes."

Kira paused a moment, staring into space. "After that, the only thing I really remember is a bumpy ride and a gravelly voice telling me to stay quiet and he'd see me to safety. The next thing I knew, you were opening the crate."

Another long moment of silence passed before she glanced over at him. "Zeke, I didn't stow aboard your ship. At least not on purpose."

"Okay..." he conceded. "I know now who's responsible for putting you on board."

"You do?"

He nodded. "The same man who found your comb."

Gibby had indeed saved Kira's life, a heroic act for the proud old coot who takes his citizenship so seriously. But stashing her onboard *Solar Wind* was a huge mistake. Dragging his hand through his hair, Slater's gaze unbidden dropped to Kira's breasts, noting for what had to be the two-millionth time how she tented yet another one of his damned shirts.

With a ragged sigh, he looked away. He should never have kissed her. What the devil was he to do with her now? One minute he was as mad as all hell. And the next minute... The next minute he was staring at her chest.

He wondered bleakly if there was some sort of limit as to how long a man could remain in a state of semi-arousal. Damn, he hated redheads. Shoulda never kissed her.

"So, now you know," Kira said. "And I sure hope you've had all your questions satisfied, because I'm fresh out of answers."

He managed a grin. "As long as there's nothing else I should know, I'm satisfied."

"There's nothing else."

"Well, I want you to know I'm genuinely sorry to hear about your father."

"Thank you."

"He was a good man," Zeke added.

"Yes. He was."

"Now, I've got some good news for you. Frank has graciously offered up his cabin for your use."

"Frank? But...Zeke, I can't take his cabin."

Slater's eyebrows rose. "You really don't have many options, Legs. It's either that or share mine. Of course, if you're interested, I'd be more than willing to scoot over to make room for you." It was all he could do to keep from reaching for her, but he managed one of his rascal smiles instead--one of those teasing, half smiles he was sure would hide the damn urgency behind his pretense of an offer. If she only knew the thoughts that had been tripping through his mind.

"Gee thanks, Slater, but I think I'll have to pass on your invitation. Now if it's all right, I'd like out of jail. I want to find Frank and thank him personally for his generous offer."

Zeke was grinning. "You sure I can't change your mind, Legs?"

"Positive. Now am I free to go, or what?"

The audible snick of the lock being disengaged was her answer.

~ * ~

One week later:

It was mid-morning, ship's time, when a gray planet known as Aden loomed before them in the view screen. Without even looking, Slater was aware of Kira as she quietly ascended the stairs to the helm.

He refused to look at her, afraid to see her in another one of his damned shirts. God help him, for his own sanity he was going to have to do something about her clothes. Kira was disrupting the ordered flow of things on board. It seemed the simplest pullover only accentuated her breasts. Frank managed to bank his interest well, but young Steve Talbot was a complete goner. And as for himself... More than once she'd personally caught him staring. At her chest for godsake, like some randy fool still wet behind the ears.

"Kira, grab a seat," he said a bit gruffly. "And strap in. We're about to leave hyperspace."

"You can take this empty one right here, darlin'," Frank broke in, patting the seat next to him. "Never mind him," he added, unmasked laughter in his tone, "he's just a little cranky this mornin'."

Refusing to rise to the bait, Slater's eyes narrowed as he entered a final directive. A soft chime sounded and a computer-generated voice calmly announced the upcoming procedure throughout the vessel. Several minutes later came the resulting moment of nausea as the ship's screens blurred and the *Solar Wind* slipped out of Stellardrive.

While confined to a planet's atmosphere, *Solar Wind's* power source came from conventional booster jets. Once unleashed into the void of hyperspace, however, a secondary drive system called Stellardrive took over. As a result, Stellardrive made it possible to arrive at their destination in a matter of weeks as opposed to years.

But it was the highly illegal fuel-charger, combined with the ship's powerful weaponry that made *Solar Wind* not only unbelievably fast but damned dangerous. Despite her harmless freighter appearance, she was a fully armed warship.

With a sigh, Zeke made an adjustment then leaned back in the seat. What he needed was to get Kira off ship. But since that wasn't an option at the moment, the next best thing was to see about a new wardrobe before he and Talbot went out of their ever-lovin' minds.

"All systems, green," Frank announced, his attention riveted on the console.

Scanning the readouts, Slater opened the COMLINK, tapped in a frequency and spoke into his mike "This is *Solar Wind*, Delta Beta, five-niner-five, requesting a planetary approach vector."

Having taken the empty seat next to Frank, Kira sat quietly through the verbal communication between *Solar Wind* and Aden's largest settlement, Port Jahara. At last Zeke swiveled to face her. "Kira, we've got approximately three hours before hitting dirt. I don't know about you but I'm starved, and there's a few things we need to go over."

Leaving Frank in charge, Zeke escorted Kira toward the galley.

CHAPTER ELEVEN

The pungent aroma of coffee and Frank's cooking teased their senses as they entered the galley.

"Coffee?"

"Please." Kira's attention was caught and held by the sight outside the round view port.

Returning with two steaming mugs, he took a seat across from her and slid one of the mugs over. "You ever been to Aden?" he asked, gesturing toward the view port where a sandy gray globe hung against the blackness of space.

Kira shook her head. "No. Is that where we're headed?"

"Hmmm. And I've been thinking...maybe you should go shopping."

Her eyes widened.

Slater grinned. "I realize it will be an unpleasant task..." Reaching across the table, he fingered the rolled sleeve of the oversized shirt she was wearing. "But you really need your own things, Legs."

"But I don't have any credi--"

"It wouldn't make any difference even if you did," he cut in, guessing her concern. "The only thing they'll accept here is their own scrip or ship's credit."

"What about putting the charge on Major Metals?" she asked.

"Uh, uh. They won't accept it. Besides, I'm not leaving any trails. You're to use ship's vouchers for any purchases."

"But, I can't just accept--"

"Don't worry, Major Metals will get the bill."

"You're actually going to trust me off-ship this time?"

"Hell no. There's only one way you're getting off, and that's if I have your word you'll stay with Frank and not go sneaking off. I'm not exaggerating. They've got some really weird customs here. You get yourself into a jam, and I may not be able to pull you out."

"You have my word."

"Word on what?" he pressed.

"That I'll stay with Frank."

"Excellent." Zeke rose from his chair and headed for the cooktop. Within minutes he was back with a plate for each of them.

"Zeke, where's Frank from? I mean, he's not exactly your standard crew member, if you know what I mean?"

Slater barked a laugh. "Well, that's one way of putting it. He's from Earth. That much I know. We've pretty much kept our pasts to ourselves."

"You've known him for a while, haven't you?"

Shoveling a forkful into his mouth, he reached for the bread. "I've known Frank for about twelve years now."

"Well, he certainly can cook--and doctor, too. You're very lucky to have a First Officer who's so diversified."

"We agree on that."

A moment of silence fell between them.

"Zeke?"

"Hmm?"

Her expression had turned to one of concern. "Your arm. How is it?"

"Sore as all hell, but I'll live."

"Are you still putting that special salve on?"

"Acuel?"

She nodded.

"Hit and miss. Why? You offering for the job?"

Her reaction amused him. He watched a play of emotions cross her face. Then, as if accepting a challenge, she asked, "The salve's in the med kit?" At his nod, she added, "After lunch, I'll change that bandage for you."

The rest of their lunch was spent in small talk, and surprisingly enough, even a bit of laughter. Eventually, Kira rose to her feet and headed for the storage cabinet containing the medical supplies.

"What is it I'm supposed to be looking for?" she asked, her back turned to him as she bent to open one of the medical kits.

While shamelessly staring, Slater carefully eased his arm out of his shirt. The view from the back was prime.

"Zeke?" She'd turned her head and was looking at him. Waiting.

"Uh, it's, uhmm...I'm sorry, Kira. What was it you asked?"

With a sigh, she straightened. "The Acuel. What's it look like?"

"It's not labeled, but you can't miss it. It's the only thing in a small black jar."

"Okay. I see it."

By the time she returned to his side, Zeke had succeeded in removing the left side of his shirt. Setting everything down on the table, Kira pulled up a chair and with an air of proficiency, eyed his bandaged arm. "You should be using a sling until this heals."

"You've been talking to Frank, I see."

She laughed. "I'm sure he told you the same thing?"

"That's an understatement."

"Well, he's right. Hold still while I cut away these bandages."

"You need all those?" he asked, his gaze narrowed on the small collection of cleansers she'd managed to find.

"Don't tell me you're nervous?" When his look turned suspicious, she laughed and braced herself as the last of the bandage fell away to expose the gruesome gash across his left arm. Kira carefully studied the raw injury then rose to get a basin of hot water.

"Do I detect a hint of distress in that warrior-like façade of yours?" came his mocking drawl.

"Actually, I'm just fine, Slater." Returning to his side, she dropped a cloth into the steaming water, and with a knowing smile asked, "How about you?"

"Just hurry up. I haven't got all day."

Getting down to business, Kira began gently cleansing Zeke's wounded arm. Within minutes, she was satisfied and reaching for the

Acuel ointment. "I'm impressed with the healing that's already begun," she said, removing the lid. "Frank says Acuel salve is a miracle."

"You could say that, but unless you've got some private reason for wanting me in undue agony, may I suggest you apply Nervatrite first?"

"Nervatrite," Kira echoed. "Yes, I knew there was something else Frank had used." Hurrying back to the med kit, she quickly retrieved the topical anesthetic, Nervatrite. Within moments she was putting the finishing touches on the fresh mediwraps.

Two hours later, she was seated in the U-shaped cockpit, wide-eyed with curiosity as Frank manned the NAVCOMP and Zeke handled the main controls.

The closer they got to Aden, the larger the swirly gray planet became. Turning her eyes to the small view port to her left, Kira listened to the verbal communications between Steve Talbot and the spaceport. Gradually, Aden became so large it completely filled the window.

A bark of static hailed a greeting over the com. "Welcome to Port Jahara, *Solar Wind*. You are cleared for Docking Bay 11. Please initiate your descent."

"Understood," Zeke replied as Frank entered the designated coordinates.

Before long the blackness of space began giving way to Aden's luminous aura. They were entering the planet's gravity, and from the view port Kira watched the starboard wing as it began to burn. Soon flames were licking off the leading edge of the wing as the ship continued easing down through the various layers of atmosphere, Once again a curious orange glow filled the cabin, and at regular intervals a soft chime sounded as it signaled designated drops in elevation.

Dark splotches on the planet's surface slowly became the shaded sides of towering dunes. Beyond that, more sun-drenched dunes stretched out for as far as the eye could see.

Soon the *Solar Wind* was gently banking into a turn. Kira felt the subtle vibration when Zeke reversed the ship's thrusters, and within moments the ground was rising up to meet them.

Port Jahara was no different than any other industrial spaceport. It consisted mainly of docking bays, each one a hub of activity as longshoremen moved freight to and from darkened cargo holds.

Geysers of dust, stirred up by the thrusters, coiled about them as the ship made its way across the landing zone. And before long Zeke was guiding *Solar Wind* into its designated bay where he gently lowered it onto its landing jacks.

Fascinated by his practiced fluidity at the controls, Kira observed Zeke's bronzed hands as they danced across the keyboard, powering down and securing the ship.

Frank turned to Kira, his mouth cracking into a wide grin. "Hot dog! Looks like you and I are goin' shoppin', darlin'." She couldn't help the resulting smile. As always, Frank's enthusiasm was contagious.

In what seemed like minutes, Zeke was reaching for his holstered gun and strapping it on. "Don't forget your promise, Kira."

"I won't."

"Then, if we're ready, let's go." Slater palmed the main lock and stepped out first. Kira was next. Instantly a blast of desert heat engulfed them. The descending whine of the *Solar Wind's* powerful thrusters had her clapping her hands over her ears. Standing at the top of the boarding ramp, she ignored the stench of hot metal and exhaust as she took in the barren surroundings in one sweeping glance.

Just as it had appeared from space, Aden was hot and desolate. Mid-afternoon sun radiated off the surface of the landing zone in scorching waves. The heat was intense enough to wilt even the most rugged of men.

Zeke's black leathers may have appeared hot, but Kira knew that looks were deceiving. Being made of taubear hide meant they were insulation against heat as well as the cold.

"This place will blister the hide right off ya, if you don't protect yerself from the sun," Frank drawled, his voice raised against the descending noise.

Kira nodded and shouted back, "He offered me a set of leathers, but I turned him down."

"Not ladylike enough for y'?"

She laughed. "Actually, they were so big I was afraid I'd trip. But he did give me a special lotion to put on that protects my skin against the heat."

Frank grinned. "'Bout time he started treatin' y' with a little more care. Lord knows he's been actin' like a rogue bull paka lately."

"Hey!" Zeke yelled up at them. "You two going to stand there all day, or what?" He was waiting at the base of the boarding ramp, staring up at them through his dark glasses. Dragging her eyes away from him, Kira began making her way down.

"Two hours?" Frank asked as he stepped off the ramp. By now the descending whine was almost to a tolerable pitch.

"Sooner, if you can. I don't want to stay dirt-side any longer than we have to." Zeke's gaze slid to Kira as he added, "If she can't buy the market out by then, I don't know what to tell her."

"Oh, please. I'll hardly be buying the market out."

Zeke laughed. "We'll see."

Frank touched her arm. "Either way, darlin', I'd say we'd better get started."

"And Kira?"

She turned back. "Yes?"

"Stay close to Frank and don't be striking up a conversation with anyone but the marketers."

She sighed. "Yes, Zeke."

"I mean it, Kira. This place speaks its own language of which Frank knows little more than the basics. The vendors will be the only ones able to communicate with you. You understand?"

"Yes, Zeke. I promise I won't be trying to talk to anyone."

"Don't worry, Boss, I'll keep an eye on her."

~ * ~

The heat was unbearable. The air was heavy with an ever-changing mixture of incense, exotic flowers, ripening fruit and the unmistakable odor of foreign textiles. An occasional breeze carried the reek of animals, obviously stalled somewhere in the heat.

A tight press of canopies over open-air stands lined the street on both sides. Haggling voices ascended into the sweltering afternoon air-- merchants hawking their wares, shoppers dickering for prices. Their disputes and bartering were conducted in a mixture of languages that Kira neither understood nor recognized. At the moment she was trying to decide whether to buy the bright multi-colored gown in her right hand or the teal jumpsuit in her left.

"How much?" she asked holding up the gown.

The marketer's voice rose above the din. "For you, my beauty, one hundred filo. And that's a steal."

Frank's gaze narrowed and he snorted in disgust. "Come on, darlin' there's plenty more places on down the strip."

"Wait! Wait. Seventy-five!" the man called out.

Kira glanced up at Frank before answering. When he slowly shook his head, she turned back to the merchant. "Still too high. Make it forty and you got yourself a sale."

"Forty," he sputtered. "No, no. You rob me." He paused to ponder another counter then said, "I tell you what. For you, I make it sixty."

Getting into the spirit of things, Kira didn't bother to glance at Frank for guidance. Instead, she calmly set the colorful garment back down on the table, lifted her chin and said, "Fifty. One filo higher and I walk."

After a moment, the merchant's dark brown face cracked into a wide smile of acceptance. "Because you are beautiful. Fifty filo it is."

Frank presented a credit plate, charging Kira's purchase against the ship's tab. Within moments they were working their way on down the strip. "Y' handled that good, darlin'."

Kira beamed with satisfaction. "I did, didn't I?"

Fragments of bright sunlight sliced through the cracks between the stall's canvas tops, casting wedges of blistering light across both merchandise and shoppers. Kira's fascination grew as she took in everything from clothing to handcrafted jewelry to tethered animals as well as exotic flowers like the fragrant bouquet she'd purchased and tucked into the crook of her arm.

"Oh, Frank, wait." Her arms loaded with purchases, Kira stopped in front of a display of handmade jewelry.

"Darlin' I'll be right with y'." Not ten feet away, at the next stall down, Frank was in the process of purchasing a supply of pipe tobacco.

Temporarily forgotten was the fate that life had recently dealt Kira. For the moment the burden had been lifted as she took in everything with candid pleasure. Presently her attention was caught and held by an unusual necklace hanging off the end post of a display. Odd how the translucent gray depths of the unusual gems drew her thoughts to Zeke. Strange how they reminded her of his smoky eyes and how yesterday in his cabin, his eyes had shimmered with passion just as these gems were shimmering. At the memory, a curious tightening coiled in the pit of her stomach.

Neither Kira nor Frank noticed the man standing nearby, his hungry gaze riveted on Kira. In fact, Kira was so caught up in her reverie she never noticed anything until a massive dark shadow fell across the table of handmade baubles.

Glancing up, she discovered that a large man had stepped between her and Frank. It was hard to judge his age with half his face covered. He was both fearsome and striking with his olive skin and dark eyes. He emanated wealth from his black flowing aba to the black headdress that partially covered his face.

With an air of nonchalance, Kira forced her attention back to the merchandise, using the maybe-if-she-ignored-him-he'd-go-away method.

He didn't. In fact, there was an air of possession about him that was setting off a host of inner alarms. Anxious to escape his presence, Kira stepped back. In tandem he followed her motions, closing the distance between them.

Just then he spoke in a voice that was deep and commanding. And though Kira was unable to understand the words, she did indeed recognize the force of an order. "Sorry," she said, not about to comply with whatever he wanted of her. "I don't speak your language."

He wasn't dissuaded. Again he commanded her, this time gesturing to her left hand.

A quick glance in Frank's direction confirmed her fear that Frank hadn't noticed the confrontation yet. With a hard swallow and a helpless shrug, Kira tucked her hand beneath her purchases and repeated, "I don't understand you."

The man continued to babble on, his jet-colored eyes dancing with carnal interest.

"I must be going," she said, panic building. But her way was instantly blocked by an accomplice when she tried to pass. Operating solely on bravado now, Kira lifted her chin and took another step backward. "I suggest you let me--"

On an indrawn gasp, her words died in her throat when the man blocking her way caught her wrist in a vise-like grip. "Let me go!" she cried, unable to jerk her arm free.

Ignoring her feeble protests, the man proceeded to flip her hand over, his dark gaze dropping to the underside of her wrist.

"Let go of me, you lizard!" Kira struggled vainly to free herself. They were looking for something, and whatever it was it was scaring the hell out of her.

Finally, piercing black eyes lifted to recapture hers, and after what seemed an eternity of eye contact, the man in the black aba recited what sounded to be some sort of declaration.

Believe me, Kira, they've got some weird customs here. You get yourself in a jam, and I can't guarantee I'll be able to pull you out. Zeke's warning thundered through her mind.

CHAPTER TWELVE

A wall of people blocked Slater's view. The cargo had been loaded and he was anxious to be on his way--to put a void of space between *Solar Wind* and this godforsaken place. The last thing he wanted was to miss the rendezvous with those spectrometers.

"What's happening?" he asked a bystander in native tongue.

"A bonding rite's being challenged."

"Oh, yeah?" Why did he have this sinking feeling? Although he knew very little of the bonding rite, he knew it was an old tradition occasionally embraced by the smaller settlements.

As he recalled, according to custom, any female without a brand on the inside of her wrist or a male escort at her side was fair game. It was just one of several reasons why he'd taken Frank aside and insisted he not let Kira out of his sight.

Zeke pressed closer, trying to see past the gathering crowd, straining to hear what was being said. It was then he heard Frank's unmistakable voice raised in anger.

Shortly thereafter came another distinctive voice, "I said, take your hands off me!"

"Ahh Maann." With his mind racing and adrenaline raging through his veins, Slater pushed his way through the crowd until he could see into the center opening.

Sure enough, there she stood, toe to toe with a tall olive-skinned warrior whose beefy hand was wrapped about her wrist. Another warrior held Frank at bay, and a third man was looking Kira over as though she were merchandise. The thing was, this third guy appeared to be more than just a warrior. Slater frowned, trying to remember what that particular style and color of headdress meant.

Then it hit him. Hell, he was a damned Shakari. No wonder the bodyguards. Geez, Kira, why pick a lowly warrior when you can have a Shakari. Now what?

Damn, he hated redheads. Nothing but trouble.

His gaze slid to Frank. The old man was still arguing.

Well, shit. Having quickly calculated all possible options, Slater pushed his way through the remainder of the crowd and stepped into the opening. "She's mine."

Instantly Kira stopped her struggling and twisted about to face him, but Slater's eyes were locked in silent challenge with the man who seemed to be in command.

Again he spoke in the native tongue. "I said...she's mine."

"And what proof have you of this claim? I see no token of ownership. She bears no brand of right or title, no shroud about her head. You were not at her side when I first came upon her."

"True..." Slater pulled his stare away, centering it upon Kira. "She's mine just the same, and I claim both her and the unborn child she carries in her belly." He waited to see what the Shakari would do with that little tidbit of news.

"She is with child?" he asked, regarding Slater with piercing intensity.

"She is," he lied.

The man frowned. "And you are not bonded with her?"

"Nope." Peeling off his sunglasses, Slater made a production of cleaning them with the end of his shirt.

"Then, this child... It is not yours?"

Slater shrugged. "Can't say for sure, but since I'm the one who's been with her the most..." Leaving the sentence hanging, and with an air of supreme confidence, he lifted the sunglasses toward a shaft of light, inspecting them for smudges. "Yeah, I figure it's mine."

Several moments of silence passed while the Shakari mulled things over. "She has been with another besides you?" he asked in transparent astonishment.

Satisfied, Slater put the sunglasses back on. "Oh, I'd say about half the crew." He watched a dark scowl form on the Shakari's tanned face as he turned to stare at Kira.

The crowd grew still.

Slater could only imagine what the man was thinking. From his expression, he obviously believed Kira to be a whore. And that was just fine. Whatever it takes to shake his interest.

Meanwhile, unaware of the slur that had just been bestowed upon her character, Kira's eyes went from Slater to the Shakari to Frank. "What are they saying?"

"Damned if I know. But I'm sure the Boss is trying to negotiate your freedom."

"So, what do you say, chief? Tell your watchdog here to get his hands off her, and we'll be on our way?"

Several moments of silence passed before the Shakari drew his gaze away from Kira. "Because of her great beauty, I am willing to shelter both her and her child with my name and my home."

"I don't think so, buddy," Slater muttered beneath his breath.

"Zeke, why do I have this feeling you're making things worse?"

"Stay out of it, Kira."

"But he wasn't scowling at me until you got involved."

"Everything's under control then, is it?" Zeke's gaze slid purposefully to her entrapped wrist.

"Well, at least he wasn't looking at me the way he is now. What did you say to him?"

Slater drew in a deep breath and let it out in a sigh. "Nothing to be concerned about."

"What did he say to him?" she asked, directing the question to Frank.

"Beats me. Myself, I never did learn the language."

"There seems to be only one way for us to settle this," the Shakari said. "Because we both lay claim to her, I challenge you in the ancient way for possession of this woman."

Once again Kira tried wrenching her arm free and failed. "The least someone could do," she sputtered, "is find out what he wants."

"I know what he wants, Legs."

"Then give it to him. Charge it to Major--"

"He wants you."

She fell silent.

"Capt'n, it wasn't her fault. I'm the one who walked ahead t'--"

"She was warned, Frank."

"But, I'm tellin' y', I walked away from her. Not the other way around."

Slater turned to Kira. "We do this my way, or you're on your own. No interruptions, no arguments and no questions."

"Yes, yes. Anything. Just make him get his hands off me."

"And that's another thing. When you're released, stay right where you are. For godsake don't come running over here."

"If you think I'm simply going to--" At his look, the words died in her throat.

Slater's gaze returned to the Shakari. "Okay, let's get this over with. I've wasted enough time as it is."

As promised, Kira remained quiet while Zeke and the Shakari haggled out the details. Soon the meaty grip on her wrist fell away, and as instructed, she remained in place, eyes locked on Zeke as he turned and made his way over to Frank. Speaking in undertones, he sent Frank back to the ship to wait.

At last, he came to her side. "This way," he muttered with a nod that directed her away from the marketplace.

"Am I free now?"

"Hardly." They were proceeding toward an awaiting ground runner. "After you." Inclining his head, he indicated she enter the air-conditioned vehicle.

"Where are we going?"

He settled in next to her. "To a bonding challenge."

"Bonding chall--"

"Don't even ask."

"Look, this is not my fault. I didn't do anything wrong."

He made no reply.

They followed a winding road for approximately fifteen kilometers before cresting a hill that overlooked an oasis on the other side. In silence, Kira's gaze was fixed upon a large cluster of white tent-like structures spread out across the valley floor.

Soon the ground runner was making its way down into the basin. Skirting the main portion of the settlement, they came to a halt before the largest pavilion of all. A guard came forward to open the vehicle's door and usher them inside.

Incense hung heavy. Muted lighting was offset by bright jewel-colored panels of iridescent cloth draping the walls and ceiling. Coordinating pillows were clustered about low tables, and in the center, an arena-like area had been cleared of all furnishings. "Zeke," Kira whispered, "what is this place?"

Her answer came in the form of a dark, quelling look. Catching her by the arm, he pulled her close. "Kira," he began in a lowered tone, "if I don't happen to come out the winner here...I want you to know you'll be okay. You won't be hurt."

"Zeke, you're scaring me. You wouldn't leave me here, would you?"

"Not without exhausting all resources, no. But, if it comes to that, and until I can figure something out, you've got to promise me that you'll do exactly as you're told. You understand?"

She nodded woodenly.

"Say it!"

"Yes. I understand."

"Dear god," he breathed, "I hope so...I sure as blazes hope so."

Kira glanced uneasily at the two weapon-toting dark-clad men standing sentry at the entrance. Before long, a young olive-skinned woman with almond eyes approached and gestured for Kira to follow her. As if sensing her impulse to decline, Zeke's low-voiced command had her graciously accepting.

Ducking beneath flowing panels of shimmering gossamer, she reluctantly trailed behind as the young woman led her away to an area where colorful pillows were piled about the floor. At the girl's bidding, Kira slowly sank down onto a cushion. Another young woman appeared soon after, carrying a platter of food, which she placed on the low table before Kira.

Both women seemed no older than herself. Both were strikingly beautiful with their smooth sun-kissed skin, black hair and dark eyes. Allowing her gaze to wander, Kira took in the area. The panels of cloth shimmering along the walls and ceiling were in rich hues of topaz, ruby and sapphire. They hung from carved poles supporting the structure. A shiny brass-like brazier burned in the far corner and a thick luxurious carpet of indigo and emerald covered the entire floor.

A soft tittering drew Kira's attention back to Zeke, who was presently being attended by three veiled young women dressed in a rainbow of semi-sheer colors. A trill of amused giggles erupted when one of them brazenly reached up and touched a lock of his sun-kissed hair-- the color obviously a novelty.

Even more of a novelty, however, was Kira's own reaction to their blatant interest and curiosity. In truth, it was taking every ounce of willpower to keep from rushing over and batting their curious hands away.

"Your master has accepted the challenge for your ownership," came a heavily accented voice.

Kira whirled about to find the same girl who had set the platter of food before her. "You speak my language?" she asked, relief surging through her.

"Yes." The girl came forward, this time bearing a tray with an enameled carafe and a small cup.

"Please..." Kira pleaded, "why have we been brought here?"

With calm reserve, the young woman set the tray down and began pouring amber liquid into the cup. At last, she turned to Kira. "My master desires you," she said simply. "Your master must either relinquish you or accept the challenge for your ownership."

Normally, Kira would have been quick to correct the usage of the word master, but decided to overlook the slight in this instance. Finally, with great hesitancy, she asked, "This...challenge thing...what will it entail?"

The serving girl shrugged and replied in a gentle tone, "Each challenge is unique. Each contest is decided accordingly." She then quickly added, "But a fight to the death is very rare."

"Fight to the death?" Kira's gaze immediately shot to Zeke.

"It's very rare," the young woman repeated. "Some challenges are decided by bravery, some by endurance, but most are decided by the first draw of blood."

That thought was not exactly reassuring either, considering the recent wound to Zeke's left arm. The initial loss of blood had to have weakened him. The partially healed wound itself would have left his muscles stiff and painful. Kira was sure he'd never be able to fight at his full capacity.

More laughter drew Kira's attention. Once again straining to see across the dimly lit chamber, her eyes narrowed as a bevy of tittering young women gathered about Zeke and began divesting him of his jacket and shirt! Worse was the fact that he didn't seem to be doing a thing to stop them.

The sight brought her surging to her feet. "What are they doing?" she asked, hating the telltale dismay in her voice. But before the girl could respond, the exterior flap opened, casting a blinding shaft of bright hot daylight across the murky interior. Immediately the women attending Zeke hushed their giddy chatter and set to quickly finishing their task.

The man who had challenged Zeke had entered the chamber. One end of his headdress was draped about his neck and right shoulder, while the other end was wrapped about his head in turban fashion and secured with a string of fire gems. Unlike before, however, his face was now uncovered, and from a distance, Kira discreetly examined his features. To her surprise, he appeared older than she had first thought. She watched as he approached Zeke, their low-voiced discussion inaudible. Then Zeke nodded in solemn agreement to something.

"What's happening?"

"The challenge is about to begin. Come. Sit."

With great reluctance, Kira did as she was asked, once again sinking down onto a cushion as the rival warrior turned away and gracefully made his way to the opposite side of the enormous tent. Several young women gathered about him and began methodically removing his headdress and aba. His dark hair fell to his shoulders, and as his eyes lifted over the top of the industrious women, his attention was riveted solely on Kira.

Feeling uncomfortable beneath his lengthy perusal, Kira broke eye contact, her gaze flicking back to Zeke. Stars, what sort of contest had he agreed to? How would he fare with his injured arm? Though Zeke was a good two inches taller, both men were near equal in build, and given the fact that Zeke's strength was bound to be impaired, Kira felt certain it would not be a fair match.

"What happens if he loses?" she asked.

"If your master loses, then you will remain here, well cared for in the master's harem."

Appalled, Kira stared at the young lady. These women were little more than glorified slaves. She'd die before she'd be anyone's slave. No matter who won, no one would ever own her. Ever!

As if sensing her thoughts, the young woman added, "You and your baby would have a good life here and want for nothing."

That brought Kira's head around. "Baby? What are you talking about?"

"They are about to begin now. We will talk later."

Baby? With a scowl, her eyes slid back to Zeke, piercing the distance between them.

All was soon forgotten when the women began to move away from Zeke. He'd been stripped to the waist. Kira watched as he made his way to the center of the tent, to where an arena had been quickly prepared for the event. Zeke's left arm still bore the mediwrap she'd fastened earlier that afternoon. Attached to his left wrist was a curious looking leather manacle.

"The sakin has been chosen for this contest," the young woman whispered from behind.

A cold knot formed in Kira's stomach as she studied the vicious saber-like weapon each man held in his right hand.

"It's an ancient weapon," the girl explained. "They are only used now for occasions such as this."

"But it looks deadly. Are you sure somebody isn't supposed to die?" Kira held her breath as the men approached each other, eyes locked. One of the guards stepped forward and attached a single strap of leather to their manacles, tethering their left wrists together. The length allowed no more than six feet of separation before growing taut.

Torchlight glinted off their blades as both men grabbed a fistful of strap and squared off. The challenge had begun.

For several heartbeats the two men grimly regarded one another, gauging the other's strengths and weaknesses. Then the Shakari made the first move by jerking hard on the strap, nearly pulling Zeke off balance. With a sharp intake of breath, Kira bounded once again to her feet as Zeke avoided a slashing stroke of the warrior's weapon. "That thrust was intended to draw more than blood," she whispered.

Quickly gathering his composure, and with the skill of a warrior himself, Zeke retaliated, his own weapon coming around in a sweeping arc that narrowly missed his opponent's right thigh. The air clanged with the sound of metal striking metal, reverberated with the shouts of violent tugs on the strap and echoed with the grunts of hard thrusts and resultant parries.

Every jolt on the strap was brutal as each man tried to throw his opponent off-balance. Kira wondered how Zeke's arm was faring, how his strength was holding up. She'd watched him sustain several vicious yanks, muscle-wrenching jerks that were bound to have been excruciating to his injury. It would only weaken him further.

As if anticipating his opponent's next move, Zeke lunged forward, levering his left shoulder into the warrior's midsection. The force of the blow sent the man stumbling backward.

Muted light glinted off the sculptured muscles of Zeke's back as much as it did the steel blade he wielded. The grueling competition dragged on in an endless blur of flashing sabers as two equally muscled men dodged the advances of the other. Kira knew it was only a matter of time before the demanding intensity would eat away at Zeke's strength, slow his movements and make him vulnerable. To her horror a spot of dark crimson had already begun forming on the mediwrap, the exertion having undoubtedly reopened the wound.

Suddenly, Zeke's weight shifted, and with lightening speed, he skillfully hooked the back of the warrior's knees with his leg. The action brought the man down hard onto his back, knocking the wind from his lungs with a gasp.

Immediately, Zeke was on him, chest heaving, muscles tense as he pressed his knee firmly into the belly of his opponent.

Kira held her breath as the deadly point of Zeke's weapon hovered menacingly over his opponent's throat. From her vantage point, Kira watched something terrible flare in the depths of Zeke's eyes, as if invisible shutters had cracked open to reveal a passion so stark and black it was frightening. And then the look faded to one of inner turmoil. Suddenly, as if coming to a decision, Zeke quickly brought the descending blade down, nicking the flesh of the warrior's exposed chest.

First blood had been claimed.

He'd won. Kira's knees nearly buckled with relief. Zeke had won. Her eyes remained on him as he slowly rose to his feet and offered a hand to his downed opponent, helping him up. Breathing hard, both men stood toe to toe, staring at one another.

Then a large grin suddenly split the face of the Shakari. Clapping Zeke on the back, he said something in his native tongue.

Kira turned to the serving girl who was still standing beside her. "Are we free to go now?"

"Your master has won, but he cannot claim you just yet."

"But, can I go to him?"

"Soon."

Kira's glance swung back to the two men, once again encircled by a cluster of scantily clad females. Several girls surrounded their master, one attending the slight wound to his chest as two others rubbed him down with fluffy towels. All the while, another bevy flocked about Zeke in much the same manner. Feeling oddly possessive, Kira watched through slitted eyes as they hovered over him, slavishly toweling down every virile inch of his sweat-slickened torso. Next, the soiled mediwrap was removed from his arm and a new bandage fastened in its place. Within minutes Zeke was back into his shirt and reaching for his leather jacket.

Kira's gaze shifted as the Shakari turned to speak to Zeke. Whatever he'd said was met with a bark of laughter and an emphatic "No way in hell!" That much she heard in the tongue she understood.

A discussion followed from there, both men equally determined as they stood their ground. Several minutes of debate passed before the warrior finally grinned and once again clapped Zeke on the back. A decision must have been met, yet Zeke didn't look happy as he began wrenching his jacket on with jerky motions.

No longer waiting for permission, Kira bolted across the plush indigo carpet and drew to a halt at Zeke's side.

"Can we go now?" she whispered.

He looked down at her, his gaze shuttered. "Not quite, Legs."

CHAPTER THIRTEEN

"No matter how hard you rub it, it's not coming off." His mood was as black as the leathers he wore.

Kira squirmed in the seat beside him. "Well, I want it off. You're the one who agreed to this. I didn't."

He ignored her, keeping his eyes focused out the window of the ground runner. Hell, married. A familiar jaw muscle ticked at the thought. He always figured someday he'd settle down, but not--not like this. And certainly not to a slip of a girl still wet behind the ears. Good gods, it was the most outlandish ceremony he'd ever seen. Kira had been whisked away by a bevy of giggling females where she had been bathed, perfumed, fussed over and finally brought to him--like a sensual gift wrapped up in a rose-colored sari that revealed far more than it covered. Also included in the "wedding package" was a night in the marriage tent, which included all the wine he could drink--compliments of the Shakari himself. But that part of the ritual Zeke tactfully declined. Hell, he wasn't about to consummate this ridiculous charade. They were so behind schedule as it was, he wondered how they'd ever make up the time.

At last the ground runner drew to a halt at the far edge of the landing zone. With a muttered curse, Slater climbed out first, offering his hand to Kira.

As angered and provoked by the sheer absurdity of it all, he should have resisted the urge to watch her step from the ground runner. But watch he did. Took pleasure in it, in fact. After all, Kira was his wife and if he wanted to look at her legs--or anything else that happened to be exposed--by the gods he'd look. He'd earned that right.

First, came two shapely and unbelievably long legs, followed by an equally enticing body, clad in a shroud of translucent hot pink.

Without warning, a flash of heat surged through his veins. He knew he should look away, knew he should heed the alarm blaring somewhere in the back of his mind. Kira aroused a fire in him that was as urgent as it was unexplainable. Dammit, he hated redheads.

Hard as it was to admit, he hadn't been able to get her out of his mind since the day he first found her hiding in the cargo bay. And though this wasn't the first time he'd seen those long legs, this time it was worse. Much worse. Visions of his wife's tantalizing skin, luscious curves and bare legs would be pure hell in the nights to follow.

All the more reason to get her off ship as soon as possible.

The silent voice snapped him out of his thoughts. "Let's go," he growled. All he wanted was to get the hell back to his ship and be off this Godforsaken planet. Far too much time had been wasted, and too damn much was riding on the upcoming rendezvous.

A second look at Kira's filmy-clad body had him thrusting his jacket at her. "Here, put this damn thing on!"

Kira put it on without comment. Though it did nothing to hide her legs, it at least covered the rest of her.

"This way," he muttered, steering her up a flight of stairs that took them onto an upper level landing deck. Waves of heat radiated off the hot surface and in the distance *Solar Wind's* image undulated and shimmered in the midst of a glistening watery mirage.

Half running to keep up with his long strides, Kira tried again to talk to him. "Okay, since it won't rub off, how do I get this stupid thing off?"

He shot her a twisted smile. "You don't."

Kira caught his arm. "What do you mean, I don't?"

"Just that," he said without breaking stride. He smiled blandly. "Think of it as a souvenir, Kira." Leaving her to trail behind, he picked up the pace.

Married. Anger raged through him over the time that had been wasted on a stupid, idiotic contest of ownership. Hell. Marriage was the last thing he wanted in his life.

So what if she has the longest, sexiest pair of legs you've ever seen?

They skirted a cargo ramp. "Look," he offered, "if it makes you feel any better, I'm not any happier about this than you are."

"Then why did you agree to it? And, furthermore, did you tell him that I was pregnant?"

"Yes," he answered frankly--almost spitefully. He could feel her staring at his back.

"Why? Why would you say such a thing?"

"To dissuade his interest in you, Kira." He refrained from elaborating on how he'd further sullied her character with the impression of her being a ship's whore.

"Well, obviously, it didn't work, did it?"

"No. The fool was besotted enough to take both you and your supposed unborn babe into his fold."

Silence fell between them as they advanced toward the ship.

It was one thing watching Frank and Talbot make fools of themselves, but to have a stranger... He refused to finish the thought. Jealousy was an unfamiliar emotion. And jealousy over Kira was one he refused to acknowledge, let alone indulge in.

"And who, if I might ask, did you say was the lucky father? You?"

"All right," he said, breaking stride long enough to turn and face her. "Since you asked, I explained that you weren't sure, but that I was the one who had been with you the most so I was willing to claim the child."

"What?"

"There. Now you know it all." Once again he resumed his trek toward the *Solar Wind.*

"Of all the egotistical, conceited... Just when did you tell him this?"

"At the market."

"I knew it! I just knew it!"

"Things were moving pretty fast, Legs. I had to say something to try to get him to drop his interest."

"So, you told him I was your whore?" She had broken into a sprint to catch up with him. "I knew you'd said something terrible from the way he was looking at me."

"Sorry. I didn't have time to concoct much of a story."

"No, you sure didn't. We're getting this annulled, you know."

"I got news for you. This ridiculous farce means absolutely nothing. It was terminated the instant we left his presence."

"Good! Because, just in case you had plans of...of consummating this stupid--"

That turned his head, and with a slow smile he drawled, "If I'd wanted you, sweetheart, believe me I'd have had you by now." He didn't dare look at her after that one. Didn't need to. Her sharp intake of breath said it all.

Hell, married!

They were approaching the ship when Slater reached for his remote and punched in a code. Instantly, the ramp emerged from a dark narrow rectangle below the main hatch and extended slowly to the ground.

Two things hit them the instant they entered. The first was the blessed coolness of the ship's climate-controlled interior. And the second was, "What the devil took y' so long?"

Retrieving Kira's purchases that had been stacked near the entry, Frank handed them to her along with her bouquet of flowers, which he had put in water. "Here y' go darlin'. I rescued 'em for y'." He then turned and followed Slater down the corridor. "Don't go tellin' me all this time y' were sippin' tea with his Royal Highness." He stood in the doorway to Slater's quarters, his old man's eyes peering beneath bushy eyebrows-- missing nothing, watching his captain undo the leather tie from his leg and remove his gun belt. "So, did y' tell His Majesty that..."

Slater tuned him out. He already had one bitch of a headache, and listening to Frank go off on one of his lectures was about as far from a cure as one could get.

Brushing past his First Officer, he made his way to the helm and dropped into the captain's seat. "How long before rendezvous?" he asked as Frank ascended the stairs.

Frank moved to the NAVCOMP and tapped in a series of numbers. After a moment he replied. "If we push 'er hard, rendezvous with the Star Runner comes up in exactly four hours and thirty-one minutes."

Zeke nodded and studied the controls. "Cutting it damn close," he muttered.

"Yep, so if there's anyone else yer plannin' to have a little social hour with, may I suggest--"

"You're out of line, Frank. Just enter the damned coordinates."

"Already done. Three hours ago," he added testily.

"Cargo sealed?" Slater asked without taking his eyes off the controls.

"Yep, that, too. Three hours ago."

Within minutes the *Solar Wind* was responding to Slater's commands and roaring skyward, leaving Aden, its strange culture and the legalities of marriage far behind.

~ * ~

"Hot damn!" Frank's voice drifted out of the ship's lounge, having just heard the news.

"Don't look so happy, old man. The instant we left port, that ridiculous marriage became nonexistent."

"Whatever y' say, Boss," Frank said, still grinning.

Slater absently studied the figure-eight design on the inside of his wrist. It meant nothing. Just a stupid tattoo.

He glanced back up at Frank. "Anyway, what I needed to ask you is: could she continue using your cabin for a little while longer?"

Frank studied the smoke trailing off the stem of his pipe. "I have no problem with that, but I suggest you come up with a good reason to have 'er in yer cabin by the time we take-on the Star Runner. The last thing we need is to have 'er loose and about."

"Yes. She's in my cabin now, ridding herself of that godawful perfumed oil they bathed her in. She mentioned being tired and wanting a nap. I'll tell her you need the use of your cabin, and for now she can nap in mine."

Truth of the matter was, Slater's cabin was the only one that could be locked from the outside. Short of locking her in a cargo pod, it was the only place to ensure Kira's isolation during the upcoming raid.

Reaching for his mug, Frank rose from his chair and ambled over to the beverage dispenser. "By the way, we received a message from headquarters while you were havin' tea."

"Oh, yeah?"

"Somethin' about a memo from Celeste."

"Celeste?" Slater groaned. "God save me from women. Now what?"

"Y' gotta give 'er credit. She's managed to get herself on board, even if it is through the magic of a memo-vid."

Slater slid him a retiring look.

Without further comment, Frank absorbed himself in the task of refilling his mug. Zeke had the distinct impression he was more likely stifling a belly laugh than anything. Finally, with coffee in hand and a smirk safely concealed, Frank made his way back to his seat. "I went ahead and patched it through to the terminal in the lounge for y'."

No response.

"Remember, its headquarters sayin' you need to hear it. Not me."

Slater took a breath, releasing it slowly as he rose from his seat. "This had better be important." The last thing he needed was Celeste. His entire body ached, and he was in dire need of a shower. But that would have to wait, since he'd given Kira the use of his quarters.

Thane Morgan's familiar face materialized on the view screen. "Slater, I've got a message here that just came in from somebody named Celeste. I assume you know her? Anyway, see what you make of it."

Silence filled the cabin as Morgan's face faded, and Celeste's elfin one took form. "Zeke, there's something I've got to tell you..."

Immediately an odd sensation sliced through him. The alarm in Celeste's voice was so unlike her. Celeste didn't have sense enough to be alarmed about anything. And yet there it was, staring him in the face as if it were something visible.

"...man nosing about Port Chance the day you left," she went on. "He was asking the destination of your next drop."

Frowning, Slater sat forward, his undivided attention focused on the vid screen.

"I only overheard part of the conversation, but I caught enough to know that the guy behind the desk gave out information he shouldn't have. I heard him explaining how he couldn't get past the security lock on your flight plan, but...he was able to somehow snag your first port of call."

"Here's a security picture of the guy who had asked for the information."

The screen blurred then cleared with the face of a grossly scarred man. For Zeke, the face triggered no recognition, but it would give him something to tuck away for future reference. The thing that had him concerned more than anything was the fact that somehow security had been breached. How the blazes did they learn about his first drop?

"...Anyway," Celeste was saying, "I just thought you should know." She sighed. "I miss you, Zeke. You should have taken me with you. You wouldn't have regretted it, and we could have been having so much fun by now." She smiled and lowered her voice. "By the way, did you happen to find that little souvenir I left tucked beneath your bunk? Just a reminder of what you're missing out on--"

Abruptly, the screen went blank and Morgan's face returned. "If this character's who I think he is, you got major trouble on your hands, Slater. Get back to me."

Reaching forward, Zeke put the message on pause, freezing Morgan's face on the screen.

"Trouble?" Frank asked, his pipe clenched between his teeth as he stepped inside the lounge.

"Yeah... But nothing we can't handle. Rendezvous comes up in a little less than an hour. Go ahead and ready the crew. I'm going to try to make contact with Morgan then I'll join you."

"What about Kira?" Frank asked.

"She's secure. She was sleeping when I locked her in."

With a nod, Frank turned and made his way down the corridor.

~ * ~

Kira roused from a three-hour nap, grateful Zeke had once again offered the use of his private quarters--the shower in particular. The warm spray should have been soothing, but oddly it wasn't. Instead, all she wanted was to rinse off the heavily-scented oil they'd rubbed her down with and get into something less provocative.

For what seemed the hundredth time, she glanced down at the mark on her wrist. How many times had she tried erasing it to the point of making it even more red and irritated than it already was? Revulsion swept through her at the thought of once again being branded as someone's property. It didn't make any difference that Zeke wasn't any happier about it than she. Oh, he'd made it perfectly clear, that as far as he was concerned, the ceremony, the tattoo, none of it meant anything. As to that, Kira wasn't sure whether to be grateful or insulted.

Again she rubbed the mark. Her wrist felt bruised and sore--for all the good it had done. It was no less noticeable now than it was when it was first applied. Twisting her wrist to the side, she examined the tattoo closely. It wasn't offensive to look at. If anything, it was fascinating with its iridescent colors shimmering from one shade to another as she rotated her wrist back and forth.

Figure eight, the sign of infinity, a silent voice whispered as she traced the design with the tip of her nail. A self-deprecating laugh echoed in her mind. *The last thing Zeke Slater wants is to be bound to you for infinity.*

Kira bore another tattoo. One that marked the underside of her left breast. The mark of another type of ownership: slavery. A time, long ago when deep in the bowels of some godforsaken mine, her past, present and future were little more than one day blending into the next. She numbly wondered if Zeke Slater had any idea of the penalty for harboring an escapee.

Rising from the bunk, she crossed the cabin to where her new outfits lay upon a chair. She was in the middle of deciding whether to wear the teal floor-length shift or the black jumpsuit when a subtle vibration suddenly traversed the ship. It was so faint, Kira almost didn't notice it. Almost.

Remaining still, she waited, listening, wondering if she had simply imagined the tremor beneath her feet... Or what...?

Nothing...

Quickly selecting the black jumpsuit, she finished dressing. After several minutes in front of the mirror, smoothing out wrinkles, adjusting the fit and admiring the tiny fire gems that adorned the neckline, Kira proceeded to work her heavy hair into a thick braid that hung down her back.

Again the tattoo on her wrist caught her eye, its intriguing beauty mocking her by its very presence. She'd been near hysterics when they'd applied it. Zeke had to physically hold her down, no doubt thinking she'd lost her mind. She recalled him trying to reason with her, telling her it was just a stupid tattoo that didn't mean anything. "Just let them do it, Kira, so we can get the hell outta here!"

Without warning another shockwave trembled beneath her feet, jarring her from her thoughts. Kira turned and stared at the closed entry panel. Something was going on!

This time, rushing for the door, she palmed the pad on the wall. But the door wouldn't open. Another try sent a sharp stab of fear down her spine. The panel was locked! He'd locked her in!

"Zeke!" She pounded on the panel with both fists then stopped to listen, waiting, hoping that someone would come. Silence. The only sound was the familiar hiss of the ship's ventilation.

A third tremor passed through the ship. Next came the sounds of muffled voices in the corridor and rapid footfalls rushing toward the stern.

"Zeke! Frank!" Again, she pounded on the door. "Somebody open this door!" Forcing back the rise of panic, Kira made her way to the large view port and gazed out at the star-studded blackness surrounding them. Something was happening. The conclusion had barely formed when a small portion of another ship eased into the lower right corner of the view port.

Quickly deciding not to stand around wondering any longer, she turned for the panel again, determined to get out. Suddenly, the vibration of acceleration pulsed beneath her feet as *Solar Wind* began aggressively swinging about.

Everything happened fast after that. A loud klaxon began resounding throughout the ship. Sounds of anxious voices drifted in from the corridor. "Zeke!" she called out again. Thunk. Thunk. "Somebody--" but her words were abruptly cut off when a loud crack split the air and Kira found herself tossed to the floor by a jolt so sharp it rocked the ship.

She lay there a moment, stunned. Lights flickered then went out, throwing the cabin into a moment of darkness before the auxiliary lamps came to life.

It didn't take a genius to figure out they were under attack. Pirates! The very thought sent another surge of panic through her. Clamoring to her feet, she gasped as another tremor surged through the ship. But this one was more subtle. Obviously, the *Solar Wind* was firing back.

Little good it would do, however, for surely a freighter such as the *Solar Wind* was hardly prepared to take on a confrontation with pirates! And Zeke? He would fight to the death, protecting his ship, his crew and his cargo from plunder.

And what about you? Are you ready to be cornered in a tiny cabin again? Memories came flooding back across the span of time, when six-year-old Kira huddled in a darkened corner of a cabin not unlike the one she now occupied. Silently, she had watched in horror as her family was slaughtered before her eyes. She recalled how the hoots of laughter and noise became louder as men moved back and forth in the corridor outside the cabin.

"Remain quiet. No matter what," her birth mother had instructed as she guided her young daughter into the wardrobe and secured the door. That was the last she saw of her mother.

Being confined is exactly what got her caught once before. Like prey trapped in a cage. She would not be caught again. Her gaze was drawn to the view port where, in mute shock, she watched the other ship slowly move into full view, its starboard side completely engulfing the viewport. Sidling up against the *Solar Wind* meant only one thing--they were preparing for inter-ship docking.

The fist in Kira's stomach tightened.

CHAPTER FOURTEEN

"Warning. Risk factor unacceptable on all options. Abort inter-ship docking procedure.

"Warning. Risk factor..."

"Shut that damned thing off!" Slater shouted over the blare of klaxons. But it wasn't the klaxons he was referring to. It was the sexy feminine voice of the on-board computer calmly detailing the consequences of their present course of action.

"Can't, Boss. Remember--after the last time y' busted it? They fixed it so y' couldn't disable it again."

"Two minutes to impact," the voice continued in sensuous undertones.

Muttering something crude under his breath, Slater reached overhead, activating a series of red-lit keys and continued with his endeavor to lessen the force of a collision.

"What the hell's with the bedroom voice?" he growled. The computer had been programmed to use audio only in times of emergency, and now was Zeke's first introduction to the sensuous new voice presently echoing throughout the ship.

Frank quickly tapped in the necessary numbers on his keyboard then looked up at the screen for confirmation. "Don't ask me," he said, half laughing. "I didn't do it, but I'd be willin' to bet one of them Banner boys knows about it. Probably figured y'd listen instead of killin' it like always. By the way," hc added, his eyes glued to the console, "looks like we'll be takin' a little hit when we connect. Crippled or not, they're doin' their damnedest to make this difficult."

Even under the best of conditions, inter-ship docking was tricky, but when one participant wasn't cooperating, it became downright suicidal. "Try slowing them with the Shel," Slater suggested.

"Already did."

"One minute to impact," came another sultry warning throughout the ship.

Things were moving fast. Ignoring the computer's forewarning, Slater spun his seat around and called out, "Talbot, I need a straight-up reading. Now!"

"We're at ninety-five. Alignment, in...thirteen seconds."

Slater swung back to the console. "Damn, I don't like cutting it this close."

"Thirty-seconds to impact."

"Hell, y' thrive on it'," Frank drawled, his focus still riveted on the controls.

"We've got alignment!" Talbot called out.

"Engage!" No sooner had Zeke given the command, than the ship was reeling under the violent jolt of a awkward link up.

"Docking collars are engaged," came the computer's silky confirmation.

The computer was already listing damages in order of severity when Zeke opened the hailing frequency and began ordering the seized vessel to stand down and prepare to be boarded.

~ * ~

Klaxons were throbbing as Kira slipped into the corridor. That final jolt had momentarily dislodged the electronic lock on the panel to Zeke's quarters. Seeing the opportunity, she quickly slipped out before it had time to reset itself.

Tucked in her pocket was a tiny pistol she had found stashed in the storage locker next to the bunk. It might be small, but Kira strongly suspected it carried a punch that would take a grown man down. She quickly made her way to the cargo bay where all the commotion seemed to be centered. Within moments she was inside and slipping undetected behind a stack of cargo pods.

Where did all the crew members come from? Men were everywhere, forming groups, rapidly strapping on weapons and checking energy levels. Urgency hung in the air like a living, tangible being. Stars, they truly were under attack!

"Bates, I want you and Reed right behind me. Weapons on stun."

Even before she saw him, Kira knew that familiar whiskey-smooth timbre, and with recognition came a surge of relief. Truth was, just the thought of Zeke didn't just calm her fears, it filled her with something far deeper--something she had yet to acknowledge.

Breathable air could be heard hissing into the interlock that now coupled the two ships. Action aboard *Solar Wind* was rapidly escalating into a swarm of energetic preparation as men scurried about with urgent purpose. Where had all the men come from, she wondered again?

"Kip, once we're aboard, you and Davis search out the living quarters. Frank, you know what to do."

'Search out the living quarters?' A tiny worm of alarm wriggled along Kira's spine. This was clearly no defensive maneuver.

And then Slater moved into view--all six-foot-three of him, issuing orders and organizing the men for what could only mean a full-scale assault. Instantly, Kira's eyes moved to his face, taking in the changes. Zeke didn't have...

His shoulder-length hair, once sun-streaked blonde, was now the shade of midnight as were his brows and a sinister mustache that curved about his mouth. A scar cut across his left jaw. The metamorphosis was complete, right down to black leathers and two fully loaded bandoleers crisscrossing his chest. A pistol hung low on his right thigh, and as Kira watched, he paused to adjust the energy level on a weapon. The finishing touch was a small silver cross dangling from his right earlobe. In truth, she would never have known him had it not been for his voice and the easy fluid grace with which he moved.

She was still assessing the transformation when the airlock cycled open, and with a collective shout, the crew of the *Solar Wind* charged through the interlock and onto the adjoining vessel.

Klaxons pulsed, men shouted, and above all the madness and pandemonium *Solar Wind's* onboard computer repeated emergency advice in breathy monotone throughout the entire ship.

Sinking back against the storage pods, Kira's imagination ran rampant. The scene, all too familiar, brought memories rushing back across the gulf of eighteen years. Once again she relived the day pirates had overtaken the liner she and her family had been on. And although she had eventually managed to escape, the brutality and loss of her parents would forever be burned into her memory.

Before long, Kira was pulled from the memories as the men began returning. Instantly, her instincts shot to red alert as she watched them push, carry and drag aboard everything from mining equipment to various imported commodities.

There was little doubt who the pirates were in this scenario. And the realization of it sent a tide of outrage, bitter and angry, surging through her.

All too soon, however, she learned that a pirate's plunder wasn't enough for this crew when a bedraggled assemblage of men and women stumbled through the interlock. Prisoners. It was written upon their bleak faces and the manacles binding their hands and feet. In stunned horror Kira watched yet a second group being herded through the passageway, prodded along by Frank's gravelly voice. Frank? How could he?

Zeke Slater wasn't just a pirate; he was a damned slave runner! The monster of her worst nightmare!

Thoughts spinning and gaining fury, Kira crept closer.

"Mr. Reno, I want to see what we have here," Slater called from within the interlock. "Line them up along the aft wall."

Two seconds was all it took. Two decision-filled seconds and one burst of blind courage. Her weapon in hand, Kira lunged from her hiding place, aiming at Frank with deadly accuracy. "Drop your weapons!"

Frank spun about. Shock and disbelief were written upon his grizzled face as his eyes leveled on the business end of her tiny revolver. "Kira, honey--"

"Now!"

"Okay...okay." Arms splayed, Frank carefully laid down the weapon he'd been carrying. "What in lasers are y' doin', girl?"

"Spoiling your fun, I'm afraid."

"Fun?"

To that she smiled blandly. "I have eyes, Frank. I'm not stupid."

"What's going...on...?" Slater emerged, his words trailing as Kira rounded on him, the gun aimed at his heart. Only when she realized that he had a small child in his arms did she relent, lowering the weapon to his thigh.

"Put her down, Zeke!

"Savages," she hissed, her voice so raw with emotion it was barely audible.

Slater's cool composure in the face of Kira's fury didn't waver. "She's injured," he offered quietly. "Her knee is--"

"I said, put her down!"

Slowly, he set the toddler on her feet, steadying her until she had one tiny arm wrapped securely about his leg. "There you go, Princess," he said softly, handing over the small doll he'd been carrying for her. With a slow exhale that puffed out his cheeks, he straightened and once again faced the bore-end of Kira's small weapon--which by now had been re-aimed at his chest.

"Now your weapons," Kira said, her eyes locking with his as he began lugging three guns, a mini blaster, two knives and a ripper from various places on his person. "Kick them over here. Tell the others to do the same."

Her orders were followed without hesitation, but Kira wasn't dumb enough to believe she truly had the upper hand. What she had at the moment was their captain in her sights. And for now that was enough.

"How about putting that gun down before someone gets hurt."

Kira laughed. "Hurt? Do you have any idea how badly I want to pull this trigger?"

"I think I've got a fair idea." Slater's words came slow and easy, his stolidity in the face of Kira's rage as cool and unruffled as the sultry electronic voice in the background chanting emergency instructions.

A muffled sob drew Kira's eyes briefly back to the toddler clinging to his leather-clad leg.

"Come on, Kira, you really don't want to fire that gun in here." Slater's gaze slid with lazy regard from her face to the gun and back. "Why don't you put it down and--"

"I don't give a damn what you steal or why. But when it's people. When it's ch--" her voice broke, "children..."

"Kira, darlin', y' don't understand. What yer seein' here is--"

Slave Runners. They were all in on it. And she had just started to trust them all. Zeke. Frank, even Talbot, as he stood there balancing a heavy crate upon his shoulder.

"So what is it you want?"

Her focus snapped back to Slater. "I want you to release these people. Let them return to their ship, unharmed." Gravity had since dragged her aim from his chest to his belly. Yet, there he stood with his familiar ease--looking for all the universe as though he should be sprawled in a chair instead of standing there cogitating the odds of still breathing in the next minute.

"All right."

His answer came too easily. Clearly skeptical, Kira's blistering glare lifted to his face, taking in the scar, that idiotic mustache, his black hair--and all the while adamantly ignoring how recklessly handsome he was. Even in his dark disguise.

"You'll let them go then?" she asked.

"Yes."

She barely caught the movement out of the corner of her eye. Never had time to flinch before someone seized her from behind, wrenching her arms up over her head. There was a moment of struggle before the weapon suddenly fired, sending everyone to the deck and a slug ricocheting off the bulkhead in a series of high-pitched ballistic whines.

"Somebody get that damn thing away from her!" The words were barely out before the gun was being twisted from her grip and Kira was sinking to her knees in defeat.

Her ears were ringing from the report. The air was permeated with the acrid stench of gun smoke. Voices were raised, a child was crying and through the emotional blur of it all, Kira vaguely heard Slater's deep voice calmly issuing explicit orders to his crew.

And then he was there, drawing her to her feet and propelling her toward the exit. "You little fool. Of all the brainless stunts! Do you realize you could have blown us all into the next galaxy?"

Tears of defeat and outrage slipped down her cheeks as she fought him every step along the corridor. It wasn't until they'd entered his cabin that she rounded on him, catching him squarely on the jaw with the flat of her hand. "Bastard! You deceitful--"

Moving so suddenly she flinched, he captured her wrist, drew her against him and angled her arm behind her back. "Don't ever try that again." The words were quiet and precisely enunciated through lips that barely moved.

They glared at one another for what seemed an eternity, his features hardening, a crimson imprint of her hand slowly forming on his cheek. "Everything would have been just fine if you'd stayed where you were put."

"So you could carry out your depraved deeds without a witness?"

"What the hell do you take me for?"

"A monster! That's what!"

His jaw went rigid. "You have no idea." Again, his tone was soft with menace. And in that very moment Kira realized the consequences of what she had witnessed. In essence, she had looked upon the wizard. She could identify him and his crew.

He would not allow her to live.

The hand within his grip was growing numb. Kira flexed her fingers. "You're hurting me."

Slowly he released her then moved to engage the lock on the door. "You made one bitch of an error in judgment back there, Kira." He tugged at the leather holster tie around his thigh. It slipped undone.

"By trying to free innocent people?" she snapped, massaging circulation back into her hand.

"By underestimating me." He unbuckled his gun belt. It swung free of his hips to droop from his hand. "And that doesn't even count firing that gun. Do you know what happens when a slug penetrates the hull of a ship?"

"The ship wasn't my target," she said with a toss of her head.

Cursing beneath his breath, Slater dropped the gun belt onto the nearby bunk. "If that slug had penetrated--"

"It didn't."

He stared at her. "No. It didn't. But how do you explain dodging a wild bullet to a little kid who's already been through hell?" His quiet words sizzled like drops of rain on the hot surface of a landing zone.

Up went her chin. "If your man hadn't jumped me, I would not have missed."

"And how far do you think that would have gotten you? Were you prepared to take on my entire crew?"

"If necessary."

He said nothing, but his look was condescending as he proceeded to remove the bandoleers. Gathering up the weapons and ammo, he hung them inside a nearby cabinet and secured the lock. At last he turned for the mirror and began removing the scar. "I should have known better than to trust you to stay put," he said, eyeing her in the reflection.

"And I should have known better than to trust you at all. How could I have been so stupid?"

He held her hostile stare in the mirror for several beats. "Don't punish yourself too hard, Legs. I'm damn good at what I do. Your gullibility was inevitable."

"And just what is it you do? Sell innocents into slavery? My, the profits must be impressive."

"I do all right," he drawled, matching her sarcasm. "It's a living."

"You're despicable." Quaking with fury, she lapsed into stony silence while he continued ripping off the disguise. He may have masked his true identity, yet she couldn't help notice--albeit grudgingly--that there wasn't a whole lot he could do about that damned dimple.

"You look like an idiot in that mustache," she quipped, her insolent gaze piercing the distance between them.

"You should see me in my full beard."

Refusing to rise to the bait, Kira continued to hold several moments of unblinking eye contact before allowing her gaze to slide away in disgust. Stars, she hated him. She should have shot him when she had the chance.

At last he turned to face her, minus the scar, the mustache and the earring--the dimple irritatingly in place. "You stuck your nose where it didn't belong. Now I've got to figure out what the devil to do about you. And believe me, right now the nearest airlock looks damned tempting." Releasing a compressed sigh, he turned for the lav.

Zeke Slater wasn't the sort to make idle threats. God only knew the atrocities he had already committed--savagery that would harden him to anything when it came to achieving his goal. She had witnessed enough to imagine what he and his band of cutthroats were capable of as they overtook, ravaged and plundered...even little children. That was the one that got her the most.

And what about the child?

At the moment Kira was in no mood to acknowledge the mental image of Zeke Slater gently cradling a small child in his arms.

Hardly the act of a callous slave runner.

She was in the process of denying that one as well, when a faint tremor once again traversed the ship. Crossing to the view port, she watched the connecting interlock slowly disengage and retract like a telescope until she could no longer see it disappear into the hull of *Solar Wind*. For several long minutes the two freighters slowly drifted apart. Gradually, the other ship began to nose about. But just as a cat toys with a mouse, the fleeing vessel was allowed to retreat only so far before the floor beneath Kira's feet shuddered and a fiery missile was burning its way across the void. Kira gasped as the resulting flash bathed the cabin in blinding light.

"I guarantee," came the familiar deep voice from behind, "if the tables were turned, you'd like their methods even less."

Eyes ablaze, she whirled about to find Slater watching with impassive interest. "You're killing people!"

Holding her gaze, he shrugged. "Yes, that's possible."

"How can you do this?" she cried, appalled by his cold acknowledgment and knowing full well that someone was carrying out his precise orders.

"Do what?" As if on cue, *Solar Wind* shuddered again and a second missile streaked across the blackness. Another bright flash, and by degrees the doomed vessel began listing to port.

Kira turned away from the view port to meet Zeke Slater's faintly amused gaze.

"We're crippling their ship, Kira." Shouldering away from the wall, he came forward. "They're pirates. I don't set them free if that's what you're thinking."

"You're calling them pirates?" she scoffed. "You're the one stealing innocent passengers."

His jaw tensed. "Is that what they were--passengers?" He came a menacing step closer and bent forward, his face within inches of hers. "Or were you too busy judging me to even notice?"

Kira straightened to her full height. "I know what I saw."

"The hell you do." In one swift and fluid motion he'd captured her upper arm and marched her toward the exit. "But you're going to find out."

With Kira rebelliously in tow, he advanced down the corridor. She managed to kick him and felt a moment's satisfaction at his ensuing curse. Halting before the airlock to the cargo bay, he seized both of her wrists in one manacling grip, entered a code into a security panel and guided her inside when the door cycled open.

Solar Wind's hold was ominously quiet. No crew. No chaos, and no slaves as there had once been. Rows of commandeered cargo formed narrow aisles that silently ran the length of the chamber. Tiny red lights winked at them from security vids along the ceiling, and a host of scents permeated the air as they made their way past rows of stolen cargo.

He drew to a halt before the aft wall with Kira twisting and straining against him as once again he entered a code into yet another safety lock. "Snake," she sneered, then added for good measure, "Rapist!"

Was he a rapist? No sooner had the question formed, than she found herself pressed against the bulkhead.

"That's enough! When this door opens, no more yelling. No more name-calling, and no more tantrums! Understood?"

"You can go to hell, you sorry s--"

Her breath caught as he angled his body forward, pinning her intimately between the wall and the open cradle of his thighs. With palms planted on either side of her head, he entrapped her. And then his voice dropped. "What does it take to silence you?" His head lowered. "This?"

Before she could recover from the shock and feel of his strength, he took her mouth with a fierceness that left her weak.

There was no escape. Only soul-burning submission as Zeke Slater deftly parted her lips and subjected her to the most thorough, intimate and rapacious kiss she had ever experienced.

Breathing heavily, he lifted his mouth from hers and opened it against her throat, swiftly drawing a patch of delicate skin taut against his teeth. Her knees nearly buckled when he nudged his hips against her, leaving no doubt of what was going through his mind. "And, just to set the record straight," he murmured, gently laving the bruise he'd brought forth on her neck, "I have yet to resort to rape."

Kira was vaguely aware of a hidden door cycling open behind her, dimly conscious of Slater backing her into what turned out to be a secret adjoining cargo hold. When released, she remained motionless, stunned as much by his sensual assault--the lingering taste and feel of him, as by the brusque-looking crewmen and the bustle of activity going on around her.

Along the back wall, crew members worked to rid prisoners of their shackles. To the left, makeshift pallets were being fashioned out of cargo pads. To the right, injuries were being tended, and in the air was a mix of meds and steaming coffee.

"You're...rescuing them."

Without comment, Slater's gaze moved to take in the purposeful flurry.

"I almost sh--" she swallowed convulsively, "sh--shot you."

"Ahh, here he is, little one. See?" Frank's graveled voice broke the tension as he came forward with a toddler perched on the side of his hip. His knowing eyes settled first upon Slater, moved to linger upon Kira, then shifted curiously back to Slater again.

Still clutching her doll, the tot silently, warily searched Slater's face, her cheeks flushed, her lashes dewy with tears.

"I know, I know," Frank went on, humor lighting his old man's eyes, "he's even uglier than before, but I guarantee it's still him."

Zeke's hair spilled recklessly upon his shoulders. The unruly wisp sagging over his forehead only intensified his good looks, lending a disheveled boyish charm to his appearance.

"Well, Capt'n, don't just stand there. Say somethin'. She's been cryin' for y' ever since that damned gun went off." Frank turned searching eyes back to Kira. She seriously doubted much escaped Frank's knowing eyes as she stood there with damp, kiss-swollen lips and her face aflame. To his credit he said nothing more than, "Are y' feelin' any better, darlin'?"

She barely managed a nod, her throat so tight it hurt to talk.

"As y' can see," he added, "we're in the business here of salvagin'. Not slavin'."

"But...the disguises," she whispered, noting for the first time that even Frank looked different. "It's misleading."

"As it should be. Y' see, first of all we have a shippin' business to run here. We can't just go around pissin' off the bad guys without disguisin' ourselves. Frank grinned proudly and with a sweep of his arm spanned the ship. "Even the outside of this old girl changes, thanks to a few hi-tech accessories."

"Crying? For me?" Clearly mystified, Zeke's features visibly softened as his gaze fell upon the towheaded youngster. He touched her tear-stained cheek. "Hey there, Princess."

His attention shifted back to Frank. "What about family? Any luck?"

"It don't look good, Boss. We went through the manifest three times and..." he shook his head sadly. "Nothin'."

The scene was typical. Kira knew first hand how common it was for children to become separated from family, to be herded along like animals and loaded into the stinking hold of a ship. But instead of being set-up for rescue as the *Solar Wind* was, the holds of slave ships were brutal, overcrowded and reeked of body waste.

With intense scrutiny and a final heart-wrenching hiccup, two little hands hesitantly reached out in silent appeal. Next instant Slater had the babe in his arms, her damp, tear-smudged face buried against his throat, her tiny fingers curling into his shirt.

Gently stroking the child's back, he murmured low in a dialect he hoped might be hers, yet only half-spoke himself.

Kira didn't want to deal with her feelings at the moment. Didn't want to examine the turmoil going on within, let alone admit that Zeke Slater's scent was fused with her very soul. The taste of him still lingered upon her lips. And now simply watching him--preoccupied as he was with the child--such tenderness swelled and coiled inside, she thought her heart would break of it.

CHAPTER FIFTEEN

Going through his own private hell, Slater didn't want to think about her any more. Why the hell had he kissed her? As if the first time wasn't lesson enough.

Because she'd pissed him off with her name-calling accusations--that's why. He was angry and the more he thought about, it the angrier he became. He'd been good enough to save her defiant little hide on Aden, hadn't he? Right down to a marriage he neither wanted nor had intentions of ever consummating. Yet the truth remained. A truth he wasn't facing very well--his anger had nothing to do with the fact that his gut was all twisted in knots. He couldn't remember a time when he'd been turned-on so fast as when he kissed her this last time. Fact was, he'd had one hell of a time forcing himself to stop--to keep from pressing her back against the wall. God only knew how he'd wanted to. Still did, for that matter.

The silent voice laughed. *You've wanted her ever since the day you found her hidden in the hold.*

Just the memory of those long legs stretched out on his bunk in invitation sent a rush of hormones cruising through his veins looking for release.

You shouldn't have kissed her, and you have no one to blame but yourself.

He'd kissed her with the intention of knocking her down a notch or two. It might have been different had she been willing to indulge in a little recreational sex, although he didn't have Kira pegged for that type.

And now...the last thing he needed was un-slaked lust to add to everything else.

Then slake it, the tiny voice argued. *You're married. She's your wife.*

A marriage he had no intentions of legalizing. Number one, Kira wasn't his type. And even if she was, he couldn't afford the distraction. Distractions cause mistakes.

Yet, distracted he was. Right along with every other male on board. Damn redheads.

Especially ones with long legs, huh?

Purposely glancing about, Slater shifted his train of thought from the fantasies he'd been fighting off over the past half hour to the reality around him. Reality was the stench of unwashed bodies, the moans of the injured, and the fragile weight of the slumbering child in his arms.

"If y' wanna lay that little pup down, I made a place for 'er over thar along the bulkhead." Within minutes of being in Slater's arms, the toddler had lost the battle to sleep, her head resting upon his chest.

He followed Frank over to a small pallet that had been fashioned out of cargo pads.

"Poor little tyke," Frank whispered, watching as Zeke eased the babe down onto the makeshift bed. Reflexively she stiffened then relaxed as she settled onto the soft bed. "Y'd think it'd get easier, wouldn't y'-- seein' a little kid like this and knowin' the hell she's been through."

"Yeah..." Slater rose to his full height, and they both stood there a moment considering the child--safe at last. "But then," Zeke added, "this is what it's all about, Frank--right here. No one ever said it was easy." He paused a moment, lifting his sights to scan the crowded chamber. Kira was nowhere in sight. "So, where'd she go?" he asked.

"Who?"

Slater refrained from rolling his eyes.

Frank grinned. "She's right over there, Boss."

He followed Frank's gaze over to where Kira was helping one of the crew members hand out energy bars.

Kissing her was the dumbest thing you've ever done if you aren't going to follow through, the tiny voice whispered.

"Sure seems t' be useful at this sort of thang, don't she?"

Slater didn't answer. His taciturn face remained unchanged. "Frank," he said at last, "I'm going to leave you in charge for a bit."

~ * ~

Unlike the child who had fallen asleep so easily in Zeke's arms, Kira's response was just the opposite. Zeke Slater addled her brain and left her feeling anything but relaxed and sleepy. Truth was, her mind and body were still dealing with the lingering aftershocks of his kiss--even in spite of her excitement over the rescue.

"Seen enough?" Zeke had moved up behind her.

She turned to face him, the top of her head barely clearing his chin. "Oh, Zeke, this is so wonderful! I owe you such an apology. I had no idea."

"You weren't supposed to know, Kira."

"I'm sorry for the things I said. Please forgive me."

Without comment he stared vacantly at the box of energy bars in her hands. Then, swearing softly, his eyes swept back to hers. "Let someone else finish up here. We need to talk."

"But, I'd--"

"By simply being on board you not only put yourself in danger, this entire mission is at risk."

"I don't understand."

"What do you think would have happened if they had overtaken us instead?"

"That's not the point now. These people need--"

"That's exactly the point. I don't want you involved. It's as simple as that."

"But I'm already involved. I'm helping--"

"Riley!" Slater called out, his gaze never straying from Kira's face.

"Sir?" The crewman had conveniently busied himself nearby.

"Think you can handle this on your own?"

"Yes, sir."

Before Kira knew what he was about, Zeke had taken the bars from her hands and set them down. "There. Now you're uninvolved." Catching her arm, he began steering her back toward the exit. Within moments they were entering the ship's tiny lounge.

"Have a seat," he said, motioning to a nearby chair.

Kira woodenly sat down while he bent to retrieve an object that had fallen to the floor at some point during the mêlée. At last he came to stand before her. For several moments he said nothing, just stood there. Kira flinched when he finally reached out to touch a tender spot on her cheek--another bruise to add to the collection. Only this one had been obtained during the struggle over the gun.

With a soft curse, Zeke raked a lank of hair off his forehead and sank down on the edge of a bench across from her. "Look at me," he said, bracing his forearms on his knees and leaning toward her.

The last thing she wanted, let alone needed, was to look at him. Absently she studied her clasped hands, her nerves still raw. The heat of his kiss had stoked a fire in her belly that stirred to life every time she looked at him.

"Kira. Look at me, please." The gentleness in his voice drew her.

"I'm sorry you're caught up in all of this," he said. "Technically, you were supposed to have been off ship by now. But as we both know, that didn't happen."

Kira's gaze slid away.

"Look at me, dammit!"

She did, and again felt her pulse quicken.

Releasing a compressed sigh, he continued. "I appreciate your willingness to help, but the less you're mixed up in our affairs, the better it is for you."

She had always hated it when someone presumed to know what was and wasn't best for her. "You make it sound as though handing out energy bars is a perilous task. Besides, wouldn't you say the danger is long past?"

"The danger is never past."

"I don't even know what to call you. Is Zeke even your real name? Or is that too much to ask?"

His mouth curled up slow at the edges. "It might be."

She sniffed. "That figures."

His attention was focused once again on her cheek. "I never wanted you hurt." His expression held so much regret, her heart tripped.

His look suddenly changed, his gaze discerning, as if assessing her in some manner.

"What?" she asked after a drawn out moment. "Why are you looking at me like that?" she asked, rising to her feet.

Zeke stood up as well, his expression still probing. "I'm trying to decide just how sharp you are--whether you're more dangerous knowing the little you do, or if I dare explain anything more."

"What do you mean?"

"I mean, I've got a decision to make. As it stands, you know just enough to be a problem. The question is, if I elaborate on a few things, will it solve the problem or complicate it? If I make the wrong decision and you screw up, we could all end up dead."

"I don't understand."

"I don't doubt it, but the hard fact remains, we've had a shadow on our tail ever since we left Port Chance. If you're the one they are after and I set you off ship, you won't stand a chance. Yet, if I don't set you off, your very presence could jeopardize our mission."

"You keep saying that. How can I possibly jeopardize your mission? All I want to do is help with the rescued."

"First of all, not all of the crew members are as honorable as Frank or Steve Talbot. Eventually, someone's going to mess up because his mind's on doing you instead of his job. Either that, or you'll end up being in the wrong place at the wrong time--just like you were a couple of hours ago."

"But now that I know what you're doing, it will be different."

He cocked her a questioning brow. "And what exactly are we doing, Kira?"

She stared at him. "You just showed me what you--"

"Not even close. You have no idea what's going on here, and what little you do know makes me extremely nervous."

"I know you're one of the good guys, and that's really all that matters."

"Yeah, I'm a regular saint."

"And as far as the crew is concerned, they've all been considerate and polite--all of them, Zeke. You speak of them as if they are undisciplined hoodlums."

"Most of them are. My crew has been hand picked for their skills, not for their respectability and manners. They've been carefully screened by an assessment that determines other things besides etiquette. The first being whether we can trust them to remain on our side, and then for the job they've been hired to do. It doesn't make them gentlemen nor my personal friends. Take Riley, for instance--the crewman you were helping--he's good at what he's been hired to do, but I wouldn't trust him alone with you for one minute."

"Even though I'm your wife?" she asked skeptically. "You're saying he would--"

"You can bet on it."

"Oh..." Kira sat down, unable to ignore the chill snaking down her spine. Riley seemed like such a nice guy. She decided not to ask what exactly he'd been hired to do.

Several moments passed before Zeke spoke again. "Today I saw a side of you I never would have believed existed."

That brought her head up.

"You have more blind courage and determination than most men I know, and you're sure as hell a lot tougher than you look. Since my gut tells me I can trust you, I've decided the answer to my dilemma is to put you to use."

Kira's expectant eyes shot to his face. Had he changed his mind? Would he let her stay on board until they reach Echo?

"But it's important you understand a few things before you go jumping to conclusions," he added.

"I'm listening."

"First of all, to answer your question, my name really is Zeke Slater. For appearances' sake, I'm simply a cargo pilot. But in reality, my crew and I have been secured by an alliance of merchants to recover stolen merchandise. We work in Recovery Operations with the Interplanetary Law Enforcement."

Kira blinked. "You're a cop for the ILE?"

"Not exactly, but in a sense, yes."

"That explains it then."

"Explains what?"

"Why even your ship becomes disguised."

"Disguised?" He frowned. "Well I wouldn't know anything about that."

Kira smiled knowingly. "I take it Frank must have told me something he shouldn't have? Zeke, don't you see? When we get to Echo, maybe you can help me find--"

"Weee...aren't going to Echo, Kira."

"But..." She felt the bottom give way. "You said you were going to put me to work."

"That's right, and I will. Just not on board my ship."

"Where, then?"

"I'm putting you off at the Containment Base--it's where we discharge the stolen cargo along with the rescued people."

"Just like so much excess baggage, you're dumping me off too," she muttered beneath her breath.

He sighed. "I'll pick you up on the trip back. Besides, I thought you might want to be there for the little girl. She's going to need someone."

Before Kira could utter another word, he had changed subjects.

"Okay, now your turn. Your dramatic reaction in the cargo bay could use a bit of explaining."

Kira rose to her feet. "I said I'm sorry."

"You were seconds from nailing me, Legs."

"That's because I thought you were--"

Zeke slowly shook his head. "What I saw wasn't rational anger. You didn't just want me stopped. You wanted me dead." His eyes narrowed. "Why?"

"I told you."

He moved forward, "There isn't a doubt in my mind," he said very distinctly, "if I hadn't had the child with me, you would have put a hole through my chest without a second thought."

"That isn't--"

"It was in your eyes, sweetheart."

Several heartbeats of silence passed. "You won't believe me," she finally said.

"I think you've said that before, and I said try me."

Silence hung heavy as Kira sat back down and quietly gathered her thoughts. "Okay," she said in a voice little more than a whisper. "But what I'm about to tell you no one else knows. No one," she emphasized.

He acknowledged her with a curt nod. "All right."

She was quiet for several beats before drawing a deep breath and lifting her gaze to meet his. "I'm...I'm not who you think I am."

That got his attention. Zeke immediately took a seat across from her. "What do you mean by that?"

"I mean, Renn Delaney is--was," she corrected, "not my real father. I'm adopted."

"Okay," he said, questions no doubt whirling through his mind, yet Zeke remained silent, watching her, waiting for the rest.

"I was six years old when my world came crashing down around me," she went on. "At the time we were on board a commercial liner...my real parents and I," she clarified. "I don't remember where we were going. I just remember it being a happy time until...we were set upon by pirates."

A muscle in his jaw clenched, but Zeke didn't interrupt as Kira began unraveling the details of a story no one else knew except Renn. Gradually bitterness seeped into her tone. "Do you know what it's like watching your parents murdered right in front of you?" she asked, her eyes locking with his.

He muttered a soft curse and reached for her hand. "Kira--"

But she cut him off. "All because they dared to fight for their freedom." It had been years since she had dredged up the memories of that day, allowed herself to remember, to feel the grief, the pain...the stark terror that had ripped through her terrified child's heart back then. With a determined breath, she continued. "My parents had hidden me in a nearby storage locker and made me promise not to make a sound."

She paused, staring into space as she relived a portion of the past only she could see. "I tried so hard, but I couldn't keep from crying. Even now...I can hear the screams--"

"Enough." Zeke pulled her up into the circle of his arms. "It's all right, sweetheart," he said gently, tucking her head beneath his chin. "I think I can fill in the blanks."

There was incredible compassion in his resonant voice--deep and sensual to the feminine ear pressed against the wall of his chest.

"Tell me how you came to be with Renn."

Several heartbeats passed before she finally spoke. "I was added to their collection of human cargo." She looked up at him. "So you see...I do know what it's like to be crammed into the stinking hold of a slave ship. And I know the nightmare that waits at the end of the voyage."

He drew her close and Kira knew he understood, knew exactly what she was talking about. In his line of work, he'd no doubt seen the same scenario countless times.

"So, how did you meet Renn?" he asked again, resting his chin on the top of her head.

"I was nine by the time I was singled out for another auction. A small handful of us were lucky enough to be considered trustworthy." An empty laugh escaped with the word. "It meant we didn't have to be chained up like animals. We were conditioned, as the term went--the shining example of the benefits of positive behavior." With a labored breath, Kira continued. "I'd heard rumors that some of us had been pulled from the mines to be sold into prostitution." She paused to collect herself.

"That's when I knew I had to escape, or die trying." With very few interruptions, he listened as Kira skimmed the details of the story. "Being small for my age, I'd managed to sneak into an air duct shortly before they came to get us. And I remained there until long after everyone had gone."

"Weren't you afraid that one of the others would rat on you?"

"No. Even if only one of us were to escape, it was considered a victory by all. By the time I finally crawled out and slipped off ship, it was dark--the perfect cover for finding another hiding place."

"And that's when you met Renn?" he asked after a long span of silence.

Kira nodded. "I was hiding behind a stack of cargo pods when he found me." She laughed softly. "And I was terrified of him."

Slater smiled in understanding.

Pulling away she looked up into his face. "He took an enormous chance, Zeke," though she didn't need to explain. It was common knowledge--the fate of anyone who dared to aid an escaped slave. She lifted her gaze to meet his. "Can you now see how I overreacted when I saw you and your crew pilfering cargo and people from the other ship? I truly believed you were a slaver."

"Yeah...I understand," he said drawing her once again against him.

Kira swallowed, sensing an odd mixture of both supreme safety and imminent danger in the arms of this man. Choosing not to speculate on the danger part, she focused all thought on the steady thunder of his heartbeat beneath her ear. Closing her eyes, she breathed in the heady mix of scents surrounding this tower of strength holding her in his embrace-- the lusty scent of leather and something so blatantly masculine, so intensely Zeke, her insides gave a funny lurch.

"I know you believe me responsible for Lance Gerard's death," Kira went on. "But Zeke, there was nothing I could have done to prevent what happened. I was inexperienced at the time, and in-training under Lance's tutelage. "

Zeke frowned. "What do you mean, in-training."

"Back then, I was in my teens and introduced to a small group of people who had formed an underground network of secret routes and safe houses for rescued and escaped slaves."

"Yes, I've heard of the underground rescue group," Zeke offered. But I didn't know you were involved, let alone Gerard."

"Yes. Lance was one of the founding people. And when I expressed a desire to join the cause, he offered to personally train me."

Zeke released a breathy whistle. "What did Renn have to say about your association with this group of rebels?"

"He didn't like it." With a heavy sigh Kira glanced up to meet Zeke's eyes and sadly added, "I think I was responsible for most of his gray hair."

"I'm sure you're right on that one."

"He bailed me out of spaceport detention at least a half dozen times."

Amusement flickered in Zeke's eyes. "Yes, and at Renn's request I recall securing your release myself...and more than once."

"And each time I knew you were angry," she whispered.

"Damn right. Had the decision been mine, I would have let you sit there a while and learn a lesson." His expression stilled and grew serious. "But it seems all this time I've misjudged you, Kira. I had no idea you were trying to rid the universe of slavers.

Zeke lifted a hand to caress her upturned face. "Will you promise me something?"

She nodded. "Yes."

"Promise me that you will bury this memory along with this dangerous life you've been living. And in its place remember the good times with your real parents and with Renn. Remember, he not only rescued you, Kira, he cloaked you with his name. You are his legal heir now."

As Kira listened, there was something in his manner and tone of voice that soothed her. Here he was a ruthless privateer, a man who seemingly knew no fear and possessed the same lethal skills as his enemies. And yet...the compassion she sensed in him reached deep inside to touch her heart.

"No one person is going to win the war over slavery," he went on. All we can do is stop it when we see it."

Kira's breath caught when his gaze lowered to her mouth and his thumb slid over her bottom lip in a slow glide--his touch curiously rough and yet soft at the same time.

If she was expecting him to be the plundering pirate as he had been in the past, she couldn't have been more wrong. This was nothing like the calculated moves he'd forced upon her earlier

"You've put in your time, Kira. Now it's time to run Renn's half of Major Metals."

Suddenly, all thought vanished when Zeke lowered his head to brush a soft kiss across her mouth. "Promise me you won't look back any more," he said in a low whisper.

With a sigh, Kira dropped her forehead to his chest. "I'll try."

~ * ~

"Good. That's all I ask." Overcome with tenderness, he rubbed her back and nestled her closer to his heart. Knowing now what she had been through at the hands of slavers--imagining the hell she had experienced as a child--had him aching inside. How often had he come across the same sort of situation in his line of work--the child he'd rescued today being simply another example.

The need to make Kira his was as powerful as any he'd ever known, yet he released her and sat back, putting space between them. She looked lost, confused and so damn sexy it was all he could do to keep from reaching for her again. Damn, he wanted her. No, he wanted to be rid of her, rid of the responsibility and complications she posed just by being on board. But she'd stoked a fire in him and unfortunately desire wasn't something that simply retreated upon command.

This one's different, isn't she?

Shutting out the inner voice, Slater admonished himself about letting Kira get to him. He knew better than to get caught up in her troubles. They'd been sharing tight quarters over the last few weeks. That was it; he wasn't thinking clearly. At some point he'd lost his emotional distance.

At some point? The silent voice laughed. *The instant you first kissed her, you lost your emotional distance, pal . A guaranteed suicide.*

And that first kiss had come when he'd been so hell bent on teaching Kira the merits of intimidation.

"Some lessons are best not learned at all." Only now did the truth of Frank's solemn response hit him full force.

That first kiss had changed everything. He'd stepped over the line and broke a resolute rule.

No one knew better than Zeke how emotional involvement could cause hesitation when a split second decision is crucial; how it could trade self-confidence for doubt. How easy it is to lose your nerve when someone special is in the picture. He'd always prided himself on keeping his relationships with women strictly physical because the complications of involvement could mean the difference between life and death. The very fact that he was uninvolved is what made him so good at what he did.

It hadn't always been that way, just ever since he'd taken on this new direction in life. He prided himself on keeping his relationships with women uncomplicated, and it was the reason he'd kept things simple with beautiful Celeste.

CHAPTER SIXTEEN

One week later:

Zeke opened the COM link. "This is *Solar Wind*, Delta Beta, five-niner-five, requesting an approach vector."

They were a little over an hour out. With the child on her lap Kira had been observing Base 72 on the main view screen, watching it grow closer, noting how it sparkled like diamonds against the backdrop of space. Zeke had explained that the glittering effect was actually the sun reflecting off countless solar panels. He'd gone on to say that the containment base was essentially a glorified refueling station. The ILE had purchased, renovated and enlarged it into a massive, oddly shaped configuration with passage tubes linking a multitude of storage and housing portables.

"See that, Aylie?" Kira asked, drawing the little girl's attention to the structure on the screen. "That's where we're going, honey." Kira had named the toddler, Aylie, after a wildflower as blue as the little girl's eyes. For Aylie's benefit she tried to sound excited and cheerful. For now facial expressions and tone of voice were the basic communication tools between her and the child. Zeke was able to communicate somewhat better in that he knew a little of her language.

~ * ~

Solar Wind's main lock hissed closed, sealing the ship behind them. The pressurized tube connecting the ship to the base was roughly eight feet in diameter and ran for approximately 100 feet before linking *Solar Wind* to one of the base's many docking rings. At Zeke's request, Kira had waited until all the rescued people and confiscated cargo had been unloaded and recorded. Once the initial chaos had died down, he returned to escort her and Aylie. It was best this way, he explained, knowing the chaos would bring back disturbing memories for both her and Aylie.

With Aylie perched on one hip, Zeke escorted the two ladies into an enormous collection area. Picking up the pace to match his stride, Kira remained at his side as they made their way down one of several long aisles. Thousands of mysterious cargo pods were stacked in rows on both sides. Every now and then, dim passageways would cut at right angles between the stacks of pods to disappear toward distance walls. For Kira, once again the sights and smells triggered memories just as it had on the *Solar Wind* when the people were brought on board. She stifled a gasp as a wave of sheer black fright swept through her.

As though sensing her panic, Zeke reached for her hand and squeezed it gently. "You okay?"

Kira nodded, forcing a smile. The base may have been set up for rescue and rehabilitation, but there were still too many parallels at this early stage for Kira's peace of mind. The wave of panic that had swept over her had been all but paralyzing.

Zeke drew an arm about her, pulling her close. "We'll have you settled in your own compartment in no time."

"Zeke, please...don't make us stay. Please."

"Honey, we've been through this before. Aylie has no choice but to stay, and I need you to stay here with her. You both will be safe."

"Aylie will be able to stay with me after all?" she asked, hopeful.

He smiled. "No guarantee, but I'll try to pull a few strings. We'll have to wait and see. She'll have to go into quarantine first. There isn't anything I can do about that."

Kira frowned. "Like for how long?"

"I don't know, Kira, but I'm going to see if I can make arrangements for you to help out around here. That way you can be--"

"This the child you're wanting?" The voice belonged to a stocky middle-aged woman whose gray hair was cropped into a no-nonsense butch and whose dull brown eyes were leveled on Aylie.

"Yes."

"And this, your wife?" she asked, with a nod Kira's direction.

Zeke drew Kira against him and responded without hesitation. "That's right."

If Zeke had admitted to having sprouted wings, Kira couldn't have been more astounded. He was no happier over their farce of a marriage than she, yet here he was joyfully admitting she was his wife.

Surprise quickly gave way to curiosity as she listened in on the ensuing conversation. Credits, it seemed, would be exchanged for her room and board at the base, but the arrangements for her to be able to do volunteer work appeared to be more difficult for some reason.

"There's no job openings."

"Then create one." With an exasperated smile, Zeke looked away. "We're talking volunteer work, not a paying job," he said, turning back to the woman. "Just give her something that will allow her to see the child on a regular basis. That's all. Anything will do."

"I'll do what I can, but I'm not making any promises as to what it will be."

"As long as it's something." With Aylie in his arms, Zeke turned and made his way toward the impound.

"We run things tight around here, for your information," the woman called after him.

"Sure do," Zeke mumbled beneath his breath. "Real tight."

"Zeke," Kira whispered, "Why does Aylie have to endure all this? I mean,

if--"

"Like it or not, if you want her to be legally free, it has to be this way. She's been coded, and unless she goes through all the proper channels--and the code deactivated--she'll be living in secrecy and constantly looking over her shoulder just like you. Do you want that for her?"

Kira sighed. "No."

"Me neither. So, let's just get this over with." He approached the counter.

"Hello, Slater. How's it going?" A slim man with graying brown hair and a friendly face seemed to know Zeke personally.

"Not bad, JD. Yourself?"

"Oh, can't complain." His gaze shifted to Aylie. "So what's going on with the kid?"

"I don't want her going through the routine procedures. There's no need since she's being adopted."

"Not a problem. We can arrange that."

Aylie buried her face against Zeke's chest and began to cry when JD came around from behind the counter.

Zeke murmured something soft in a language Kira didn't understand and the crying was reduced to a pitiful tear-streaked face as Aylie watched the stranger scan a tiny tattoo on the inside of her arm then place a band around her small ankle.

"So, who's adopting her?"

"I am," Zeke answered.

"No," Kira piped up. "I'm the one adopt--"

Zeke smiled. "JD. This is my wife, Kira. We're both adopting her."

"No," Kira broke in again, wanting to make sure she was the one adopting Aylie. "I'm the one adopt--"

JD barked a laugh. "You're married, Slater?" He turned to Kira. "What a pleasure it is to meet you."

"Thank you."

The woman that Kira had dubbed Butch had followed them over. "Just because you're cutting corners doesn't mean the child won't go through the same routine as everyone else. Four to five months is the average quarantine and process time."

Unaware of her predicament, Aylie playfully made a grab for Zeke's nose. "I sure would like to see the process go a little faster than that." he said, capturing Aylie's tiny fingers and pretending to munch on them. "I was hoping to be able to make a sizeable donation when I returned for the child."

"Donation?" the woman repeated, intrigued.

"Yes," he said, "but I'm afraid it will only be three months by the time I am heading back this way again. Sure would be handy if the child were ready by then."

"Three months, huh...?" Rubbing her chin pensively, she made a production of thinking things over. "Hmmm. What size of a donation did you say you had in mind?"

Zeke adjusted Aylie's position, deftly evading her inquisitive little fingers as she reached for the small twin looped earrings in his right lobe. "I was thinking along the lines of five hundred."

"Five hundred? Well, I'm sure we can work something out to your satisfaction. In fact, I will personally see to it that the child is ready for you when you return."

"What about my wife?"

The woman's voice dropped considerably as she spared Kira a glance. "I'll see what I can do."

"Thank you."

~ * ~

"How much longer before they're finished?" Zeke asked impatiently. "Never could understand why they take so damn long finalizing everything."

"Shouldn't be too much longer." Frank made his way back into the helm. "Half hour from now, and we'll be nothin' but a memory."

"I certainly hope so. I've been back a half-hour. They should have had everything wound up by now."

Goodbyes had been hard. Zeke remained until Aylie was officially taken away. Her pleading tear-filled eyes evoked the most helpless feeling he had ever known. Jaw set, Kira had remained cool during the entire ordeal. As soon as Aylie disappeared from view, she turned and melted into the circle of Zeke's arms, her face buried against his chest. He vaguely remembered kissing the top of her head. The next instant...a gentle knuckle beneath her chin lifted her face for his branding kiss. One more kiss that imprinted her as his. One more kiss that should never have happened.

~ * ~

"Uh, Boss...I dunno, you might want to take a look here." Frank's eyes were fastened on a pulsing red indicator. With a flip of a switch, an exterior vid cam snapped to life and they both stared in mute wonder as a single figure made her way through the connecting tunnel. "That who I think it is?"

Without comment, Zeke's eyes narrowed on the feminine figure stalking toward the *Solar Wind*, her thick russet ponytail bouncing with every step.

"Thought y' made arrangements for--"

"I did. What the devil is she doing back?"

Half grinning, Frank turned back to the controls. "Least she ain't hidin' in the hold this time."

Releasing a compressed sigh, Zeke bounded down the short flight of stairs. "Is there no mercy?"

"Y' married 'er. Need I remind y'?" His teeth were clamped about his pipe stem and his mouth was on the verge of a smile.

"Kira and I are not married, Frank. I'm getting tired of repeating myself."

"Well yer both wearin' proof o' the fact that y' are."

"You're speaking of the tattoos, I take it?"

"I am. And I ain't stupid. That ceremony may 'ave been gawd-awful, but I'll wager my paycheck it's as legal as any. Yer married to 'er, Sport. Like it or not."

Ignoring him, Zeke turned and headed for the entry port. The main hatch cycled open, presenting a view down the long corridor that connected *Solar Wind* to the base. With the exception of the walkway itself, the tubing was transparent, offering an unimpeded view of the surrounding star-studded blackness. "What are you doing back?" he asked as Kira drew near.

"That woman!" she said through her teeth as she stalked on board.

He followed her inside, turning to seal the ship behind them. "You were supposed to remain there until I returned. What happened?"

"I don't even want to talk about it."

"It was all arranged, Kira. Why are-- What the hell happened?" Muffled mechanical sounds could be heard as docking collars and all umbilical ties with the base were being disconnected from the ship.

"Everyone better grab a seat, we're about t' depart," Frank called out.

They both ignored him. "Well, Zeke, for your information, what you thought was all arranged, apparently wasn't. And, furthermore," Kira went on, "I was told I would not be allowed to see Aylie until you returned. Rules." Kira stressed the word with a furrowing of her brow and a stubborn jutting of her jaw.

"Who told you that?"

"That woman you made the arrangements with." Her mouth trembled and she swallowed hard. "Now...who's going to be there for Aylie?" she asked brokenly.

With a heavy sigh, Zeke looked away. Lost for words. "She'll be all right, Kira. She'll be taken good care of."

"By strangers."

"Yes, I was hoping to bend a few rules and keep you and Aylie together, but it seems we'll have to go with Plan B."

"What? You've got another place to dump me?"

Without response he turned toward the helm.

"Zeke--"

"Legs, Echo happens to be four weeks from here. Do me a favor, would you? Put that busy little imagination of yours to work and see what you come up with by the time we reach Echo."

Several heartbeats of stillness ticked by before he added, "Somehow I doubt either of us would last that long."

"I don't know about you, but I assure you, I could."

A weaker man's ego might have been cut to the quick with that one, but Slater had the audacity to laugh. "Just the same, I'm not taking you to Echo."

The floor beneath them began to vibrate. Catching her by the arm, he quickly guided her to a seat and helped her strap in before heading for the command chair.

~ * ~

On Board the Moon Runner:
Twenty-two hours behind *Solar Wind*:

The distorted image of Grant Preston wavered on the ship's comscreen. "I've got a bit of news that might be of interest to you."

"It had better be good news." Kendyl's gruesome features hardened. "Someone just took out one of our freighters--after emptying the entire cargo bay."

"Then this should be music to your ears," Preston added. "I just got a solid confirmation on the *Solar Wind*. Both Slater and Banner are the official registered co-owners. It took some real digging as they're both assuming an alias on the legal stuff."

A mass of twisted skin tugged itself into what passed for a satisfied grin. "Did you find out where they're based?"

Preston shook his head. "That's the interesting part. The company seems to be classified to the hilt. Even my connections weren't able to break through."

"I'll wager they're based out of Acacia," Kendyl snarled. "Both of them come from there."

"That may be true, but--" The comscreen fluctuated, obscuring both Preston's image as well as the last of his words. The wide base of cliffs bordering Major Metals Mines on Echo would often times play havoc with the transmission.

Kendyl leaned forward and made an adjustment, clearing the reception as best he could from his end. "You're breaking up. Say that again."

"I said if the Delaney girl's with him, like I'm banking on, Slater will be heading for Echo before this run is over."

Kendyl's eyebrows rose, "What makes you say that?"

"You see," Preston said, grinning, "the girl not only trusts me, she's running scared."

"And who better to run to than her daddy's trusted partner," Kendyl added.

"You got it. And accompanying her will be none other than Zeke Slater--alone and unaware. I think our two guests deserve a welcome party."

Kendyl laughed. "Don't start the fun without me."

CHAPTER SEVENTEEN

To Kira's surprise, the next two days passed without incident. She even managed to stay out of Slater's way. Though in truth, it wasn't Slater she was afraid of, it was her own wanton reaction to him. That's what scared her most. Each time he had kissed her--including that first turbulent kiss--she hadn't wanted him to stop. And, he knew it. He knew it!

Frank had proven to be a true friend, in spite of the fact that she had held a gun on his captain with every intention of shooting him. Often Frank would join her in the lounge for coffee and a moment of conversation.

The laser-impressed mural on the feature wall of the lounge was breathtaking. It took up the entire wall, floor to ceiling. Indirect lighting softly illuminated the illustration, literally bringing it to life.

Kira had lost count of the times she had stood mesmerized by the image of the magnificent stallion running free and wild across a star-studded galaxy. He looked so real it was as if she could reach out and touch his silky coat and flying mane.

"He's beautiful," she remarked, captivated by the picture.

"Yep. His name's Thor," Frank drawled. He went on to tell Kira a little about Zeke's horse. How he'd been transported from Earth as a yearling and given to Zeke on his sixteenth birthday.

"Does he still have him?" she asked.

"He does. In fact, you'll get to see 'im for yerself. Boss keeps 'im stabled with the same people you'll be staying with."

Frank meant well, but he might as well have said that Slater would be stabling her right along with his horse. Pushing the irritating thought aside, she said, "Now that you mention it, I think I saw a picture of a much younger Zeke riding this very horse."

Frank's eyebrows rose a notch. "Did y' now?"

Kira laughed. "When I asked him about it, he seemed irritated."

"Well, don't go takin' it personally, darlin'. He's irritated with just about everyone and everything these days."

Kira laughed again. "Don't worry, Frank. Once we hit port--wherever that might be--I'm sure Zeke will find a cure for his crankiness."

"Think so, huh?" Frank's raspy laugh drifted into the corridor.

~ * ~

Although the onboard computer had already transmitted much of the necessary information to Port Imperial's spaceport, Zeke opened the COM link for verbal communication. "This is *Solar Wind*, Delta Beta, Five-niner-five requesting a planetary approach vector."

Two hours later, the planet Acacia took up over half the view screen. At Frank's insistence, Kira sat in one of the extra seats in the cockpit.

"When yer approachin' Acacia," he said, "it's like comin' upon a giant emerald in the sky." And he was right, for the planet truly looked like a glowing green gem set against the black velvet of space.

The comset chimed and a voice announced, "Please initiate your descent."

"Understood," Slater replied, and assumed control from the ship's computer.

Through a side viewport, Kira watched the tip and leading edge of *Solar Wind's* starboard wing start to burn as the ship penetrated the protective membrane of Acacia's atmosphere. Within minutes the entire wing was on fire, flames streaming off the back edge, licking past the view port and casting an eerie orange glow inside the cabin.

Eventually the blackness of space gave way to the bluish hue of Acacia's daytime aura, and the flames intensified. Below, a vast continent of green could be seen covering nearly all of Acacia's southern hemisphere.

Other than Zeke's occasional communication with either Frank or the spaceport, the only other sound was a soft decent chime that sounded at regular intervals.

Soon, they were skimming high over an immense body of water. A mountain range loomed on the curve of the horizon.

"See that settlement nestled at the base of those mountains up ahead?" Zeke's deep voice pulled Kira's attention away from the view port to the master screen. "That's Port Imperial," he explained, "Acacia's capital."

It was one of the few times he had actually spoken to her conversationally since they left the containment base. In truth, she suspected he had made as much of an effort to avoid her as she had avoiding him.

Her gaze strayed reluctantly to Slater's profile. Without even trying, the man radiated a sensuality that drew her like a magnet. The memory of his embrace, the heat of his kisses and stormy gaze brought back all the butterflies she had tried so hard to deny and bury over the last few days. Her sights moved to his sun-kissed hair. Several careless wisps spilled across his forehead. Swept-back sides descended to touch broad shoulders straining against the grain of the black shirt he was wearing. From there Kira's gaze traveled to his hands as they danced fluidly across the controls. He did have nice hands, she grudgingly allowed.

And you're legally bonded to this man, a silent voice reminded.

Though Kira couldn't see it at the moment, she knew on the underside of his left wrist, Zeke Slater bore the mirrored image of the tattoo she wore. Unwittingly, her gaze dropped to her own wrist as she contemplated the meaning, her denial, and Slater's echoing words that as soon as they lifted, this farce of a marriage was terminated. Was it really annulled the minute they left Aden, she wondered. Regardless, they would both forever bear the marks of their reluctant union.

The comset chimed, and Slater leaned forward, opening video communication with Port Imperial. "Slater here."

"*Solar Wind*, this is Imperial Control. You have confirmation for docking bay one-zero." The voice belonged to a middle-aged, heavy-set woman. When she smiled, her eyes nearly squinted shut. "Zeke, darlin', it's good to see you again."

"You too, Shara."

"Nick said you'd be in today. I'm to let him know when you arrive. Your berth is ready and waiting below. The drone should be there by the time you set down. You know what to do, hon."

"That's a roger."

The screen went blank and within minutes, Slater was killing the ship's forward motion and firing reverse thrusters. Another ten minutes and the proximity alarm sounded as the ground rose up to meet them. With a gentle thump, he eased the *Solar Wind* onto her jacks while jets of air stirred up the dust around them.

Kira's gaze traveled back to Zeke, once again lost in a perusal that began at his sun-streaked hair and settled at last and lingered much too long on a hard-muscled thigh clad in black leathers. She had just caught her lower lip between her teeth when she sensed Frank's gaze. A quick glance in his direction confirmed her worst fears. He'd seen her ogling the captain and he was grinning. Grinning.

Jerking her gaze away from Frank, Kira directed it toward the view port. Heat scorched her cheeks as she kept her attention focused on the spaceport outside. Let him think what he wanted. Whatever it was, he was wrong.

Frank leaned forward to flip a switch on the console. "Switchin' to exterior vid."

Kira's eyes once more were drawn to the exterior monitor as a small robosphere moved into place, the words, "THIS WAY" flashing in bright neon. With an adjustment on the console, Slater fired the thrusters, lifting the *Solar Wind* mere inches off the burn-scarred surface of the LZ and slowly began trailing after their robotic escort.

When the robosphere came to a halt, its message changed to read, "KILL THRUSTERS." Zeke gently eased the *Solar Wind* back down onto the decking, shutting down the ship's forward propulsion as instructed.

It was early morning and the sun had barely crested the horizon of Port Imperial's distant mountains. All four external vid screens were on, showing different angles of the darkened spaceport. Silhouetted outbuildings were nestled at the far end. In the foreground sat the main terminal, its domed skylight aglow with inner light. Dark, partially-lit shapes of other ships and a scattering of greenish float lights dotted the landing field. Turning toward the viewport, Kira watched as robo loaders scurried back and forth across the LZ. Without a doubt, Port Imperial seemed a huge cut above the spaceports she had seen so far.

Before long, a marked jolt preceded a grinding vibration. Kira's eyes widened as the ship slowly began sinking below ground level. Rock walls, inching their way upward, moved past the view port. They were perched on an immense elevator that was taking them below the surface.

When there was nothing left to see but solid rock, Kira's glance returned to the vid screen as the wall finally opened up into a massive underground hangar. Row after row of various sized ships ranging from commercial freighters to private yachts lined the aisles in uniform procession.

Another jolt indicated the elevator had stopped. The robosphere hopped off, its sign flashing "THIS WAY". In compliance, Slater once again fired the thrusters, lifted the ship inches off the surface and slowly trailed after the drone. The entire process took nearly an hour before they were finally led into a berth.

~ * ~

At last, killing the drives, Zeke eased the *Solar Wind* onto her massive jacks. With a covert glance Kira's direction, he unfastened his safety harness and rose to his feet. The moment he had thought would never arrive was finally here. Three weeks with Legs had been enough to drive him to drink. In truth, he was too close to the edge and seriously doubted his ability to last another day.

"Frank, I'll be spending the night. You want to let the crew know they can have shore leave? I don't care what they do or where they go, just as long as they stay out of trouble and are back here by 0600."

"You got it, Boss." Frank's gaze shifted to Kira. "Yer gonna like the Banners, darlin'."

"All set?" came Zeke's deep voice as he left the helm and joined Kira at the base of the steps.

Kira turned to Frank, offering him a timid smile. "I'll bet you'll be glad to get your cabin back again."

"Nah. It hasn't been inconvenient, darlin'. With me and Talbot takin' opposite shifts, one of us is comin' when the other is goin'."

Kira laughed. "You wouldn't tell me even if it was inconvenient. Just the same, thank you for allowing me the use of your cabin."

"All my pleasure, honey."

Zeke turned for the main boarding hatch, picked up Kira's bag and tucked it beneath his arm. "Shall we?" he asked as the hatched cycled open.

Once again the familiar fumes of a spaceport greeted them as Zeke ushered her out of the ship and down the ramp for what he truly hoped to be the very last time.

"Stay with me and watch your step," he shouted over the descending whine of *Solar Wind's* turbines. Fuel and service lines cluttered the decking as they made their way toward the open passageway. From there, Slater caught her elbow and guided her to the terminal where they entered a set of doors and caught an escalator up to the second level. "Someone should be waiting for us outside," he told her as they passed through a revolving door and out to a waiting area.

A large circular drive spanned the front of the terminal. Ground runners moved in and out of the morning traffic, vendors were scattered about, setting up their displays--everything from flowers to handcrafted items.

A gust of wind kicked up, ruffling Zeke's hair down over his forehead. "This way," he said, cupping her elbow and guiding her toward a vehicle that had pulled up to the curb.

"You been waiting long? Came a deep voice from the driver's seat.

"Just got here." Slater ushered Kira inside then climbed in after her.

Half turning to glance over his shoulder, the man's focus slid from Zeke to Kira--and lingered.

"Clint," Zeke began, "Meet Kira Delaney. Kira, Clint Banner."

Greetings were exchanged as Zeke slid the door closed. Clint turned back to the controls, and within moments they were pulling into traffic and picking up speed.

Within half an hour the city was far behind and the scenery was whisking by in a blur as they followed a winding road up into the foothills.

CHAPTER EIGHTEEN

Zeke and Clint were absorbed in a conversation she strongly suspected was guarded. That was fine, for at the moment Kira's mind was on Aylie. Was she okay? Was she scared? Who was caring for her, and how long before she would be released?

Ignoring the hard-muscled thigh pressed against her own, Kira turned her gaze toward the window and the passing landscape. At last the vehicle turned off the main road onto a long tree-lined drive that was flanked on both sides by pastureland. Within minutes they were pulling around a circular drive where they drew to a halt beneath a portico. "I'll let you two off here."

"Thanks," Zeke said. "Is Tressa around?"

"Yeah. When I left, all three of them were up in the solarium..." he grinned, "talking babies again." Clint's eyes shifted to Kira, sweeping over her face with unmasked approval. "They're anxious to meet you, Sunshine."

Kira smiled politely, wondering what all Zeke had said about her.

Climbing out first, Zeke turned and extended a hand to her. From there, they made their way up a short set of stairs where a double-doored entry swung inward, and a gentleman greeted them warmly.

Kira's eyes widened as she took in the breathtaking interior. The front entry was basically an atrium. The vaulted ceiling was completely sky-lighted and the walls were paneled in rich wood. Potted plants and even a couple of unusual-looking trees in enormous planters gave the foyer a masculine, almost woodsy atmosphere. With a gentle touch, Zeke guided her up the wide-carpeted staircase and down a hall that opened up into a crystalline-domed solarium.

Instantly, two beautiful women were at his side. One was very pregnant with dark auburn hair in a loosely woven braid. The other was a classically beautiful blonde, whose motherly once-over of Zeke belied her youthful appearance.

Having given them both a welcoming hug, Slater stood back and smiled warmly at the younger pregnant woman. "Well, look at you."

"I know," she pouted. "Just look at me. I'm fat."

"You look gorgeous, as always." He drew her into his arms and with a grin, added softly, "And he'd better be treating you good."

"He is."

"I still say you're too good for the likes of him."

She laughed. "I know, and I remind him of it every day."

"We all do," the blonde chimed in emphatically.

Kira stood off to the side as the amicable small talk continued. From the pictures she'd seen, she knew before introductions had even been made that the pregnant woman in Zeke's arms was Tressa Banner and "the likes of him" had to be none other than Zeke's partner, Nick.

"Tressa, Delta," Zeke began, turning to Kira, "This is--"

"You must be Kira." The blonde's warm voice cut in, grasping Kira's hand in both of hers. "I'm Delta Banner."

Tressa stepped forward with an extended hand. "And I'm Tressa. Zeke mentioned he was bringing someone with him." She laughed. "But he didn't tell us nearly enough. We've been dying to meet you."

Kira's response was lost amid a cry of delight as a flash of teenage femininity dashed across the chamber to throw herself into Zeke's embrace. "You're back! Nick said you'd be getting in today." She stepped back and asked. "You'll be able to stay for a while, I hope."

"Not this time, I'm afraid." He turned to Kira. "Kira, this is Rachel Banner. Rachel, Kira Delaney."

"Hi," she said with an outstretched hand. "My friends just call me Rae."

~ * ~

Once introductions had been made and Kira was in good hands, Zeke excused himself to join the rest of the men: Clint, Nick, and the youngest of the three Banner brothers, Marc.

So far Nick was the only one married. But then, that wasn't counting the joke of a marriage to Kira that Zeke refused to acknowledge. He absently rubbed the mark on his wrist at the memory.

Actually it was funny just thinking about Nick being married. It hadn't seemed all that long ago that Nick and marriage were two words you just never used in the same sentence. Nick Banner. The name was synonymous with a variety of colorful descriptions ranging anywhere from rakehell to black sheep. Not that the other two Banner boys hadn't created their own reputations within the community. Nick, it seemed, always took perverse pleasure in giving the wagging tongues of Port Imperial something to talk about. At the time of their marriage, Tressa truthfully had been too good for him. Everyone knew it--especially Nick. She was the best thing that ever walked into his miserable life.

"We were just talking about you," Nick announced, as Zeke entered the room.

"All good, I hope."

"Hell no," Clint snorted as he pulled away from the wall he'd been leaning against.

Zeke made his way across the room to clasp hands with each of the brothers. "Thanks, guys, for coming together on this."

"No problem," Clint replied. "Fill us in."

"I've already told them what I know," Nick said.

"Unfortunately, I don't know a whole lot more." With a sigh, Zeke settled hipshot on the edge of a nearby desk. "First of all," he began, "I believe we're looking at the tip of an iceberg here. Secondly, I'm damn near positive Grant Preston--Delaney's business partner--is involved somehow."

"So, it's true, Delaney's dead?" Nick asked.

"All we need is a body." Zeke went on to explain about Renn's mysterious death and how Kira began running into botched-up ledgers, lost files, overpaid billings and unauthorized orders. "There's not a doubt in my mind--someone's tampering with the records."

"So, what makes you think Preston's involved?" Clint asked.

Zeke took off his jacket and hung it across the back of a nearby chair. "I may not have all the pieces together yet, but I've got a pretty good handle on the picture. Hell, the majority of the shipment and slaves we pillaged off that last freighter were earmarked for Major Metals. Not exactly Delaney's style. Besides, I personally happen to think its a little odd the ledgers got messed up right after Kira refused Preston's offer to buy her out."

"What if..." Clint hesitated then began again. "In the process of trying to learn the business, what if Kira accidentally--"

"She didn't," Zeke interrupted. "In order to delete information out of the system, she would've had to give a command along with a password. Besides, there's more--"

The door opened, and a familiar face entered--Dawson, who had worked for the family since the boys were small. "Coffee, gentlemen?" At their mumbled thanks, he offered each one a steaming mug. Setting a large carafe down on a nearby table for easy refills, he quietly exited the room.

Zeke eased into a nearby chair and hunched forward, his forearms resting upon his thighs, his mug of coffee suspended between his parted knees. "The night Kira ended up onboard the ship, she was running from a biker with a T-30. The guy had been lying in wait for her at Major Metals' parking lot where he took a shot at her, missed Kira, and ended up killing a security guard. From there he chased her to the spaceport.

"When we hit dirt on Lilo," he went on, "two thugs were waiting for her--"

"You lost me," Clint interrupted. "How'd she end up onboard the ship?"

Zeke released a sigh. "It's a long story. I'll tell you later. But in the process of trying to save her hide, I ended up getting winged with a coated slug."

That brought Nick's head up. "Coated? As in poison? How come you're alive?"

"Luck, and an excellent First Officer."

"So how'd they know you were headed for Lilo?" Marc asked.

"I can thank Celeste for that."

"Celeste?" Clint and Marc asked in unison.

Zeke slid a quick glance at Nick. "I take it you didn't tell them?"

Nick lit up a thin cigar and blew a lazy stream of smoke into the air. It was painfully obvious he was doing all he could to keep the smirk off his face. "I thought I'd leave that for you to tell."

Zeke's gaze flicked back to the two brothers who were waiting with bated breath.

Might as well say it and get it over with.

"Celeste is--" His jaw clenched as he began again. "She's an acquaintance from Port Chance."

"An acquaintance? You want to expound upon that, Slater?"

"There's nothing to expound upon, Clint. She's someone I enjoy looking up when I'm in port."

Marc grinned knowingly. "In other words, you get laid, she gets paid?"

Zeke laughed out loud. "No. It was never a paid arrangement. Besides, how would you know about such things at your tender age?"

Marc bristled visibly, bringing on even more teasing laughter from Nick and Clint. At twenty-four, being the youngest of the three, Marc was generally the target for their jokes.

At last, Clint turned back to Zeke. "I guess what I don't understand," he began, determined to eek out every scrap of information, "is how's this Celeste person responsible for you getting shot on Lilo?"

Nick's eyes danced with suppressed laughter. Anchoring the cigar at the corner of his mouth, he winced against up-trailing smoke as he turned to refill his coffee.

In an attempt to get them off their present topic of discussion, Zeke quickly explained Celeste's double-dealings. Despite her story of the young clerk giving out classified information, Zeke knew there was no way he could have known anything about *Solar Wind's* itinerary without a code. No, Celeste sold him out.

Clint frowned. "Yeah, but... I guess what I don't understand is how she knew you were headed for Lilo in the first place?"

Nick quietly watched from the sidelines as the merciless bantering continued. At last, all joking aside, Clint asked, "So...any ideas on this burn-scarred character?"

"I'll lay you odds it's Kendyl," Zeke answered.

"Kendyl?" Clint asked. "Why would you think--?"

"Gut instinct," Nick interjected. "No one actually saw him die that day on Steel." His gaze moved to Marc. "In fact, you were the last one to see Kendyl alive."

Marc nodded. "That's right. He was running for his ship minutes before it blew. But I can't imagine him living through that inferno."

"But what if he did?" Zeke suggested.

Nick blew a stream of smoke toward the ceiling. "He'd be out for revenge. That much I can tell you."

"So, you think he's connected with Preston?" Clint asked.

Zeke shrugged. "Hell, I don't know. Anything's possible. But if he is...I can't see Kendyl's motivation being anything other than his own revenge.

"This is what I'm thinking," Zeke continued. "Preston gave Kira her chance to sell out. When she refused, he got tired of waiting and arranged to have her eliminated." Zeke fell silent, a familiar tick in his jaw working. Finally, he said, "What I wouldn't give to have three minutes with him and a copy of that partnership contract."

"Three whole minutes?" Nick scoffed. "There'd be nothing left of him."

Zeke grunted in agreement. "Exactly. You see, in the event of both Renn and Kira's deaths, Preston would become the rightful owner of Major Metals."

"Does she know how you feel about Preston?" Marc asked.

Slater shook his head. "I'm not ready to lay that one on her just yet. She thinks he's going to help her through this." Slater's lips curved into a cynical smile. "If my instincts are correct, he'd help her all right-- right out of it."

After a long pause, Zeke spoke again. "Here's what I have planned so far. I've still got that shipment sitting in my hold for Major Metals, to the attention of Preston himself. I intend to personally deliver his payload."

Nick jerked the cigar from his mouth. "You're crazy if you go in there alone. Besides, if Kendyl's--"

"I have no choice. Oh, and another thing--I want to leave Kira here. She's not going to like it, but I'm hoping that maybe Tressa can convince..." Zeke's voice trailed off at the three smirks aimed his direction. "What?"

"Tressa's not exactly the one to convince Kira to follow orders," Nick said with unmasked amusement.

Zeke knew all too well that Kira and Tressa had more in common than he wanted to admit.

"Hell," Marc chimed in, "she'd encourage Kira to do whatever she damn well pleases."

Laughter drifted out into the foyer as Zeke looked helplessly at Nick.

"Don't look at me. It's all I can do to keep Tressa toeing the mark."

That comment earned a resulting snort from Clint. "Right. In case you haven't noticed, you're the one toeing the mark these days."

Another round of masculine laughter--this time at Nick's expense.

The next hour was spent finalizing the details and laying a plan that would begin first thing in the morning when Zeke left. Nick produced a topographic map of Echo's northern hemisphere.

"Where the devil did you get your hands on something this detailed?" Zeke asked, examining the chart with avid interest.

"Let's just say, the source is part of our internet. Goes by the code name of Black Fox."

"Black Fox," Zeke repeated. "Should I know him?"

"Hell, this guy's so deep in the system, he could be your own brother and you wouldn't know it." Nick smiled easily. "From what I hear, he's full-blooded Creohen and has developed his abilities to their fullest extent, if that tells you anything."

Creohen was a name given to a select group of Earth colonists who, nearly fifty years ago had mined the coveted Creoh ore. Tressa was part Creohen. Her grandfather had been just one of the many young miners affected by the raw mineral. By the time they discovered the irreversible gene-altering side effects, the damage had been done-- damage they soon discovered would be passed on to offspring. Tressa possessed the Creohen ability--the gift of feeling emotions...namely Nick's. After two years of marriage, Nick generally found himself scrambling to keep at least a few emotions private.

It was unanimously decided that Tressa would be of no use in convincing Kira to follow orders.

"Remember, just take the bull by the horns." A mock frown of rigid control was plastered on Nick's face.

"That's right," Clint interjected. "You gotta let her know who's boss."

"Right," Zeke muttered, raking a hand through his hair.

Clint's eyes shot to Zeke's hand. "What's that on your wrist, Slater?"

Zeke nearly groaned aloud. "Nothing. It's simply a--"

"Nothing?" Nick challenged. "Let's see it."

With a heavy sigh, Slater extended his arm, wrist up for inspection. Past experience had taught him long ago that he might as well get it over with. If he didn't, they would all just overpower him and see it anyway.

Two heartbeats was all it took before the frown of curiosity melted into the smirk of comprehension. "Damn," Nick muttered incredulously. "You're...married."

"The hell I am."

"The hell if you're not," Clint interjected, craning his neck to see. "That's an Aden bonding symbol, my friend. I know what I'm looking at."

"I don't give a damn what you call it. It was terminated the instant we lifted off that godforsaken planet."

Nick simply stared at him, his half-smile growing larger by the second. "It's damn legal, regardless of what planet you're on."

"So, who's the lucky lady?" Marc asked. "Anyone we know?"

Silence.

"Kira," Clint offered into the silence.

Zeke laughed out loud. "I said I'm not married."

"Yep, and what do you want to bet she has a matching sign on her wrist?" Nick added.

Clint released a breathy whistle. "I congratulate you on your taste in women."

"She'd be a good match for you, Clint," Zeke quipped, tiring of their bantering. "A damn good match."

The words had barely cleared his lips when the door to the study opened. "Something sure must have been funny," Delta said. "A couple of those boisterous outbursts could be heard clear upstairs."

"Come on in, ladies," Clint drawled, his eyes on Kira as the women entered the study chamber.

Zeke set his coffee down. Nick rolled up the map. For now, tomorrow's plans would be set aside in lieu of an evening that promised good food, good company and a much needed calm before the morning storm.

All four men together at once was enough to take a woman's breath away. Tressa had already braced Kira for the initial jolt of meeting the Banner men. 'The disarming trio,' she called them. There certainly was no doubt but that they were related. The Banner stamp was clearly etched in each one.

Nevertheless, it was to Zeke her gaze returned. Zeke, who immediately came forward, caught Kira gently by the hand and escorted her across the room. "Kira, I'd like you to meet my business partner, Nick Banner. Nick, Kira Delaney."

CHAPTER NINETEEN

A grin broke across Nick's handsome face as he offered his hand. "The pleasure's all mine, Kira."

"Thank you." Kira recognized him immediately from the pictures she'd seen in the memory crystal. However, something about him seemed a little less reckless now than when he had appeared in a couple of those pictures with Zeke. No doubt the result of Tressa, marriage and a baby on the way.

"And," Zeke continued, "you've already met Clint."

"Yes," she said, meeting Clint's luminous eyes. Now this one, she'd already decided, was dangerous. Clint was the first born, Zeke had explained earlier. And Kira easily imagined that when it came to the affairs of the heart, Clint Banner was an accomplished heartbreaker.

With unabashed boldness, Clint's eyes held hers as he captured her left hand. "Kira," he murmured silkily. In less than a heartbeat, he'd cleverly managed to expose her wrist. Kira hadn't even realized it until he broke eye contact long enough to briefly glance down. His eyes were dancing when he shifted his focus to Zeke.

Ignoring Clint's amusement, Zeke led Kira over to the third Banner brother. "And this is Marc."

From a distance she suspected it would be hard to tell the brothers apart. Even their voices were alike. Marc greeted her with a nod and the gentle mention of her name, and looking into the third and final pair of sapphires, there was no question in Kira's mind but that the youngest rebel of the family, Marc Banner, was just as much of a heartbreaker as

182

his two older brothers. She suspected their methods might be a little different, but the end result would surely be the same.

Glancing away she found Clint watching her with a lazy regard that melted into a nod and a disarming smile. Meeting his stare, Kira smiled back. A woman would have to be crazy not to see straight through that one.

"Well," Delta said, as she came to the rescue, "now that we've gotten all the introductions over with, what do you say we leave these men to themselves. I want to check on the dinner."

Zeke's look was pensive as he watched Kira turn to leave.

"Boy, I don't know, Zeke," Clint began. "That symbol on her wrist looks pretty damn official to me."

Zeke groaned aloud. "Well, it's not."

"You know..." Clint went on in a baiting tone, "she just might make a good match for me after all. Did you really mean what you said about being welcome to her?"

Slater's brief hesitation brought the place down with another round of rowdy laughter.

Having left the men to resume their raucous camaraderie, Delta quickly checked on the preparations for the evening's meal. Afterward, the women took a leisurely tour of the home where Kira was shown the room that would be hers.

The tour ended up outside and included the stables. "The horses are my husband and daughter's hobby," Delta explained. "Five mares and one stallion had been originally selected and shipped from Earth."

With its warmth and aroma of sweet hay, the stable had been especially fascinating for Kira. She'd seen horses before, but mostly in pictures. On the rare occasions when she had seen them live, it had never been up close.

"Would you like to see Zeke's horse?" Tressa asked as they made their way to a large box stall at the end of the barn. "This is Thor."

Silence. Then... "He's as magnificent in life as he is in the mural on board ship."

"He's eighteen years old," Rae added. "But you'd never guess it. He acts younger than most of the four-year-olds around here."

Kira enjoyed the relaxed female companionship of the three Banner women. During the flow of conversation, she'd learned that Delta was the stepmother to Clint, Nick and Marc. Their mother had died shortly after Marc had been born. As a friend of the family, she'd volunteered to help Max in caring for the boys until someone permanent could be found. Two years later, she and Max were married, and eventually Rae was born.

Kira laughed. "Three boys. I can only imagine that was an undertaking."

Tressa joined in her laughter. "Those were practically my same words."

Later, in returning to her room, Kira found that a fragrant bath had been drawn and waiting. For the first time in what seemed a lifetime, she allowed herself the luxury of forgetting everything unpleasant.

After her bath, Tressa offered to help fix her hair, pulling it back in a cascade of curls down her back. The beautiful aqua gown she wore was also Tressa's, a dress she said she wouldn't be wearing in a long while. Never in all her life had Kira felt so feminine, so...sexy.

"You look beautiful," Tressa said as they both stared at the stunning results in the full-length mirror.

"Thank you. And so do you."

"Me?" Tressa laughed. "The only thing I look like is fat."

"No, you're not. You may not see it yourself, but you literally glow." At eight months pregnant, Tressa was a vision of femininity and it was doubtful Nick saw her as fat. "Just from the way he looks at you," Kira went on, "I can tell Nick is absolutely crazy about you and the way you look."

"Just wait until Zeke sees you," Tressa sighed, beaming at Kira with approval.

Kira shot her a disbelieving look. "Don't hold your breath. I can pretty much guarantee he won't even notice. Besides, he couldn't dump me off here fast enough."

Tressa grinned. "My, that too sounds familiar. The dump-you-off scenario is a sure sign, you know." She caught Kira by the arm. "Come on, we can talk on the way."

"What do you mean, 'a sure sign'?" Kira asked as Tressa led the way down the wide stairway.

"Let's put it this way, I'd be willing to bet that you're far more than just a passing acquaintance. Zeke's never brought a woman back for us to meet. Ever."

Kira huffed a soft laugh. "He's not exactly bringing me back for everyone to meet. The only reason he's doing this is because he used to work for my father and...well, for the time being he's stuck with me."

"Oh, yes," Tressa whispered, "I believe I also heard that exact line too. This way," she said, directing Kira toward an open set of doors. "There's one more Banner you have yet to meet."

"Not another brother?"

"Stars, no." Tressa laughed. "The galaxy couldn't handle another Banner male on the loose. No, I want you to meet their father, Max. He was gone when you arrived this afternoon."

The instant they entered the large dining room, the smell of freshly brewed coffee greeted them. Place settings were in order; a young serving girl was carefully pouring wine into each goblet and tantalizing aromas wafted in from the kitchen.

Tressa led the way past the table and through an open doorway out onto a veranda where Zeke and Nick were engaged in conversation. Kira immediately noted that Rae was hanging on Zeke's arm, a look of pure adoration in her eyes. Funny how it bothered her. After all, what did she care? She certainly had no feelings for him.

"Rae, have you seen your father around?" Tressa asked.

"Yes, I saw him in the study not twenty minutes ago."

It was obvious, judging from the death grip Rae had on Zeke's arm, the young beauty was enchanted with him. Kira didn't want to know if the feelings were mutual. Rachel Banner was pretty enough to catch any man's eye with Delta's blonde hair and delicate features along with those Banner trademark eyes.

Zeke glanced away from his conversation, his eyes meeting Kira's. With unmasked approval, his gaze traveled downward then back up. Kira's stomach coiled.

"Rae," Tressa went on, "should we miss him somehow, tell him to stay put. I want him to meet Kira before dinner."

"I will."

Zeke's galvanizing gaze held Kira immobile, once again stirring up butterflies.

"This way," Tressa said. Once they were back inside, Tressa turned to Kira, unable to keep the satisfied smirk off her face. "Did you see the look on his face?" she whispered.

"Who?"

Tressa laughed out loud. "Who indeed. His jaw was on the floor, Kira, how could you miss it? She laughed. I knew it would be. I took you out there just for that reason."

"You didn't."

"Of course, I did." Tressa continued leading the way through the home. "I knew where Max was all along. I just wanted to see the look on Zeke's face when he saw you."

Kira rolled her eyes and began laughing. "I still say you're wrong."

"Not the way he was looking at you," Tressa whispered as they approached the study. "You stole his breath, my dear."

"Door's open."

Max Banner sat behind a large desk as the two ladies entered. Clint was leaning nonchalantly against the hearth. Obviously they had been in conversation.

"Are we interrupting?"

"Not at all. Come on in, Tressa."

"I wanted you to meet Kira."

Immediately, Max was on his feet and coming around the desk to grasp Kira's extended hand. "Kira, it's good to meet you. I hope the ladies are helping you to feel at home here."

"Thank you, and yes, they are." Kira instantly realized the origin of the notorious Banner trademarks. Looking far too young to be their father, Max Banner was just as charming and just as strikingly handsome as his three sons. Then her eyes slammed into Clint's. Suddenly the corners of his mouth lifted, and pushing away from the wall, he made his way toward them.

"Brace yourself," Tressa warned softly. "God's gift to all women approaches."

"Ladies, you do look enchanting this evening," he said, drawing to a halt before them. His gaze shifted specifically to Tressa. "And I mean it when I say you've never looked lovelier than you do at this moment."

Tressa closed her eyes in amused supplication. "Oh, Clint," she sighed, "would it make you feel any better if I were to tell you that you were my second choice if Nick had turned me down?"

At that they both broke into laughter, and Tressa commented that dinner was about ready.

A challenging gleam lit Clint's eyes as he focused his attention on Kira. "Kira, since I seem to be running second place to Zeke, would you at least allow me to escort you to dinner?" At her consent, he offered her his arm.

Why didn't it surprise her when he took a seat right next to her? Zeke was still nowhere in sight, nor was Nick. It wasn't until everyone was seated and dinner was about to begin that the two men came in from the veranda. Nick took his place next to Tressa. The only place left for Zeke, however, was down near the end on the opposite side of the table from Kira...right next to Rae.

All through dinner the table buzzed with conversation centering mainly around business and Zeke's encounters over the last five months. Rae seemed to hang on every word Zeke had to say.

Clint, on the other hand, kept Kira entertained with small talk and clever remarks that had her laughing most of the time. She suspected that much of Clint's attention was entirely for Zeke's benefit. Nevertheless, for the time being she allowed herself to enjoy his company.

Several times she'd glanced up to find Zeke's gaze riveted on her, though he seemed unconcerned over Clint's charming and undivided interest.

The camaraderie among the family members was tangible. There was little doubt but that Zeke was as much a part of the family as any of them. According to Delta, he'd grown up with all three boys, although his friendship with Nick had been the strongest.

After dinner, the men migrated from the table into a nearby den, taking their manly conversations with them. Zeke eventually challenged Clint to an energetic game of good old-fashioned billiards on an elaborately hand-carved antique billiard table that had been imported from Earth. The women moved into a small room across the hall where a quieter conversation centered on the events of the day, and...babies.

Though everyone had gone out of their way to make sure Kira felt welcome, she couldn't help the wave of melancholy presently sweeping through her. She'd never known the close ties of having a sibling. It had always been just her and Renn. And now even he had been taken from her.

Eventually, conversation dropped to a lull, and excusing herself, Kira moved out onto the covered porch. The evening was warm. Darkness had settled in and the air was heavy with the fragrance of night-blooming flowers, many of which hung in pots off the louvered support beams. Her focus moved to Acacia's three moons hanging low on the horizon. Occasional peals of gentle laughter drifted out into the night air, mocking the emptiness she felt deep inside. It was nobody's fault. Part of it was reality once again surfacing. The other part she strongly suspected was the wine breaking down her resolve, lowering her resistance and her strength to hold the tears at bay.

Thor, a silent voice whispered. He'd cheer her up. Having made a decision, Kira made her way down a short flight of stairs and followed an illuminated pathway that rambled through the landscaped grounds. The stable and outbuildings were brightly lit as she approached them. With a timid touch of a small keypad, the door slid open and she quietly entered the stables. Once inside, low lighting came to life and Kira glanced around, her eyes adjusting to the dimness. The only noises were the soft sounds of snuffling and munching coming from the horses. The fragrant, sweet scent of hay teased her nostrils as she quietly made her way deeper into the barn. Thor was gathering the last few blades of alfalfa off the floor when Kira came to stand before his stall.

Lifting his head, he watched her curiously, ears flicking forward, listening as she spoke to him in gentle tones. Seconds ticked by as the two of them studied one another--Kira, awed by the captivating beauty of Zeke's horse, and Thor, curious about the stranger who spoke softly and kept her distance.

Finally, he blew through his nostrils and lazily ambled over to the door. When he poked his nose through the bars, Kira backed up two steps. Still, he watched her beneath the heavy curtain of his long forelock.

Just like his master, she thought. Raw male virility lay within the heart of this magnificent animal.

Finally gaining a small measure of courage, she reached for a tiny clump of hay from a nearby stash and offered it to the velvet muzzle sticking through the bars. She nearly giggled aloud, watching as he gently lipped it from her hand. Problem was, all too soon those liquid brown eyes were again riveted on her.

"I can't give you any more," she said quietly.

"Thor's a moocher."

Kira turned abruptly to find Zeke coming up behind her.

"Hey there, boy." With his attention fully trained on the horse, he asked, "What happened Kira? Get bored?"

"No, I just...needed a moment to myself."

Zeke unlatched the top half of the stall door and slid it open. "How ya doin', big guy?" he murmured as he stroked the stallion's neck.

Kira stepped back when Thor stretched his neck in her direction.

"He won't hurt you. He thinks you've got more for him to eat, that's all."

A nervous giggle escaped as she took another step backward, avoiding Thor's probing nose as he searched for another morsel. With the few times she had actually seen a live horse, she'd forgotten how big they were.

"Mind your manners, boy." Slater's tone lowered to a gentle command as he directed the horse to back up. "Remember what I told you about being gentle?" Reaching into a nearby tack box, he withdrew a brush, slid open the lower half of the stall door and entered. Kira watched as Zeke began working the brush down the horse's sleek body.

Feeling a strange tugging at her heart, she remained where she was, her breath suspended as she watched this magnificent man--this ruthless pirate who had it within him to order open fire upon a freighter, knowing that people--albeit pirates--would be killed. This gentle man, who cradled a small child in his arms and carried her to safety. This man who now seemed to be at complete peace with his horse. And what a pair they were, these two males--equal on every level. Surely God could not have made a finer specimen of either species.

Kira caught herself watching the play of muscles across Zeke's back and shoulders as he worked the brush across the horse's withers. His remarkable coloring, his height, even that air of supreme confidence set him apart from most men, a self assurance that could only be born of experience. A spark of heat coiled low in her belly as a stray thought cut across her mind. Was Zeke Slater as merciless a lover as he was a pirate? Her breath caught as she recalled the impact of his stolen kisses.

"Do you ride?"

The question gave her pause.

"Would you like to ride Thor sometime?"

Kira shook her head. "Oh...I don't know how to--"

"He's gentle. Besides, I'd be right there with you." Leaving the thought hanging, he returned to his task.

"What about you?" Kira asked. "Do you ride him much?" It was a stupid question. How could he ride his horse when he spent months off-planet?

Zeke smiled, but didn't answer for a moment. "I used to ride him quite a bit," he finally said, methodically flicking the brush across the length of the horse's back. "Back then, I usually needed an escape from one thing or another. Now Rae's taken over Thor's care for me."

For reasons Kira didn't want to examine, the mention of Rae's name sent a twinge of jealousy surging through her. Naturally, she thought, Rae would take care of Zeke's horse.

He likes that," she said, stepping a little closer.

Slater laughed. "Thor likes attention--period."

Determined to overcome her hesitation, Kira worked her way closer, until she was standing in the doorway of the stall. There she remained, watching as Zeke worked the brush over Thor's sleek coat. "He really is beautiful. Frank said he's called a paint horse."

"That's right." Zeke moved around to the other side and continued working the brush. "Did he also tell you about his markings?" He stepped in front of Thor and drew his creamy white forelock aside, exposing a patch of golden tan that covered his forehead and ears. "See how the color covers the top of his head?" he asked.

"Yes."

"It's called a war bonnet. And the patch of color on his chest is called a shield. On Earth many Native American tribes would consider Thor magical simply because of his markings."

"Magical? Like how?"

Zeke shrugged and returned to grooming Thor. "He's called a Medicine Hat horse. Supposedly his rider is protected from harm."

Kira opened her mouth to respond, but her words were cut off when Thor stepped forward, once again stretching his long neck to touch her with his nose.

Willing herself not to back up this time, she stood still, even as the big animal tentatively lipped at her arm with his soft muzzle.

"What should I do?" she whispered.

Zeke had stopped his work to watch the byplay. "Pet the pushy devil," he said.

Lifting her hand, Kira gingerly stroked Thor's face.

Slater laughed. "He won't hurt you. Go ahead and pet him."

"I did."

"Hell, Legs, you call that petting?" Kira's eyes widened as he came forward. "I'm afraid that's not going to do it." He shook his head, a hint of a smile touching the corners of his mouth. "Here, let me show you how easy it is."

Was it her...hearing more in his tone, reading more in his look than what was actually there? Ogling him as she had, it was entirely possible she was letting her imagination run wild. Or maybe once again it was the wine that had her feminine curiosity piqucd. Regardless, Kira ignored the tiny voice telling her it was time to return to the house.

With deliberate ease, Zeke moved in behind her. "There's a right way and a wrong way to do some things. Take grooming for instance," he said, holding the brush for emphasis. "Thor loves being groomed. But there's a secret to doing it right."

Fascinated, Kira listened as he continued. "Number one, you've got to have a good stroke. Without that, the results aren't nearly as satisfying."

A warning bell sounded with that one, but Kira was unable to do anything but stand there.

"Here, let me show you," he said. Taking one of her hands firmly in his, he gently set the brush in her palm then placed it on Thor's neck.

She tried putting the brush down, but his fingers curled about hers preventing her from releasing it. "Zeke, I really don't--"

"It's all in the touch," he breathed against her ear. He flattened the palm of her other hand on the horse's neck just slightly above the one holding the brush. "Don't you agree, Legs?"

Kira swallowed, appalled and intrigued at the same time. The double meaning was all too clear.

"It just takes practice to get good at it," he said, "but the secret is in a strong down-stroke and a good follow-through. Like this..." Guiding her hands with his own, he ran her through a practice session, brushing with one hand, smoothing the coat behind it with the other.

"See? That's all there is to it. Want to try it again?" Before Kira could voice an answer, Slater was lifting her hands to repeat the process.

Somehow, through it all, he'd maneuvered his body to where he was pressed up tightly against hers, his thighs intimately embracing her backside, his arms completely encircling her as he took her through the steps once again. "Just remember," he murmured, his voice hardly more than a rasp against her ear, "a smooth down-stroke and slow repetitions."

CHAPTER TWENTY

Zeke knew he was treading on dangerous ground, but he couldn't seem to help himself. Blame it on Acacia's triple moons rising on the horizon, or maybe the wine. Blame it on the madness that had plagued him ever since he'd first kissed her. Hell, it really didn't make any difference. For all he knew, some mystical goddess of love was playing havoc with his mind. Truth was, he'd tasted Kira and now he wanted--no, he needed more.

He hadn't counted on her being here when he came to the stables. Dammit, he'd left the house to get away, to find peace, to rid his mind of Kira and the memory of her in his arms and the sweet kisses he'd stolen. Instead, here he was, lethally hard--and her in his arms again.

Why the devil did she have this effect on him? She was sexy in an untutored, innocent way. But he'd seen just as hot--even bedded his share. And yet, he'd been nearly crazy with jealousy this evening--a response he never would have thought himself capable of.

Oh, it was all a ruse on Clint's part--he knew that--a challenge to get a rise out of him. A familiar muscle clenched along his jaw. It had worked, too, but he'd be damned if he'd let any of them know it.

Tomorrow couldn't come fast enough. The sooner he got away from Kira, the better for both of them. As for right now... There's nothing he wanted more than to lay her back in the soft hay and ease the ache in his loins. Her soft scent and the heat of her body had already overloaded his senses beyond reason. Under normal circumstances he would have laughed at himself. But things were far from normal. He could never remember wanting a woman as badly as he wanted sweet Kira right now.

Brushing a heavy dark lock aside with his chin, he placed the lightest of kisses on her nape and muttered, "I came here to get away from you."

Slowly turning her about, he found her willing mouth and nearly groaned aloud when Kira passed her tongue over her lips. Foolish as it was, his predicable body tightened to unbearable readiness. If she only knew the thoughts raging through his mind, would she still be standing so pliant, so willing and trusting in his arms?

Surprise colored her face when he deliberately backed her against the wall. She gasped as his hands cupped her face, tilting it up to him. He couldn't resist smoothing his thumb over her lower lip. It was such a soft, supple lip. "God in Heaven, you're beautiful," he rasped, begrudging the truth of his words.

He felt a shudder course through her and again his head lowered to nip at her, catching the fullness of her lower lip between his teeth and drawing it into his mouth. He wanted her. But what right did he have to her, to drag her into a life that promised nothing, nor offered any guarantees that he'd even walk away from the next encounter?

But for the moment--for right now, his muddled brain wouldn't think on that. All he could concentrate on was sweet, sweet Kira who was staring up at him with a gaze that nearly became his undoing. Tonight, he'd taste her just once more. Then tomorrow he'd be gone and she'd be out of his life and, God willing, out of his blood.

With that he lowered his head, taking her lips again, this time in a fevered kiss that left him reeling and her clinging as if she'd never let him go. He swallowed her moan, the soft cry drowning out the last chance of reason. The only thing that mattered was here--now--and the woman in his arms.

Take it easy old man, a tiny voice cautioned.

Zeke drew back, his seductive gaze moving over Kira with deliberate examination. She smelled of flowers and tasted like Heaven. He looked down at her through heavy-lidded eyes, his breathing shallow. "You have any idea what I've been going through these past weeks with you on board?"

He felt Kira tremble at his confession, and with a low growl dipped his head, blazing a trail of soft, slow kisses along the arch of her jaw to the sensitive hollow beneath her ear. From there, he worked his way back to her mouth. "I've been goin' outta my mind," he whispered against her lips. Again, he felt Kira's body jolt when he touched the tip of his tongue to her lips and sought entrance, teasing and taunting his way past the barrier of her teeth. With ease born of experience, his hands moved for the fastenings at the back of her gown, and one by one began working them loose.

What are you doing, Slater? a silent voice asked. Is this what you want? To slake your desire on her like...this? In a damn barn?

No, it wasn't at all what his rational mind wanted. But right now Zeke wasn't exactly thinking with the rational part of his body. His eyes veiled beneath lowered lids, he pulled back, desperately trying to douse the fires of need burning within--at least long enough to say what he had to say. He'd give Kira fair warning of his intentions. If she was smart, she'd turn and run. If not, he'd have her, and to hell with the consequences.

"I want you, Kira" he said bluntly. "Right here. Now." The next words came reluctantly, through gritted teeth. "And, unless you feel the same way, I suggest you turn around and run."

"Zeke, I--"

"Now, Kira."

~ * ~

Playing with fire, Kira made the mistake of looking into his eyes. His raw expression took her breath away, and her heart along for the ride. A muscle tensed along his jaw. The ruthless pirate had returned, and Kira knew instinctively that this time she was the plunder he was after.

It was one thing to flirt with danger but quite another to face it head on. With her own nerves in turmoil, Kira drew in a shuddering breath. She should go--run back to the safety of the house and leave him out here to cool off. Yet, mesmerized by his rakish good looks and the heady realization of the power she held over this man, she swallowed, torn--knowing what he wanted from her, yet at the same time reluctant to walk away from him.

Her tumbling thoughts were abruptly cut off when his hands plunged into her silken tresses and he drew her head back, again lifting her face to his. "Time's up," he whispered.

Kira thrilled to the feel of his warm lips, reveled in the masterful way he kissed her. His mouth was persuasive as it slanted across hers with sweet possessiveness, stoking a flaming need that left her desperately hanging on for dear life.

Somehow the fastenings down the back of her gown were undone, and Kira felt his calloused hand slip inside to rest against the small of her back. Her legs were jelly, nearly buckling with the desire surging through her veins. And even if she'd been thinking about stopping him before, she was lost when his hand moved down to cup a rounded cheek and pull her intimately into him.

Reflexively, Kira's nails dug into the back of his neck. Dear Lord, when had she wrapped her arms about his neck?

His hungry gasp filled her with a heady sense of power. "So sweet," he rasped against the arch of her throat. His teeth gently nipped her tender skin, his tongue following in penance, licking away any traces of pain. Murmuring something indecipherable yet clearly suggestive against her ear, he pinned her against the rough wall, wedging his knee between her legs. The confines of his trousers did nothing to conceal his need, and Kira moaned in feeble protest as the hem of the dress she was wearing rose shamelessly in the process.

Suddenly, his kisses turned gentle, passionate...and oh, so very tender. And whatever he wanted from her, Kira was trembling and ready to give.

As though sensing her willingness, Zeke reached between their bodies and single-handedly began undoing the studs on his pants. "You know how long I've wanted this?" he whispered.

Thor ambled over the threshold, taking advantage of the open stall door as he gathered up particles of hay off the floor. Suddenly, his ears flicked forward, his attention fastened on the lovers pressed against the wall across the aisle.

Three open studs were as far as Slater got before the force of a head-butt sent him and Kira both stumbling into a mound of loose hay.

Muttering a string of curses, Zeke looked up into a pair of big browns peeking through a curtain of white silk. The horse had dropped his head in humble repose, but Zeke wasn't fooled for a second. "You all right, Kira?"

She was laughing. "Yes."

Instantly, Zeke bounded to his feet. "Why you disloyal, traitorous, lowdown, sneaky son of a duce."

Thor slowly began backing into his stall.

"Thaaat's right. You'd better get in there if you value your life, you shifty traitor. I've half a mind to haul your sorry ass off to auction."

Kira was still laughing.

Once the horse was secure, Zeke returned to her, lowering himself down beside her on the hay. "You sure you're okay?"

"I'm fine, but you've got hay all over you."

Zeke leaned forward, plucking a piece from her hair. "And so do you, Legs."

"Zeke..." she whispered, suddenly sober, "I hope this place doesn't have security cams."

"It does," he whispered back.

Eyes darting about for evidence, Kira jumped to her feet and began brushing herself off. "Oh, no--"

"But--" He came up beside her, "they're not engaged at the moment."

"Are you sure?"

He laughed. "Yes. I'm sure."

"Oh, Zeke, can you just imagine the scene it would have recorded?" Removing several more pieces of hay from her dress, she added, "We'd never live it down."

Zeke's amusement faded. At the moment, everyone's laughter was the least of his concerns. What was it about her that had his brains between his legs? Once again he'd allowed things to get out of hand. Lack of self-control was not only a new experience for him--it was as unwelcome as all hell. Even worse was the fact that only a very small part of him felt thankful that the stallion had interrupted them. The other part strongly resented it.

He adjusted the fit of his pants then gently turned Kira about so that he could refasten the tiny closures down the back of her gown. "There," he said as the last fastener came together. He turned her so that she faced him again. "Except for a little hay here and there, you're as good as new." Bending his head, he gave her a sweet, tender kiss. "There's nothing I want more right now than to make love to you." He kissed her again, a mere brush of his lips over hers this time. "But we'd better head on back 'fore someone gets a search party organized."

~ * ~

Shaken by his blatant admission, Kira quietly walked at Zeke's side, her hand in his as he escorted her back to the house. Had it not been for Thor, she would have willingly submitted to this man and his practiced seduction. Did Zeke know how close she'd actually come to yielding? How was it he could bring out such extremes in her, and so quickly? It was as if he held a key to a lock she didn't even know existed.

Clint glanced up as they entered through a side door. A blind person couldn't miss his knowing look of assessment. Already he was thinking the worst. Kira sighed inwardly, thankful his gaze was focused on Zeke instead of her. Not that Zeke cared. It was obvious that Clint's licentious conclusions didn't bother Zeke in the least.

She'd no sooner recovered from Clint's appraisal when they were facing Nick's arched brow. Shoving away from the wall, he made his way toward them. "Hey, Slater," he began in a lowered tone, eyes glittering with laughter, "next time you romp in the hay, pal, make sure you brush yourself off."

Zeke hastily retrieved the telltale piece of hay off his pants. "Better?"

"Much." Nick's expression sobered. "By the way, Dad's looking for you; I think he's still in the game room. He's got a slew of charts on Echo to go over with us."

Zeke's gaze flicked to Kira then back to Nick in a silent plea to take her off his hands. "Where are the women?" he asked.

"You go on ahead," Nick said as he stepped forward. "Kira and I will track them down."

With a nod of consent, Zeke quickly turned and made his way to the game room.

"You really don't have to baby sit me, Nick. Just point me in the right direction and I'm sure I'll find them."

"It's my pleasure. Besides, I think I know where the ladies are. Let's go see if they're still there." With Kira at his side, Nick led the way down the hall toward a drawing room off the main entry.

"There you are," Rae said when they entered. "We were wondering where you'd disappeared to."

With a light touch on her arm and a polite dismissal, Nick turned and headed back the way they had come, leaving Kira with the feeling she had just been deposited.

Rae came forward. "Mom was just saying all your travel pacs were lost somehow at the spaceport."

Kira felt her face flush at wondering what all Zeke had told them. "Yes," she said, following through with the lie. "Can you imagine?"

"Come with me." Before Kira realized what she was about, Rae was leading the way to her room. "You and I seem about the same size," she said, "and I've got a closet full of clothes--half of which I've never worn."

"Oh, I couldn't--"

"Yes, you can." Rae laughed.

"Just let her do it," Tressa chimed in, having tagged along. "Before I became pregnant, I was the recipient of Rae's hand-me-downs."

"It's true," Rae added. "I love shopping, and every now and then I need to clear things out." At Kira's look of hesitancy, Rae continued, "At least take a few things to hold you over until your pacs are found. These for instance," she said holding up a pair of blue pants. "Nothing fancy, just a pair of good ol' Levis." Rae tossed them on the bed along with a couple of t-shirts. "And, this..." She tossed another shirt on the bed. "The color will be stunning on you."

"Really, I can't--"

"Nonsense," Rae laughed again. "Just ask Tressa. It's the only way I can justify my shopping sprees."

"Yup," Tressa said as she settled on the edge of the bed. "It's true. Some of my favorite things used to be Rae's."

Torn by a barrage of conflicting emotions, Kira numbly watched as Rae held up several more items for her approval, and a small pile began forming on the bed. Despite all the fuss over Rae's castaway clothing, Kira kept thinking about the plans being discussed by the men. Zeke had said nothing about plans for Echo, except that he had a delivery--no doubt the instruments he'd picked up in Port Chance. And now all of a sudden the Banners were dragging out detailed charts? For what purpose?

"...and I'm thinking that this color would be beautiful on you. What do you think, Tressa?"

Lost in her thoughts, Tressa glanced over at Rae. "I uh..."

"I was saying this color would be beautiful on you."

At last Kira turned to assess the growing stack of clothing, "Oh Rae, this is far too much. I'll never be able to--"

"Sure you will. Oh!" She held up a crimson jumpsuit, "I've never worn this and it would look great with your hair." Rae grinned. "I know because Tressa once borrowed a gown this color, and the two of you have about the same color of hair."

"And this!" Rae held up yet another jumpsuit, this one in royal blue with sparkling gems outlining the neckline. Rae smiled warmly. "You've just got to take this one, Kira. I guarantee you will drive Zeke to total distraction."

Rae's lack of jealousy had not gone unnoticed. The kindness of sharing some of her most beautiful things with a potential rival were not the deeds of a woman madly in love. Maybe she had misjudged Rae's affection for Zeke.

Despite her growing fondness for Rae, all she could think of was getting to her room and being alone with her muddled emotions--thoughts and feelings that revolved around her need to get to Echo, and a man who drew her to him one minute and pushed her away the next.

"I want you to have these things. Besides, you'll..."

Rae's voice faded as Kira's mind wandered once again. What difference would it make what she wore? If the truth were known, she'd bet there was a broken heart over Zeke Slater in every port across the galaxy. One thing for sure, their farce of a marriage certainly put no claims on him.

Kira felt Tressa's hand on her arm. "I know you're worried," she offered with quiet emphasis. "May I ask why you're not down there getting in on it?"

Lifting her eyes to meet Tressa's, Kira said, "I believe I was banned from the discussion."

At that, a look of complete incredulity passed over Tressa's delicate features. "Excuse me? From what little I understand of it, this is your corporation they're talking about. And you were told you couldn't sit in on it?" she asked in total challenge.

"Well, not in so many words, but I was definitely disposed of nonetheless."

"Disposed of?" Rae repeated indignantly. "You mean by Nick?"

Kira shrugged. "He was very sweet and polite about it, but he was definitely getting rid of me."

"What do you think, Tressa?" Rae asked, with an all-business frown. "I'd say it's time we joined the men in the War Room, don't you?"

Tressa stood up. "Let's go."

Zeke was the first to look up as Rae, Tressa and Kira entered the room.

"Gentlemen," Rae said smoothly, "please, carry on with what you were doing. We just thought we'd see what's going on."

Clint rolled his eyes heavenward. Marc muttered something beneath his breath, and Nick blew a stream of smoke into the air and grinned.

All five men were poring over an array of papers spread out on the billiard table. A cloud of blue smoke hovered over their heads, compliments of Nick and Marc, who both had small cigars shoved into the corner of their mouths.

"Kira," Max said with a warm smile, his deep voice inviting as he extended an arm to her. "Come over here by me, honey, and I'll try to explain a little of what we're doing."

Several detailed maps were spread out on the billiard table, overlapping one another, "See this red circle," he asked.

Kira nodded.

"That's Port Ore. And over here is Major Metals Mining. As long as Zeke has a routine delivery here," he said pointing to Port Ore's Spaceport, "he's going to go ahead and try to find out a little more about some of those problems you've been having."

"Good. And with me along, he won't have any trouble getting through security," Kira said, "because I have a clearance."

No one even looked up.

Max cleared his throat. "I am sure you could be a great deal of help, Kira, but because of the attempts that have already been made on your life, it's best if you remain here until Zeke's has a chance to check things out."

"But Grant will be there. I'll be safe with him," she reasoned.

No response.

Kira glanced about the table. "Surely, you don't suspect him of something?" she asked, her accusing gaze landing on Zeke.

"No, of course not. It's just that it never hurts to be cautious," Max offered conversationally.

"Where, may I ask, did you get your hands on these?" Rae interrupted, leaning over the billiard table and inspecting one of the 3-D survey maps. "I've never seen anything so detailed. Where did you get them?"

Clint grinned and shook his head. "Never a dull moment..."

Marc's gaze shifted to Max, no doubt curious as to how his dad was going to handle Rae.

Max glanced up and said patiently, "It's nothing you need to concern yourself with, Rae."

The ladies were allowed to stay, but Kira personally had never heard so much doubletalk in all her life. It was painfully obvious that the discussion had become guarded. And on top of it all, Zeke hardly acknowledged her, keeping his gaze focused on the maps, his coffee and virtually everywhere else except on her.

Just as the men had obviously hoped, the discussion became so boring and so uninformative, the women eventually left.

Kira did not see Zeke again that night. Not that she had expected to, but with his plans to leave early in the morning, he at least could have said goodbye. She supposed that what they had experienced earlier in the barn had meant nothing more than a chance at quick sex. And why not? She'd certainly been willing enough.

She wondered about Zeke and the tender side he hid so well. Unbidden, the image materialized of his hard face when he stood by her side at the view port and watched the *Solar Wind* fire torpedo after torpedo upon the pirate freighter--an act undoubtedly being carried out as a result of his direct orders. Men were dying on board that ship with each hit, yet there had been no mercy, no compassion from a man she'd found capable of both. The contradiction almost frightened her.

"Kira," Frank had said gently, "he did what he had t' do."

"But did he have to kill them?" she had asked.

"Technically? Yes. It's a warnin' t' others who prey upon this trade way." Frank took her hand in his. "Kira, it goes with the job, darlin'. His ability to carry through is also what makes him able to command men, some who would just as soon cut y' down as t' look at y'. It's a fine line, honey, between a privateer and a pirate."

Kira thought about it. "You mean those men in the back are--"

"No." Frank shook his head. "Not those men. But, every now and then we have that sort as part of our crew."

When she started to glance away, Frank's gravelly voice drew her back. "And when we do, y' think a weaker man would have control over 'em?"

Kira sighed, her mind brought back to the present. No, she supposed a weaker man would have no control at all over a rough crew.

CHAPTER TWENTY-ONE

Solar Wind:
En route to Echo:

Slater hadn't intended to leave without saying goodbye to Kira, but by the time he and the Banners had called it a night, it was too late to go knocking at her door. And when he left this morning, it was too early. So he did the only thing he could think of: he left a voice message for her.

It was better this way anyhow, he told himself. It would only have made matters worse to see her again. She would have just begged to go with him. Actually, it surprised him that she hadn't pestered him about it since they'd arrived on Acacia.

With a heavy sigh, Slater loaded a music rod into the entertainment center--something smooth and moody. The slow haunting wail of a synthesized guitar with a deep bass pacing out the tempo suited his mood. Reaching for the decanter of Terran whisky, he poured a small swallow into a glass.

There was another reason why it was best he didn't see her again, a reason Zeke wasn't in the mood to face at the moment. Never had his nerves been so raw from fighting primal desire. The lust rampaging through his veins had its origin the instant he'd lifted the lid on that produce container and found her inside. Like it or not, Kira aroused a fire in him that would consume them both if he didn't extinguish it.

He'd pledged three years to this mission--this life of privateering. Yet, lately he'd found himself lured from his purpose by a most unlikely decoy--Delaney's little hellion. Damn if he knew why she fired his blood so. And of all the inconvenient times, this was the worst. It wasn't as if he was some untried youth still learning to control lust, yet even now he wanted her with an all-consuming hunger.

Drawing a deep breath, he did his best to calm the surge of desire that had begun to hum through his veins. Maybe if he ignored it, it would go away.

No, a silent voice laughed, *maybe if you get good and drunk, it will go away.*

He'd always been in control when it came to women, particularly since he'd accepted this mission. There simply was no place in his life for someone special. Number one, it would undermine his ability to face death square on. And that, Zeke knew, was the very edge that made him so competent, so damn dangerous at what he did.

So why now, when women had been nothing more than quick liaisons?

He tossed back the drink he'd been staring at for the past five minutes, savoring the burn--while elusive memories of past dalliances danced through his mind--echoes of lilting laughter and fleeting memories of himself placing his lips to the arched neck of some female while his body surged like a raging river into hers. And all the while reminding himself he didn't miss the warm intimacy that comes with trusting and caring...and loving and being loved.

So if he didn't miss it, why the devil did he keep finding himself envying what Nick had with Tressa? The pride of knowing her belly was swollen with his child, the anticipation of a baby, soon-to-be-born...the love and idolization in Tressa's eyes whenever she looked at Nick.

Did you not see that same love in Kira's eyes last night? a silent voice taunted. *You could have had her so easily.*

Once again he relived the memory of Kira in his arms, the rush of pink staining her cheeks, the taste of her sweet lips, the soft velvet of her skin. All it would have taken was an invitation, and he could have had her on board with him right now.

Redheads, Zeke all but moaned. Especially ones with sexy, long legs.

So why the devil hadn't he followed through? He was no damn hero. Heroic martyrdom had never been his 'forte. Slater raked a hand through his hair, knowing that visions of tantalizing skin, luscious curves and sexy long legs were going to be pure hell in the nights to come.

With a private breath of desire, he allowed himself one final indulgence, envisioning her young, lithe body lying beneath him. He could still see the wonder in Kira's eyes last night, could still smell the delicate fragrance of flowers emanating off her heated skin. Just the memory alone invoked immediate and idiotic results.

Focusing on the smooth song presently filling the lounge, he reached for the decanter. The heady vapors as he poured another small swallow were as potent as its taste. Yeah, maybe getting good and drunk would purge her from his soul. He sat there gazing numbly into the glass, as if expecting some miracle to evolve out of its amber depths.

You know exactly what it's going to take to purge her from your mind and ease that ache in your loins.

Deep in his locked-away heart, in the safe place where he kept his conscience and innermost thoughts, Zeke Slater also knew exactly what he'd left behind and why. If he made love to her once, once wouldn't be enough. It would only whet his appetite and he'd crave her all the more. A risky gamble that scared the hell out of him--and a risk he wasn't willing to take.

But she's your wife, the silent voice argued. *You have every right to make love to your...wife.*

Wife. The word stuck in his throat. Even as his gaze dropped to the emblem on his wrist, he renounced the very union the iridescent design symbolized. A union he'd been forced into. Deny it all he wanted, nothing changed the fact that Frank was right. He was just as married to Kira as if they'd been joined in a traditional ceremony.

Ah, God, married.

"Y' got that music loud enough?"

Zeke groaned in reaction to the one voice he least wanted to hear at the moment. Frowning into his glass, he ignored his First Officer, which wasn't easily done. Shit, he hated being at loose ends like this.

"I said, y' got that mus--"

"I heard you," Zeke snapped, irritably. "I happen to like it just as it is."

Frank stood in the open archway, his coffee mug in hand, pipe stuck between his teeth and the sweet aroma of tobacco drifting in the air. With a raised brow, the old man studied his captain before saying around the stem of his pipe, "Well, I can see yer cantankerous mood is even fouler than usual. Maybe we should make fer the next port so y' can remedy the cause."

Strained silence filled the room despite the melancholy sound of the saxophone crying out its sad message. Zeke felt the familiar muscle tug along his jaw. "And I suppose," he began with low-voiced composure, "you think you know the cause?"

"I think we both know the cause," Frank drawled.

Slowly glancing up, Zeke met Frank's steady look. "Meaning?"

"Y' really thank I need t' define it?"

Well aware of Frank's judging eyes, Zeke reached for the shot glass and raised it to his lips. His temper was short fused, and as usual he was finding the old man's opinion exasperating. Swallowing the drink in one burning gulp, he defiantly wrist-wiped his mouth. "Go for it," he rasped. "You're so sure you've got it all figured out."

"Hell, y've been stalkin' 'round here like a rogue bull paka ever since we lifted. Anyone with half a brain can figure it out. Y've gone nova over that little gal, and yer just too stubborn to own-up t' it."

Slater's eyes narrowed. "You're way off base, old man."

"Am I? Then prove it. Go slake yer frustrations--and yer ill temper along with it at the next port so we can all git back to normal routine 'round here."

It was a dare. Plain and simple, and one the old man knew full well Zeke would not accept. Frank turned for the galley across the way then stopped. "And, jist in case yer wonderin', alcohol ain't gonna cure what's eatin' away at yer guts right now."

"Well, I wasn't wondering," Zeke replied nastily. Hell, nobody had a better excuse to get roaring drunk than he did at the moment. Belligerently refilling the shot glass to the top for Frank's benefit, he wrapped his fingers around it and sat there staring into its amber depths.

And though he was tempted to purge Kira from his mind, he decided against it. Frank was right, as much as he hated admitting it. Finally, with a heavy sigh he shoved the glass away and rose to his feet. "I'm heading to my quarters."

Frank shrugged and stepped aside.

"And by the way," Slater muttered, "the alcohol helps."

"Nope," Frank drawled in all seriousness, "it only dulls the edges, son. Only the edges."

The heavy thud of Slater's booted heels echoed down the corridor as he made his way for his cabin. He'd learned long ago not to take too seriously every baiting remark Frank made. Nevertheless, it rankled that the old man was usually right-on when it came to seeing through to his true feelings--not to mention his motives. But this time, he told himself, Frank was wrong. Dead wrong.

Gone nova over Kira. Hell, he'd made his choice. He'd settle down someday, when he was good and ready. In the meantime, he was damn good at what he did, and no woman was going to undermine his plans, or his skills.

No matter how long her legs?

Zeke knew something was amiss when he first entered his quarters and heard the shower running. With a broad sweep of the cabin, his eyes took in a travel pac lying open upon his bunk, a few lacy items hanging over the edge. From there his stunned sights riveted on the half-closed privacy panel of the lav.

"Is that you, Zeke?" came a familiar voice.

Kira.

"You'll never believe where I had to hide this time," she called out. "I'll be out in a second." The sound of the shower stopped, replaced with the hiss of the body dryer.

Frozen in place, Zeke simply stood there, staring at the privacy panel. And here he was beginning to think that between the booze and Frank running interference, he just might survive.

Within minutes the panel slid open and Kira emerged...dressed in another one of his damned shirts. Exasperated, yet intrigued at the same time, Zeke boldly took in every stunning detail. Starting at her bare feet, he inched his way up shapely long legs that disappeared beneath a thigh-length shirt--his shirt. He knew he should back off now, before it was too late. But then, it was already too late.

This is you're wife, don't forget.

"I hope you don't mind me using your shower," she said in a voice that sounded a million miles away and fading fast. "If you could have seen how messy I was, you'd..."

Slater's lazy inspection continued upward, only to stop with insulting regard upon up-tilted breasts that boldly stated she was wearing nothing beneath the shirt. Zeke didn't miss the message. By the time his focus rested upon her face, he was beyond noticing whether Kira's dark auburn hair was hanging loose or pulled back in a thick braid.

"How the hell did you get past security this time?"

Undaunted by his irritation, Kira took a seat in a nearby chair and chattered on while digging through her travel pac for a pair of slippers. "Actually, it was quite simple. I knew Frank wouldn't be leaving the ship while we were at the Banners, so before you and I left the ship, I simply borrowed his security badge as my ticket back on board."

"You stole his badge?"

"No. I borrowed it," Kira clarified. "I brought it back. No harm done. He never even missed it."

"What made you think he wouldn't need it?"

"I heard you tell him to remain on board."

Zeke looked at her in total disbelief.

"I borrowed it before we took off. And as you can see, I brought it right back. But trying to get back on board was not easy," she rattled on. "I had to hide behind some smelly lubricant vat for nearly an hour. Honestly, Zeke, you wouldn't believe..."

Kira's chatter began fading again as Zeke's attention returned to her legs--long...sexy...legs. And when she leaned down to slip on one of her slippers, he received a brief but thorough glimpse of what lay beneath the shirt. His shirt.

"You have no idea just how good that shower felt. Believe me..."

The buzzing in his ears had turned to a roaring as though he were standing too close to a launch deck.

Suddenly, Kira stopped talking and stared up at him, her look suspicious. "I know you're mad, but if you'll--"

"I'm not mad."

"You're not?" Seemingly relieved, Kira rose to her feet and approached him. "Good, because there was just no way I was going to stay on Acacia. Not when I knew you were headed for Echo."

Bleary-eyed and badly in need of a shave, Zeke gazed down into his wife's expressive face and intense green eyes. Wife. Odd how he didn't choke on the word this time.

"Oh, Zeke," she prattled on, "if you'll just give me half a chance, I promise you won't be sorry. In fact, I'm a quick learner. If there's anything I can do to be of use..."

Again, Kira's voice faded into oblivion. His eyes settling on her parted mouth, Slater's primed body was about to shift into automatic pilot.

~ * ~

The intensity with which he was regarding her made her nervous. Despite her inexperience, Kira recognized the look with instinctive clarity. Strange how she felt weakened, yet exhilarated all at once. Unmistakably alive, and yet at the same time she sensed she was about to be hurled into the farthest reaches of the galaxy.

"I'm sure we can work something out," he breathed, his deep voice alarmingly smooth.

Kira swallowed, unable to drag her eyes from his. Never had she felt so helpless, so out of control as she did at this moment with this man. After last night she could no longer deny that her feelings went beyond the big brother mentality--far beyond. Zeke Slater was anything but a safe haven. He was dangerous, and it was odd how that very thought sent a thrill down her spine. What a change these last weeks had brought about. She hardly went to bed anymore without dreaming of being in his arms, fantasizing that he would see her as more than just an annoyance out of his past.

For what purpose? That cynical inner voice was laughing again. *That he might desire you...surely not love...you?*

A heated flush swept clear to her hairline as her mind and heart sluggishly acknowledged the silly illusion. Any minute now, he would mock her; remind her once again that she was little more than excess baggage, a damned nuisance who had cost him much in credits, time and aggravation. Plus, by law, she was still a slave. Were he ever to be caught with her in his possession, it could mean a variety of severe penalties.

She started to step back.

Zeke grabbed her arm. "You shouldn't be here, you know that?" The roughness of his tone, the raw desire in his eyes stole her breath. Kira swallowed, unable to speak. Heat from his hand sluiced through her like a fire. Once again, her body was turning traitor, and there was nothing she could do about it, even if she wanted to.

"You have any idea what you're doing to me?" His voice sounded hoarse. Tormented.

If it was anything similar to what he did to her, she had a very good idea. A searing flame shot through her as she glanced down at his bronzed, callused hand imprisoning her arm. They were so opposite.

He was bronzed. She was fair.

He was hard. She was soft.

He was lethal...and again, the very thought sent a bolt of lightning to the pit of her stomach. Was it fear or intrigue? She was finding it harder to differentiate between the two.

Kira lifted her eyes. Tawny sun-streaked hair was swept back, spilling over his collar like liquid. He was the most ruggedly handsome man she'd ever set eyes upon. Oh, yes, she had a very good idea what he might be feeling.

"When I was eighteen," she began in a breathless whisper, "our little team of rescuers received an anonymous lead that an escaped slave was hiding inside a restricted zone. I volunteered to cross the barricade and search for her." She shrugged and smiled lamely. "We had no way of knowing it was a set-up. Or that once I crossed the boundaries, the lance of a stun-laser would flash out of nowhere."

Zeke's grip on her arm loosened.

"The first blow knocked me to the ground. The second drove the air from my lungs. I could hardly breathe. There was a terrible roaring in my ears, and every nerve ending in my body was on fire."

With still gray eyes he searched her face and listened.

Kira released a deep, shaky sigh and went on. "When I'm with you--when you touch me, she swallowed then whispered, "I feel like that all over again."

His grasp on her arm fell away.

There, she'd said it. Fearing his laughter more than anything, she dared not so much as a single breath while awaiting his reaction.

A gamut of emotions moved across Zeke's face. Not one of which even remotely suggested amusement. Cool gray eyes searched her features. A tremor lanced through her when he reached out and caressed her cheek with his knuckles.

"Kira." There was tenderness in his husky voice, softness in his gaze...and he'd called her by her name. Not 'Legs.'

The next instant, her left hand was being lifted and turned over. And when his focus dropped to the indelible design on her wrist, she swallowed. Knees weakening, Kira nearly moaned aloud when he brought her hand to his mouth and pressed his lips into her palm. From there he moved to her wrist, and with a kiss so tender it nearly curled her toes, he reverently embraced the very symbol that bound them together.

The roaring in her head returned. Breathless and spellbound by his slow gentleness, Kira closed her eyes, nearly crying out as a rush of longing surged to every nerve ending in her body.

"Mot Siante," he muttered thickly, taking her face in his trembling hands. Lowering his head, he took her parted lips in a slow, drugging kiss.

Kira melted into him as he slid one arm around her waist, drawing her up against his body. She could feel his open palm splayed across her lower back, pressing his hard angles against her soft ones.

"I want you," he whispered roughly against her mouth.

Her knees nearly buckled. She wanted him too--wanted to know this tender side that he hid so well behind stormy emotions and a ruthless façade. Wanted to know what it felt like to be made love to by this man. Yet, what did she know about the ways of love? The years before Renn's death had been so caught up in helping out on the rescue team, there'd never been thought, let alone time for romance.

With a low growl, Zeke's hand slid down to cup her bottom, pulling her intimately against him. The action brought her hips even harder against his taut thighs and hard length.

So physical.

So explosive.

So dangerous.

And deep inside--where no one could see--Kira's inexperienced little heart was suddenly scared to death.

CHAPTER TWENTY-TWO

Introducing Kira to an exquisite form of torment, Zeke ran his tongue softly across her lips, moistening them, parting and probing before slowly easing inside. Growing more insistent, he demanded a response she could no longer deny, and she reveled at his low growl of pleasure when she touched the tip of her tongue to his. But then...just when it was starting to get interesting, he tore his mouth from hers and buried his face against the arch of her neck.

"You think I've forgotten that day you shared your secrets with me? How I held you?"

Kira didn't reply. She couldn't.

"Do you have any idea what it cost me not to have you then--and again last night?"

His voice roughened. "It's nearly cost me my sanity. I can't get the taste of you out of my mind. It's all I think about--when I should be concentrating on other things."

His voice lowered to a growl. "I came to the stable last night to get away from you." Gently entangling his fingers in her hair, he eased her head back. "To try and forget...this." Reclaiming her lips, he crushed her to him. It was no gentle kiss this time, but a fierce possession. A branding.

"I want this damned thing off." Catching the hem of the shirt she was wearing, he began tugging it upward, but in frustration ended up ripping it apart until she stood completely exposed to him--naked, trembling and pink with embarrassment. No man had ever seen her naked before.

"Di'aja," he murmured softly, and for a long moment Zeke stood there watching her, studying her beneath hooded eyes, his expression indecipherable. Eternity seemed to pass before he finally said, "Ever since I found you hiding in the hold, I've been going out of my mind, wanting you."

He had? She would never have guessed. She could tell he had been fighting for control but assumed it was anger and frustration. Not...not passion. And to think she could do this to him was as thrilling as it was frightening.

But then that little silent cynical voice returned, reminding her of her inexperience, her lack of skill. What did she know of lovemaking--of his kind of passion? Would he be disappointed? Would he find his desire dampened by her lack of knowledge and inability to please? Suddenly, fear surged through her, overriding the passion Zeke had stirred to life. Acutely aware of her nudity, she tried covering herself.

"Don't," he groaned. It was said with the force of a command, yet his tone was clearly an appeal. "You're sexy as all hell, baby. Let me look at you."

Unable to deny his husky plea, Kira's hands fell to her side.

Zeke groaned.

She trembled.

"Kira," he said gently, as though sensing the extent of her innocence. "Don't be afraid, honey."

It wasn't him she was afraid of. Her fear of him was long past. No, it was her own inexperience that scared her. Yet, here she was, stark naked as he towered over her, his broad chest and shoulders blotting out all else within her line of view. Face unshaven and hair spilling over his shoulders, he looked like a cross between a bronzed savage and a pagan god. And he said don't be afraid? She was terrified.

Zeke reached out and gently brushed the swell of her breast with one knuckle.

Kira swallowed, or at least attempted to. Lowering her gaze, she watched him touch her again--noting how tanned he was against her own flesh. The visual alone stole her breath. His very touch weakened her.

"Would you stop if I asked?" she whispered breathlessly, watching as he drew his callused thumb across a tip.

"You want me to stop?" he asked in languid challenge.

She couldn't answer as again he passed his thumb across the taut, sensitive bud.

"Hmm? You want me to stop, Kira?"

She nodded. "Yes." But it was so weak it was hardly believable, even to her own ears.

"Then why are you shaking?"

Still speechless, she raised her eyes to his and found his stormy gaze searching her features.

"Tell me to stop, and I will." Again, he lightly traced one finger across her nipple, watching her reaction. When she drew in a sharp breath, he bent to take her lips again. "Just say the word, honey," he murmured against her mouth.

Her lips were tender from his kisses. Her heart was pounding and getting louder.

"Dear God, you're beautiful," she heard him breathe. Pulling away from her, he slowly began unbuttoning his shirt, never taking his eyes from her.

Losing the battle to embarrassment, Kira snatched up the torn shirt he'd ripped off of her and clutched it to her chest. Though it hardly sufficed as a shield, Slater would have none of it.

"Don't hide from me, baby." Gently taking the tattered scrap from her hands, he tossed it aside. "You have no idea how sexy you are." Her knees weakened another notch as he finished unbuttoning the shirt he was wearing, pulled it free of his pants and dropped it.

Forbidding her eyes to follow the dusting of hair trailing downward, Kira lost her breath at the taut-muscled wall before her. Recently, she'd lain awake in the night fantasizing about being held and loved by this man. But never had her imagination conjured up the bronzed perfection that faced her now.

Several old wounds had left their marks across his chest and midsection. Yet it was the jagged half-healed wound on his left forearm that caught her eye and sent a lance of guilt and regret straight to her trembling heart. "Does it still hurt?" she whispered.

He looked at her, confused. "Does what still hurt?"

"Your arm."

He shrugged. "Only when I've used it too much." With tenderness he cupped her cheek, his look galvanizing. "It's you that makes me hurt."

Kira glanced up into gray eyes that were regarding her with a sharpness that sent her pulse skittering. "I--I'm afraid that I'm not very good at this," she whispered before she could stop herself.

A slow, lazy smile tugged at the corners of his sensuous mouth as he drew her into his arms. "Then I'll just have to teach you as we go." Pulling her closer, he molded her body to his and brushed a gentle kiss upon her forehead. "Don't worry," he murmured in a tight voice. "We'll take it slow."

He took her mouth again, flooding her senses with the lingering taste of the liquor he'd been drinking, the scent of leather, cold steel and something she couldn't begin to name. The combination was so heady and so sensual an odd lurching coiled in the pit of her stomach.

"You're driving me crazy," he groaned. And the proof was a blatant hardness straining beneath taut leathers against her belly.

When she was sure her legs would buckle, he swept her up weightlessly into his arms and started for the shadowed bunk. "Zeke..."

"Shhh. Let me take care of you, baby."

Kira locked her arms about his neck and turned her face into the curve of his shoulder. "You might be disappointed," she whispered as old insecurities taunted her from the edge.

She felt his dimpled smile against her temple. "You think so, huh?" Laying her down on the bunk, he followed her down, bracing splayed hands on either side of her head. Again, he murmured something in a language she didn't understand, and her insides clenched at the smoldering flame she saw in his eyes. His mouth found hers again and the only sounds were the steady hum of the ship's drives, the hiss of life support and the pounding of her heart at his kiss, his touch. Stars, his touch--Kira gasped as his mouth and hands explored and played over every inch of her body, finding sensitive places she never even knew existed.

She held her breath when he discovered the unalterable tattoo of slavery marring the underside of her left breast. He asked no questions--made no comment. Comprehension registered briefly upon his features as his fingertips traced the coded numbers that certified she was someone else's property. Then, before she could inhale, Kira felt the warmth of his mouth upon her--there, laving the very imprint that would seal his fate if he were ever caught with her in his possession. Once again, reaching for her left wrist, he brought its underside to his lips for yet another burning kiss. It was a graphic statement that needed no words as he paid homage to the very symbol that confirmed she belonged to him, and him alone.

Returning his attentions to her body, Kira gloried in the shocking exploration of his gentle hands as he skimmed her breasts, her ribs, her waist and tightly clamped legs. In an onslaught of kisses and soothing words he coaxed her into relaxing, sweet-talked her into unclenching those sexy long legs. Then, as soft as a whisper, he touched her--there--a touch so gentle and so reverent it was barely perceptible. Kira held her breath, acute embarrassment warring with curiosity as he slowly, tenderly initiated her into the magical world of erotic sensation. A world he had mastered long ago.

Sighs turned to moans as Slater paced himself to her responses. Taking his time, he methodically strung her out until she was all but crying for release. Only then did he rise from the bed, never taking his eyes from her as he began, one by one, undoing the straining fly of his pants. Eyelids heavy, Kira could not look away as his splendid nudity was revealed, his muscled body, supple and sleek. A distinct tan line rode low on his hips, and she noticed several old scars upon his abdomen, another on his thigh. And then...and then her gaze fell on the fully aroused length of him. "Blazes," she whispered. Intrigued and yet at the same time knowing a rush of feminine fear, Kira's eyes shot back to his face. Zeke's expression was intense and she knew in an instant that he was allowing her that moment of curious perusal.

Embarrassed to find herself staring, Kira closed her eyes as he returned to her, the bunk dipping beneath his knee, his scent heaven as he bent to kiss her. "Kira, don't be afraid. Look at me, baby." She opened her eyes to find him hovering over her, half on and half off the bunk, his hands on either side of her, bracing his weight. He was magnificent--the rawness of his very image reminiscent of some mythical deity seducing a planet-bound mortal. "We'll take it real slow," he whispered.

Sun-streaked hair cascaded recklessly about his neck, face and shoulders. Hooded gray eyes regarded her with an intensity that stole her breath. She gasped when his knee shifted, once again coaxing her clenched legs to open for him. "*Etal dionte.*"

Gentle pressure, a skillful hand, and soft exotic words. It was a killer combination that cajoled Kira into relaxing. "That's it, honey," he whispered, continuing the onslaught as he eased himself into the cradle of her thighs.

Kira found herself gazing up into eyes that were hot with desire. He was stunning, the whipcord muscles of his chest rising and falling with each breath. Her throat ached to tell him--to tell--she couldn't even remember what she wanted to say. It was hard to talk when her breath kept catching. Slipping her hands over the flex of hard biceps, she clung to him like a buoy in the midst of a storm.

"Zeke?" The question ended in a low moan as his mouth closed with exquisite delicacy on the tender tip of her breast. He exercised no discipline when it came to using his tongue, even as his sex gently caressed her.

Again and again he glided against her, readying her to receive him, sending shards of pleasure radiating through her with each stroke. "Zeke," she whispered, "I'm not experienced in--I don't know how to--" Again her breath caught. It was a stupid confession anyway. As if he hadn't already noticed.

He grinned and shifted his weight to heighten the contact. "Experience isn't always better," he answered, and Kira melted, shocked by the pleasure that was building inside.

"But," she added brokenly, "I would know better how to please you if I--"

"You already please me. Heaven help me if you were more experienced."

"But others--"

"Aren't my wife." He stopped and lifted his head from her breast to look at her. "They aren't my wife, Kira." And then his mouth was slanting across hers, his tongue sliding past the barrier of her lips--even as he carefully entered her delicate and incredibly tight body.

It was inevitable, this moment of tender conquest. Kira was in so far over her head that she never even realized she was drowning until--

Inhaling sharply, she froze.

Zeke stopped, his breathing shallow as he rested his forehead against hers and silently waited. Several long, tense moments ticked by. Her small trembling hands clung to his arms. She could feel the powerful sinews standing out like cords as he supported his weight off her.

"*Dionte*," he whispered against her ear. He then kissed her tenderly, leisurely exploring her lips, his tongue teasing the corners of her mouth. "*Nodoni.*"

Kira's eyes fluttered closed as once again she slipped beneath the magic of murmured words in a strange and alien language.

~ * ~

If she only knew how unsure he was of himself at this moment. Never had Zeke known such overwhelming tenderness. This was Kira-- his wife. His control slipping fast, he advanced slowly, his senses jolted by her tight heat. Damn, he hadn't even thought about her being a virgin. "Kira," he murmured unsteadily, wishing he had the strength to withdraw right now.

She didn't answer. Her hands were at his hips, wordlessly urging him on. It was enough to completely shatter what little control he had left. "Honey," he whispered against her throat, "I promise it will only hurt this once." Feeling like a bungling youth, he withdrew slightly, then with a quick thrust he sank deep within her.

Kira gasped and caught her lower lip between her teeth. Moments passed as Zeke waited, hardly daring to breathe while allowing her time to adjust.

~ * ~

For Kira, with her eyes squeezed tightly shut, it was a time for serious reevaluation. *So this is what all the giggling and fantasizing is about? This pain? This burning fullness?* Far as she was concerned, sex was vastly overrated. Although she had to admit the first part was wonderful--the kisses, the touching, the whispered words that set her heart to pounding. But this... It certainly wasn't the heaven she'd expected.

At last her eyes flew open. "Is that it?"

Zeke, the brute, actually started laughing. And Kira, certain she was the brunt of a cruel joke, did her best to shove him off. His superior weight, however, kept her pinned in place. And the worst of it was they were still intimately joined. Humiliated all the more, she stiffened, desperately trying to ignore the tinge of pleasure that was slowly replacing the pain. "So, now that you're done," she snapped in a tone of pure disappointment, "I insist you get off of me and let me up."

"Who said I'm done?"

"Blazes, don't tell me there's more?"

In answer, he moved within her--ever so slightly. Embers of pleasure burst into flame, eliciting a moan from Kira's lips. "Oh yes," he murmured as he began moving with shallow rhythmic strokes, "I'm afraid there's more." He kissed her tenderly, his tongue teasing the corners of her mouth.

The transformation from pain to pleasure was swift and startling. As quickly as it came, the pain was replaced by waves of hot pleasure.

"Wrap those sexy long legs around me, honey," he whispered against her ear. She did as he asked, and he eased deeper and deeper still until he was fully seated. At last he took a shuddering breath. "Ah, baby," he murmured, "are you for real, or am I dreaming?"

His words were a blur, barely discernible through the heat that was beginning to throb through her veins. Kira caught her breath and held it. So this was the magic--this giving and taking between a man and woman. She was lost to the feel of his invasion, the force of his powerful body slowly and carefully increasing in momentum with each stroke. And he'd called her his wife... His wife.

Zeke controlled the pace, dictating the moves, as Kira gloried in the pleasure of his touch and the steady glide of his possession. Raising her arms above her head, wanton and vulnerable, she sobbed his name, over and over...urging him on with a combination of age old instinct and untutored innocence.

Slow and gentle, he made love to her, never once breaking the tempo he'd set. "That's it, sweetheart," he murmured, his breath warm against her throat. She felt him smooth back a stray lock of damp hair then pressed his mouth to her brow. "Stay with me, honey." Every stroke, every sigh, every whispered endearment impelled Kira higher toward a nameless summit.

"Baby, you feel so damn good." His rough voice made her breath catch. Forcing her eyes open, Kira found him watching her, his jaw clenched with a fierceness of will, his focus entirely on her, the tempo and the rising swell between them.

What would he think tomorrow, she wondered. How did she compare? The thought had barely formed when he picked up the pace. And then there was no more thinking. The spasm hit her hard and by surprise. Crying out his name, she tumbled over the edge, suddenly weightless and free.

Zeke followed close behind, his lips pressed to her throat as he spilled into her the essence of his need and love.

Nothing mattered now, Kira thought dreamily. Nothing but this fierce warrior, this privateer whose sweat-dampened body was pressing into her. She could feel his heart pounding against her own, hear his labored breathing in her ear. His hair tickled her face, a tawny mane she vaguely recalled dragging her hands through.

She sighed, loving the scent of his hair, the scent of him, feeling incredibly sated and amazingly drowsy. For several long minutes, they lay joined until with a soft moan of protest, Kira felt him slowly withdraw, the bunk shifting as he got up.

"Zeke?"

"Be right back."

Languid with fulfilled pleasure, her eyes had drifted shut again by the time he returned.

"I should have shaved," he muttered.

Kira lifted her heavy lids long enough to see him opening a small black jar.

"This will help soothe the burns on your skin," he said. The next thing she knew, a silky, fragrant smelling ointment was being gently smoothed onto her cheeks, her lips and her breasts.

"Ummm," she sighed with a groggy smile. "What is that?"

"Acuel salve," she heard him answer.

"Ohhh. The same ointment we used on your arm. It smells nice." She felt the bunk shift again and peered up to find Zeke leaning over her, a frown marring his handsome face as he smoothed another lock away from her eyes. "Are you alright?"

"I'm perfect," she breathed. "Just per--fect."

He laughed softly. "Yes, that you are." Within moments Kira felt his weight settle down next to her, his arms pulling her into his embrace.

~ * ~

All too soon Kira had fallen asleep, leaving Zeke alone with his thoughts. Cradling her in his arms, he stared vacantly up at the metal ceiling, its satin sheen mirroring their images in a murky sort of way. Eyes narrowing with interest, he studied the blurred reflection overhead, noting the differences in skin tones and hair color as their bodies blended together. Ah god, why did temptation have to seem so right with her?

It was only a matter of time before reality reared its ugly head, as he knew it would. His commitment, the vows and pledges leered at him from the shadows. Reason washed over him in gut-wrenching waves.

Kira sighed and curled deeper into his embrace, the gesture almost possessive, as if on some unconscious level she feared he might leave her. Truth be known, if he had the strength, he would leave her--run like hell and not stop running until the tenderness raging through him had ceased.

What sobered him more than anything, though, was the glow he'd seen on Kira's sweet face. She shone with all the radiance of--God forbid--a woman in love.

And what did you expect?

Everything had happened so fast he hadn't thought to expect anything. Hell, he hadn't thought, period.

Kira. Her name drifted through his mind on a whisper. With a labored sigh, he adjusted her so that her head rested on his shoulder and his arm curled about her rib cage, possessively concealing the mark of slavery beneath her breast.

Love. Ordinarily, the very mention of the word would have sent him running. He'd never before had trouble keeping his emotions in line. Why was it so different with Kira--who only yesterday was no more than an annoying teenager?

Remember Echo? Major Metals? The mission you've taken on for this woman--not to mention for the ILE? a silent voice reminded. *You'd better get the blood back up to your brain where it belongs.*

Where the devil was his sense of self-preservation? Hell, if he were smart, he'd apologize, give her back Frank's cabin and promise it would never happen again.

But since he wasn't in the habit of making promises he knew he couldn't keep, he drew Kira deeper into his embrace. God help him, he wanted her again.

CHAPTER TWENTY-THREE

Solar Wind's aft cargo hold:

"Snakes?" Marc Banner's deep voice rose several decimals in volume. "Why the hell snakes?"

Stifling his amusement, Clint turned to face his youngest brother. "Because they happen to be the one thing that will get your butt through security. That's why. They might lift the lid, but I guarantee that's as far as it will go."

"Hell. Nobody ever said anything about snakes."

"It's something I came up with shortly before we left home," Nick interjected as he made his way across the chamber.

Though the snakes were non-venomous, it was a relatively common sight to see shipments of them coming through the spaceport. The snakes were excellent hunters and often used to clear newly opened mines and surrounding areas of undesirable vermin. Nick knew about the snakes from when he'd spent two years on Echo. He'd changed a lot since then. Back then he'd work any high paying job he could--no matter the risk.

Marc snorted. "That figures. I notice you're not volunteering to climb in with them."

"And cheat you out of the honor?" Nick laughed. "I wouldn't dream of it. Besides, Slater hand-picked each one of those beauties personally." He clapped Marc on the back and added, "With you being such a ladies' guy and all, he made sure they're all females."

That brought on the chuckles--even from a few eavesdroppers.

"Very funny," Marc muttered with a look that could have dried up an ocean. "You got any more surprises I should know about?"

"Nope." Clint replied. "Other than the snakes, nothing's changed. Talbot will still be playing delivery boy until he gets you through security. From there, some guy named Logan will take you out to Major Metals."

"Who is this Logan, anyhow? How do we know he's not going to simply turn us over?"

"The only thing we can go on is that Black Fox lined him up," Nick said.

Seconds ticked by before Marc finally growled, "You guys owe me for this. Big time."

Clint laughed. "Just get your ass in there and let's try this contraption out."

~ * ~

Port Ore, Echo:

Disguised as a port maintenance worker, Matt Logan sank into the shadow of a nearby landing jack and watched Quint Kendyl make his way across the LZ. The man walked with the bold arrogance of someone who feared no one. There was a sense of brutality about Kendyl--a callousness that in Logan's opinion would make anyone think twice about crossing him.

It had been just in the last year that he'd seen Kendyl in Preston's office. More so, after Delaney had been killed. It wasn't long after, there was an influx of equipment and supplies as new mines were suddenly being established and old ones reopened. Security had been strengthened and shiploads of slaves were being brought in on regular intervals. Hadn't Major Metals always prided themselves on the fact that they used no slave labor? Hell, it was about time somebody was checking things out. A sense of pride welled in him at the thought that he would play an important role in the investigation.

~ * ~

Quint Kendyl stepped over a cluster of service lines leading into the belly of a nearby ship. He still couldn't believe his luck. Zeke Slater might not be Nick Banner, but he sure as hell was the next best thing and would be the first to die. The way he saw it, Slater was just as responsible for the raging inferno on Steel that day. The devastation had ended in the complete annihilation of Steel's docking bay, and had nearly cost him his life when the Renegade--his prized yacht--blew up before his eyes, spewing fiery fuel and entire sections of the hull in every direction.

Kendyl made his way up a short flight of stairs and out onto a parking area where Grant Preston had arranged for a company vehicle to be waiting for him.

Banner. He wanted that devil with a ferocity words couldn't even describe. The debt that man owed was about to be paid, and Kendyl intended to see that it was paid in blood. The burns he'd suffered, the days he'd lingered on the brink of death--the resulting scars. It had all festered far too long and there was only one way to ease it.

Oh, how he'd dreamed of this moment. How many times had he played out in his mind the different scenarios of punishment he would inflict upon Banner? Exquisite forms of torture, intended to maim, not kill--at least not right away, not until full retribution had been extracted and he had Banner begging for the release of death. His tight face curled into a twisted humorless grin at the very thought of testing a few of those hellish procedures on Banner's sidekick. Fitting entertainment, he reasoned, while waiting for the rescue party to show up. And there was no doubt in his mind but that Banner would come looking for his missing business partner, and when he did, there'd be one hell of a surprise in store for him.

~ * ~

One hour later, the small company-owned ground runner pulled up to the front gates to Major Metals Mining. Kendyl flashed the required credentials and proceeded on to the designated parking area. From there it was a quick trip through the main entrance of the small two-story structure and up a flight of stairs to where it opened into a large office--Preston's office.

"I didn't expect you for at least another two hours," Grant said, glancing up from his desk.

Kendyl's face was pulled in a tight lopsided grin as he settled into a nearby chair. "Let's just say I hurried. So, what's happening?"

"I have men posted at every exit of the spaceport with images of the Delaney girl, Slater and a detailed description of his ship."

"Good."

Preston looked at Kendyl appraisingly. "Remember what I said. If you kill Slater before I get that document endorsed..."

Kendyl grinned. "Believe me, I have no intentions of killing Slater. Live bait's always better than dead."

Preston nodded. "Just as long as we understand each other. I don't give a damn what you do with him, or his partner, for that matter. I just don't want my leverage or my bargaining power with the girl jeopardized. I've waited too damn long for this."

"And you think I haven't?"

"I just don't want any more screw-ups, that's all," Preston muttered.

"There won't be, I assure you. We'll know the instant *Solar Wind* touches down."

A muscle quivered in Preston's jaw as he rose from his seat. "Yeah, well, with all that's happened so far, I'd say Slater would have to be pretty stupid not to be wary. Especially if he's still got the girl with him."

"Slater's anything but stupid," Kendyl offered. "But, what reason would he have to suspect anyone here? My guess is he's on a routine delivery and dropping the girl off on the way. Fuel's too costly, and time's too valuable for him to be making out-of-the-way excursions. When he lands, we'll have him."

~ * ~

Solar Wind:

Four hours out of Echo:

The plan was to touch down at Port Ore long enough to unload three snake crates earmarked for Major Metals Mining; then the *Solar Wind* would immediately lift off-planet. Marc would be concealed inside one crate. The other two crates would each contain a volunteer--friends of the Banners, who had agreed to help at the prospect of a little action.

In spite of everything, there was one hitch that still had Zeke worried--a possible security check at Major Metals.

Dropping into the command seat, he entered a code into the MAINCOMP and waited. Hopefully their tails would be covered--even during a security check. That is, if everything went as planned...and the gods were in good moods. Zeke released a compressed breath that puffed out his cheeks. Problem was, if was a big word--especially when it came to the lives of those whose friendship went far beyond the surface.

The recent information he'd loaded into the databanks soon began flooding the system, depicting first an integrated map of Echo's northern hemisphere. He tapped a series of keys and a detailed layout of the entire tract of land owned by Major Metals Mining appeared on screen, including the positions of every shack, maintenance shed and sanitary station on site.

With a long, tired sigh, Zeke kneaded the kinked muscles at the back of his neck and studied the screen for what seemed the hundredth time, familiarizing himself with the map, memorizing important landmarks and reviewing the game plan he and the Banners had worked out.

Finally, looking away from the monitor, he rubbed his bleary eyes. How much sleep had he gotten over the last five days? Maybe ten hours at the most? If only he didn't have Kira to worry about on top of everything else. She was the one glitch in the entire plan. Dammit all, she was supposed to have been safe on Acacia, smelling flowers, riding horses and enjoying the friendship of the Banner women, not traipsing halfway across the galaxy to one of the most rugged and untamed planets in the system.

One thing about it: Miss Stowaway wouldn't be setting one foot off-ship. She'd be staying safely aboard under Frank's eye--even if it meant locking her in the cabin. He refused to think how he'd tried that tactic once before.

The last thing he needed was to have her involved any more than she already was. Bottom line: he didn't trust Preston. Renn's partner or not, gut instinct said the man was up to something--something Renn had possibly discovered and was ultimately killed over. Everything was just a little too coincidental. At one point, he'd considered sharing his concerns with Kira then decided against it.

Zeke tapped in another key and the screen switched to reveal a detailed illustration of every exit off the property. Clint and Nick would be disrupting the security on the closest gate to Preston's office.

So far, the only things he had to go on were the screwed-up company ledgers, part of which included purchase orders that Kira never okayed. And another thing was the voice duplications Frank had discovered. Someone was ordering equipment--and lots of it--under Kira's name and using a nearly identical voice pattern.

Slater absently worked the protesting muscles of his injured arm. As for the attack on Lilo, he had his reservations. He wasn't sure he bought the idea that they were simply two slimeballs out for a good time at a young woman's expense. Maybe to an untrained eye they appeared as such. But they were both too heavily armed for his peace of mind. Poison coated slugs were not only illegal--they were not easily accessible. The way he saw it, if Preston was trying to rid himself of Kira, then the attack on Lilo was most likely another failed attempt.

"Won't be long now," Nick said, taking the short flight of stairs two at a time.

Zeke released a heavy sigh and swiveled about to face his friend. "We passed their robo sensors about an hour ago. *Solar Wind's* made contact with Port Ore and we've locked in an approach vector. Should be hitting dirt in a little over three hours."

"Good." Nick dropped into the co-pilot's seat. Patting his pockets, he found one of his small cigars, bent his head and lit up. "They've just finished with a trial run on the crates back there. Everything's a go," he added, releasing a stream of smoke overhead.

That brought a grin to Zeke's face. "I can just hear Marc."

Nick burst out laughing. "Never was a happier guy. Out of all three crates, his was the only one cursing."

Still grinning, Slater reached for his mug of coffee. "Did you remind him that talking containers almost never make it past security?"

"You should have heard him after Clint pounded on his crate and told him to shut the hell up. If he thinks it's bad now, wait 'til he gets to share his space with the snakes."

One of the sweet benefits of privateering was the confiscation of interesting spoils off enemy freighters. As an example, the crates the men would be hiding in were far from an average run-of-the-mill shipping crate. Instead, they were specially designed double-walled smuggling crates. Though not necessarily intended for concealing a man behind its false inner panel, it was, nevertheless, a viable option if the man folded his legs and curled into a tight ball.

Nick quickly ran through the plans outlining their objective. "Even with the words 'Live Snakes' plastered on the crates," he said, "it's still possible some hotshot inspector will call a full-blown inspection."

"All right," Zeke said, pondering the consequences, "as planned, the top half of each crate will contain the cages of snakes. But, what if we leave one cage empty, the door ajar suggesting a loose snake somewhere inside?"

Nick nodded in agreement. "That should discourage even the most ambitious inspector."

"And, by the time they arrive at Major Metals," Zeke went on, "we'll be returning dirtside disguised as the *Revenge*. The coordinates are already locked-in for that isolated LZ at the south boundary." Zeke didn't like the idea of bringing the *Revenge* dirtside; it was too damn risky. But unfortunately, transforming the ship into the *Revenge* was the only way to raise *Solar Wind's* hidden weaponry to the surface of her hull. No way in hell were they going back down unarmed.

Frowning, Nick absently watched smoke trail off the tip of his cigar. "Just exactly how much does Kira know about our plans?" he asked pointedly, his gaze lifting to meet Zeke's.

"Enough."

"You mean enough to bring this operation crashing down around us if she--"

"I can handle Kira."

Directing a stream of smoke toward the floor, Nick leaned back in the chair and studied his partner for a thought-filled moment. Finally, he said levelly, "All I can say is, you'd better be damn sure of her." Slowly shaking his head, he added incredulously, "Whew...first Celeste, now Kira. What's with you and women, lately?"

Zeke groaned, wondering the same thing.

"So, have you decided yet what you're going to do with the little wife while you're off-ship?"

Zeke ignored the taunt. There was no doubt where the conversation was headed from here. The bantering had been virtually non-stop from all of them ever since Kira was discovered on board. Even if he hadn't bedded her, just the looks on their faces alone said they wouldn't have believed it. No, there was only one thing to do: ignore the whole lot of them. But God help him, it wasn't easy. One thing he'd learned over the years about the Banners: there was no backing off...especially when they knew they were right.

Still waiting for an answer to his question, Nick sat forward. "Surely you're not thinking of taking her with you?"

"Hell, no."

"I trust you intend to have her well guarded?"

Again Slater ignored him.

"Look, Zeke, if she's anything like Tressa--"

"Frank will be watching her," Zeke snapped. Leaning forward, he tapped in another key and brought forth the ship's log.

"Frank?" Nick jerked the cigar from his mouth. "You can't be serious. She'll have him eating out of her hand before we even clear the gates. And by the time we get back, she'll either be off the ship or at the helm. One of the two."

"You have a better idea?"

Nick cleared his throat. "Not at the moment."

Zeke didn't respond. Instead he focused on updating the log on the computer:

Stopped on Paradise, long enough to pick up the shipment of snakes. Time loss recovered, putting us once again on schedule. Decision was made to keep... He paused before completing his thought. ...Frank on board with Kira once we set down on Echo.

"But then again," Nick added into the silence, "I suppose under the circumstances Frank's your safest bet. After all, it is your wife we're talking about here, isn't it?"

Eyes narrowing, Zeke looked up from the MAINCOMP. "You're pushin' it, Nick."

"Just agreeing with you, that's all." He punctuated the sentence by blowing three lazy smoke rings into the air.

With a muttered oath, Zeke rose to his feet. "Whatever Kira and I have--or don't have between us--has absolutely nothing to do with my decisions on running this ship. You got that?"

"What you have between you is marriage, pal."

Nick's placating tone was grating. His narrowed eyes and cocky grin said he was well aware of it, too. Slater reached for his mug. "You know...I'm only going to say this one...more...time. The only damn reason Kira and I are bonded is because I didn't happen to have a whole lot of options to choose from. As soon as we get back to civilization, it's over. Period."

"Oh yeah? And, in the meantime, what is she? Your mistress? Exactly what's her role, Slater?"

Slater stopped mid-stride. A heartbeat later, his boots echoed down the corridor.

~ * ~

It hurt. It shouldn't have, but it did. Kira sank back into the shadows of a small storage alcove as Zeke stormed past. She'd overheard enough of the conversation to understand the exact meaning behind Zeke's response to Nick's accusation.

And just who the hell was Celeste? Obviously, someone else in his life.

You foolish, lovesick girl. Did you think you owned his heart? the silent voice laughed.

Taking a deep breath, Kira swallowed hard, willing the tears not to fall. And here she'd been looking for him to tell him that she'd just made a batch of temberberry biscuits under Frank's tutelage. What a joke. If they weren't in flight, she'd walk out of Zeke Slater's life this very instant and never look back. Furthermore, if he thought she was staying on board with Frank, he was sadly mistaken.

~ * ~

The heady aroma of temberberry biscuits teased his nostrils as Zeke entered the galley. Frank's been busy, he thought, reaching for one of the tasty treats. Refilling his mug, he made his way to a nearby table and eased into a chair. Plain and simple: there was no room in his life right now for the demands of a commitment. Once they got back to Acacia, the vows they were forced into would be renounced and officially recorded.

What about the tattoo on her wrist?

If it can be erased, he'd pay to have it removed.

And the loss of her virginity? the silent voice taunted.

That was the one thing he could not pay for--or erase. And it was the one thing he truly regretted, despite the fact she'd been sharing his bunk ever since. He cursed the lust that held him prisoner. Kira was a flash fire he couldn't douse. No matter how much he hated the weakness in himself, there was no stopping when it came to taking her into his arms each night.

Reaching for his mug, he leaned back. Somehow he'd find a way to make it up to her.

CHAPTER TWENTY-FOUR

Port Ore, Echo:

It was nighttime on Echo when *Solar Wind* touched down. Easing the ship gently onto her landing jacks, Slater killed power and began putting everything else on standby. All four external vid screens revealed different angles of the surrounding landing zone. On the port side, darkened silhouettes of other ships sat within their berths, each pad outlined by a ring of bluish-green float lights. Beyond, on the starboard side, stood the blocky shape of Port Ore's single-level terminal building.

The soft chime of the comset heralded a gravelly voice. "Ground Control to Delta Beta, five-niner-five. Please stand by for a routine customs inspection."

"Customs inspection?" Frank muttered. "When did they start performin' routine customs inspections?"

Slater swore under his breath. He was afraid of something like this. Why so efficient all of a sudden? He might have expected it if they were a tramp freighter or if he'd come in as the ominous-looking *Revenge*, but as squeaky clean as the *Solar Wind* appeared, Customs almost always left them alone--at least when it came to a complete security scan.

"Damn good thing we're clean," Frank mumbled, leaning forward and depressing a series of keys that set the NAVCOMP on standby.

With a heavy sigh, Slater touched a keypad on the control panel. "Ground Control, this is Delta Beta, five-niner-five. That's a roger."

The tap of another key put Slater directly into the ship's intercom. "Looks like we're getting the V.I. P. treatment. I suggest you boys clean house and disappear back there. And make it fast."

"Nick here. Let me guess. Customs?"

"You got it. And they're requesting a full look-see."

"Terrific. Try to stall them as long as you can."

"I'll do my best." Zeke rose from his seat. "Frank, give me five minutes then deactivate manual override to the ship's hold and lower the loading ramp."

"Good as done, Capt'n'."

Slater quickly made his way down the corridor, past the storage bins, the common lav and the cabins.

He was just hurrying through the circular lounge/galley when Kira called out coldly, "I take it we're finally there?"

"We are," he called over his shoulder. He could have sworn she sounded pissed about something. He'd noticed it earlier too, but had little time to worry about it then, or now, for that matter. Customs inspectors were notorious for their ill-temper and lack of patience.

Hitting the entry pad with his fist, the lock to the hold cycled open and lights snapped to life the instant Zeke entered. Just as it should be, *Solar Wind's* cargo bay was cool, shadowy and hushed. Nick, Clint and the other volunteers were safely tucked away in the private smuggler's hold behind the aft wall. Zeke glanced toward the secret entry to that hold, finding it safely hidden behind a façade of crowded storage bins rising from deck to ceiling. A touch of a button from either cargo bay moved the camouflage in or out of place.

Zeke's roving eyes quickly grazed the chamber for anything suspicious, but found nothing. The three crates labeled 'Live Snakes' were stacked near the exterior hatch, ready to be unloaded along with the equipment that had been originally picked up back at Port Chance. All were tagged for Major Metals. From there he moved to the crates, giving each one a light tap. "Everyone all right?" The answering replies gave little doubt as to which crate Marc was sequestered in. His caustic aversion to the snakes was about the only thing that put a half grin on Zeke's face. "Okay, listen up all of you. We've been tagged for a customs inspection, and things are going to take a little longer than expected. So quiet from this point on."

"Boss, Customs runner approachin' now," came Frank's voice over the intercom.

Zeke moved to the wall and pressed the touch pad. "On my way." Before turning, he hit the intercom again, linking both cargo bays. "Nice job, guys. We look real clean."

"Now for a slide-in-slide-out inspection," Clint replied from the other side.

"Exactly." Disengaging the com, Zeke released a compressed breath of air and turned for the exit. Once again he made his way back down the corridor, through the circular lounge/galley and past the cabins. He'd just arrived at the main lock when a loud bong sounded on the hull, followed by a husky voice announcing, "Inspector Martin here...open up!"

Zeke had learned long ago there were only two kinds of customs inspectors: honest ones and corrupt ones. Of the two, corrupt was always preferable. Honest inspectors were notorious for being picky and meticulously thorough. In short, they were a major pain in the ass.

An indicator light switched from red to green as the outer hatch cycled open. Slater touched a button and a tiny vid screen came to life as the inspector stepped through the outer hatch and into the small interlock chamber separating the outer and inner hatches.

Zeke nearly groaned aloud. One look was all he needed to know that the inspector on the other side of the inner hatch meant one bitch of a headache before this ordeal was over. With a compressed breath that puffed out his cheeks, Zeke slid into the cocky hotshot persona he played so well at times like this. Patting his pockets, he found the trusty pack of cigarettes he kept for just such occasions, withdrew one, bent his head and lit up. There was a fine line between looking too straight, and looking a little too shifty. The idea was a hit somewhere in the middle. At last, palming the lock, he stepped back and waited for the inner hatch to cycle open.

"Inspector, welcome aboard," Slater drawled, releasing a lazy stream of smoke into the air. All the reasons for having quit smoking several years ago came slamming back in one nauseous wave.

Inspector Martin greeted him with an insulting once-over as he stepped through the inner hatch and glanced about. He had an ingrained look of snobbery. Roughly six feet tall and impeccably neat in appearance, his navy blue uniform fit him flawlessly--right down to his highly polished police-style gun belt. Every hair on the man's slick dark head seemed to be lying obediently in place, including his perfectly shaped mustache.

Not a good sign.

"You're master of this vessel?" Martin asked, activating his transacomp.

"The one and only. Blake Helford's the name," Zeke lied, using the fictitious name he operated the *Solar Wind* under.

Martin looked bored as he carefully entered information into his transacomp. "Okay," he said with a jaded sigh, "first let's have a look at your registry, itinerary and the cargo manifest."

Shoving the cigarette into the corner of his mouth, Zeke produced the required but carefully doctored data strip, which the inspector accepted and slid into a slot on his transacomp. With a touch of a key, information began filling the mini-screen. Though most of the information was false, it was a flawless piece of work and another sweet benefit of being a privateer.

"This gonna take long?" Zeke asked with deliberate impatience. With a crooked grin, he added, "You see, I gotta hot little muff I'm supposed to meet in about--"

"Ship: *Solar Wind*," Martin interrupted, "registered to one Blake Helford on Earth."

"That's right," Zeke responded. "And, like I was saying, I'm supposed to--"

"It says here your flight originated on Earth at the Phoenix Agricultural and Hydroponics Research Complex where you took on fifteen thousand pounds of fresh citrus."

"That's right," Zeke replied again.

"The most recent port of call," the inspector continued in an all-business tone, "Terra Four."

"Correct."

One patronizing eyebrow rose. "Fresh fruit? What the hell does someone do with fifteen thousand pounds of fresh fruit before it spoils?"

Slater did his best to smile smoothly. "I didn't ask, Inspector. I make it a practice to do my job and collect my credits at the end of the run."

Martin glanced back down at the screen again. "It says here you're headed for Elrod after you leave here."

No response. The man was really starting to get on Zeke's nerves. At this rate, they'd be here all night.

"Is that correct?" Martin asked again, this time looking up at Zeke for the answer.

"Yes, sir," Zeke replied.

"You understand with all the smuggling going on, we can't be too careful these days," Martin added self-righteously.

"Of course."

"Personally, if they'd just waste them when they catch them, it would have those idiots thinking twice about loading contraband into their holds."

"Yes, sir," Slater added gravely. "I'm sure it would."

Martin lowered his slick dark head and finished his entry. "Well, Mr. Helford," he said with a nod toward the bow of the ship, "shall we see what we have aboard?"

Zeke waved him on with a sweep of his arm. "After you, Inspector."

They were just passing the cabins in route to the helm when the entry to the captain's cabin slid open and Kira stepped out. "Oh, Blake," she said in a voice so smooth no one but Zeke would have picked up on the contempt behind it. "Why, I was just coming to look for you. I've changed my mind, and I'll be getting off here after all."

Zeke went still. Then, quickly regaining his composure, he smiled and said lightly, "Honey, I don't think that's a very good idea."

"I'll be just fine, Blake," Kira said, emphasizing his fake name with each use. She was dressed in a pair of blue jeans, a yellow T-shirt and a brown leather jacket--something Tressa or Rae had obviously given her. A backpack was slung over one shoulder.

"This is really not a good place to get off, Sunshine." He kept the smile on his face, his voice lightly pleasant. "You know father's expecting me to keep you safe." He turned to face Martin. "My sister," he explained with a shrug. In undertones he added, "She's headstrong."

Martin smiled and nodded sympathetically. "I know what you mean. I have two sisters just like her."

If looks could kill, Zeke would be dead by now. With a huff of a sigh, Kira simply stared at him. "Do yourself a favor and don't lose any sleep over me. Okay?"

He reached for her, caught her by her wrist and pulled her close. "What the hell's the matter with you?" he whispered.

"You'd better let go of me, Zeke," she whispered back. "Now."

Martin cleared his throat. Slater turned to face the inspector. "She seems to be feeling ill," he explained, his teeth all but clenched. "Allow me to see her to her cabin."

With that Kira delivered her parting shot. "Nooo..." she moaned, seemingly on the verge of bursting into tears. "Please, Blake. Don't make me go back. We've been sharing your cabin these past few weeks and...sniffle, sniffle. I can't...I just can't do this anymore." More sniffling. "With you being my brother and all...it...it just isn't right."

That brought Martin's head up, his beady eyes piercing the distance between them.

Instantly releasing her, Zeke remained frozen in place. Kira had cleverly managed to maneuver him into a very difficult position, leaving him only one way to avoid detainment at best, and arrest at worst. As much as it scared the hell out of him to turn her loose, he had no choice. "You damn well better watch yourself out there," he said quietly.

Up went Kira's chin. "Your concern is touching."

That comment only deepened the frown of confusion on Slater's face as she swept past him, palmed the lock and exited the ship. Both men were left frozen in place and staring at the hatch cycling closed behind her.

"Well..." Martin's voice broke the silence as he turned to assess Slater. "That was all very interesting."

"Yeah," Zeke muttered, dragging a hand through his hair. "Inspector, shall we proceed? The sooner we get this over with, the sooner I can get back on schedule."

Martin began his inspection at the helm and slowly worked his way back. Whatever Slater might think of the man, Martin wasn't stupid. The inspection of *Solar Wind* was one of the longest and most thorough Zeke had ever been put through.

The haughty inspector asked him about everything from how large a crew he carried to the extra equipment installed in the helm--the very controls that transformed *Solar Wind* into the *Revenge*. But that query was easily explained away as Slater's answers were well rehearsed. After all, it wasn't the first time he'd found himself clearing up an inspector's suspicions about all the extra toggles and switches.

The man was a smuggler's worst nightmare. Looking under, over, behind and around everything, Martin worked his way toward the stern, leaving absolutely nothing to chance. At the officer's insistence, Zeke was forced to take up random deck panels leading to open crawl spaces, and even remove the fasciae off nearly every piece of equipment, thus proving the electronic guts were actually inside.

And all the while Kira was foremost on Zeke's mind. Was she still wandering about alone in Port Ore's ragtag spaceport? Had some slimeball already tried picking her up? She didn't even have a weapon on her.

"Helford, you with me? I said, open this one up too."

Electrodriver in hand, Zeke lowered himself to one knee and began removing the screws holding yet another fascia in place. Customs inspections were always a little unnerving, even under the best of conditions. But, this was going beyond unnerving. Zeke was becoming increasingly fearful the closer they got to the hold. The sonovabitch just wasn't giving up. At this rate it would only be a matter of time before Martin discovered the secret smuggler's hold in the back, find Nick and

Clint hidden there, and eventually uncover Marc and the others tucked away in the snake crates. It wouldn't make any difference to say they were connected with Interplanetary Law Enforcement. The ILE would simply deny any connection, and they'd all be arrested regardless.

And, somehow he had this sinking feeling you don't buy your way out of an Echo prison.

Between his distress over Kira and his growing concern over Martin's uncanny ability to smell out a scam, the rock in his gut felt the size of a man's fist and growing. He resisted the urge to drag his hand through his hair--a telltale sign of nervousness. Even his damn hands were shaking by the time they reached the ship's hold.

Overhead lighting snapped to life as they stepped into cargo bay. The space was filled to half capacity with various sizes of crates and shipping modules lining the scarred deck in neat rows. A massive walk-in refrigerator sat in the far corner, and the three snake crates were positioned directly to the right of the cargo hatch. Slater swallowed as Martin stood there glancing down at the manifest on his transacomp, then gazed about for confirmation.

"What's in the refer?" he asked.

"The citrus you asked about earlier."

"Open it."

Steadying his nerves, Zeke led the way to the refrigeration unit, placed his thumb on the print lock and heard a soft click in response. Pulling the door open, he stepped aside. "Tangerines. Oranges. Grapefruits. You ever tried an Earth-grown orange or tangerine, Martin?" he added, forcing himself to sound calm. In truth, the guy scared the hell out of him. All he could think about was getting rid of this jerk and finding Kira.

"Tangerine?" Martin repeated. "No. I can't say that I have."

Zeke reached in and retrieved a couple of tangerines. "Here," he said, tossing one to Martin, which the man caught single-handed. "Once you try one of these babies, you'll understand why I have fifteen thousand pounds in my hold."

Feeling more like gagging than eating, Zeke eagerly began peeling the rind from his own chilled tangerine. The tangy scent of citrus filled the air as he tossed the rind into a nearby waste receptacle. At last breaking the small fruit into juicy segments, he popped one into his mouth. "Problem is, it will spoil you for anything else," he said around his mouthful.

It was obvious this guy was a die-hard, and nothing--no matter how tempting--would dissuade him from his purpose. Martin's only acknowledgement consisted of a patronizing smile and a vague nod of thanks as he tucked his tangerine into a small pouch hanging off his shoulder. His attention immediately returned to the inspection.

Slater just hoped to hell the sonovabitch didn't go through the hold with the same thoroughness he'd inspected the rest of the ship. At Martin's nod, he led the way up one aisle and down the next, all the while answering questions, while Martin checked off the manifest. Surprisingly, he didn't appear too concerned about the three snake crates, nor did he seem particularly interested in any of the storage racks that lined the bulkhead. Nevertheless, the man was shrewd, and Slater was well aware of it. All it would take at this point was one small slip-up, one tiny sign of being overly anxious or just one too many nonchalant distractions to have Martin calling in a swarm of customs officers to rip the place apart.

At last having adequately toured every aisle, Martin stood near the hatch, entering his final comments into the transacomp. The heat was far from off, and Slater knew it. If anything, Martin would be on his guard more than ever.

Retaining his cocky air, Slater forced himself to reach for the pack of cigarettes in his breast pocket. He'd managed to ditch the first cigarette before retrieving the tangerine. "You smoke?" he asked, extending the pack in invitation.

Martin shook his head. "Never picked up the habit."

With a nod of understanding, Zeke withdrew one, bent his head and lit up. "You've been doin' this for awhile, haven't you?" he drawled with deliberate admiration in his tone.

"Fifteen years at it," Martin boasted. "And there aren't many who have escaped my notice over the years."

"Now, that I can believe," Zeke said, releasing a lazy stream of smoke into the air. "Your skills show, Inspector," he added, wincing against up-trailing smoke. "Yep, I have to say, if I were a smuggler, you'd have me pretty damn nervous."

As hoped, that comment earned a delighted chuckle out of Martin as he glanced back down and made a final entry in his transacomp. "Well, Mr. Helford," he finally said, turning for the exit, "looks like you run a clean ship."

"Thank you, Inspector, I try my best." Zeke followed the man back up the corridor where they came to a halt before the main hatch.

"Yes, well, unfortunately there are those who don't." Releasing a feigned sigh of fatigue, Martin palmed the lock and added, "And that's where I come in."

"You just keep up the good work," Zeke replied sanctimoniously.

Martin accepted Slater's outstretched hand. "Thank you, Captain."

It was all Zeke could do to keep from shouting expletives as the hatch cycled closed. With panic rioting through him, he turned from the main entry and sprinted for the hold.

"Kira's off ship! I'm going after her!" he announced as Nick and Clint emerged from the hidden chamber.

"The hell you are!" they said in unison.

CHAPTER TWENTY-FIVE

"We have clearance," Frank announced and waited for Zeke's command to lift.

No response. Lost in a private world of hesitancy to leave Kira behind, Zeke stared numbly at the controls.

Finally, Frank swiveled about to face him and stared. "We gonna sit here all night or what?"

Silence.

"What do y' want me to tell 'em wer doin'? Havin' a little picnic?"

Zeke turned to his First Officer. "Take 'er up."

Navigational lights flashing, thrusters screaming, the *Solar Wind* lifted off Echo's surface.

It had taken some serious persuasion on the part of both Clint and Nick to convince Slater not to go dirtside in search of Kira. Oddly, Frank had kept to himself during the exchange. In fact, now that Zeke thought about it, the old man had very little to say about anything over the last several hours--an unusual occurrence, and one that gave Zeke the distinct impression that Kira wasn't the only one mad at him about something. With all that had been going on, Frank obviously hadn't had the chance to vent his thoughts yet. But soon enough, he would. There was little doubt of that.

"Initiate the R.C.S.," Zeke said, flipping an overhead toggle, "and give me an immediate scan reading."

Frank's hands moved to the controls to tap in the directive. "Delta two-eight-niner, and..." his eyes shot to the next panel, "Chicago-one-seven-one. She'll top out in...twenty-one seconds."

It wasn't long after that the ship's thrust decreased sharply, reducing the "G's" that were pressing them into their seats.

Zeke leaned forward and entered a series of figures into the console. "Leveling off at zero-zero-three 'til we're clear." His gaze remained fixed on the digital readouts. "Begin switch-over on my mark. Five...Four...Three...Two...One...Mark."

Fingers danced across keyboards, soft chimes proclaimed the completion of procedures and indicators pulsed their response as the *Solar Wind* began the intricate metamorphosis of transforming itself into the dark and ominous *Revenge*.

"You've got to admit," Nick said, "it was a rather creative effort on her part."

Zeke ignored him.

"Cosmetic switchover complete," Frank interjected. "The *Revenge* is up and runnin'."

Zeke engaged the exterior vid and began running a visual on the ship's hull. No longer was the *Solar Wind* shiny silver. As if by magic, its color had been transformed into a menacing blue-black. The christened name was now reading in harsh blood red letters *Revenge*. "Dammit all, I should be down there looking for her," he muttered. "Not up here."

"They'll find her," Nick assured him. Though Zeke strongly doubted Nick's mind would be so easily pacified were it his wife down there instead.

More entries were made into the MAINCOMP by all three men. Buttons were pressed, toggles flipped and soon massive weapons blisters began rising to the surface of the once harmless-appearing exterior hull.

Inset panels on each wing opened up, bringing with it a complete automatic weapons system. At other points along the hull, doors slid open revealing gaping torpedo vents. The *Revenge* was not only fearsome in appearance, she was armed to the teeth and as dangerous and fast as any pirate vessel out there.

"That little gal wouldn't be down there right now y' know, if it weren't for somethun' y' either said or did." Frank's eyes remained on the controls, but his voice reeked with contempt.

Zeke's head came up slowly as he turned to face the old man. "What the hell are you talking about?" he asked quietly.

It was obvious Frank was deliberately stalling as he calmly tapped in another command and waited for the MAINCOMP to confirm. At last he looked over at Zeke and regarded him for what felt like an eternity. "The little thang had gone lookin' for y' to tell y' she'd baked yer favorite biscuits."

Zeke focused on his face, thinking all of a sudden that his First Officer looked as though he had aged twenty years in the last couple of hours.

Frank's tone slid into a deeper twang, his words carelessly drawled as he continued. "Next thang I know, she's cryin'...only she's tryin' real hard to keep me from knowin' it. Y' either did or said somethun'..." The last sentence was tossed out in a tone of pure disdain.

Zeke swallowed as seconds ticked by, then. "Ohhh shhhit!"

"What?" Nick asked.

"She overheard us."

"Overheard what?" Nick asked, clueless.

"Well, she sure as hell heard somthun'," Frank cut in.

The resulting hush was tangible as Nick and Zeke stared at one another.

"*Weapons are fully integrated*," came the sensuous voice of the ship's MAINCOMP echoing into the tense silence. "*Transformation complete.*"

Nick frowned as he stared at Zeke. "What all did we say?"

Dragging a hand through his hair, Zeke's mind raced as he tried recalling what Kira might have overheard during the badgering between Nick and himself. And then the words tumbled through his mind. 'The only damn reason Kira and I are bonded is because I didn't happen to have a whole lot of options to choose from. As soon as we get back to civilization, it's over. Period.'

With the memory came the feeling that he'd just been kicked in the gut. How could he tell her--make her understand that the things he and Nick generally toss back and forth meant nothing? Hadn't he given Nick just as much grief over Tressa before they were married?

"I've gotta find her, Nick. She's down there right now because of me."

"Believe me, I know the feeling. I've been there. But listen to me, if she were still at the spaceport, Clint and Steve would have found her and we would have heard from them by now. Since we haven't, that means she's found a ride out to Major Metals."

Zeke sank back into the seat. "We've got to stop her before she gets to Preston."

"That's right. And the only way we can do that is to get there first."

High in Echo's atmosphere, under the guise of the *Revenge*, coordinates were set for a hundred and fifty kilometers south of Port Ore--a secluded LZ not far from the mining headquarters.

~ * ~

The ragtag terminal was little more than a large three-sided shed. Port Ore was a dirty mining port, geared for the needs, not the comfort of its clientele.

The first thing Kira had done was to find a wall of comphones and make a call out to Major Metals. It was good hearing Grant's voice again, and he seemed genuinely happy to hear hers.

"My God, where are you, honey?" he'd asked so tenderly it nearly made her cry. And when she told him she was standing in the middle of the terminal, his words were, "You stay right there, honey. I got a man in picking up supplies as we speak. I'll page him and have him bring you back when he comes."

Fanning herself, Kira closed her eyes, leaned back in the seat and tried to ignore the heat, the humidity and her nagging thirst. Anything, however, was preferable to staying on board with him.

"You Delaney?"

The raspy voice sliced through Kira's thoughts. Opening her eyes, she found herself contemplating a scuffed pair of work boots. From there, her gaze quickly moved northward, up a pair of grubby-looking brown trousers and faded navy blue shirt to a hardened face partially shadowed beneath a tipped-back miner's hat and several days growth of beard.

After a moment's hesitation she answered, "Yes."

"Boss says you need a ride out to the mines."

"Yes, I do."

"If you're comin' with me, then, let's go," he muttered. At that he turned and began making his way toward the open end of the terminal, leaving Kira to grab up her backpack and trail after him.

~ * ~

Two of Echo's moons were rising on the horizon, making the night sky glow as though it were early morning. Kira glanced out the open window of the tiny shuttle. They were flying low, following a rushing river as it snaked its way beneath them. Geometric patterns of moonlight danced on the water's surface, sparkling like the jewels of so many Echo legends. There was no shore on either side; instead, dense jungle began at the water's edge, rising up off the floor into a thick canopy of green.

Kira's mind drifted, remembering the times when Grant Preston used to make frequent trips out to the home office. Back then, it seemed Grant and her father were closer than they'd been in recent years. With an inward sigh, she focused on the scenery skimming below and looked forward to seeing Grant again.

Twenty minutes and the distance between Port Ore and Major Metals had been covered. Soon, the small aircraft was gliding low over the top of a thick canopy of vegetation. Veering sharply to the left, they began approaching a private landing zone, a clearing in the dense vegetation outlined by a circle of glowing float lights. Seconds later, the ground was rising up to meet them.

Kira bent to get through the doorway, stepped out on to the wing then jumped to the ground. The air was heavy with the spice of steamy damp soil and the overpowering fragrance of night-blooming flowers. Actually, the scent in the air was the first thing she had noticed earlier when she'd first stepped off the *Solar Wind*. The intoxicating fragrance was so contradictory to Port Ore's harsh, squalid little spaceport she had waited in.

"Hurry it up, I haven't got all night."

Gravel crunched beneath her feet as Kira quickly hoisted her backpack over one shoulder and began following the pilot across the LZ toward a small two-story building. A bird wailed soulfully from the jungle behind her and was immediately answered from the other side of the landing zone. Insects hummed, filling the air with an orchestrated drone that almost seemed to pulse.

"Kira!" With a frown of concern creasing his brow, Grant Preston rose from his seat and came around from behind his desk. "What in a renegade's name--what brought you out here all alone, girl?"

"I need your help."

Preston crossed the room and enfolded her in his arms. "And whatever it is, you've got it," he said, giving her a light kiss on the forehead. "But...why have you risked your safety coming out here like this?"

Kira's gaze shot to a man lounging in the shadows against the back wall of Grant's office. Their eyes met, and instantly an unexplained jolt shot through her.

"Here, have a seat, honey," Grant said, directing Kira to a nearby chair. He turned toward the stranger. "Mr. Kendyl, would you get Miss Delaney something cool to drink?"

"Certainly." Kira felt the man's lingering gaze before he turned away.

"All right, darling," Preston went on, "tell me what all's going on."

Kira briefly explained her struggle with the company records. "Have you had anything like this happen with your records at this end?" she asked.

Preston shook his head then smiled. "You sure it isn't just a few complications that come with trying to pick up the pieces. You've been through a lot, you know."

Kira shook her head. "I don't think so, Grant."

The man he called Kendyl soon returned with a glass of chilled water, which Kira gratefully accepted. "Thank you." It was then she noticed his scarred features. Trying not to stare, she concentrated on ignoring the tiny voice inside her head screaming: Danger!

A runaway imagination, that's all it was. That and Zeke filling her head with suspicions about everyone and everything.

"Kira, let me introduce my foreman, Mr. Kendyl."

"Hello," she said as he nodded his acknowledgement.

"Kira is Delaney's daughter," Grant explained.

Referring to his deceased partner as simply, Delaney, seemed a bit impersonal, Kira thought. Besides, Grant never used to call him Delaney. It was always, Renn.

"Kira, honey," Grant continued, "anything you have to say is perfectly okay to say in front of Mr. Kendyl here." Preston shot Kendyl a knowing glance then added, "You might say he's more or less a...business consultant."

Lifting her gaze, Kira watched Mr. Kendyl's scarred features pull into a parody of a smile, sending another ripple of caution through her. Unable to pinpoint the reason for such a feeling, she took a sip of the cool water, hoping to calm her nerves along with her thirst. "Okay," she began. "I strongly believe someone's also trying to impair the records at the home office.

"Impair. As in...sabotage?"

Kira shrugged. "For lack of a better word, yes. Look, I realize I don't have a lot of past experience to rely on when it comes to taking over Dad's half of the business, but...somebody's doing something. I no sooner get the records all straightened out and in a matter of days they're right back in the same mess again. Besides, you, yourself, mentioned sabotage in your message to Dad, which I just found. Did you, by the way, ever find anything out about that?"

"Message?" Grant's face was a blank. "I don't recall...wait. Yes, I do remember now. "Your dad and I checked it out after he got here." He shrugged. "We ended up deciding my worries were over nothing. Like I say, you sure it isn't just the stress of all you've been through, plus trying to learn the business all at once?"

Kira couldn't help but notice the condescending smile and dismissing tone. Her cheeks flamed. "I'm not stupid, Grant."

Preston's expression stilled. "I didn't mean to imply that you were, honey."

"The kind of trouble I've been running into has nothing to do with being inexperienced. Besides all the double invoices, someone's been using a voice duplication system and ordering equipment under my name that I know nothing of."

Preston's flash of eye contact with Kendyl didn't go unnoticed. "How'd you find that out?" he asked. "That they're using voice duplication, I mean?"

"A friend ran a computer check on it for me."

Preston's brow rose. "Anyone I know?"

"I doubt it," Kira replied, refusing to drag Zeke's name into it.

"I see." He weighed her with a critical squint. "Kira, why didn't you at least send a memo torp off to me?"

"I did. Two of them, in fact."

He shook his head slowly. "I never received anything from you. Believe me, I had no idea." With a sigh, Grant turned his back and gazed out the window. "So, how'd you get here anyway? It's not like you can just hop on the first commercial liner bound for Echo."

"An acquaintance brought me."

That turned Preston's head back around, his face sobered into what appeared as indignation. "You mean to tell me, somebody you know not only brought you to this hellhole, he simply dumped you off in port?"

"Not hardly. I smuggled on board his ship for starters. And then when we got here, he wouldn't let me off because it's too dangerous, he said. So, I left on my own."

Preston shook his head. "Where's that little girl I remember? Over night you've become a young woman, Kira, making decisions and taking matters into your own hands."

She felt her cheeks flush. Neither physically nor emotionally was she the little girl he once knew.

"So this...friend. He still in port?" Kendyl asked, breaking into the conversation for the first time.

Kira didn't like the anxiousness in his voice and wondered what difference it made to him anyway. She shrugged. "I doubt it. He was running behind schedule as it was."

"Well, your friend is right," Preston calmly agreed. "It is too dangerous for you to be off-ship."

"Believe me, it couldn't be any worse than what I've already been through," Kira interjected. "Someone was actually shooting at me in Major Metals' parking lot. That's when I decided I had to come to you. And then when we made a stop on Lilo, two men attacked me."

Preston looked properly astonished. "You mean your life has been threatened?"

Kira nodded. "Yes, twice that I know of."

"Honey, this whole thing is too dangerous. I want you to rethink your decision about selling your half of the business to me."

Ignoring his suggestion, Kira pulled the backpack off her shoulder and set it down at her feet. "I brought all the rods for the ledgers. I'm hoping that you can make sense out of them."

"Don't you worry, we'll get to the bottom of this," he said, then added, "but, please, just think about what I've said. I'll pay you well, honey, and then you'll be done with this kind of worry."

"Grant, I can't give up Dad's part of the business."

The condescending smile was back. "I understand the commitment you feel, just give it some thought, okay?"

The comphone rang. Preston made his way to his desk. "Preston here... Where? How long ago?"

For several heartbeats Kira's gaze remained on Grant's hardening face.

"How the hell would anyone know about that place?" he said.

Feigning a lack of interest, Kira cast her gaze to the floor and listened as Preston's tone of voice became more malicious during the exchange. Then, through clenched teeth came a response that sent a chill down her spine. "I'm on my way."

Hanging up the phone, he walked over to Kendyl where he spoke in quiet undertones. Immediately, Kendyl turned for the door and Preston returned to Kira's side. "Kira, darling," he began almost too sweetly, "looks like I'm going to be working all night after all. Let me show you my guest hatch. It's not exactly home, but it has a shower and a bed." He smiled amiably. "Somebody might as well get some use out of it."

Kira rose to her feet. "Okay," she sighed, knowing it wouldn't do any good to argue the point.

Preston reached for her backpack. "Thata girl," he said. "And tomorrow, we'll take a long look at those records of yours."

She nodded, allowing him to guide her out the door and into the sultry night toward a small cluster of cabins.

~ * ~

Kendyl hit Slater with a massive open-handed blow. "You're a tough bastard, aren't you?" he drawled.

Slater lifted his bleary gaze and glared insolently at his captor. Never would he have recognized Kendyl, had it not been for Celeste's description and warning.

"It's been a while," Kendyl went on. "But I imagine I don't have to remind you of that, do I, Slater? I'll venture you remember Steel as if it were yesterday."

Zeke offered no response.

"I'm right, aren't I?" Clasping his hands behind his back, Kendyl slowly circled Zeke's trussed body. Leaning forward, he proudly inspected the puckered scar above Zeke's right shoulder blade. "Nice trophy you got there." He came back around to continue his taunting. "Just to keep the records straight, that was my slug you took in the shoulder that day."

Zeke simply stared at him through pain-dulled eyes. Blood dripped from his swollen lip. There was an awful roaring in his ears, and his ribs hurt so badly it was an effort just to breathe.

"Since I couldn't quite get Banner locked in the crosshairs of my scope, I sighted-in on you instead." Kendyl paused and considered Zeke, his features hardening into a mask of cynical incredulity. "You impressed me. You see, that slug should have dropped you in your tracks, and instead--all you did was stumble a bit upon impact."

Zeke averted his eyes. He knew what was coming next. Beyond the vendetta over his burned-scarred body, Kendyl felt cheated and intended one way or another to exact his pound of flesh. With an inward sigh, Zeke knew whatever perverted tactics Kendyl had planned, he'd be damned lucky to survive it.

"Are you listening to me?" Kendyl's wheedling voice intruded once again upon his thoughts. "I said, I'm going to enjoy entertaining myself with you while waiting for your 'rescue party' to show up. And when he does...I'll have you both."

Well, at least Kendyl had answered one of the questions tumbling around in Zeke's mind--whether Nick had fallen prey to a similar fate.

Prior to landing the *Revenge*, they had run a full scan on the perimeter, finding nothing beyond the usual lower life forms and the single guard at post about a mile and a half from the LZ. Nick had taken off on foot to meet up with Clint and Marc at a nearby rendezvous point. Zeke had found the jet bike stashed in the underbrush just as Black Fox had said it would be for the trip from the LZ to the mining headquarters. He was halfway there when he came upon a flagger stopping on-coming traffic for a massive ore hauler just starting to move out on to the roadway. He should have smelled a trap and ordinarily would have, but his mind was on Kira--just one more reason for believing that attachment and love were weakening forces.

"Sorry about the delay, mister. Hope you're not in a hurry," the flag woman had called out as she approached him.

He'd just opened his mouth to ask if he could quickly slip on through before the hauler actually took over the road...but he never got the chance. The woman was aiming a small needle gun at him. When she fired, Zeke felt the sting as the dart entered his thigh. The next instant, a wave of nausea rolled over him, and as though in slow motion, the bike began toppling, taking him with it in a fall that seemed to last forever. Zeke vaguely felt the shock of impact, heard himself grunt as the bike careened over him, pinning him beneath its weight.

"Noth--ing per--son--al, mis--ter. Just fo--llow--ing or--ders," came the woman's distorted voice as if talking in slow motion from a great distance.

Drugs...she'd used drugs, he acknowledged numbly. He searched for remorse in her eyes but found none as he sank deeper into layer after layer of dark oblivion.

Zeke surfaced briefly at times, gathering bits and pieces of reality before sinking back into the void of unconsciousness. He vaguely remembered being carried by rough hands and tossed into some kind of vehicle, followed by a long, bumpy ride. He tried picking up on snatches of conversation along the way, but somehow the effort of trying to listen was more than he could accomplish. The last time he was pulled under, he didn't resurface until he awoke to find himself trussed up in what appeared as a small maintenance shack.

His head throbbed and someone had clearly delivered a vicious kick to his side while he was out.

Escape was impossible. In the beginning, Zeke had struggled against his bindings, but the only thing it got him was several bruising blows in punishment.

"Payback's are a bitch, aren't they, Slater?"

Zeke tried to tune out the man's wheedling voice.

Kendyl laughed. "Actually, it was fortunate my men screwed up on Lilo. This is much better."

Zeke looked up. "Your men?" he managed to grit out. "Those were your men who attacked Kira?"

Kendyl shrugged. "A couple of incompetents. You were their target, by the way, not the girl."

Zeke closed his eyes. Damn...and he'd been so sure it was Kira they were after.

Kendyl's expression turned to a mask of stone. "There's three people I've dreamed of having at my mercy: Nick Banner, you and whoever's been raiding my ships. Up until an hour ago, I didn't know which one of you I wanted the worst. Now I realize, of course, that you and the pirate are the same. I figure I can wait for Banner."

Zeke didn't respond. How the devil had Kendyl connected him to the *Revenge* already? Not only was the landing zone remote, it was overgrown with vegetation. Their sensors had picked up no motion detectors or human life forms in the vicinity.

"Ah, I can see you're wondering how I managed to nail your identity. Actually, it was quite simple. One of your lovesick crewmen wanted to play hero for the girl's sake. Kira, of course, has no idea of his heroics."

Zeke's glance slid away. Talbot.

"I do believe the poor fool was in complete disapproval of your bedding Miss Delaney. Tsk--tsk--tsk." Kendyl shook his head in mock censure. "Yep, it's pretty bad when the ship's captain can't even whore with the bitch of his choice."

Zeke felt the familiar tug in his left jaw. If only he could get free of his shackles.

Kendyl went on, his voice mocking. "With a little--shall we say, persuasion, your man told us all about the *Revenge*. Of course, you understand, we had to eliminate him. A traitor is a traitor, no matter whose side he's on."

They killed Talbot, Zeke realized numbly. "If you're looking for Banner to come to my rescue," he managed weakly..."he doesn't even know I'm here, so you're in for one hell of a long wait."

Kendyl laughed out loud. "You think I'm stupid? Of course Banner knows you're here. He'll show."

The man was sick, there was no question about it. Months of seeking vengeance had twisted Kendyl's mind into something so evil his burned exterior couldn't begin to compare with the ugliness inside.

At Kendyl's nod, the man waiting for orders came forward.

Zeke's mind reeled. There wasn't a damn thing he could do but take whatever was about to be dished out--and hope to God, he'd live.

"Shall we see if you're as tough as your sidekick?"

"Why don't you suck vacuum, Kendyl," Zeke snarled, and grabbing hold of the chains above the manacles, he called upon a supreme amount of strength, hoisted himself up, kicking out with both feet at Kendyl. It was a narrow miss, costing him dearly as an explosion of white-hot pain shot across his injured ribs.

"Ahh, you want to play rough?" Kendyl's voice was dangerously soft as he calmly stepped back out of Zeke's reach. With that, he turned and nodded to his accomplice.

Zeke tensed, bracing himself as Kendyl's goon stepped forward, holding what looked to be some sort of nerve rod.

"Sonofabitch..." Zeke whispered, trying to kick the instrument away as the man advanced on him. His efforts were of little help. The instant the end of the rod made contact with Zeke's bare chest, excruciating, mind-numbing agony surged through him in pulsating torment.

CHAPTER TWENTY-SIX

Kira knew something wasn't right the instant Preston got off the comphone. She might be inexperienced when it came to running her half of the company, but she wasn't a total idiot. They were up to something--he and that Mr. Kendyl.

For her safety, Preston had said he would be locking her in. Yet, something about his placating tone said her safety had nothing to do with it. They were deliberately excluding her...from what? Kira gave the door's palm plate a few fruitless pushes, then resorted to going through a daily log lying upon a small desk. When that enterprise failed to turn up anything of value, she opened the top drawer of the desk. She knew better than to snoop, but insult and rebellion were high on her list of emotions right at the moment.

The drawer ended up holding nothing more important than a few receipts, a couple of carbon pencils and a note pad. With a sigh, she glanced about the sparsely decorated room. There just had to be a way out of this place. She hadn't gone through hell and back just to be locked away in Preston's hatch once she got here.

Turning for the door again, Kira quietly studied the palm plate. There's got to be some way... With a sharp intake of breath, she remembered the time she'd been locked away in Zeke's cabin and how security had been disrupted allowing her to escape. With that memory, an idea began to percolate. What would happen, she wondered, if somehow she were able to short out the palm plate? But another search of the tiny cabin yielded nothing she could use to pry open the cover. At last, in desperation, she stripped off the belt from her jeans and began frantically working the edge of the buckle beneath the plate. Within a matter of minutes, the plate was forced off and the controls vandalized.

Echo's heavy night air greeted Kira once again with a mixture of exotic scents and muggy warmth. High overhead thousands of stars twinkled-- diamonds of light against a curtain of dark velvet as she quickly hurried across the clearing. A night bird called out in the distance.

The door to the site office was locked, Preston and Kendyl both gone. Since she hadn't heard a ground runner leave, they must have walked. Swinging around, she scanned the surrounding area then began walking toward a small building at the far end of the settlement where a lone ground runner sat outside.

Soft lighting spilled through the shed's two windows and open doorway. Skirting around a crop of thick undergrowth, Kira heard raised voices. A knot formed in the pit of her stomach as she broke into a run.

Upon reaching a side window, she carefully peered inside, stopping cold at the scene before her.

Nooo, she moaned inwardly. Zeke.

His head hung lifelessly to the side against a raised arm and Preston and Kendyl were arguing over something. A third man was standing by. In his hand was some sort of a rod.

"Look," Kendyl said, "I've told you before, I have no intention of killing him." He stalked forward, gripped Zeke's shaggy mane in his fist and wrenched his head up. A low groan emanated from Zeke's throat. "See? I told you. He's not dead, just unconscious."

Barely able to suppress the moan welling up in her own throat, Kira turned away from the window, pressing her back against the wall.

"Shut up! Just shut up," Preston growled, their heated voices continuing to drift outside. "I've about had it with you, Kendyl. You pull another stunt like this, and you're out. You hear me?"

Numb with horror, Kira choked back a sob of anguish. Why were they doing this to Zeke?

"Does Preston know you're out here?"

Kira's eyes flew open to find a stocky man standing before her. Unable to find her voice or an appropriate answer, she started to bolt but was instantly stopped by a meaty hand gripping her arm.

"You're not going anywhere, sweet-cakes. Uh..." he hollered out, "we got company!" With that, he began towing her inside.

Preston's face registered obvious shock when their eyes met, but then he quickly masked it. "Kira," he said smoothly, "please..." He motioned to her with his hand. "Come, join us."

"Grant, what are you doing?" she cried. Blinking tears, she started to rush to Zeke's side but was halted once again. "Let go of me!" At last, she leveled accusing eyes on Preston. "Why are you doing this to him?" Her gaze drifted back to Zeke. "Release him!"

Preston calmly shook his head. "Kira, Kira, Kira. You should have stayed where I put you," he said, coming to stand before her. With a heavy sigh he glanced at Zeke then back to her. "I wasn't going to expose you to this. Not unless it became necessary."

She stiffened. "What are you talking about? That's the man who brought me here!"

"I know," Preston replied, in that same unemotional tone that said her wishes meant nothing.

Kendyl laughed and slugged Slater in the side for emphasis, the effort gaining him no more response than a half groan.

"Have a seat, Kira." With no more than eye contact from Preston, the man gripping her arm shoved her into a nearby chair.

"Please," she sobbed. "I beg of you, Grant, stop this."

"You know, I think we might have something here," Kendyl drawled, taking in Kira's tear-streaked face with amused interest.

With a low groan, Zeke stirred, his eyelids fluttering briefly, then closing again. Kira watched his throat work as he swallowed, watched an agonized frown crease his brow as pain began breaking through the threshold of reality.

"Please..." she whispered again, turning beseeching eyes upon Preston.

"Sorry," Kendyl said with a twisted grin and a slow wag of his head. "Slater and I have an old score to settle." He turned and picked up a cask of water and tossed it in Zeke's face, bringing him coughing back to consciousness. "Slater, can you hear me?"

~ * ~

Another low groan as Zeke lifted his swollen eyes and tried focusing. "Go to--hell," he muttered through gritted teeth.

"Tsk, tsk. Such talk. And in front of a lady, nonetheless." Kendyl turned to face Kira. "I'll tell you what--" He paused, deliberately struggling for her name. "Kira, is it?" When she did no more than glare at him, he smiled and continued. "You just might be able to persuade me into a little negotiation. You interested in hearing more?"

"Now wait, just a damn minute," Preston interrupted, "I don't want--"

Kendyl held up his hand. "Don't worry. What I have in mind is a package deal. You're included."

"Damn you!" Zeke growled, wrestling to free himself as awareness of Kira's presence slowly settled in. "I'm going to--frigging kill the both of you," Zeke promised, before choking again.

Kendyl turned amused eyes on Zeke. "You're hardly in a position to threaten anyone."

Gathering his senses, Zeke closed his eyes briefly. When he opened them again, Kendyl was studying Kira where she sat, her face tense with fear and shock.

At last Kendyl's gaze returned to Zeke. "Besides, if my hunch is correct, I think the little lady, here, just might be willing to bargain for your life."

"Lay one hand on her--" Zeke's words were cut off by a backhanded blow delivered by Kendyl's goon.

"Nooo!" Kira cried, leaping from her seat. Again she was shoved back down. "Please," she sobbed, "don't hit him any more!"

"Touch 'er and I'll...kill you!" Zeke managed to choke out, straining against his bindings.

Kendyl ignored him. "So, what do you think, honey, you willing to bargain? Or do we leave your lover to his fate?"

"No, Kira!"

"He's not my lover," she spat defiantly." He's my husband."

"Husband?" Preston repeated.

Kendyl's eyes gleamed as he slowly turned to face Zeke who was suddenly stock-still and very much alert. "Well, well. How very interesting." His mouth curved into a smile of satisfaction. "I just hate the title, 'widow'," he drawled, his eyes still focused on Zeke. "Don't you, Mrs. Slater?"

"Your conditions?" Kira asked without hesitation.

"Nooo!" Zeke growled, again thrashing for freedom. But his efforts were non-productive and ended the instant Kendyl's man hit him again. "It's me...you want," he gasped brokenly. "Leave her...the hell...out of this."

Kendyl grinned. "Mrs. Slater, shall we talk business?"

"Kira, noo--umph!" Again, Zeke was silenced.

~ * ~

Marc Banner unfolded his long legs and climbed up out of his crate. "No offense," he grumbled, working a cramped thigh muscle as he rose to his full six-foot three height, "but, next time Slater wants a favor, remind me to--"

"You're none the worse for wear," Clint interrupted. "Get your butt in gear, Marc. Nick will be expecting us to have that gate opened."

He turned to Matt Logan, the one who'd met them at the spaceport with the papers to claim the three crates of snakes. "Logan, you take the rest of the men and see what's happening in the mines."

"Gentlemen," Logan said, his attention returning to the men, "Echo's not exactly a walk in the park during the day, but it's a visit to hell at night and forgiveness isn't even a word in the vocabulary. If you screw up, it could mean your life."

Clint's solemn gaze scanned the face of each man, finally coming to rest on his hotshot youngest brother. "And if you forget that for even one damn second..." He left the sentence hanging.

"Okay," Logan said, "Any questions before we leave?"

The men all muttered their acknowledgement before parting.

Broad leaves were pushed aside as Clint and Marc made their way along an overgrown trail that led away from the warehouse toward the closest perimeter gate. Again the air was heavy with an odd combination of decayed vegetation and the rich fragrance of exotic flowers. Pushing forward, the two men found themselves slipping instinctively into a defensive mode--the only way of life on Echo. Hands hung near their holstered weapons, ears listening for anything unusual, and their eyes taking nothing for granted.

Twenty minutes passed before they reached the perimeter. A twelve-foot high fence marked the exact location, and the familiar hum of electronics indicated security was indeed on. An overhead floodlight illuminated the surrounding area with a large circle of light.

~ * ~

Roy was a big guy. In fact, he was so big when he propped his crossed ankles up on the security console, his oversized work boots obscured a big portion of the plot screen. Between that, the porn-mag that his face was buried in, and the music booming through his earbuds, Clint and Marc were furnished with a period of grace as they approached the guard station.

"You want me to do the honors?" Marc whispered.

"Make it quick and no heroics, you understand?"

Marc grinned. "You want quick? You got it." He turned and silently began working his way in behind the guard's station. With a last look around, he emerged from the darkness and in one lithe move, jerked the guard out of the station, gripping him in a neck lock before the guy even knew what was upon him.

"I'm afraid I don't have time for formal introductions," Marc said pleasantly, having jerked the earbuds out of the man's ears, "but would you mind disengaging the security on the gate for me--please?"

Refusing to cooperate, the guard struggled for freedom, his bulk gaining him no leverage, however. Marc reached around, found his target on the side of the man's neck and twisted. "I suppose we can do this the hard way if you insist," he said close to the man's ear. "By the way," he added in an amiable tone, "that weakness you're beginning to feel about now is caused from lack of blood to your brain. You'll be clinically dead in about two minutes unless you decide to change your mind."

Ten seconds and the man's struggles stilled, and he nodded as best he could.

Marc smiled, loosening his hold. "Whadda guy," he drawled, cordially patting the guard on the back. "I just knew you were the reasonable sort."

Within a matter of minutes, security was released, the guard was unconscious, and Nick, who'd been waiting in the shadows, was racing through the gate. "I think they've got Zeke! I overheard two guards saying something about using a dart gun on someone."

"Damn," Clint muttered. "They must have Talbot too, because he never made it out from the spaceport as planned."

"The first place I think we should check is headquarters."

"That's thirty minutes from here."

A crack of static came from somewhere inside the guard's station. "Unit Four, come in..."

Silence, as all three Banners stared first at the empty station and then at the man collapsed just outside the doorway.

"Base to Unit Four, Brenda here. Come in you miserable son of a-
-"

"Four to Base," Clint said, activating the transmitter. It was a reckless gamble, but hopefully the static would cover his voice enough to pull it off. "Cool your jets, would ya? Can't a guy take a leak, dammit?"

"To answer your question, Unit Four: no, you can't take a leak, or whatever the hell else you're doing. You missed check-in, reptile breath."

"Uh, sorry."

"Listen up. I've got a message from headquarters. Some idiot's landed out on the old LZ. So stuff it back in your pants and keep a sharp look out for anything unusual going on out there."

"You got it."

"Yeah, you're going to be the one getting' it, greeg bait, if you don't keep your fly zipped and get your damn act together out there."

"Yes, your mamship. Unit four out."

"Mamship?" Nick whispered, shaking his head. "Mamship?"

"You actually think they bought that?" Marc asked.

"Buy it?" Nick cut in. "Hell, they've probably got half the security on their way."

"So, what the devil are we standing here for?" Marc asked. With that, all three men broke into a run for the warehouse where Logan had left a ground runner for their use. A half hour later they were pulling to a halt on the outskirts of the mining headquarters.

~ * ~

Zeke awoke slowly, awareness returning by degrees, layer upon painful layer. So, how long had be been out this time: Three minutes or three hours? They'd used that nerve rod on him again. He vaguely remembered the water they'd thrown in his face and the brief moment of renewed consciousness before slipping back into darkness, Kira's screams echoing in his mind.

Kira. Was she all right? Struggling against another wave of beckoning peace, Zeke fought to remain conscious. Easing his eyes open to the barest of slits, he scanned the room through the veil of lashes. Kira was still sitting in the chair, a man standing guard at her side. Kendyl and Preston were converging off to the side, their voices barely audible. Kendyl glanced up, studied Zeke for a moment then returned his attention to Preston.

"I'm tired of waiting," Kendyl snarled. With that he turned and began making his way toward Kira. "When Slater finally comes around," he added, wrapping his hand about Kira's wrist and jerking her to her feet, "let me know. I want the privilege of seeing the look on his face when I tell what an easy score his little bride is."

"Nooo!" Kira screamed. "Let me go! Grant! Please..."

He shrugged dismissively, and she turned back to Kendyl. "You can't do this!"

"Oh, but I'm afraid I can," Kendyl replied, "and whatever else I damn well feel like."

Again Kira turned pleading eyes on Preston as Kendyl dragged her toward the door. "Grant, please!"

"There isn't a damn thing he can do," Kendyl snarled.

"Why are you doing this?"

"Why?" Kendyl echoed, a diabolic smile cracking his face. "I'll tell you why. Because it will drive Slater crazy just thinking about you in my bed. Your lover owes me a debt, sweet thing, and I intend to see it paid--in blood." He jerked Kira forward. "Don't make me drag you, 'cause I will."

It was all Zeke could do to keep from struggling against his bonds--it would do Kira no good and would only serve as entertainment. And so, he continued feigning unconsciousness, hanging lifelessly by his wrists, watching beneath slitted lids as Kendyl propelled Kira out the door. If he had any hope of helping Kira, he would have to stay conscious.

Mumbling something to one of the guards, Preston turned and followed Kendyl out the door.

Zeke carefully scanned the inside of the shack. From his vantage point, it appeared there were only two men left: the goon who'd used the nerve rod on him and the one who'd been standing guard over Kira.

Zeke bided his time, keeping his breathing shallow and his body lax, hoping to lure their notice and curiosity. It was an effort that cost him dearly as he silently envisioned Kira in that monster's possession.

"Wouldn't y' think he'd be comin' around by now?" one of the guards asked.

Easing his slitted eyes closed, Zeke held his breath and willed his body to relax as one of the thugs cautiously approached.

A meaty finger jabbed into his chest. "If you ask me, I say 'ee's already dead."

"He ain't dead," came the other voice, laced with irritation. Zeke listened to the sound of footsteps as one of the men walked around him. The next instant, a fist slammed into his side. It took every ounce of will just to keep from groaning.

"Whad I tell ya? Ee's dead," the first man spoke up.

"And I say he ain't. Go get some water."

"Yeah, it brung him around the first time." With that, the sound of retreating footsteps were heard, followed by silence.

Zeke wanted in the worst way to crack his eyelids to see who remained. But even the tiniest movement, if noticed, could give him away.

Absolute silence.

Seconds seemed like hours as Zeke waited, taking shallow breaths that just barely sufficed his need. At last, slowly opening his eyes to tiny slits, he ventured a peek through lowered lashes. Just as he figured, the thug who'd used the nerve rod on him was the one left. Now, if he could just lure him in for a closer look before the other guard returned.

As if reeled in by a magic line, the man cautiously stepped closer, studying Zeke with the same cautious scrutiny that one might approach a sleeping snake.

Dead silence.

Zeke held his breath, relaxed his muscles and hung perfectly still. Yet, hidden beneath the slackened façade was an animal of prey, whose every nerve, every fiber was tense with the mixture of anticipation and adrenaline. Come on, you sonofabitch. Come on. Just--one--more--step.

The hush was tangible, the only sound was Zeke's heart pounding in his ears as the man continued staring at him, studying him, waiting for one little slip up, one little blink, just one tiny breath.

"You can't be dead," he muttered cynically.

Eyes peering through veiled slits, Zeke remained motionless, hardly daring a breath. And then the mistake he'd been waiting for happened.

That one fatal step closer.

In a blur, Zeke grabbed the chain above his wrists, hoisted himself up, caught the thug in a leg lock about his neck and squeezed with bone-crushing strength. Ignoring the man's grappling hands and futile struggles, ignoring the searing pain of bruised ribs, he hung on, squeezing as if he were strangling the very devil himself. At last the resistance ceased and the man's body went limp. One more vicious clench of his leg muscles for good measure, and Zeke let him drop to the floor with a thud.

After that it, was just a matter of disregarding the pain in his side as he pulled himself up the length of chain until he reached a large grappling hook in the ceiling. Within seconds he'd slipped the chain off the hook and dropped to the floor. There was still just one small problem. His wrists were shackled, and somebody had the key.

"Here's the water," came the voice of the returning guard. "For all the good it will-- Umph!"

CHAPTER TWENTY-SEVEN

The guard never knew what hit him. As he came through the door, Zeke was waiting around the corner, both fists clenched for a two-handed blow that rendered the man unconscious before he even hit the floor. From there, Zeke awkwardly rummaged through the pockets of both men until he found what he was looking for--the key to the shackles. Odd, neither one was armed with a gun. Obviously they must be good with the knives they both carried.

Within minutes he had confiscated one of the knives and was heading for the exit. Suddenly sensing someone was just outside the open doorway and with nerves wire-tight, Zeke prepared for round three.

Suddenly, a dark-clad figure cautiously stepped over the threshold.

Exploding out of the shadows, Zeke put all of his power and weight into one massive blow that caught his opponent straight across the jaw. The force of it hurled his victim back through the doorway, out onto the stoop where he slid down the steps on his back and landed with a dull groan.

Zeke moved to the open doorway, ready to take on anyone else if he had to. That's when he saw Nick lying at the base of the steps. Out cold.

"Zeke!" Clint lowered his weapon. "What the devil..."

"I had no way of knowing," Zeke said, rushing to Nick's side. "Here, help me get him up before someone comes."

Within moments Nick was heaved to his feet, one arm slung over Clint's shoulder and the other over Zeke's. A groggy moan escaped as they moved into the shadows toward their hidden ground runner.

"What hit me?"

"Zeke," Clint supplied.

Still dazed, Nick looked over at Zeke. "Thought we were on the same side."

Zeke couldn't help smiling. "My humble apologies."

"Yeah, that's easy for you to say," Nick grumbled as they eased him down into the front seat where he began gingerly rubbing his swollen jaw. "Anyway, I thought they had you,"

"They did. Now they've got Kira." A hard knot tightened in the pit of his stomach just saying the words.

Nick cursed. "If Kendyl's involved in this--"

"He is," Zeke ground out. "In fact, I'll wager Kendyl's the one pulling Preston's strings." Zeke anxiously glanced down at Nick then back to Clint. "Look, I can't stay. I gotta go after her."

Clint nodded and pulled the extra gun from his waistband and handed it to Zeke. "Here, take this. We'll be along shortly. Just give us a minute to catch up before you go doing anything stupid."

With a muttered thanks and gritting his teeth against the pain in his ribs, Zeke swept the area with a glance. Having dredged up a mental image of the blueprint Fox had provided them with, he took in his surroundings and decided they were at the south end of the mining settlement. Now to find Kendyl. Damn, what if he'd taken Kira somewhere in a ground runner?

~ * ~

From the moment Kendyl first wrenched her to her feet, Kira had resisted him every inch of the way, digging her heels in as he dragged her out the door, down the steps and into the night.

"You want to do this the hard way, sweetheart?" he shouted, having taken only so much of her defiance. "That's fine. We'll do it the hard way." And with that he caught her about the waist and tossed her over his shoulder like a sack of feed.

The pressure of his shoulder cut into her midsection, driving the air from her lungs. Kira gasped for breath as she dangled over him in an undignified heap. Squirming and kicking, she finally doubled her hands into fists and pounded on his back until a cruel pinch stung her into a brief moment of submission.

"Put me down." Warring emotions whirled through her head-- confusion, fright, helplessness and most of all, outrage at his insultingly splayed hand that still remained on her bottom.

Kendyl laughed. "I'll do more than put you down, sweetheart."

Preston was tagging along several paces behind. "Grant, please!" Kira pleaded. But he only shook his head.

Within minutes, they'd arrived at the main complex, but instead of going up to Preston's office, they turned and descended a short flight of stairs. With the touch of a pad, a door clicked open and lights came to life the instant they crossed the threshold. Still shouldering Kira, Kendyl crossed the room and dumped her on the couch.

"Preston has been generous enough to offer his executive accommodations for our use," came Kendyl's mocking voice. "I say that was real nice of him now. Don't you?"

Kira could only stare, a mixture of fear and rage coursing through her. It didn't take a genius to know what he intended to do to her. And if this monster expected her to surrender, he was in for a big surprise.

Her horror must have shown on her face, because Kendyl smiled as if reading her mind. "There's nowhere to run."

"Why are you doing this?"

"Why?" he asked. "You see this face?"

Kira's gaze remained unblinking upon Kendyl's distorted features. Despite the scars, she could almost imagine that at one time he might have been a handsome man.

"Not a pretty sigh, huh?"

Still, no comment.

"Unlike mine," he said, towering above her, "your skin is flawless." He stepped closer and reached out to cup her cheek then laughed as he caught her hand before it connected with his face.

"Your beloved husband and his sidekick were the ones responsible for this, and I intend to collect."

"But first, we're going to take care of something," Preston interjected, who was still standing in the doorway.

"Later," Kendyl snapped, his cold eyes holding Kira immobile.

"No. Now," Preston insisted. "In your rush for revenge, you've lost track of the real reason for this little escapade."

Ever so slowly Kendyl pulled his gaze away from Kira. "All right," he said calmly. "Business first. Then pleasure."

Preston was already heading for his office upstairs when Kendyl returned his attention to her. "Kira," he began, "you remember that bargain we talked about?"

It was said in challenge and Kira boldly lifted her eyes to meet his. "I remember," she said flatly, calling upon that cool, aloof composure-- that protective façade that somehow always got her through difficult times. Renn had always told her, 'Honey, carry your fear and pain inside your gut. That way when you look your enemy straight in the eye, only that deep core within knows how scared you really are.'

And right now the lust in Kendyl's ice blue eyes had her scared.

"The negotiations between you and Preston are on behalf of Slater only," he sneered. "I'm afraid it won't change your fate." Kendyl grinned and added spitefully, "You see, the man working him over as we speak knows of ways to make a person long for death."

'Carry your fear and pain inside your gut.' Again, Renn's words came tumbling through her mind as Kira simply looked at Kendyl through hate-filled eyes. "You won't get away with this."

He laughed. "I've already gotten away with it. I have you, don't I?" he boasted. "I have Slater just where I want him. And soon..." his expression turned to a mask of stone, "...very soon, I'll have Banner."

Kira exploded off the couch, making a run for the door. Suddenly, his hand lashed out so quickly, she had no time to react. The blow across her cheek sent her spiraling backward where she lay, stunned.

Kendyl turned briefly as Preston reentered the suite and made his way to the computer.

Pain knifed through Kira's jaw. Her eyes were watering and the metallic taste of blood was on her tongue. Kendyl moved to stand over her, shoulders shaking with laughter.

"Lesson one," he gritted out. "Don't try to escape again. As you can see, there's consequences."

"Why don't you keep your hands off the girl until we get business taken care of," Preston said, his eyes trained on the monitor as he entered information into the terminal. Kira sensed more annoyance than anything in his tone, certainly not concern or mercy. Finally, his gaze slid to her.

"If you want to save that new husband of yours," he began, "all it will take is for you to authorize the transfer of your half of the company over to me."

"What?"

"You heard him," Kendyl leered. "It's really quite simple. If you want mercy for your lover, you're going to have to buy it with your half of the company."

"Right here, Kira," Preston added, indicating the information on the screen. "All we need is your approval in three places."

"I'll do no such thing!"

With a sigh, Kendyl shot her a satisfied smile. "I was just hoping you'd say something like that."

"What he means," Preston interjected, "is that he intends to turn loose the forces of hell on your man. You see, he's been holding back until you made your decision. I'm afraid there's nothing I can do now to--"

"Wait," she cried. "Please, I'll endorse whatever you wish."

Preston's faint smile held a touch of mocking sadness. "Wise choice."

Kira studied the familiar face of her father's business partner. "I don't know you anymore," she choked out brokenly.

Impassive eyes met hers. "You never knew me in the first place, Kira," came his cold response. "And for that matter, neither did Renn." Shaking his head in feigned regret, Preston sighed heavily.

"Unfortunately, when he started snooping around, I had to lure him here to eliminate him."

Stunned by his blatant admission, Kira's jaw dropped. "Eliminate?"

"That's right, and if you want to save that man of yours from a similar fate, I suggest you surrender your half of the company. Now."

"You killed--my father?"

"Right here, Kira," he said, indicating the ID Scanner.

Without another word, she woodenly came forward, numb with shock as she placed her palm on the ID pad. The results were immediate as the scanner read, identified and recorded the approval of the forfeiture of her inherited half of the company.

While Preston readied another document for her authorization, Kira froze as Quint Kendyl eased in behind her, his body insultingly close. The brazen hand on her backside was a grim reminder that her fate would not change.

And why would it? Who would stop him? Certainly not Grant. And what good would it do if she tried to fight him? Her last attempt at defiance had earned her a bruised jaw for the effort. But it wasn't the pain that halted her so much as the fact that she'd gain nothing.

"Take your hands off of her," came a barely leashed, but familiar voice.

CHAPTER TWENTY-EIGHT

She'd have known that voice anywhere: rich, deep, and as thrilling as thunder. He'd escaped! Relief swept through Kira at the sight of his shadowed silhouette standing in the open doorway.

Weapon drawn, he slowly crossed the threshold. So commanding in appearance was he, Kira ceased breathing as all six foot three inches of him emerged out of the darkness by degrees. As a rising sun casts its brilliance upon a darkened landscape, the interior light inched its way up long leather-clad legs, narrow hips and a breathtaking torso exposed in all its glory by his open jacket.

Then, as he stepped fully inside, the light found his face.

Inhaling at last, Kira fastened her sights upon Zeke's sun-bronzed countenance, marred only by the scrapes and bruises he'd received earlier. That air of lazy nonchalance she'd come to know so well was back in place. His long, lean frame looked relaxed, almost indolent, but Kira wasn't fooled for an instant. Despite that careless façade, a barely leashed fury vibrated just beneath the surface--a ruthless purpose that she'd only briefly glimpsed when they were attacked on Lilo and again when he'd ordered the annihilation of that pirate freighter.

Slater's steady gaze never left Kendyl's face. "Step away, Kira," he said, his voice no more than a husky whisper.

With lightning speed and bruising strength, scarred fingers closed around Kira's wrist. "She's not going anywhere," Kendyl snarled, jerking her in front of him--a maneuver that left Kira the one staring down the muzzle of Zeke's weapon and forcing him to adjust his aim.

"Ah...Quint Kendyl..." Nick drawled as he and Clint stepped through the doorway behind Slater, guns trained on both Kendyl and Preston. "What an unpleasant surprise. And all this time I'd hoped you were enjoying your stay in hell." There was no question what Nick was doing. Running interference with meaningless small talk would hopefully defuse the moment and cause Kendyl to be careless.

"Small galaxy, huh, Nick." Kendyl replied, drawing Kira even tighter against his chest.

Nick shook his head in feigned disappointment. "And then to find you hiding behind a woman..."

Kira felt Kendyl's body vibrate with silent rage.

"I guess what I don't understand," Clint asked, "is why steal your own shipments?"

"Simple," Nick filled in. "Heat's off when you become a victim just like everyone else. Besides, bankrupting all the little guys out there, you end up taking over their claims and still get their ore. Then you turn around and sell it for a tidy sum."

Despite the guns on him, Preston started clapping slowly. "Very, very good. Between not having to pay for it, the insurance reimbursement and the eventual net on the black market, we more than double our profits. It's a win-win situation."

"I doubt Delaney knew about this," Zeke cut in.

"Immaterial. The records show we're losing our shirts from piracy. Delaney came out to discuss security measures. By then, of course, I already had most of the mines switched over to slave labor." He grinned. "He started snooping around...I had no choice."

Kira moaned, the implication more than she could take.

"And all the time you'd been collecting the allocated salaries coming out of the home office," Nick added.

Preston shrugged carelessly. "That too."

Kira choked back a sob and struggled for freedom, vowing to kill Preston personally. It took more than Kendyl's arm tightening to stop her efforts. It was the subtle jab of a weapon in her back that brought her struggles to a halt.

"Enough!" Slater said, his gun now trained on Preston, his eyes fixed on Kendyl. "You going to turn her loose, or do you need a little persuasion?"

"Why don't you take a flying leap about five hundred kilometers straight up, Slater, and take a deep breath."

Zeke's eyes never left Kendyl's for even a blink as he gently eased the trigger back, sending a slug of white-hot lead into Grant Preston's thigh. Bug-eyed, Preston dropped to the floor, bellowing out his agony.

Tension was tangible. Kira could feel it radiating through Kendyl's body, see it barely bridled in Zeke's gunmetal eyes that never left Kendyl for so much as a blink.

Preston was gripping his injured leg and moaning. The fast-spreading blood staining his trousers was a sure indication that an artery had probably been hit.

"Gee, Preston," Clint drawled, "that looks like it hurts."

The sandy-haired man was glaring at Slater. "You shot me!" he growled, followed by a string of foul oaths.

"That I did," Zeke agreed, "and if I were you, I'd be convincing your partner here to let Kira go."

"The next slug, I guarantee will do worse." There was no trace of hesitancy, no vestige of mercy in Slater's calm but arrant warning.

"All right! All right! Anything," Preston muttered pitifully, his sights rising to Kendyl. "Let her go, Quint. Dammit, let the girl go!" When he lifted his hand off the wound, the resulting geyser of blood had him instantly clamping back down. "Ohhh..." he moaned, "I'm going to bleed to death."

"No, you're not," Kendyl snarled, and in a blur he turned and shot Preston with the small revolver he'd been pressing to Kira's back. "There," he said, his scarred face pulled into a satisfied smile. "I've just removed your bargaining power, gentlemen."

"Not quite!" came a voice from behind him.

As if by magic, Marc emerged from around the corner. How he'd gotten there, where he'd come from was anyone's guess. In a flash he was ramming Kendyl with a full body slam that sent the three of them--Kira included--crashing to the floor in a tangle of arms and legs. The force of the impact knocked Kendyl's gun from his hand as a full-scale brawl developed.

Closest to Kira, Clint rushed to help her up and out of harm's way. "You okay?"

She nodded, as Kendyl's huge fist connected with Marc's jaw. From instincts born of many brawls with two older brothers, Marc Banner didn't waste time returning the courtesy.

"Why doesn't somebody help him?" Kira cried frantically.

"And rob him of this moment?" Clint shot back. "We'd never hear the end of it."

"But, what if--"

"Don't worry," he interrupted with cocky assurance. "We'll be moving in for the kill shortly. In the meantime, we're letting Marc work off a little frustration."

Chairs and tables in the comfortable suite scattered; floorboards groaned as the men rolled back and forth. Marc got in two more solid punches and was in the process of putting Kendyl's head through the paneling when Nick and Zeke found an opening in the fight and moved in.

As if the very fires of hell were licking at his heels, Kendyl miraculously managed to free himself long enough to produce another hidden weapon. With a snap of his wrist, a small mini slug-gun materialized in the palm of his hand and Marc became the easiest target.

"Drop the gun!" Zeke shouted, bringing his own weapon to bear. But before the words were out of his mouth, Kendyl had fired.

"Nooo!" someone shouted.

In horror, Kira saw Marc's body jolt, the force slamming him back against the wall where he slid to the floor in what seemed in slow motion.

Amidst the chaos of shouting and Kira's screams, Nick and Zeke simultaneously opened fire upon Kendyl--who dropped at their feet in a heap.

"Marc! Ah, God, noooo," Nick moaned, dropping to one knee at Marc's side. Clint was lifting Marc into his arms.

Kira took in the tragedy before her, her heart wrenching. A dark crimson spot stained the carpet where Marc had been lying. Marc, with his devil-may-care smile and go-to-hell persona.

Six feet away lay Kendyl, and beyond him Preston.

Suddenly Zeke was at her side, drawing her trembling body into the security of his embrace, and turning her face away from the scene. For a long while neither of them spoke.

Was it worth this hell bent trip to see Preston? a silent voice asked. *It could have just as easily been Zeke lying there.*

You wouldn't listen, would you? You just wouldn't listen. Right down to disregarding his order to stay on board the ship. You knew his concern for your safety would have him following, storming the very gates of hell, if necessary, to keep you safe.

In the rush of anguished realization, Kira saw the full extent of her foolhardy, thoughtless act. If it hadn't been for her, maybe none of this would have happened.

Zeke's arms tightened about her.

This was all her fault. All of it. If it hadn't been for their close bond with Zeke, none of the Banners would have been involved--and Marc wouldn't have been shot.

Before long the sounds of activity and tense, hushed voices reached the threshold of Kira's awareness, Kira pulled away from Zeke. With tears stinging her eyes she watched with numb awareness as on-site paramedics tried to talk Clint into releasing his brother. At last he rose to his feet with Marc's limp body in his arms. From there he carefully laid Marc onto an awaiting gurney. Nick and Clint hovered protectively over their youngest brother as they followed him outside to the ambulance.

"Wi--will he be all right, do you think?"

"I don't know," Zeke breathed. Suddenly setting her away from him, he gave her a quick once over.

"I'm all right," she said in answer to his unasked question. She looked up at him and added on a breathless sob, "Zeke...I'm sorry for--"

Drawing her back into his embrace, she felt his lips brush her brow. "I know," he whispered.

"You Slater?"

Glancing up, Zeke found a young man making his way around a toppled chair and broken lamp. "Who wants to know?"

"I'm Logan, Matt Logan," he said, extending a hand in greeting. "I'm the one who met your people at the spaceport."

Several heartbeats passed before Zeke accepted the young man's outstretched hand. "Zeke Slater."

Logan glanced about the room, taking in the bodies of Kendyl and Preston still lying where they'd fallen. "Geez, what the devil happened?"

"All hell," Zeke replied.

Logan shook his head slowly. "Sure hope he's going to be all right. Marc's a good man. Not many I know would squeeze in with those snakes." His gaze slid to Kira. "Are you Miss Delaney?"

Kira nodded slowly. "Yes."

"If you'll come with me, there's someone who wants to talk with you."

"Can't it wait?" Zeke interrupted.

"I don't think so."

"It's all right, Zeke, I'll be right ba--"

"Kira, honey?"

Kira's gaze lifted to find Renn Delaney bracing himself in the open doorway--thin, weakened, but very much alive.

"Dad!" And then she was in his arms, their joy momentarily chasing away the tragedy and violence--the hell they had both been through over the last few months.

~ * ~

"We discovered him in one of the mines," Logan went on. "Preston had him working as a slave. Something about forcing his hand to sign over his half of the company..."

Zeke's attention was divided as Kira and Renn turned and made their way out of the suite.

She never glanced back.

CHAPTER TWENTY-NINE

The console keys clicked beneath Slater's fingertips as he methodically went through the pre-lift procedures. "Bow thruster port."

"Check," came Frank's response.

"Bow thruster starboard."

"Check."

"Midship thruster, port..." Within minutes, the preflight routine was accomplished and Frank was announcing clearance to lift. The subtle vibration of ignition soon became a low rumble, and then the ear-piercing scream of lift-off.

Nearly five hours had passed since the incident at Major Metals. After a general check over at Port Ore's emergency clinic, Zeke was released with doctor's orders to take it easy on the trip home. His injuries consisted mainly of bruises and a pulled tendon in his left arm. Surprisingly, he had no broken bones or internal injuries.

After leaving the clinic, Zeke and Nick spent over two hours with interplanetary police in a grueling interrogation session. It wasn't until Kira and Renn showed up and validated his statements that he was released. Preston had obviously succeeded in snowing even the law, as several local boys were ready to jump to Preston's defense when Zeke had begun unraveling the mutinous plot to take over Major Metals. Steve Talbot had yet to be found, and probably never would be.

The longer it took, the more detailed things became. All it would have taken was one wrong answer and Zeke would have found himself facing a whole new set of questions explaining his double identity.

"Y' know, I don't get it," Frank said idly. "If Preston had Delaney all along, then why the devil was he after Kira? Once Delaney signed over his half, wouldn't that automatically put Kira out of it?"

Slater smiled. "Yes, but Delaney refused to relinquish his half, and when slavery wouldn't force him into it, Preston decided to go after Kira. Either kill her or get her to sign off her half."

"So you were the wild card Preston hadn't figured on," Frank added.

"So it would seem." Zeke leaned forward and made a minor adjustment to the controls. Coordinates had been set for Quade's world--specifically to take Kira and Renn home.

With Steve Talbot assumed dead, it was just Zeke and Frank manning the helm. He could have drafted someone into Steve's position from the extra crew members on board...but right now, he just wanted to be alone.

Clint and Nick had remained dirtside with Marc. The small emergency clinic was primitive by comparison to the medical center on Acacia, but Marc was alive, and until he was strong enough to be moved, there was no option but to keep him there.

Renn Delaney had also been given a once over, grumbling the entire time. "I'm fine," he'd argued. "I just want to get the devil away from here." And technically he was fine, other than obvious exhaustion and weight loss. His release finally came with strict orders for rest on the trip home and to see his own physician for a complete physical once he got there.

So far, with Kira playing a cross between a nursemaid and sergeant, Renn had no choice but to relax and allow her to wait on him.

Zeke had seen very little of Kira since they'd lifted off Echo. Actually, it was good he was taking her home, though he was still trying to convince himself of that fact. After all, this was exactly what he'd been wanting from the day he first found her on board. With a wearied sigh, he reached for his mug of coffee. The decision facing him now was one of the hardest he'd ever had to make.

Let her go. You can't afford to get any more involved. Remember, detachment is what makes you so damn good. Let her go.

"Let 'er go, Boss."

Zeke all but choked on his coffee as Frank ascended the short flight of stairs to the helm. "...What?"

"The ship," Frank clarified. "I'll take over for y'."

With a muttered acknowledgement, Zeke rose from his seat and turned for his quarters. A muscle clenched along his jaw as he mulled over--for what seemed the ten thousandth time--the thought of Kira having been in Quint Kendyl's possession. It had been on his mind constantly, replaying itself with heart-stopping clarity. In truth, he'd never been so scared in his whole damn life. And never wanted to be that scared again.

So, what the hell was he anyway? In love? What else would explain the heaviness he felt inside? Why his chest hurt like it did?

Lying face up on his bunk, Zeke came to a decision. He could not risk Kira's life for his own selfish reasons. He had to let her go--get her back home where she belonged. And that meant having to watch her leave. He tried ignoring the wave of heartache that washed over him at the thought. One way or another, he had to end it before he did something crazy--like beg her to stay.

He should have returned her to Acacia the instant he discovered she'd stowed back on board, but he didn't. The temptation of her standing there in nothing more than his shirt had been his undoing. If only he hadn't yielded--consummating a marriage he would all too soon be dissolving. He just hoped Kira would understand, especially when he, himself, wasn't sure he understood.

~ * ~

Kira was alone in the lounge when Zeke joined her. For the past five minutes he'd been going on about how Renn would be needing her now. Kira stood behind the bench in front of the viewport, clinging to the back rest with both hands. She couldn't look at him, and fought the overwhelming urge to put her hands over her ears. Relentlessly, he went on, his voice calm and pragmatic as though he were discussing the coordinates of their next destination instead of the direction her life would be taking. Leveled, that's how she felt--as if there was nothing left of her broken heart but pieces.

"Once we're back in Port Chance," he went on calmly, "You'll be able to help Renn recuperate, and then the two of you can begin restoring Major Metals to its former state. If you'd like, Frank has concocted a story to explain your presence with me. Renn won't ever have to know, or anyone else for that matter--about the marriage, that is. I will personally handle all the arrangements for having it dissolved."

Avoiding his eyes, Kira turned to face him. Nothing in Zeke's countenance indicated he felt anything beyond a desire to be rid of her as discreetly and diplomatically as possible. In fact, Kira had the distinct impression he was more relieved than anything. There was no mention of love, or even a hint of regret over the intimacies they had shared.

"I see," she said, failing miserably at matching his cool indifference. Where was her own veneer of nonchalance that always seemed to get her through times like this? "Tell Frank thank you for the offer, but I'd just as soon Dad not know anything about me ever being-- with you." A heartbeat of eternity passed before she managed through a thick whisper, "I'll figure out what to tell him."

"As you wish."

What she wished was the love and heart of a privateer named Zeke Slater, but a simple "thanks," was all she could get out. Her throat closing, Kira found it difficult to continue and turned her attention back to the view port and the star-studded blackness beyond. The silence that fell between them was broken only by the now familiar sounds of the ship and the occasional laugh of a crew member drifting in from the galley across the way.

It was a good name, *Solar Wind*--the phenomenon for which Zeke's ship was christened. For the solar wind emanates straight off the sun's fiery surface at a horrendous speed, dragging bits and pieces of the sun with it as it streaks into outer space.

In many ways, Kira likened Zeke to the solar wind, dragging with him bits and pieces of her broken heart. She despaired of ever truly capturing his love.

Frank's pipe smoke drifted in from the corridor, pungent and fragrant as it blended with the other familiar scents of the ship. In the reflection of the view port, she could see Zeke standing behind her, his face as shadowed and just as obscured in the dim lighting as the emotions he had tucked away inside.

She'd known this moment would come eventually. Zeke had never been anything but honest and up-front with her. So why hadn't she been more prepared? And why did it have to hurt so?

"Kira," Zeke's voice intruded upon her thoughts, "Please realize that I am only concerned for your safety."

"Is that right?" She whirled around, sudden anger flushing her cheeks. "Concerned, Zeke, or burdened? I didn't notice you being too concerned while I was sharing your bunk."

Kira knew she had cut him with that one. Zeke was staring at her with an expression she was afraid to interpret. It hovered somewhere between astonishment at her audacity and fury at her assessment.

When she turned to leave, he caught her arm. "Dammit, Kira, this...occupation comes with no guarantees that I'll walk away from the next confrontation. I won't have you caught in the middle of the next crisis."

Without another word she twisted from his grasp and made her escape down the corridor toward her newly assigned quarters--Frank's cabin again.

What he didn't know is that the decision to sleep elsewhere had been made long before her dad ever entered the picture; the catalyst, of course, being the overheard by-play between Zeke and Nick just before they arrived on Echo.

Kira's vision was clouded with tears by the time the door closed behind her. The next instant she was face down upon the bunk, her hands curling into the soft cover. It was hard to know what exactly hurt most-- the rejection, or the implication that what they'd shared meant nothing more than a regrettable experience. And, he did regret it. He wasn't fooling her for an instant with his lame excuses of concern for her safety.

At least she'd made it to the cabin before succumbing to tears--an odd experience lately--tears. She'd never been one to give in to them.

"Kira?"

Sniffle.

She heard the panel hiss open. "You know you really should learn to lock your door," a deep voice drawled behind her.

Hastily swiping the tears off her cheeks, Kira turned over to see Zeke standing in the open portal. "Get out," she snapped. "I don't feel like talking right now."

"So I gathered." The door closed behind him as he stepped inside anyway.

Kira sat up. "I said--"

"I know." Zeke crossed the tiny cabin, coming to rest at the foot of the bunk. "It's just our discussion back there ended a little abruptly."

"Oh? You weren't finished?" She managed a careless shrug. "I was."

Silence deepened until Zeke finally cleared his throat and said, "Look Kira, if you think this is any easier for me--"

She halted him with a raised hand. "Please, spare me the lies. Besides, don't you have other things you should be doing?"

"I don't like leaving you--especially like this."

"What? The tears?" she asked. "You overrate yourself, Slater. These tears have absolutely nothing to do with you," she lied coolly.

One eyebrow rose.

Kira schooled her features. "I've been given back the one person who means the most to me, and we're on our way home."

Zeke's mouth curved into a sardonic smile. "I see."

Kira looked away. Why didn't he just go and leave her alone. He'd said what he had to say. Married or not, she'd known from the beginning it wouldn't last. He'd made it perfectly clear where she stood.

"Ah...Legs..."

"The name's Kira."

Zeke sat down beside her. "Kira, I can't take you with me...much as I'd like."

"I don't remember asking."

His hands settled on the slope of her shoulders and gently he pulled her against him. "I think your stubbornness is what I like most about you." His fingers slipped beneath the silken mass of her dark hair as he caressed her. "It's what kept you steadfast at times when the bottom dropped out of life."

Predictably, that deep, easy voice and merest of touches sent a tremor chasing down her spine. But Kira held fast to her anger--the only thing left shielding her vulnerable heart. No way would he smooth things over with sugarcoated words.

Ever so tenderly Zeke began applying a light pressure with his thumbs, drawing lazy circles across her shoulders and base of her neck. Oh, how she wanted to drop her head forward, giving him better access to her neck and spine--but she'd die before she gave him the satisfaction of thinking he could control her so easily with a few words or his touch. A shiver chased through her when a daring hand found and explored the sensitive lobe of an ear. Instantly pulling away, Kira turned to face him.

Zeke regarded her with an intensity that made her stomach flutter before he finally said in a faintly amused voice, "Contrary to what rumor may have it, I don't generally make a habit of allowing stowaways to remain on board."

"No, you only seduce them if you want information. Besides, if you will recall, I insisted on being set off at the nearest port."

"Yes, you did. And I suspect we both would have been better off if I had." He softened the truth of his words with a grin. "And knowing you, you'd have had both Preston and Kendyl begging for mercy before you were finished."

Kira studied Zeke's face--his exquisite face--now swollen, cut and bruised, and her eyes filled with tears. In the space of just a few weeks, he'd been shot, forced into marriage and now beaten. And if that wasn't enough, his friend, Marc, had been seriously wounded, and young Steve Talbot was probably dead. The image of Steve flooded her mind. Both he and Frank had always been kind to her, especially during the times when Zeke seemed to be at his worst. Kira knew that for Zeke the pain of having lost a member of his crew had to run deep. It's said that a captain's first responsibility is to his ship and crew, and knowing Zeke, he wouldn't take that commitment lightly. It was no wonder that he'd be anxious to rid himself of her.

"Anyway..." Zeke pressed, "you'd be on your way back home by now. Which is exactly what's happening."

"Only one minor difference. I wouldn't be married, let alone to a man who sees me as excess cargo."

Slater hesitated, then raked a hand through his hair. "If you're referring to the conversation between me and Nick, I'd like to explain--"

"I don't need or want your explanations, Slater. Besides, your conversation with Nick is only part of it."

With a groan, Zeke clapped a hand over his eyes. "Damn," he muttered, "I'd hoped for just a small amount of understanding, but I can see that isn't going to happen. Kira," he said, removing his hand, "unintentional as it was, I hurt your feelings. And I am so damned sorry. You have no idea."

Kira sat very still. Hurt feelings? Glancing down at her entwined fingers, her gaze moved to the brand on her wrist--the symbol that made her his.

"I know," Zeke said, guessing at her thoughts. "Don't worry; I'll see what I can do about getting that removed for you."

"Good," she muttered. "The sooner the better."

Kira didn't look up at him. Couldn't at the moment. He might be able to get the brand off her wrist, but what about the one on her heart?

"Kira," he said gently. "I'm returning you to Quade's World for one reason only. Honey, it's too damn dangerous for you to remain aboard the *Solar Wind*."

Dangerous for whom, she wanted to ask. It was obvious he was ridding himself of her as delicately as possible. And she didn't doubt for an instant but that in his line of work and resulting connections, he would know all sorts of ways to get out of something as sticky as marriage.

"Something else is bothering you," he asked sincerely. "What is it?"

What could she say? The truth? That she'd fallen hopelessly in love with him?

As if he understood her inner turmoil, Zeke said nothing. Instead he drew her into his embrace. And for what seemed an eternity he held her close. Rocked in his arms, Kira listened to the steady beat of his heart, the even rhythm of his breathing and silently lost the battle against her tears.

He held her until she stopped crying, then gallantly offered a corner his shirt on which to wipe her eyes and nose. "You know, you really shouldn't make a habit of weeping," he said lightly. "Your nose is as red as a flare."

She pulled away from him. "Gee thanks."

Zeke laughed softly and gently squeezed her. "Kira, I guarantee by the time you get home and settled back in, you'll see the reason in this."

"I already do," she said and pulled away from him.

"Ah, Kira..." leaving the words hanging, Zeke tucked a finger beneath her chin and tilted her face up to his. She didn't fight him. Something flickered across his face--a subtle change in those stormy gray eyes. Kira caught a brief glimpse of...regret? Desperation? It was a look she'd never seen before. But then he squelched it. And as quickly as it appeared, it was gone, hidden beneath that veneer of cool resolve.

~ * ~

Port Chance, Quade's World:

"It's much better this way." Zeke dug his fingers into the smooth railing at the threshold of the open hatch, unable to look at Kira. The last thing he needed right now was to see the shadows in her eyes, the faint trembling of her lower lip that she was trying so hard to control.

"Yes," she agreed quietly as she moved out onto the top of the boarding ramp.

"They'll be notifying you when Aylie is ready for adoption," he added.

Kira nodded.

"I figure around five months by the time she goes through quarantine and all."

"All right." Kira released a sigh and looked out across the landing zone. It seemed like a thousand years ago she had ended up on board his ship. And now...

"In a few days, all this will be behind you."

Raw fuel drifted on the breeze. A company ground runner was located near the base of the gangway. Renn had already been escorted off ship and was now sitting in the back waiting for Kira to disembark. Soon, she would be safely home.

"I-I suppose I won't see you again," she said without looking up at him.

Zeke hesitated. Would he see her again? Promises were easily made, and so damn hard to keep. She was already hurting. How could he tell her he'd see her again when he had no idea what the hell might happen tomorrow?

A sudden breeze swept auburn tendrils of hair across her throat and he resisted the urge to brush them aside.

"With being committed to another year of working for the organization," he said, "I can't promise I'll see you soon."

"I understand." Her voice was hollow.

Damn. Why couldn't he just say what he knew she needed to hear? Three little words that could be said so easily. But now was not the right time; later, when he'd see her again. By then he'd be free of this commitment and--if she's still willing to listen, he'd tell her exactly what's in his heart.

"They're waiting, Kira," he said bluntly and took her by the arm. Instantly, the brief contact jolted him--even through the leather jacket she wore.

Without a doubt, this intoxicating woman standing before him would not be available by the time he returned to Port Chance.

"They're waiting," he repeated almost gruffly and gestured toward the gangway where Frank stood ready to escort her off. It was all he could do to keep from drawing her into his arms for one last time. Instead, he said stiffly, "Take her, Frank," and pushed her, ever so gently, into the old man's hands.

Kira pulled away. "Really, I don't need an escort."

"Well then, Boss," Frank quickly interjected, "if I'm not needed here, I got things yet t' do before departure." At Zeke's nod, Frank turned to Kira and took her hand in his. "Kira, we're shor gonna miss yer bright and shinin' face around here, darlin'. You take good care o' yerself, and that little one too, when y' get her. Y' hear me?"

"I'm going to miss you too, Frank," she said, leaning forward and giving Frank a kiss on the cheek. "Promise you'll watch over him for me?" she whispered against his ear.

"That goes without askin'." With a curt nod of dismissal, Frank turned and rigidly retreated through the main hatch.

Releasing a heavy sigh, Kira glanced down at the awaiting ground runner. "Well...I'd better go. They seem to be getting impatient."

Following her gaze, Zeke saw the driver standing in wait beside the open rear door. Renn signaled him from inside. It was obvious the man was anxious to be on his way. "Yeah, looks that way," Zeke said.

When Kira's gaze lifted to meet his, an intense pain coiled in the pit of his gut. Ah damn, how he wanted to reach for her.

"Zeke, did--did I thank you for saving my life?" she asked belatedly.

He shrugged, "Think nothing of it."

Kira smiled faintly. "All in the line of duty, eh Captain?"

Zeke managed a grin. "Something like that."

For several heartbeats, neither of them said anything. Then finally Kira said, "Well...goodbye." Her whispered voice was barely audible above the distant roar of a departing freighter.

Unable to force anything more than the mention of her name past his constricting throat, Slater gave a terse nod and pivoted on his heel, disappearing through the hatch before losing the last thread of resistance and the reasoning that compelled him to send her away in the first place.

He never turned to glance back. Just the thought of watching her walk out of his life tightened the fist in his gut.

~ * ~

The ground runner slowed to a stop upon reaching the edge of the landing field. Kira swallowed convulsively, longing for just one last glimpse of Zeke as she turned her gaze out the back window. But it was too much to hope for--the only ones to be seen were spaceport personnel hovering about the ship like bees around a giant flower. The *Solar Wind* sat sleek and low within its designated circle of float lights. A tiny red beacon pulsed on her belly. A flashing strobe punctuated the tip of each swept-back wing. There was little doubt but that she was being readied for immediate departure.

"Honey, after we get settled, I thought maybe you could update me on some details over lunch," Renn said, breaking the silence,

Briefly turning, she managed a bright smile. "That sounds like a wonderful idea." But in reality she didn't want to think about details, or anything else, for that matter. Numb from sleepless nights and an aching heart, she could only stare miserably out the back window until the vehicle swung onto the main thoroughfare and the *Solar Wind* slid from her view. With a hard swallow, she turned back around. All she wanted now was to get home and crawl into her big soft bed.

"Are you okay, sweetheart?"

Her smile was genuine when she again turned her gaze upon Renn's worried face. "I'm fine, Dad. Just tired...that's all."

Drawing his arm about her, he added reassuringly, "What do you say we postpone lunch and save the details for another time. And instead, why don't you get some rest."

Laying her head on his shoulder, Kira nodded.

"It's over, honey," he whispered.

Yes, it was indeed over. In more ways than one. She'd come so close--so very close to begging Zeke to take her with him. She had called upon every ounce of willpower she possessed. But in the end, it left her with the one thing no one could ever take from her: her dignity. Her pride.

With a sigh, her gaze returned to the side window. Yes, it was all over and she would be fine. After all, she was a survivor, wasn't she?

CHAPTER THIRTY

Having left the helm for a routine check before lifting, Zeke made his way down the narrow passageway toward his cabin.

He should record this scene and add it to the memory crystal, he thought bleakly as he entered his quarters. Let's see, it could be captioned, The Discipline of an Idiot, or any other appropriate title utilizing the word idiot, or fool, or--

Slater's dismal thoughts slammed to a halt at the faint noise coming from the open lav.

Kira. She wouldn't dare sneak back on board. He frowned. Would she? But how could she, when he'd watched from the viewport as the ground runner disappeared around the corner?

Besides, how could he ever muster up the courage to send her away a second time?

"That you, Boss?"

Frank. Zeke's knees nearly buckled with relief...or was it disappointment? He wasn't sure. Hell, either way he was losing his mind.

"Be outta yer way in a flash, Capt'n'," Frank muttered, poking his head out the door. "Just checkin' ship's supplies, addin' a few things to the restockin' list while we're here."

It was good Frank hadn't waited for a response, because Zeke's throat at the moment was too taut to reply. Crossing the cabin to his desk, he sank into his cushioned chair and leaned forward, bracing his weight on his elbows and his forehead in his hands. This was insane, this self-made hell. Would he ever be free of Kira's memory, he wondered?

At last, rubbing a hand over his tired eyes, he remained in his cabin long after he heard the unmistakable sounds of preparation for departure. Frank's gravelly voice could be heard barking orders from somewhere down the corridor. He barely remembered the old man leaving his quarters. The familiar muscle clenched in his jaw. No matter how hard, or whatever it took, he had to shake off this depression. There was no other option but to send Kira away. And too damn much at stake now to be wallowing in self-pity over it.

With a sigh of determination, Zeke rose from his chair and made his way toward the helm.

~ * ~

Three weeks later:
Port Chance, Quade's World:

"Are you looking for a special star, or just wishing upon the first one you see?"

Kira turned to find Renn standing in the doorway.

"Neither," she replied, extending her hand in invitation.

She smiled brightly. "Besides...my wish came true when I got you back."

"It did, huh?" Accepting her offered hand, Renn moved to stand beside her. "Then why is it I have this feeling you've still got a wish or two left in your heart?"

Kira laughed and squeezed his hand. "Only for your speedy recovery, Dad."

"I see." Renn glanced thoughtfully up into the evening sky. "Funny thing about wishes," he said. "They're supposed to come in threes. And if that's true, then that still leaves you one wish to go."

Again, Kira laughed. "Yes, I suppose it would."

"So...any ideas what your third wish would be?" Renn asked smoothly and waited for her answer.

She turned to face him. "How about for the continued recovery and success of Major Metals?"

"Oh, no, you don't. That's my wish. No, sweetheart, this one's got to be strictly for you."

"Strictly for me? Hmmm," Kira lifted her gaze heavenward in mock consideration. "Let me see. Then I'd probably wish for a--I know, how about a nice long vacation to somewhere quiet and beautiful...far, far away?"

Renn slowly shook his head.

"What's the matter with that? It sounds pretty good to me."

"It sounds wonderful, little one, but are you sure that's the wish your heart would make?"

Choosing not to respond, Kira returned her gaze to the stars. Did her father have any idea that his little girl wasn't his anymore but a woman who'd fallen head over heels in love with a pirate? What would he say if he knew that she had given herself to this man--with no regrets? Or that she missed him with all her heart and wondered if he ever thought of her.

"Kira, for godsake, I wasn't born yesterday," Renn blurted out as if reading her mind. "You think I don't know you've been brooding over Slater ever since we left his ship?"

Kira could only look at him. There was no arguing. Her arguments would be just lies anyway. And besides, when it came to lying to him, she never was any good at it. "You've known?" she finally asked.

Renn nodded. "From the moment I first came aboard his ship."

Kira's eyes welled with tears.

"You love him. And you feel he doesn't return that love. Am I right?"

Swallowing, she looked away.

"Seems to me, for someone who doesn't care, he sure took one hell of a risk."

"All in the line of duty," she said. "I overheard a conversation between him and Nick. I know how he really feels, Dad." At the moment she didn't want to admit that Zeke had apologized for the stupid conversation she'd overheard between him and Nick.

Renn simply smiled.

"Dad, he's not the same man he was back when he used to work for you. I could tell you things--" Realizing she was about to cross into forbidden territory, Kira stopped mid-sentence.

"I'm aware of that, honey," he said, earning him a sidelong glance of disbelief. "Oh, I may not know all the details, but I know he's up to his neck in trouble most of the time." Renn shrugged. "We talked quite a bit on the way back." He smiled and added, "He'd often show up after you headed off for bed."

Kira absently rubbed her wrist. Regardless of what Zeke chose to reveal to him, trouble was hardly the word she would use to describe Zeke's life. Courting death was more like it.

"Funny thing about symbols like this one," Renn murmured, gently capturing her hand and turning it over for his inspection, "they generally come as a matched set--and I understand no two pair are alike." He frowned in contemplation. "You know, I could have sworn I saw the mirrored duplicate of this same design imprinted on Zeke's wrist."

"Dad, it's not--"

"You think I don't know what this is--what it means?"

She swallowed hard. "But...it's...not what you think. I mean... Dad, Zeke was backed into a corner at the time. We had no choice."

Renn's brow arched.

"It was the only way he could...protect me," she blurted out then added, "Besides, he promised to have it removed as soon as possible."

"I see..." Renn's voice trailed into a heartbeat of silence while Kira tensed. Finally, he lifted his gaze to meet hers. "I'm not even going to ask the one question foremost in my mind right now, because--number one it's none of my business. And, number two, just from observing you two, I think I already know the answer."

Neither denying nor confirming his suspicions, Kira remained silent while Renn went on.

"You say he promised to have it removed?"

"Yes. As soon as possible."

"Don't you find it a little odd he didn't bother to make the necessary arrangements before leaving?"

"If he promised to have it removed, he'll have it removed."

"Did he look you straight in the eye when he said it?"

"What?"

"Or was he studying the ground between his boots?" Renn lifted his gaze to the horizon, still faintly warmed with dusk's afterglow. "What if he doesn't want it removed?" he asked distantly.

"That's ridiculous. Zeke has made it perfectly clear what he wants."

With a shrug, Renn turned to face her. "And what do you want, Kira?"

She started to look away and Renn gently cupped her jaw, returning her focus. With understanding and compassion, loving brown eyes met troubled green ones. "What if you're seeing exactly what he wants you to see?"

Kira lowered her eyes in confusion.

"Look beyond the surface, Kira," he said. "Look and listen with your heart, not your eyes or ears." Releasing her, he added, "You understand what I am trying to tell you?"

Swallowing, she simply stared up at him before slowly nodding. "You're saying, you think he--"

Renn shook his head. "You're the only one who can determine that, honey."

"Oh..." The word came out on a whisper of air.

"Well," Renn said on a sigh, "I think I'm going to call it a night." With a gentle squeeze of her hand, he turned away, heading back into the house.

'Look beyond the surface. Listen with your heart.' His words echoed over and over again through Kira's mind. How could she see beyond the surface, when the surface was all Zeke Slater ever showed her? And especially when the surface wasn't always a very pleasant side to see. How many times had she been bullied or insulted? *You're a stowaway,'* he had once drawled. *'You have any idea what that means, sweetheart?'* From there he'd gone on to explain how interplanetary law put a stowaway completely at the captain's mercy...and how at the moment, he wasn't feeling very merciful. Zeke's ruthless counsel was so opposite of the loving advice Renn had just given her.

But wasn't that just after she trashed his cabin? Kira winced at the memory of Zeke trying to keep his temper in check while standing in the midst of a mess that looked to be the work of a crazy person.

Look beyond the surface, Kira, beyond that rough exterior. Beyond the warnings and insinuations that had never once been carried out.

Even the memory of Frank's straightforward declaration ambled through her mind. *'Any other captain and you'd have already been a ride-under for him and half his crew by now.'*

Listen with your heart.

A soft evening breeze lifted tendrils of hair off her neck and face as Kira stood in silence listening to the din of inner voices.

For someone who doesn't care, he sure went out of his way and took a hell of a risk in your behalf.

She recalled Lilo--would never forget the heart-stopping image Zeke had made, standing there so calm and ominous as he ordered her assailants to drop their weapons and let her go. The slug he'd ended up taking that night almost killed him.

How could she ever forget Aden and the desert warrior he'd taken-on when most men might have left her to her fate. Recalling the mandatory bonding ceremony that followed his conquest, Kira's gaze dropped to her wrist. Back then, the thought of another brand on her body or the very idea of belonging to anyone but herself had scared her beyond words.

Absently, she traced the intricate design, its iridescent details oddly glowing in the semi-darkness. Funny how feelings change--how the very thought of not belonging to Zeke Slater now left her feeling empty and hollow inside.

Then there was Echo. For as long as she lived, Kira would never forget the sight of Zeke, battered and bruised, as he hung from an overhead beam while Kendyl ordered his torture. She recalled him, during a time when he had been in the most pain, begging her not to bargain with them on his behalf--could still hear his voice, pleading with her until his protests were silenced with a blow that rendered him unconscious.

Inhaling sharply, Kira blinked back tears at the memory and the dawning realization that the fear and agony she'd seen in Zeke's eyes had nothing to do with physical torture, but from the mental anguish of seeing her in Kendyl's clutches.

'You're the only one who can determine his feelings, honey.' Renn's counsel drifted through her mind. *'Listen with your heart.'*

Dare she even think it? Had his persistence and the pragmatic handling of getting her off ship been as hard on him as it was on her?

Did Zeke love her?

~ * ~

Morning sun streamed through the skylight of the breakfast room with a cheerful glow. Renn glanced up from his daily news bulletin and smiled as Kira entered the room. "Good morning, honey. You're looking exceptionally radiant this morning."

"Thanks, Dad, and how are you feeling?" she asked, taking a seat at the table.

"I'm doing a little better each day." Renn returned to his reading as a servant approached offering a platter of fresh fruit for Kira's selection.

"Come to any conclusions last night?" he asked, keeping his eyes trained on the bulletin.

"Sort of," she replied, selecting a small cluster of juicy spin berries, a delicately textured fruit named for their unusual pinwheel of color.

Renn's head came up out of the news, one eyebrow raised. "Sort of?"

"All right. Yes."

Setting the bulletin aside, Renn reached for his cup of coffee. "And...?"

Anticipation hung suspended while Kira finished making her selection off the fruit platter. "There's no 'and'."

"I see... Decide there's nothing there--nothing worth salvaging?"

Kira used the edge of her fork to slice through the purplish flesh of a locally grown melon and replied without looking up. "I didn't say that."

"Forgive me. What did you say?"

With a sigh, she stopped and glanced up at him. "Simply that I will wait for him."

"Wait for him. Hmmm."

Kira shook her head to the offered tray of sweet rolls, dismissing the attending servant with a smile.

"Yes, when his commitment is over," she said, turning back to Renn, "I'll be here."

"And what do you plan on doing while you're waiting?"

Kira laughed, halting her fork half way to her mouth. "I'll soon have Aylie to keep me plenty busy."

"No more gallivanting about the spaceport looking for escapees?"

Kira leaned back in her chair. "Well, of course I'll help with the group--just not in the same capacity as before."

"Kira," he said on a sigh, "you see these gray-hairs?"

"Oh, Dad--"

"Most of them are caused from worry over you, honey. It's true," he persisted. "For a while--when you were spending nights down there--I didn't know if you were dead, in jail, or just plain kidnapped again."

"I won't be spending nights down there anymore. I won't be helping with the rescues anymore. Instead, I'll be helping to get the survivors into recovery.

That wasn't the answer he was looking for. She could see it in the thinning of his mouth.

"Let me see if I understand this correctly," he said. "While Zeke's off risking his life to rid the trade ways of pirates and slavers, he's thinking all the while that you're safe here at home."

"But I will be." She laughed lightly, "Besides, how do you know he's even thinking of me at all?"

A corner of Renn's mouth twisted with exasperation. "The point is, you're risking your life no matter how safe you think your position is with that group. And the crazy part is it's for basically the same cause."

Kira shrugged. "That's true."

"Kira..." Renn's tone softened. "There's no doubt in my mind that Slater's got his backside well covered during his encounters. But, who the hell's covering yours while you're out waging war on slavery?"

She smiled. "Dad, really. You can hardly call it waging war. Like I say, I'd be--"

"No, I've been doing a lot of thinking about this, and last night I came to a very hard conclusion." He paused and she saw his eyes narrow with emotion. "I've decided--Dammit, Kira," he blurted out. "I'd rather it be Zeke Slater watching your back than one of those hell-bent renegade friends of yours."

Kira simply stared at him without speaking--stared until the silence dragged on unbearably. "Just what exactly are you saying?" she finally asked.

"Exactly what you think I said." A server materialized long enough to refill Renn's coffee then disappeared. "And before I go any further," he continued, "I need to know if you're interested in hearing more?"

"Go on," she said cautiously.

"Okay. First of all, I've found out that the *Solar Wind* is sitting in port right now on Acacia."

At the mere mention of Zeke's whereabouts, her heart did a queer little dance. "He's at the Banners'?" she asked, failing miserably at masking the anxiousness in her voice.

Renn shrugged. "All I know is his ship's been in port three days."

Neither of them spoke for several moments. Then Kira murmured, "I wonder if Marc is back home." When she lifted her gaze, Renn was studying her intently.

"What???"

He shook his head. "Nothing."

"Surely you're not suggesting--"

"Aren't I?"

Kira met his eyes directly, unable to believe what she was hearing. The faint clatter of dishes behind the closed doors of the steward's pantry was a dead giveaway that their conversation wasn't private.

Finally, she set her fork down. "Even if I was interested in this little fiasco of yours, you're forgetting one minor little point. He doesn't want me."

"I'm not so sure about that."

Kira swallowed, her throat tightening with emotion.

"Do you want to be with him, Kira?"

Silence. Then came her whispered, "Yes."

"Zeke is a man of principle. He's committed himself to this...mission, for at least another year. He won't back out on his own. If you love him, go after him. Change his mind as only you can."

CHAPTER THIRTY-ONE

One week later:
The Banner Home--Acacia:

"Move him out, Rae!" Zeke shouted. "Show him you mean business--that he can't get away with doing whatever he feels like doing."

Rae Banner stepped forward and cracked the whip in the air. Instantly, Thor gathered his haunches and took off on a canter, head high, tail raised and flying as he circled the paddock. The whip, Zeke had carefully taught her, was never to touch the horse, but to merely pop and keep him moving.

"Good," Zeke shouted over the pounding cadence of hooves and the whuffing of Thor's breathing. "Now, turn him."

This time Rae took a step sideways, as if to move into his path. With a snort, the stallion skidded to a halt, turned on his haunches and took off at an extended trot in the other direction.

"See him looking over the fence, Rae? He's not thinking about you right now. He's checking out those fillies in the far pasture. Now, show me how you're going to gain back his attention."

Again Rae popped the whip and took a step, again forcing the big animal to whirl about on his haunches.

"That's it. Good."

Frank ambled up next to Zeke and draped his arms over the top rail. "How's Marc this mornin'?"

"Better," Zeke replied without taking his eyes off Thor and Rae. "But the body's healing faster than the attitude, if you ask me."

"Thank he'll ever walk again?"

"Doc says yes. I say all he needs is a pretty therapist."

Frank chuckled. "I'm just glad to hear the boy's gonna be all right."

"Yeah. Getting shot in the first place was a stupid mistake that should never have happened. We'd all been so willing to stand back and let him have his moment of glory--and he was ahead too. Not a damn one of us saw it coming--but we should have."

"Turn him Rae!" Zeke called out. "That's it."

"Little gal seems to be holdin' 'er own with 'im."

Eyes trained on the horse and Rae Banner, Zeke opened his mouth to respond, only to call out instead, "Very good! Now drive him on. Did you see him look at you instead of daydreaming about all those pretty girls? Next time he does that, remember to lower the whip. Relax and give him the opportunity to turn toward you."

"You gonna let her have 'im?"

Zeke shrugged, still not taking his eyes off the action. "Probably. God knows, he needs the attention."

"You're doing good!" he called out again. "Remember you're not there to wear him down. You're there to show him how much easier it is to give in than to keep charging around the paddock. He knows what you want, he's just too damn stubborn to submit."

Another thirty minutes passed while Rae drove Thor around the paddock with the whip. Finally, his flanks heaving, the big stallion stopped and turned to face her.

Zeke said quietly, "Lower the whip Rae, but be ready to drive him on again the instant he starts to take his eyes off you."

Nostrils flared, head lowered, Thor simply stood there peering at Rae through his silky long forelock. A decision had been reached.

After several minutes, Zeke instructed her to circle him slowly. At first the stallion followed her with his head then began slowly pivoting in a tight circle to keep her in view.

"Verrry, verrry good," he said softly. "Thor's earned himself a little attention. Go ahead and pet him. Talk to him. Then I want you to turn your back and start walking away."

Rae followed his instructions and Slater grinned as the big stallion proceeded to follow her about the paddock like an enormous puppy. After that, she cooled him off and led him back to the stable. Soon the small crowd that had gathered at the fence dispersed, leaving Zeke and Frank still standing there.

Again the conversation returned to Frank's favorite subject as of late--Kira.

"Did I ever tell y' how much y' remind me of that horse o' yers," Frank drawled.

No response. Not that Zeke expected his silence to stop the old man.

"That little darlin's in love with y' and y' know it. But just like that horse, yer too dad-blame stubborn to give in. Instead, yer chargin' half way across the galaxy trying to get away from 'er." He shook his head and mumbled, "Just lucky for you I'm not thirty years younger."

Though he couldn't prevent the lopsided grin, Zeke didn't respond. He'd heard it all a hundred times if he'd heard it once, although this--this comparing him to Thor--now that was a whole new twist in tactics.

Frank had only just begun. "Y' hear that?" he asked and waited.

With a sigh, Zeke took the bait. "What? The horses?"

"Nope," Frank answered. "Beyond that."

Zeke listened. "I don't hear anything."

"Thaaat's right," Frank drawled. "Y' don't hear a damned thang, do y'? And let me tell y' somethin' else, that's exactly what yer gonna go right on hearin'. Nothin', until the day y' die in the middle of some blazin' battle."

Silence.

Y' know...nothin' can be a mighty frightenin' sound, especially at my age. Though, at the rate yer goin', I suppose y' don't have to worry about that do y'? You won't last this long."

Zeke said nothing, just stared out across the paddock.

Frank removed his pipe from his pocket and puffed it to life. "You keep pushin' yer luck like y've been doin' and she ain't gonna be there when y' change yer mind."

Lifting his sights, Zeke gazed out across the distant hills, the horizon or whatever else happened to catch his eye. How many times had Frank lectured him? Hell, the trip back from Port Chance had been one continual sermon on life--in particular, his. Everything had been thoroughly covered from privateering, to marriage, to babies. One would think he'd have learned to tune the old man out by now.

A light breeze teased his hair, ruffling it across his forehead. Raking a hand through it, he pondered a sixty-three-year-old man who'd not only made his share of mistakes over the years, but knew first hand what it meant to live with the consequences. He recalled a story Frank had painfully spoken of only twice, the first time being several years ago, a time when both of them had been drinking. The second time was much more recent--a week ago to be exact--with Zeke being the only one doing the drinking.

Frank had been young and cocky when love tapped him on the shoulder. Like Zeke, he'd been too foolish to grab the best thing life had ever offered him. Oh, his reasons for avoiding commitment may have been different than Zeke's, but the results of that decision would leave its scar for the rest of his life.

"Lisa was the prettiest thang there ever was," he'd said. *"I was twenty-two and she was just twenty. We lived together for several months and it was good. But eventually, I started gettin' restless--started thankin' about all the places I hadn't seen yet and the women I hadn't..."* He'd paused. "So...one day I took off. Just upped and said goodbye."

Zeke recalled thinking how old and hollow-eyed Frank had become as he unraveled the story. And with this last telling, there seemed to be even more guilt-ridden details than he remembered Frank telling before.

"It took me three years t' come t' my senses and realize I'd turned my back on the only good thang in my worthless, miserable life." He'd paused for a moment then went on. "When I got home, I learned she'd given birth to my son eight months after I'd left." He'd paused again and his voice hardened. *"My boy was not even a year old when a band of renegades killed 'im and kidnapped Lisa. I'd learned only that they'd sold*

'er into slavery, but by then leads were cold. I was never able to track 'er down." Bitterness had turned the old man's voice raw.

"Frank, I'm sorry," Zeke had said, and meant it.

"I ain't lookin' for yer pity, son. The only reason I'm tellin' y' is so you won't go makin' the same mistake with Kira. If y' love 'er, then either give up this life or bring 'er with y'. But don't walk away from 'er. She may not be there when y' get back. And if y' lose 'er like I did my Lisa..."

A distant chuckle drew Zeke from his silent reverie. Turning his gaze toward the sound, he watched Nick and Tressa, hand-in-hand, ascend a short set of stairs onto the veranda. Nick--married and soon to be a father. Just the thought alone was incredible. Who would have dreamed...?

And likewise, who would have dreamed that he, too, would be married? And now that he thought about it...was he so damned sure Kira wasn't carrying his child? He swallowed convulsively, unable to deny that possibility. My God, unplanned pregnancies were a thing of the past. But at the same time he knew instinctively that as a young teen Kira would not have been subjected to the physical examination that would have been a prerequisite to long-term protection. One glimpse of the emblem beneath her breast and the MedTech would know her origin. A secret, he suspected, no one knew.

Suddenly anxious, despite the peace and beauty around him, Zeke cleared his throat. "How long before *The Wind* will be ready to lift?" he asked into the heavy silence, his voice rough.

Frank's head came about, but Zeke refused to look at him.

"She's ready now, Boss, 'cept for that shipment of sensors for Quad-tech. And they're scheduled to be loaded tomorrow."

"Load them now."

"They're not even on the dock yet."

Finally, Zeke glanced over at him. "We're leaving the hell tonight, Frank. Call Ted and pull in our marker if you have to. Do whatever it is you have to do, just get the shipment on board."

"Not to worry, Boss." Frank never asked why the all-fired rush. The grin Zeke happened to catch said he knew damned well why.

~ * ~

Achingly familiar sights and scents enveloped Kira the instant they came through the main lock of the *Solar Wind*.

"I can't believe how easy this was," Rae whispered as the hatch cycled closed behind them.

Kira smiled knowingly.

"No one should be on board," Rae added. "The ship's been undergoing some sort of maintenance thing. Zeke and Frank have both been staying out at the place and everyone else, I heard, was given shore leave." She glanced about the entry. "I always wondered what the ominous *Solar Wind* looked like on the inside."

Kira laughed softly. "If we had time, I'd give you a tour. You wouldn't believe the living quarters."

"I know. We have to hurry." Rae lifted the remote for emphasis. "I need to get this back to Frank before he misses it. By the way, I'll tell Marc you were asking about him. He'll be glad to--"

"No, you will not! The mention of my name would be the last thing he'd want to hear. Dear Lord, he must hate me."

Rae's smile vanished. "Oh, Kira...is that what you think?"

"Well, wouldn't you feel that way?"

"Kira, nobody in this family--especially Marc--blames you for what happened. In fact, I understand the first question Marc asked after regaining consciousness was if you were all right."

Kira swallowed, blinking back instant tears. "He did?" she asked in a tiny voice.

"Yes, he did." Rae's expression stilled. "So are you going to be all right?"

"Yes, I'm just nervous." Scared was actually more the word.

"You got everything?"

"Yes, I've got everything. Now get, before Frank misses his remote."

Rae smiled warmly. "I still say you should have chosen that sexy negligee--the one with the--"

"I know, but it just wasn't me. Now, go!"

"Okay, okay. Remember, they'll be loading up sometime this evening, so you'll need to be on your guard just in case Zeke's involved. You don't want him finding you before they take off."

"Just as long as he doesn't jettison me out of the first airlock when he does."

"Are you kidding? He is miserable, Kira. I've honestly never seen him so quiet, so down."

Masking a thrill of hope, Kira replied, "He's probably just got a lot on his mind."

Rae laughed. "Yeah, you silly goose. You."

"Well..." Releasing a compressed breath, Rae gazed at Kira with a smile of pure satisfaction. With open arms the two women embraced. "We've managed to get onboard, my dear. Now the rest is up to you."

"I can't thank you enough for all your help."

"You're right, you can't," Rae whispered. "Just knock his socks off, Kira Slater, and make this all worth the effort we've gone to." With that, Rae Banner palmed the lock and disappeared through the main hatch.

Kira Slater. An odd tingling coiled in the pit of her stomach at the sound. With a sigh, she turned for the corridor and Zeke's cabin. "I'll do my very best," she whispered.

And heaven help him, a silent voice added.

A painful rush of emotion swept over her when she entered Zeke's cabin. Time flashed backward for an instant as she remembered the first time she found herself on board the *Solar Wind.* How angry he'd been at discovering her in the first place.

Then there was the second time she'd managed to sneak on board, and with that memory came a swooping feeling in her belly. Never would she forget stepping out of the lav and finding Zeke standing there--his look changing from utter disbelief to unadulterated hunger. And damn the consequences, she'd been so ready.

For the first time in months, Kira felt a sense of peace, although it hadn't been a tranquil voyage getting here. She'd agonized the entire way whether or not she was doing the right thing. Then, as planned, Rae met her at the spaceport and somewhere between then and now she'd come to terms with her doubts and emotions. Even if Zeke didn't want her, she would be fine.

~ * ~

"I'll bring you back a therapist when I come," Zeke said, grinning. "What do you prefer? Blonde, Brunette, or redhead?"

"Hell," Nick interjected, "bring him back one of each.

"Sounds like a helluv'an idea to me," Clint added on a chuckle. The three of them were gathered about Marc's bed.

"Fine, then one of each it is, Zeke confirmed. "Let's see, the blonde could specialize in hydro-therapy, and I'll make sure she brings her rubber ducky."

Marc's eyes began narrowing with amusement.

"And the brunette," Zeke went on, "well...let's see...she could specialize in aroma-therapy. So if you prefer a particular scent, let me know and I'll make sure that's all she's wearing."

Marc's mouth began to twitch.

"And the redhead. Ahh, the redhead...now she'll need to be skilled in physical therapy--the specialized kind."

Eyes glinting with deviltry, Clint expounded. "You know...muscle manipulation?"

That did it. Reluctantly, that notorious Banner trademark emerged upon Marc's handsome face, and with it a roar of masculine laughter drifted out into the hallway.

"Get outta here," Marc groaned, trying to stifle his laughter and grip his injured side at the same time.

"I'm gone. But you just make sure you're ready when I get back." Zeke turned for the door.

"Hey, Slater!"

Zeke turned, "Yeah?"

"You just make sure you bring Kira back with you. That's all I gotta say."

Zeke's smile faded as he drew in a breath that suddenly made his lungs ache. "I'll do my best, Marc," he said on an exhale.

CHAPTER THIRTY-TWO

What would she say when she saw him? With her heart in her throat, Kira couldn't sit still. In fact, she was making herself a nervous wreck. Two hours had passed since they'd left Acacia. Not that she'd expected him to head straight for his quarters the instant they'd left port, but waiting for him like this had her jumping at every sound.

All lights had been left off except for the subtle indirect lighting along the floor, and even that she had dimmed. So there she waited, showered, perfumed and draped in a shirt that belonged to him. Oh, she could have chosen any one of the three beautiful negligees Rae had tried to talk her into. They were all new, created by an Acacian designer and ordered on a whim--five boyfriends ago--when matrimony had first entered Rae's mind.

Kira, however, knew from firsthand experience Zeke Slater's shirt would be all that was needed for this undertaking.

Again, she took another glance in the mirror, pinching her cheeks for added color. Her dark russet hair had been freshly washed and brushed until it shone. She'd chosen to leave it unconfined this time, to flow wildly down her back and over her shoulders. The young woman staring back at her from the mirror looked and felt more like a sacrifice about to be offered up to some pagan god.

Kira swallowed. Was she really doing this?

She'd rehearsed her lines--several of them, actually. They'd ranged from the sultry "It's about time you came to bed," to the more direct "You and I have some unfinished business, Slater."

It was ridiculous, actually--this nervousness. After all, it certainly wasn't the first time she'd sneaked on board his ship. Nor was it the first time he'd seen her wearing his shirt. So why was it so hard now? Why couldn't she just pose a casual stance like before and greet him with that calm assurance that had never failed her until now?

Why? Because, it's not the same this time. You no longer need a ride to some distant port. This time you're a woman in love, a warrior ready for battle if necessary.

And God help Slater when he walks through that door.

Clasping her shaking hands, Kira took a deep breath and made her way to the bunk where she tried sitting down to wait, but after a few breaths, she was up and pacing again. Though most of her felt warmed to the core at the very thought of seeing him, a smaller part--with a very loud voice--had her all but dashing for a safe hiding place until they made the next port where she could quietly sneak back off.

Her stomach felt as if it dropped several inches when she heard Zeke's rich voice in the corridor.

He's here! Kira jumped to her feet then quickly sat back down-- the lines she'd rehearsed so thoroughly, slipping from her mind like sand through splayed fingers.

The next thing she knew, the panel slid open and Zeke Slater's silhouetted form stood frozen in the doorway, half-in, half-out of the shadows. One hand gripping the doorframe, the other was still braced on the palm plate. The golden god she'd so carefully prepared herself for had arrived--and it was all Kira could do just to swallow.

Dressed in dark leathers, his glorious sun-streaked hair spilling down to rest upon his shoulders, he was the most exquisite creature she had ever known.

If only she could read his expression. Bright light from the corridor behind cast his face in shadow, and it was next to impossible to make out his features.

"Well? Are you going to just stand there or what?" It wasn't one of the lines she had rehearsed.

Without saying a word, Slater stepped inside. The panel hissed closed behind him, and with casual ease, he leaned back against the door. Kira's breath caught as she realized that the exit was now blocked.

She still couldn't read his expression in the dim light. But there was one thing she didn't have to see to know--those stormy grays were leveled on her.

Was he glad to see her? Was he furious? Stars, the silence. What was he thinking? Why didn't he say something, grab and kiss her? Even one of his cutting comments would be a welcome reprieve. Somehow, this wasn't going at all like she had planned as she sat there suddenly feeling the fool with his damn shirt inching up her thighs--just as it had that first day.

So what did you expect? That he would melt at your feet in hot desire? Maybe you should have also thought about how he'd hiked you over his shoulder that first day and hauled your ass on down the corridor to a temporary cabin of your own.

One thing she knew for sure, it wouldn't happen again. If she was moving out, dammit, she'd be moving on her own two feet. Bolstering her courage, Kira cleared her throat. "Before you say one word, Slater," her tone suddenly defensive, "I intend to be a part of this operation of yours whether you approve or not. Dump me off at the next port, and I'll find my way right back onboard. And don't think I can't."

One eyebrow rose. That much she did see.

Undaunted, she continued. "Just in case you're wondering...the only reason I'm here in your cabin is because I wasn't sure which one to take." It sounded stupid even to her own ears, but she trudged on. "So, if you think you're going to haul me out of here like before, you'd better think again. Just tell me where to put my things."

The lock clicked into place.

Kira's stomach lurched.

With unnerving composure Zeke pulled away from the door and began unfastening the leg tie on his gun. The belt buckle came next until the holstered gun was in his hand. He turned and hung it on a hook near the door. Then, with the lithe grace of a sleek dark animal, he began to move toward her through the shadows. Kira sat back down, her legs ridiculously weak.

When he stopped, he was so close to her she was forced to let her head fall back in order to look up into his face. And the way he was looking at her made her heart skip a beat.

"And d-don't think you can bully me into changing my--"

"Ah, Legs, I've missed you." His voice sounded hoarse, near breaking as he drew her up and cradled her face between his palms. His hands were rough against her face, yet Kira welcomed the feeling.

"How the hell did you manage to get on board *this* time?"

Suddenly breathless, she whispered, "I don't think you really want to know."

His head lowered and Kira felt a grin pressed against her mouth before he fully kissed her. "You're probably right," he murmured in a deep, rough-edged voice. "I must admit, you certainly deflate my ego when it comes to security around here."

Lifting his head, he sobered and took her hands in his. "Kira," he began, "I know I've made a lot of mistakes. And, I'll probably make a helluva lot more before my life is over, but I'd--"

Shaking her head, Kira interrupted. "It's not going to work, Zeke."

He frowned. "What's not?"

"Sugared words."

"Is that what those were?"

"Not yet, but they were coming."

"Ahh." Before she could catch her breath, he'd pulled her to him. "Then maybe I'd better try a different approach."

Was it the look in his eyes that stole her breath away? The intensity in those steel grays that promised both heaven and hell in their depths? And, in order to get one, Kira knew instinctively that she'd have to endure the other.

Without another word, he was gently lowering her upon the bunk. "There... That's more like it," he murmured, easing down on top of her as he braced his weight upon his arms. "I don't know about you, Legs, but I can think a helluva lot better like this."

"Wha--what are you doing?" she asked, focusing on his dimpled grin in the murky light.

"What do you think?"

She swallowed. "But--"

"Shhhh." He lowered his head and kissed her thoroughly. "You want something else besides sugared words? First, you're going to listen to what I have to say. And every time you interrupt, I'm going to silence you the only way I know how. With this..." Again, his head lowered and he moved his mouth leisurely and oh so thoroughly over hers, teasing, seeking, letting his tongue glide ever so lightly over her lips until timidly, they parted.

But instead of taking advantage of her tempting invitation to deeper intimacy, he dragged his mouth from hers. "And if that doesn't do it," his voice sounding raspy, "I'll have to resort to this..." Again, that dimple flashed, but Kira hardly noticed before he'd pinned her even deeper into the mattress, settling intimately against her as her legs were being nudged apart by one leather-clad knee. The shirt she was wearing had somehow become rucked up to her waist.

"There..." he nearly groaned. "That's much better."

Kira wasn't so sure about that. Maybe he could think better, but she sure as stars couldn't. The only thing between them now was leather. And that was doing little to conceal the hot, hard ridge pressing intimately against her. He knew it too. The intensity in his smoky eyes blatantly said he knew exactly what she was feeling. But it was the dimpled grin, fading by heart-stopping degrees that stirred up the butterflies all over again.

In a frantic attempt to gather her scattered senses, Kira closed her eyes. But all that did was shut out everything but the feel of him, his scent and taste. When he bent to kiss her again, she felt the abrasion of his unshaven face and detected a hint of liquor upon his lips. She inhaled and he filled her to bursting with his lusty essence--a heady mixture of leather, steel and something so blatantly masculine, another lance coiled in the pit of her stomach. If fragrance were to have a color, she numbly decided, Zeke's scent would be burnt orange. Dark and warm.

"Tell you what, Legs..." he whispered against her ear, disturbing the silken hair at her temples and scattering her muddled thoughts in a thousand different directions., "Perhaps you can convince me to let you stay after all."

"I c-can?"

"Uh, uh, uh. No interrupting. Remember?" His words were smothered upon her lips, and by the time he lifted his head again, Kira was sufficiently silenced. "Now, as I was saying. If I'm convinced, there's going to be some rules." From there, Zeke went on to clarify the hard realities of privateering--the foolishness of her coming back aboard the *Solar Wind*, not to mention his own insanity for even considering to let her stay. Every now and then he'd have to stop and kiss her--whether she'd interrupted or not.

"And when I give an order, I expect it to be carried out. You understand? I won't have you questioning me, Kira, on anything. No matter how insignificant. And another thing, once Aylie is released, I'll want the two of you safe at home. My commitment will be almost over by then anyway."

She nodded, though in truth she'd hardly heard a word he'd been saying. Stars, it was all she could do to keep from dragging her fingers through the thick mane cascading like water over his shoulders.

"Good. If I let you stay, we'll be taking it a day at a time."

She nodded. "So when do I start convincing?"

Zeke grinned then bent to brush her temple with a kiss. Oh so lightly he touched his lips to her closed eyelids, her cheeks, her nose. "Anytime, Legs. You may proceed anytime," he murmured before settling a slow, melting kiss upon her mouth.

A shudder coursed through her as an all-consuming need settled somewhere in the pit of her belly. This was Zeke, her golden god, her gallant knight, her fearsome avenging angel...her gentle, noble rogue. And she was so in love, she ached with it.

Finally, with a deep breath, she began reciting the only rehearsed line she could remember. "I just happen to know the exact coordinates of a pirate freighter coming out of Capra Three." Good lord, the way he was looking at her. Did he even hear what she had said? "With my connections," she went on, "I know I could be a great help to you."

He continued to study her for several heart-stopping seconds then drawled, "Well...I must admit you got my attention. But, I'm afraid it's not quite good enough, Legs." He returned to burying his face against the hollow of her throat and murmured. "You'll have to try a little harder."

Stars, it was so hard to concentrate when he was doing things to her. "Okay..." she said breathlessly. "How about if...I promise I won't bother you?"

The shirt she was wearing had somehow become rucked up to her chin, and Zeke was busy at the moment pressing an agonizingly slow kiss upon the fullness of her breast. "You bother me," he muttered against her fevered flesh, "whether you're around or not, Legs,"

"Oh..." was all she could manage. Then gathering what strength she had left, she began again. "Then what if I promise to stay completely out of your way? In fact, what if you don't even know I'm around?" Kira giggled as he found a particularly sensitive area.

Finally, he raised his shaggy head and studied her. Time froze as she waited for his response, suppressing a bubble of giddy laugher at the odd coilings going on inside her belly.

"That isn't what I'm looking for," he said through gritted teeth. With that, he lifted himself up and began fumbling with the fastenings of his jacket, his heated gaze never straying.

Those gunmetal eyes were dark and intense beneath half-lowered lids. And his face--his breathtaking face--was framed by tousled sun-kissed hair. Stars, he was magnificent. She reached up and brushed aside a silky stray lock that had fallen over his forehead.

Urgently working down to the last fastening on his jacket, Zeke's eyes drifted closed when she pushed her hands through the hair at his temples. It spilled like liquid ribbons of gold through her fingers.

With a groan of satisfaction, he tossed the jacket to the floor. Then, grabbing the hem of his tee, he wrenched it over his head and it too joined the jacket.

"Tell me," Kira whispered, near breathless with a multitude of emotions, not one of which she could name, "what is it you are looking for? What can I do, then, to convince you?"

Every nerve ending throughout her body felt electrified as one corner of his handsome mouth rose with slow deliberation. Stars, he was incredible, she thought, dizzied by his rakish good looks. Soft light cast a sheen upon taut muscles and bulging biceps--one of which still bore the ragged scar yet in the throes of healing.

Does it still hurt? she wanted to ask. *Dare she touch it?* Overwhelmed with a sense of remorse, Kira raised her fingers to the wound that she might tenderly trace its jagged outline.

The next instant Zeke had captured her hand and was bringing her fingertips, her palm and the brand on her wrist to his lips in something just short of worship. "I'm sure I'll think of something you can do to convince me," he murmured, his voice a lazy deep satin. Moments later, the shirt that was scrunched up beneath Kira's chin joined the growing heap on the floor.

Soft murmurs and breathless sighs filled the cabin as Slater's now urgent hands moved to his belt and straining fly. The pants had barely cleared his hips when his hands stilled.

Boots. He'd forgotten his damned boots. Hell with it. Pants half way to his ankles, boots still on, and unable to wait a second longer, Zeke eased Kira back onto the bunk. Next time, he vowed. Next time he'd do it right.

"Kira, dear God I love you." The husky admission was wrung from the very depths of his soul.

The next instant, Kira's sharp inhalation filled the silent confines of the cabin as she wrapped her arms about his neck, her legs about his hips and gloried in his urgent possession.

Tomorrow, she thought drunkenly as he bore her far beyond the stars to the place of the solar wind... Tomorrow she'd tell him her secret--of the baby she's carrying. His baby.

About the Author

Carole Ann is a native of Oregon. Along with their two children, she resides with her own special hero who shares her crazy sense of humor and love for animals. The Lee family is owned by a German Shepherd named Hunter and two horses, a Registered Quarter Horse named Ace and a Registered American Paint named Nacoma.

Having always been fascinated by the thought of space travel, yet equally captivated by the romance of the tall sailing ships, Carole Ann's goal has been to integrate the two *worlds* in a futuristic romance that sizzles with both high tech as well as the swashbuckling ambiance of a high seas adventure.

Carole Ann began writing on a lark in the early nineties. While at a writers' conference In 1994, she had the privilege of meeting and submitting *BANNER'S BONUS* to a New York editor. Eight months later, *BANNER'S BONUS* was on the shelves as a Love Spell release.

As a member of Romance Writers of America, she has placed highly in every contest she has entered, and consistently earns four and five star reviews.

Carole Ann loves hearing from her readers and answers every letter. You may email her at CaroleAnnLee@aol.com

Also available by Carole Ann Lee
At Rogue Phoenix Press

Banner's Bonus

INNOCENCE MEETS HEDONISM: He's a father's worst nightmare. Yet cargo pilot Nick Banner is Jonathan Loring's *only* hope of getting his daughter, Tressa, safely off-planet and out of harm's way.

Within the tight confines of Banner's ship**,** Tressa battles a girlhood crush gone dangerous. As a sheltered teen, she secretly worshipped the hotshot cargo pilot from afar. Even his carnal reputation seemed romantic. But now, those old feelings are unsettling.

Banner misses nothing, particularly her *coy glances*. Yeah, he's noticed, and sexual tension smolders. Danger stalks them across the galaxy and when Tressa is captured by pirates, Banner finds himself willing to sell his soul to free her.